Step Forward, Harry Salt

Step Forward, Harry Salt

Ross Lowe

BEARDED BADGER
PUBLISHING CO.

First published in 2021

Bearded Badger Publishing Company Ltd
Derbyshire, United Kingdom

www.beardedbadgerpublishing.com

ISBN: 978-1-8381995-3-1

Cover Design: MOJO Creative Studio

Printed and bound in Great Britain by
Clays Ltd, Elcograf S.p.A.

For Reeganne and Astrid,
and for Mum, Dad and Sheridan
with all my love
always.

1. Commute

And there it is again, thought Harry to himself. The number seventy-five to Sheffield. Right on time, exactly three minutes late. Coinciding (as it always did), with Harry riding his barely trusty mud-spattered moped past the boarded-up windows of shops, glowing cafes and a large, blue government billboard bearing the following slogan:

> *Hang On, We'll Be Right with You!*
> *Get ready for*
> *#TheChange*

All written in cheerful, white letters above the rain-drenched high street.

Harry was tired. He wiped his visor with his woollen and annoyingly wet glove as the bus went past. The reasons he did this were twofold: partly to ensure that he didn't collide with the rusted and steamed-up Ford Focus in front of him, but also to ensure that old Doreen Twigge – the grandmother of one of his former school friends – was occupying her usual position on the pavement outside the shoe shop to give him his daily wave. Sure enough, there she was – a vision in taupe, giving a vigorous wave of her gnarled hand and a pearly white, denture-filled smile from within her clear, plastic hood. Harry returned the favour with an affectionate salute of his right hand and, with unfortunate irony, drove into the back of the Focus.

Harry's feeling of shock was immediate, as was the feeling of the handlebars of his scooter slamming into his chest. Neither sensation was a pleasant one, and while winded, Harry took a moment to weigh up which was worse – the feeling of shock, the feeling of pain or the late addition of steadily rising embarrassment – and plumped for the latter.

To confirm to Harry that he had made the right decision, two things then happened at once. Firstly, the driver of the Focus got out of his car. As he did this, Harry noticed to his right the hunched and keen Doreen Twigge waddling across the road into the oncoming traffic, handkerchief held straight out in front of her to absorb raindrops that she would no doubt use to rub Harry's reddening cheeks. Traffic was now starting to build up on either side of the rain-sodden street as drivers stared agog at the aged crone, on a mission to wipe, ambling through the beams of their headlights. Harry also became aware of angry car horns blaring behind him as the rain started to seep through his plaid work trousers.

"What drugs do you take?"

Harry's moistened reverie was broken by an exasperated voice. As his thighs clasped his scooter and he removed his helmet, he turned to be confronted by the driver of the Focus: a round man of Asian origin, in his fifties or thereabouts, sporting a tan roll-neck sweater that accentuated his rotundness in all the ways he probably hoped it wouldn't when he bought it originally.

"I beg your pardon?" replied Harry, not entirely sure why his inquisitor was so keen to learn about his medicinal needs.

"You do, do you? Then I'm sorry, but I will not be pardoning you," the man countered with a degree of incredulity and a heavy accent that Harry didn't really have the time or inclination to trace.

The rain was beginning to increase in its voracity, and to compound this, so was the amount of traffic and car horns. Harry wished desperately that he was somewhere else – somewhere dry and less stressful – but as was always the case in awkward situations such as this one, this completely failed to happen, allowing the Focus driver to question him in broken English again.

"What drugs do you take to tell yourself that it is quite okay to be driving your motorcycle inside my car?"

Harry drew in a deep and weary breath. "I don't take any drugs. Apart from crappy, ineffective sleeping pills lately, but... Oh, never mind."

"Well then, what do you like to drink?"

"I don't drink either, sorry," replied Harry, "Not often anyway. I apologise for driving my motorcycle – which is a scooter I've christened 'Darren' by the way – inside or on top of or into your car."

Within himself, Harry felt a slight glimmer of hope that this would be the end of the argument, and that he would be able to ride to work from here. Again, disappointment was swift, as any hint of a smile was instantly wiped away by Doreen Twigge's wet handkerchief. Despite everything, Harry had the presence of mind to keep his mouth closed during this procedure. A quick wipe of his helmet visor followed, along with a quick squeeze of Harry's sodden cheek.

"What you did just there was very dangerous," Doreen declared.

"Exactly!" chimed in the Focus driver. "Exactly the point I am making to him! You are not a qualified scooter pilot!"

By this point, the car-horn symphony had segued into a cacophony, and Harry noted that, in a case of wanton overkill, the cars in front of him were now joining in too.

"I am qualified! I am! I have a certificate! Give me your sodding address, I'll send you a copy to enjoy at your leisure. I'm sorry about your car, really I am, but it's not even dented. Look!" Harry exclaimed somewhat indignantly.

"It is very rusty though," opined Mrs. Twigge, throwing them both momentarily, "and your bodywork won't enjoy this rain, will it? And neither will yours, young man. I hope you're wearing a vest."

"I... er... well... yes, Doreen, I am. Thank you. Look, I'm truly sorry," Harry hurriedly added to Mr Focus, who was now ignoring him and staring off into the distance, "but if you hadn't stopped so suddenly, then none of this would have happened. The lights were green ahead and..." Harry stopped at that moment, as it became clearer as to why this frustrating series of events was occurring.

Ahead of where they were and at the centre of a number of stationary, honking cars stood a neon-clad crossing lady, marshalling the crossing with her lollipop at arm's length as an irate man gesticulated into her face. Calmly and in a resolute way that immediately triggered Harry's sympathy, she faced up to him without flinching, without even moving at all, absorbing his ire in much the same way as Harry's trousers were absorbing the rain. As she stood there, stiffly facing the angry commuter, a couple of nervous schoolchildren scurried across the road among the melee.

However, the reason Harry had stopped so quickly and refocussed his attention was not entirely due to the resolute lollipop lady or her neon uniform but rather the three determined-looking paramedics who had just sprinted past him in her direction. With keen efficiency, the taller two of the three moved towards the crossing warden while the slightly more diminutive third team-member moved towards the angry driver who had been berating her and ushered him back to his car. As Harry and his entourage watched, an ambulance emerged from a nearby street, reversed quickly to the crossing and opened its back doors. With the same silky efficiency already shown, the gleaming-wet crossing lady, lollipop and all, was carried into the ambulance by the taller paramedics before the shorter one clambered in behind them.

As the back doors slammed shut, the sirens began to blare, the row of red and blue lights began to flash, and the ambulance was gone as swiftly as it had arrived. With the drivers round and about satisfied by this early morning show of medical proficiency, or just plain glad to see the argument ended, the cars ahead began to slope off into the rainy morning.

With a quick, "Idiot!" in Harry's direction, followed immediately by an odd but nonetheless factually correct, "Old woman!" at Doreen, the disgruntled driver grumbled his way back into his Focus and departed.

Harry pushed his scooter out of the way of the traffic to join Doreen, who was now standing on the pavement, eyeing him up as if he were a bereaved twelve-year old who'd lost his first football match.

"Thank you for wiping my face," was all he could think of to say as he looked off to where the crossing lady had been.

Garden

*A*nd there it is again. That feeling of complete, unbroken seren-
ity. Far away in the distance, although I can't see them from
here, a long procession of cars sits patiently in line on the motorway, waiting for the hot summer sun to turn each individual one,
momentarily, into a gleaming, silver jewel containing a mum, a
dad, two kids and a boot overpacked with holiday clothes.

If I were upstairs in my bedroom, I'd be able to look away over
the fields and trees and beyond to see this giant, metal snake, excited in the knowledge that, in two weeks' time, I'd be a part of
that parade to the coast. I know I've got two weeks left because my
dad, ever the creative sort, made a little calendar for my wall last
weekend, with twenty-one days on it, and "Holiday Countdown"
emblazoned across the top in neat, red pencil crayon. Each night,
he comes in and, with his best rollerball pen and ruler, draws a
cross diagonally through the box bearing that day's date in its centre. So far, seven have gone, leaving fourteen remaining enticingly.

But I'm not up in my bedroom right now. I'm in the garden,
wearing my shorts and my favourite blue-and-red t-shirt, pushing
my weather-beaten tricycle round and round in a circle, humming a tune about chickens and deckchairs that I'd heard on the
radio that morning. I'd been sitting on the kitchen step, talking to
Grandma about astronomy as she did the post-breakfast wash-

ing-up. She, Grandpa or sometimes even both of them, would come over to help when my dad was busy with his projects.

"Russell Grant," I'd told her, "he's really clever, can see into space with his telescope and use his diagrams to predict the future. My favourite is Aries." I liked him much more than Patrick Moore because he was less frightening and wore nicer, more colourful jumpers, although he did seem to know less about the Giotto probe that the European Space Agency were sending up to Halley's Comet. I wasn't sure that he could play the xylophone either. Dad was very excited about this event too – almost as much as he was about our holiday – and he had promised that I could stay up late with a sleeping bag and watch it happen live on the BBC with him from the living-room floor. I'd told Grandma about this too, and I'd said that I hoped that Russell Grant would be presenting the coverage from inside the probe, but she had just carried on with the pots in the sink.

Being careful not to ride over my dad's neatly maintained and colourful flower borders, I pushed my trike into the shaded area behind the garage and stared up into the bright-blue sky above. Two white vapour trails formed a giant 'x', and for a moment again, I was giddily reminded of both my forthcoming holiday and Halley's Comet. From one of the gardens up the road, I could hear the faint beat of someone's car stereo and snatches of animated conversation from someone's house where they must have had the back doors open like ours, to cope with the irrepressible heat.

As I lifted my leg to climb off my trike, my shorts tightened slightly and I felt something pressing into the outside of my thigh. Of course – it was a red boiled sweet in a clear, plastic wrapper, given to me by my grandpa the previous week. I stood up, took it from my pocket and began to unwrap it – not easy, as the combined heat from the summer sun and my tricycle-powering thigh had made it very sticky, so extra concentration and fingernail skill were required to peel it off.

While reflecting on what a good thing it was that I didn't chew my nails like some of the other children at school, a sudden move-

ment in the bush to my left made me jump and stand rigid, my wrapper-peeling hand switching to grip one of the handlebars tightly while the other clasped the sweet. A large, black dog's head had emerged from under the hedge, and it was gazing directly at me, panting slowly, with its pink, ham-like tongue and sharp, white teeth in stark contrast to its jet-black fur. I stood petrified, rooted to the spot.

I hadn't seen this dog before. It wasn't from here. We didn't have a dog, and I didn't know anybody on our street who did either. A feeling of hot and absolute terror was already oozing its way through my body, a liquid electricity that made every fibre of my being stand alert, giving my perception a sudden and frightening clarity.

The dog drew in its tongue, ready to bark. Screaming at the top of my voice, I hurled the sweet at the dog's head, just as it bared its ivory-white and glistening teeth. I turned and ran. Upon turning, I heard from behind me the sound of the sweet I had so looked forward to seconds previously making contact with the dog's teeth, like a small pebble striking a ceramic tile. But I didn't turn back to look and had no idea how close the pursuing dog was to me. All I was focussed on was getting into the arms of my suddenly worried-looking Grandma, who had come out from the kitchen and was stood facing me as I ran as fast I could towards her.

2. Office

Harry's bottom was starting to itch. His plaid trousers were still somewhat sodden, and he couldn't be sure whether steam was rising from his damp groin to obscure his view of his computer monitor slightly, or if it was just that the screen itself needed a damn good clean. There was no Doreen Twigge and her wiping hanky in the offices of Chegwin and Blunt, he reflected to himself, and he shifted his clammy arse on his seat before turning his attention back to his murky spreadsheet.

Chegwin and Blunt was a small and uninspiring transport firm that operated a fleet of small and uninspiring shuttle buses throughout the county of Derbyshire. The fleet consisted of thirty 'Shoppa Boppa' buses, on a good week. Upon encountering a Shoppa Boppa for the first time, one was usually overwhelmed by the lack of any aesthetically pleasing features within or without it whatsoever. The white vehicles were always caked in traffic filth, apart from every third Sunday when they received a cursory wipe at Washees, the local 'drive-in, while you wait, cash only, thank you' Eastern European hand wash. The wipe had once been a fortnightly affair until a recent company budget review had revealed that Chegwin and Blunt needed to tighten their already restrictive financial belts, given the current climate and all that.

The next thing you would notice, once the beleaguered driver had clambered into his or her seat and turned the key, was the sound of the engine. This particular sound lay somewhere on an aural spectrum between 'traumatised elephant' and 'randy pterodactyl'. This hideous noise would eventually steady into a slightly more agreeable but nonetheless wrong combination of chugs, with the occasional clunk thrown in for good measure, which would continue until that unfortunate vehicle had finished its duties for the day.

Harry was one of a team of four charged with the duty of maintaining and plotting the working timetables of the bus drivers. He'd been at the company for almost three years and, frankly, that was enough. A few faces had come, frowned and gone again in that time, and Harry was now keen to head for the door himself and close it on this particular chapter of his life. He'd been secretly having a number of job interviews recently, but so far none of his applications had ended with an offer, so things were to remain as they were for the time being.

The current staff who sat around him in the office had been in place for the last six months or so. Ben, who sat at Harry's left, had been the most recent addition. Young, spiky-haired and clearly enjoying wearing a tie, Ben was overly enthusiastic when it came to stapling documents together. He was a nice lad, and Harry had enjoyed showing him the ropes, of which there were roughly four.

Opposite Harry sat Roxanne, who – like Ben – was young, spiky-haired and fresh from college. She was an artist and lacked Ben's perky enthusiasm for the job, clearly marking time before she found work elsewhere. But she had a wicked sense of humour, wore excitingly colourful clothes and lived with an unwillingness to play by the rules, which Harry adored. He had to admit that he had really quite fancied her at first, which was a fact that Roxy was now very aware of and was more than happy to exploit when necessary. Nowadays, while Harry still fully appreciated her humour, he also fully appreciated the fact that her interest in him only ever extended as far as a smile in return for a cup of badly made tea, which happened to be Harry's speciality.

The final member of the team, Alan, was a former soldier with a permanently ruddy complexion, a roaring laugh and an awful taste in shirts. His particular favourite was a bright-orange and short-sleeved affair. It set off his ginger toupee horribly and was often as much of a distraction as Roxanne's wardrobe choices, if not more so. The toupee (which Harry secretly called 'Paul') had a life of its own and would often move independently of the rest of Alan's reddened cranium. Underneath the swivelling wig and garish attire, Alan was – in his own way – quite a likeable bloke, if only for his unfortunate habit of putting both his feet into things at precisely the wrong time, when others would normally deftly swerve out of the way.

And then there was Alice. From her orthopaedic leather swivel chair in the corner, office supervisor Alice Miggington kept two beady eyes on proceedings from within her owl-like swivelling head. Her jam-jar spectacles gave her already sizeable pupils a larger-than-believable appearance, and Harry was almost certain he'd only seen her blink six times since he'd started work there. No one was quite sure how long she'd been employed by Chegwin and Blunt, but she preceded all four of the current roster-planners. In fact, very little was known about Alice other than that the management of a slick and efficient office was of paramount importance to her. She spoke rarely, if at all, about life outside of work, which led to much speculation among the team.

Alan's speculating never got much further than the belief that Alice was not in possession of a vagina or indeed a 'winkle' and was therefore neither woman nor man. A thought along these lines appeared to be close to being aired to all in the office at this very moment, as Alice strode meaningfully towards Alan's desk brandishing a sheaf of reports.

"Alan, you're missing the point," she declared.

Harry thought he noticed a discernible rotation of a few degrees in a clockwise direction by the toupee, but it could have been the light.

"I'm sorry, Alice? The point being... ?" queried Alan.

"The point. The decimal point. It's missing."

There followed a steely silence during which it felt like, for a moment at least, everyone in the world had stopped what they were doing and had zeroed their attention in on the office.

"The decimal point? Which decimal point are we referring to here then, Alice? The one on my payslip that separates the numbers representing happiness and despair?" Alan enquired.

Harry bit his lip, Roxanne let out an audible giggle and Ben touched his tie to steady himself.

Alice's eyes bulged a little, which was saying something. "I have nothing to do with your payslips, Alan. They are dealt with by the payroll department. This is the driver-roster department. Look around you. See it. Become more aware of it."

A frond of Paul the Toupee was caught in a shaft of light from the morning sun as it emerged from behind a raincloud outside and shone in through the window. It appeared, at that very millisecond, that Alan had a laser mounted on his head, primed and ready to end this confrontation in a ball of fire and carnage. Alan opened his mouth as if to say something venomous. The sun went behind another cloud, the light dimmed, and he thought better of it.

"I'm sorry Alice, I was just being... I was just being... well, I was just being," Alan mumbled.

For a brief second, Alice looked puzzled before carrying on as before. "Sheet 469A. No decimal point. According to your figures, driver David Belton worked 830 hours on 5th January."

"I bet that's how he felt, the poor bastard."

"Alan, 'bastard' is a swear word."

"Yes. Yes, it is Alice. I apologise and will use something different next time, a gesticulation perhaps or maybe a strangled sigh. Do go on."

"Sheet 502B," continued Alice, getting into her stride. "Driver

Brian Hard worked for a total of 4,029 hours during the first week of February, and took a lunch break of 115 hours on the Tuesday. This is incorrect."

"Is it?"

"Yes. Yes, it is Alan."

Harry was certain he saw Alan's toupee bristle at this, priming for attack.

"You must make sure that this level of carelessness does not happen again. If it does, then I will have to speak to my superiors," Alice warned.

By now, Alice was leaning forwards, inches away from Alan's face. His jaw was set and his gaze matched hers. Everyone else in the room was now captivated by this titanic conflict between Brown Owl and the Iraq veteran.

A further moment of silence was finally broken as Alan said, through clenched teeth, "Et woan a'en agen."

Unclenching his teeth and drawing in a deep breath through the hairy caverns of his nose, the former soldier repeated, "It won't happen again."

Alice studied him intently for a moment, as if he were a wounded shrew, blinked her beady eyes (to Harry's amazement), nodded slightly and then rotated her head to face the others in a hideous slow turn that had Ben reaching for his tie again. "This conversation is complete. You should all be working. Work."

And with that, Alice stood up straight and returned to her computer desk in the corner of the office, seemingly oblivious to the increasing air of malevolence emanating from Alan's seething form, and the ferocity with which he was now pressing the decimal-point key on his keyboard as he stared at her.

Enough, said Harry to himself. *Enough*. There had to be more to life, more purpose than this. He knew he should be glad just to have a job, given the way things were in regard to the current high levels of unemployment, the worries of an impending fertility crisis biting into the economy, and so on. Not to mention the massive uncertainties surrounding The Change, which was only weeks away.

But Harry wanted a role that employed more than just 0.001% of his brain, which was something that only happened once in a blue moon at Chegwin and Blunt. He couldn't stand to be in an office with Alice any longer. There was something odd about her lately, something that put him on edge. He didn't care much for the way she stared at him, as if she were trying to see into his thoughts.

There was, however, a possibility of salvation. His job hunt was still live, and as it happened, there was a jobs fair that very evening at the local college. In fact, he'd been counting down the days to it, mentally ticking them off on his calendar at home. *Only eight hours to go*, he told himself. Eight hours, that was all.

Another wave of tiredness hit him. There'd been something he was supposed to remember, something he'd been trying to recall recently. Something gnawing at the edge of his thoughts, but he couldn't quite reach it. He tried to focus his mind on it, his pulse-rate rising as he did so, trying to will the memory back. But it wouldn't come.

There was a black blur at the window, and Harry's attention was suddenly snatched back from the internal and given to the external, the office and his working day. He turned to look at where the black shape had been, but there was nothing there now save for the usual grey skyline of the town and the twisted church spire in the distance. He took a deep breath, looking to see if anyone else had seen anything outside, but they were each working away at their computer terminals.

Harry sighed. It was time for the first badly made brew of the morning.

Beach

*I*can just about see the grass outside. The flimsy curtains are still drawn across on the piece of washing-line cord stitched in over the crinkled, clear, plastic rectangle that makes up the tent window, but they don't quite reach fully across, thus allowing me a peep into the morning light. As I watch, Dad wanders across in his flannel shirt and cloth shorts.

His sandals. The buckles on them clink as he pads across the groundsheet.

"Watch your eyes, son," he says, smiling down at me, and he pulls the curtains apart. The sunlight pours into the tent, and from behind me, the kettle on the camping stove begins to whistle.

"Just look at that! That's a sunny day and a half!" he exclaims. He picks me up and holds me up to the window, before giving me a kiss on the forehead and setting me down again. The kettle's whistle dies rapidly as he takes it off the flame and first pours himself a cup of tea, then some orange juice for me, using the blue, plastic mugs that form part of our holiday kit. He comes over and stands beside me with his steaming mug and takes in the view.

Other tents of varying sizes are pitched outside in neat rows, framed along one side by a wooden fence running the length of the field. The sun beats down on them from a cloudless, aqua-blue sky, and the green carpet of the campsite stretches away on all sides, with other tents dotted here and there, each coupled with a gleaming car: larger tents with family-sized saloons, and smaller tents cosying up to more diminutive vehicles. Round and about, people are heading to the shower blocks, towels slung over their shoulders, and washbags dangling from their hands.

Half an hour later, we're heading out too. Dad has packed a bag with sandwiches and fruit, which sits in the boot. He's driving the car, looking handsome and healthy, with his top two buttons undone and his sunglasses on. He's already starting to tan, thanks to this glorious summer. The man on the radio is saying something about hosepipe bans.

From where I'm strapped in on the back seat, I can see high hedgerows and lush, green trees whistling past the opened car windows. Here and there are telegraph poles, and I follow the rising and sinking motion that the wires make between the poles as we whizz along the lanes. Small birds swoop and dart about, playing in the heat, as the wonderful sun shines on above them. There's something magical about this part of Wales. Something mystical about the very landscape itself. Something ancient. Something alive. Somewhere there are castles. Castles with kings. Somewhere there are stone circles and a priestess, chanting. Somewhere there are wind turbines. Indefatigable, silent sentinels atop the ridges of the hills. Watching. Waiting. Turning. Hypnotising. Even at that age, I could feel it. I could. I can. I always have.

"I can see the sea!" exclaims Dad. "Can you see it too, son?"

I peer between the seats and through the windscreen. We're high on a hill and descending. As the landscape changes and our car weaves its way through it, I work my eyesight over the patchwork of fields to a church spire, the roofs of little houses in the very distance and on to a glimmering band of ocean beyond, which joins the overarching sky. I can even make out the dark silhouette of a tanker sitting on the horizon.

It's later still. The noise of the sea, shushing against the shore, is a background to the chatter and laughter of the voices of people crammed onto the sunny beach. I'm filling a bright-orange, plastic bucket with sand and making sandcastles. Three conical mounds already stand before me, and into the middle one Dad has placed a flag made from a lolly stick and a square of newspaper. Half an article about Europe and whether bananas should be bendy or not flaps in the breeze. The sand is warm under my feet, and I dig slightly down with my toes, through the grains, to where it's cooler and more compacted beneath. Dad sits behind me, soaking up the sun rays in a hired deckchair, and to our far right a Victorian pier juts out into the sparkling sea.

"Son."

I turn round to look at my dad. Something is different. He looks sad.

"Son, we need to talk about the crash."

This doesn't make sense because it hasn't happened yet.

A slight breeze gently whips the loose sand to my left, and there's a small cry of consternation from an adult somewhere. Someone calls nearer, and there's a sudden blur of colours in the crowd nearby. Among the colours is a dark shape. I'm aware of a huge, black movement next to and in front of me, and a sudden noise. It's not right. It's not right, and it shouldn't be there.

Now my sandcastles are ruined, and I'm being grabbed roughly and quickly by the shoulders, picked up, crying, held up and crushed tightly against my father's chest. He's holding me and rocking me gently as I sob over my obliterated sandcastles.

"Shush, son; it's okay. We'll make them again," he says into my ear, his eyes darting around us. His voice sounds different again. "Shush, now... There we are... We'll build them again just as they were before."

3. Biscuits

The working day at Chegwin and Blunt was over. Workers scurried away from the functional concrete edifice into the late-afternoon gloom to pick up their kids, traipse through supermarkets, or hit the off-licences or pubs within the town. Harry was accompanied by Alan. He'd hoped to sneak into the careers fair on his own, unseen by colleagues and – most especially – Alice, but after following Harry out and accompanying him for a few yards, it soon became apparent that Alan was headed for the same event as him.

"Hadn't realised you were after a new job, Alan," remarked Harry, feeling he should strike up a chat. Despite Alan's brusque attitude and chronic political incorrectness, Harry harboured a bit of a soft spot for him. He was only ever honest, which in itself often rubbed people up the wrong way, but there didn't appear to be a bad bone in his body – apart from the dodgy knee that, according to Alan himself, had swiftly ended his military service a few years before.

"Just curious, Harry. Just curious. Keeping my options open, you know? Besides, it's always good for you to have a wingman, right?" Alan responded.

Harry frowned. "I'm not on the pull, Alan."

"No, no, course not, course not. Although a lad like you should be sowing your oats by now. Getting some action. Are you?"

"Am I what?"

"Getting any? Action, like?" Alan's ginger toupee appeared to twitch in anticipation of Harry's answer, but it was most likely the breeze.

"That's none of your business!" spluttered Harry, a little more affronted than he'd intended to let on, before adding, "and, no, as it happens, I'm not. Not for want of trying, obviously, but no. Thanks for your... concern."

Not that Harry had actually been trying. At all. Although he was tired and frustrated in all kinds of ways lately, sorting a new career out was, he hoped, going to be the first piece in a happier, more focussed and more prosperous jigsaw going forwards. But Alan wasn't likely to take that for an answer right now.

"It'll only be a matter of time, you'll see. Be patient. A nice lad like you. Clever. Kind. A lot to offer to a nice girl. You're not a silly bastard like some of the drongos out there." Alan paused, thoughtfully. "You'll have all the fanny after you, you will."

Harry had been absentmindedly sucking on a sherbet lemon until this point, and this particular revelation caused him to nearly choke on it before sending it flying out of his mouth and spinning into the gutter.

"Oh now, that's a waste," opined Alan.

For a brief second, Harry feared his burly companion was going to go and rescue the sweet and have it for himself.

They were standing still now at a pelican crossing, with the crossing man opposite illuminated in red and partially covered by a blue sticker that carried the words "Bollocks to The Change!"

The crossing light changed from red to green, and they started to make their way over the black and white-painted stripes on the tarmac. The angry bark of a dog came from a nearby street, causing Harry to jump. Alan looked about, as if checking for something, and then they crossed.

***

A short while later, they turned left along the main road for Tavener College, one of the more modern buildings in the locality. It was half-term, so any 'snowflake students' (as Alan referred to them) were safely shielded from his unfathomable ire. Once through the rotating glass doors of the reception, they padded across a large rug bearing the inscription "Welcome to Tavener College" to where a very bored receptionist sat playing a game on her mobile phone. Her focus upon the game was such that she appeared to be unaware of them.

Alan moved forwards to speak. "Excuse me, miss?"

The receptionist raised an eyebrow, but she didn't move away from the game. Alan noticed that she was also chewing gum. He rotated his head slightly to the right, straining his neck and causing it to crack loudly before grimacing.

The receptionist looked up disinterestedly into his steely gaze. "Careers fair? Upstairs. Room UC106." And with that, she returned to the game.

Alan drew a long breath. "There. That wasn't so hard, now was it?" he said with a degree of satisfaction in his voice before turning to Harry. "I swear," he commented under his breath, "customer service in this country is on the skids."

They worked their way upstairs, and as their footsteps echoed, they both became acutely aware of the emptiness of the building. The only other person they encountered was a cleaner on the stairs, who appeared to be taking a rest midway through cleaning a step, leaning on his mop, asleep.

"Sleeping on the job?" enquired Alan sniffily as he navigated his way around the prone body.

Harry stopped and stared at the cleaner for a moment, puzzled. "Hello? Hello? Are you okay?"

The cleaner didn't answer, or move, for that matter. Harry was about to say something else, but Alan had bounded round a corner at the top of the stairs and so, reluctantly, Harry nipped up the remaining steps to catch him up.

"He was a bit odd, wasn't he?" asked Harry as he fell back into step with Alan.

"The cleaner?" replied Alan dismissively, "Just overworked and underpaid, I imagine. Shagged out and grabbing a moment's kip. For the pittance he's probably earning, we can leave him to it. Mind you, if he's not started again by the time we head back downstairs, I'll clip his bloody ear, the lazy tosser. Anyway..." He pointed ahead of them at a pair of double doors on the left. "I reckon this might be it."

Jogging in an ungainly manner ahead of Harry, he pushed the doors open and entered before sticking his head back out and nodding conspiratorially towards Harry. Puzzled, Harry followed Alan into the room. As the doors shut behind him, Harry stopped to see Alan was now standing transfixed, looking towards the end of the long hall in which they now found themselves.

Following Alan's gaze, he turned to see a pretty and immaculately presented lady sitting behind a desk right at the far end of the room. A colourful display board stood by the desk, and an equally immaculate and identically dressed woman was standing by it. Both of the ladies smiled back at the boys. There was something unsettling about the smiles. They were just that little bit *too* perfect.

The lady behind the desk spoke first in a very cheery, singsong voice. "Good evening, gentlemen."

"Yes, good evening gentlemen," added the woman to her side.

There was absolute silence: no sense of traffic outside anymore, no footsteps within the building, no hum of air conditioning, nothing. Alan and Harry stared forwards. The two matching ladies in their matching business outfits smiled back.

"Good evening to you, miss. And to you too... miss," ventured Alan.

"Hello... is this the careers fair?" asked Harry.

"Oh, it most certainly is," replied the lady behind the desk through her glossy smile.

"Do come and sit, and we'll find the right job just for you," added her companion.

"You can even have a free pen," chirruped the lady behind the desk.

"A free pen. We have plenty," the second confirmed.

Harry and Alan continued to stare. Whenever one of the ladies spoke, the other followed immediately with immaculate timing. It had a somewhat disturbing effect – yet they both smiled on fixedly at the two men.

"Come and sit. We won't bite!" pointed out the seated woman.

Right on cue, her partner laughed, "Ha ha ha! No. We won't."

Neither of the boys looked convinced. Harry turned briefly to look at Alan, who was open-mouthed. The verbal-relay game continued.

"Perhaps you would care for a biscuit?"

"Or two biscuits?"

"There are plenty of biscuits."

At this, Alan sparkled back into life. "Ah, now you come to mention it, I was feeling a little peckish. Ex-army, see. I've got a big appetite." He strode proudly towards the desk, and Harry, not wanting to be left behind, followed cautiously and at a safe distance.

"Oh, Forces? How marvellous!" declared the seated lady.

"Oh, plenty of opportunities for ex-Forces, yes," appended her echo.

"I was hoping so," said Alan, taking a fruit shortcake from the plate of biscuits on the table, "That's why I came. I also brought my colleague with me: Harry."

Harry glowered at Alan momentarily, but found his attention back on the ladies immediately.

At the mention of Harry's name, the two careers advisors had swivelled their heads with disturbing synchronicity to face him. A shiver ran up his spine. Alan munched on his biscuit, non-plussed, crumbs amassing on his chin.

"Harry, have a pen," offered the lady behind the desk, indicating a mug filled with biros.

"We have plenty of pens. And a seat," added her companion, who nodded at the two plastic seats opposite them.

"A pen and a seat, Harry."

"And fill in this form."

"With that pen."

"In that seat."

"And tell us both plenty about yourself, Harry."

"Yes, plenty. If you would."

During the verbal bombardment, Harry had slowly edged himself into one of the chairs to sit facing the advisors, although he was starting to feel less like he was being advised and more that he was being dictated to. It wasn't entirely pleasant, and he noticed he was starting to feel a little sweaty, which wasn't especially ideal either.

The lady behind the desk spoke again, this time to Alan, despite her gaze remaining fixedly on Harry. "And you sir, take a seat Mr... "

"Higgins," finished Alan. "May I have one more biscuit, please?" he asked hopefully as he sat next to Harry, who was now armed with a biro and a form.

The ladies did not respond. Instead, they looked on intently at Harry who stared back edgily. Alan shrugged and took two biscuits from the plate.

As was apparently the norm, the lady behind the desk spoke first. "So... "

"So, Harry," echoed her colleague. "What is it that you want to do?"

Harry, for the first time faced with having a choice in the direction of where the conversation was headed, found himself at a loss for words. "Er, well... I want to... "

"Yes?" The lady behind the desk craned forwards eagerly.

"Erm... " fumbled Harry.

The second lady, equally keen, bent towards him. "Yes?"

Harry took a breath, looked for an instant to the ceiling for inspiration, saw a tired wasp staggering around the edge of a light fitting and fumbled on. "I want to creatively shape my er... "

The lady behind the desk beamed at him. "Do go on."

"Shape my, er... my future and take control fully of... er... "

The lady standing by the desk, who had been nodding in encouragement at virtually every syllable that Harry was managing, clasped her hands together rapturously. "This is very good!"

"Well, I want a new career," said Harry nervously, encouraged by the affirmation and now finding his stride. "Something rewarding; something demanding. Something that's going to push me and maybe take me a little outside my... er, comfort zone? I'm very good with people, and I would want to do something that can help others. I like to make things better for people, for the way they live. I want to work hard, to be challenged and to learn. I think I have a lot to offer... other people. I think."

"Yes, you do," concurred the lady behind the desk.

"A lot to offer... er... " Harry sighed and stopped, fishing for words. "Look, I... I'm sorry. I should have prepared better. I haven't been sleeping well lately, and, well, I wasn't expecting so many questions so quickly. Sorry."

As Harry had been talking, one of the ladies had glided towards him. Now she looked down upon him almost in a forgiving manner. "Oh, come now, Harry – you needn't worry. Have another biscuit. We have—"

"Plenty? Thank you," he interrupted and gratefully took one from the plate before nervously shoving the whole thing into his mouth.

"Besides which, we think we have just the job for you, Mr Salt," concluded the seated lady with a smile.

At this, Harry coughed on his biscuit, sending crumbs in all directions. One crumb landed upon the lapel of her blouse. Her smile intact, and without taking her eyes from Harry's, she delicately and efficiently curled her hand towards her neck before flicking the crumb deftly away using the long and manicured nail of her middle finger.

Alan was incensed. "Harry, that's not how you eat biscuits. You eat them like this."

Alan reached forwards for another biscuit from the plate, but Harry cut in. "I didn't tell you my surname."

Alan froze in mid-reach, and looked directly at the seated advisor. His eyes narrowed accusingly. "Are you some kind of dirty, filthy spies? What's in these biscuits? What's going on here? I demand answers!"

"Oh, we're not spies, Mr Higgins," came the immediate and somewhat haughty reply.

"No, nothing of the sort," corroborated her companion. "And currants. Plenty of currants."

"Well, what are you then? And how did you know my surname?" asked Harry, equally as perturbed.

The two ladies settled back into their original positions and paused for a brief moment.

"We're from the MOP Careers Advisory Centre. We're careers advisors. We advise on careers. That is what we do; that is what we do well, with vast experience and with clinical efficiency. And our advice to you, Harry Salt, is that a career with us could provide you with all those things you seek and a great deal more besides. We think – in fact, we know – that you could be very happy with us, and that a job at the MOP could be the first jigsaw piece of prosperity in a better life for you, moving forwards. Furthermore, your name is on your badge."

Harry looked down to see he was still wearing his Chegwin and Blunt identity pass, went to speak, froze midway through opening his mouth and then took a deep breath. "You think a job with you could be a *what*?"

"A jigsaw piece. In your life. The first piece. In a better life. Your future. A happier, more focussed one. That is what you want, right? Along with a decent wage, excellent canteen facilities and opportunities to make a difference to the world in which we all live? Moving forwards?"

Harry frowned. "Well, yes... that is what I want – exactly that, in fact – but... I'm sorry, have we met before?"

"I can 100% guarantee we most definitely have not, Mr Salt," declared the careers advisor, preening back at him sunnily.

Alan eyed them both suspiciously, before leaning to whisper behind a cupped hand into Harry's ear, "If you want my advice then remember this, Harry: never trust anyone. Anyone. About anything. Ever. That shit is fatal. Look at what happened to Neville Chamberlain after Hitler waved his little Austrian sausage in his face."

Harry turned to whisper back, "Cheers for being protective and everything, but they're just careers advisors, Alan."

"Yeah, but there's some weird shit going on at the moment, Harry. Weird as. People acting up. Everywhere. It's in the papers. Some of them, anyway. On the internet. Theories. Strange buggers like these two. I swear I'm going to get to the bottom of it."

"Yeah, well, I'd like to see what these two have to say. Maybe there's an open day at this MOP or something?"

"There's no open day as such, Mr Salt," said the first careers advisor, startling them both back into facing the desk, "but we can make you an appointment to see Mr Newman. He's the CEO of the MOP and will explain everything to you. I assume you know the cement works in the Hope Valley?"

Harry flashed them a puzzled look, something that was now a regular feature of the conversation. The cement works was a local landmark that dominated the otherwise beautiful valley near to where Harry lived and had grown up. Hated by some and loved by others, the works had been constructed over ninety years ago on the valley floor, and on misty mornings the towering chimney would rise majestically above the inverted and golden mist to greet the sun and create, along with the awe-inspiring backdrop of some of Derbyshire's more dramatic hilltops, the dream shot for any landscape photographer. Despite the industrial incongruence of the building among the dales and leas of the historic Peak District, it remained an eye-catching example of man's dependence upon the secrets held below the earth's surface, and indeed local legend held it that the works had been built on something of a sacred site, and that it wasn't necessarily a wise thing that they had.

"The cement works? Yes, I know them. Why?" enquired Harry.

"We've made an appointment for you to see Mr Newman there, next Monday morning at 9am. Please report to reception and do not be late." With those last words, she fixed Harry with a steely stare and reached over the desk to press a business card into his hand.

"But I don't know anything about cement... ?"

At this, the two careers advisors froze before erupting into a fit of high-pitched laughter, which then halted as soon as it had begun. "That is not going to be a problem, Mr Salt. Not a problem whatsoever. Monday morning at 9am. Mr Newman will see you then. Thank you, gentlemen!"

Alan and Harry looked at one another in bafflement, before the former stood, pointed accusingly, said, "I'm on to you. I know your game," grabbed a handful of the remaining biscuits, and made a swift exit through the double doors.

Harry, nodding politely to the still-grinning careers advisors, pocketed the business card and followed him as fast as he could.

Eagle

The seafront shops were slowly opening up for the new day, but I'd been awake for what felt like ages. Doors were opened, and spindly carousels filled with postcards were wheeled haphazardly out into the fresh sunshine by store owners. Further along the promenade, cafe parasols were being slotted into round tables.

I'd never seen the seaside like this. It was virtually empty, with no one on the beach save for a few early morning swimmers. Seagulls were taking advantage of the deserted pavements to peck away and help themselves to bins full of abandoned chips and wrappers from the day before. That was because most people were still in bed. But not me or my dad. Not today. Today was a treat. Today, I got to go into town early with him to get the morning paper, and I could choose a comic for myself. Not only that but we were also going to have breakfast together. Just the two of us.

We'd driven down a steep, zig-zag lane from the town centre to the beachfront, and Dad had parked up at the foot of the cliff-face. He'd asked me on the way from the campsite (I was allowed to sit in the front of the car for this journey and choose a cassette to listen to) if I wanted us to park at the top so we could use the big elevator to get down to the street level. I'd thought about it for a second before shaking my head. The elevator was fun, but when we'd tried it last week it smelled a little too much like the public toilets in the square, which had made me wheeze and choke a bit.

At the newsagent's, Dad had picked up his copy of The Guardian, and I had gone straight for the Eagle Summer Special. It was like the regular weekly Eagle comic, only it had three times as many pages. That meant two Dan Dare stories rather than just the usual one, plus a load of puzzles and other things. It would take me the rest of the holiday to plough through it.

Dad and I were already looking through it together as we awaited our beans on toast in the cafe. Dad loved the Dan Dare stories almost as much as me; he'd been an avid reader of the Eagle himself when he was a boy, and he was thrilled when it was relaunched for my generation. He had immediately subscribed me to the weekly delivery (it came every Saturday morning and was the perfect start to my weekends).

In the new Eagle, the heroic space pilot of the future, Dan Dare, was the great-great-grandson of the original Dan Dare from my dad's childhood. It was now the year 2153, and the blond, chiselled Dan was on the run in a futuristic cityscape, being chased by a flying shark called Zarkuda. At his side was Zeta, the exotic club singer with hair that changed colour.

"Dad, the future looks ace!" I declared.

"It does, doesn't it? Look at the flying taxi!" he said, pointing to the next frame in the comic strip.

"Cool. Do you think they'll invent flying cars in our time? Like, could we get our Vauxhall Viva to fly?"

Dad smiled and looked out the window to the beach and the sea beyond, which was twinkling in the early morning sunlight. "You never know, son. They're inventing all kinds of things today." He turned back to me. "Flying cars might be a way off yet, though."

"What about hovercrafts then? Could we all have those? I'd love one. We could use it on the roads and on the sea!"

"It'd be a bit noisy," Dad stated with a chuckle. "I'm not sure the neighbours would approve, if I'm honest."

He looked towards the cafe's counter for signs of our breakfast, before looking back down at the colour burst of my comic. "What *do you think the future will be like, son?" he asked me.*

I looked up from my comic thoughtfully. The bell above the door tinkled as an old couple in red and blue cagoules wandered in with a black dog on a lead, drawing the owner from the kitchen to serve them. As they decided what they wanted, I noticed that the dog was staring at me.

"Son?"

The dog was staring at me, and I was staring at the dog.

"Son, I asked you a question. Can you hear me?"

I don't remember the dog being in the cafe. But the dog was there, and it was staring at me.

"What do you think the future will be like?"

"It'll be exciting," I said, forcing myself to picture it. "Definitely flying cars. That will make it easier to get about, and to get to places quicker. There will be space stations in the sky too, but not too many or else they'll block the sun for the people on the ground."

"Good," said Dad, grinning. "That's very considerate. What else?"

"Erm... medicine will be better than it is now."

"Medicine?"

"Yeah," I continued, getting into my stride, "scientists will have made it harder for everyone to die, so that we can live longer and enjoy the future more. It'll be really hard to get ill, and if you do, you'll just go to the chemist's for a tablet that fixes everything, like cancer and flu and leprosy and stuff."

Dad nodded, impressed. "A pill that fixes everything? Good idea. So with everything fixed, will people be able to get ill at all?"

"No. There'll be no more illness whatsoever, just people living happy lives, feeling well, and being sporty and stuff. There will be loads of places to play sport too, so that everyone can keep fit."

Dad chuckled and looked at me with the warm smile I always loved – the one that shut the world and all its problems out in one go. "So, with everyone feeling fit and healthy, and never falling ill, what happens to all the doctors and nurses then?"

I clearly remember furrowing my brow at this, and feeling my forehead and nose wrinkle. "What do you mean?" I asked, with maybe a little more sass than was strictly necessary.

"Well, if everyone is fit and well, we wouldn't need doctors would we? Nobody would be ill anymore. What would they do with themselves? And what about undertakers?"

"Undertakers? What do they do?"

"They're the people who bury dead people for a living. In coffins, deep, deep in the ground," he added, putting on a spooky voice for emphasis.

The elderly couple swished past us in their raincoats, heading for a table somewhere behind us. Something was missing, but I wasn't sure what it was. They'd forgotten something; it had gone, but they didn't seem at all bothered.

"Well, they could find new jobs. I don't know, they could find things for people to do now that they're all living longer. New ways to have fun, maybe?" I was feeling a little indignant that my dad, who was a clever man, had somehow managed to find holes in my utopian vision of the future.

"But wouldn't it be slightly difficult with everybody living forever? Wouldn't the world get a little bit overcrowded as more and more babies were born, filling up a world that was already full of people?"

I was staring at a panel in the comic. Dan Dare had been forced off the ledge of a ridiculously tall building, and he was hurtling towards his doom on the busy street below.

"Well, I suppose so." I looked up, thinking. "Perhaps some people could choose to die if they wanted to. To make a bit more space for everyone. But... some people might just want to keep going and see how the world could become even more exciting than it is now... Perhaps all the other people could live underground?"

"That's certainly true." My dad nodded, still smiling. "That might be a good way to solve things. Good thinking. Ah, here we go. Beans ahoy!"

A pretty, young waitress in a blue-and-white striped apron had appeared at the table with two plates of freshly steaming beans on golden triangles of buttered, white toast, and she placed them down in front of us. I took a last look at my comic to see that Dan had survived the fall, as the road he'd landed upon was made of a rubbery surface that enabled him to bounce back to his feet and run off.

With a grin of anticipation and a wink from my dad, I smiled back, closed the comic and put it on the chair next to me.

4. Moped

Fortuitously, Harry had already booked the Monday off. For some reason, he couldn't quite recall what he'd planned to do with it, but he'd had a few days to take off that had been banked up, so it was either take them or risk losing them.

His alarm woke him early that morning, after another restless night. There was no time to ruminate on his lack of sleep or the causes. Instead, there was a shirt to be ironed, a tie to choose from his collection of three, shoes to be polished and what was, potentially, a job interview to attend. Harry was up and alert, and made his way downstairs, pushing the door to his guest room shut as he went. It doubled somewhat as a junk room now, filled as it was with carefully packed detritus from his past and a number of boxes of stuff that had belonged to his parents. Some of those boxes were filled with his dad's old work projects. He'd rescued them when clearing things from his grandma's after she had passed away last year, and he was determined to look at them properly when the right rainy Sunday came around. Somewhere outside, a dog was barking angrily at something.

Just over an hour and a disappointing bacon sandwich later (he'd never been able to make them the way his grandma had), Harry emerged through his back door with his moped helmet in hand. The morning had segued from bright sunshine to a dull, overcast sky. A light drizzle hung in the air, creating a sheen on the browned cobbles in the alleyway behind his terraced house. Darren, his moped, stood by the door, clad in a faded black tarpaulin, which Harry removed, shook and put inside the house, by the door. Two small and grubby children – a boy and a girl in matching green cardigans and red shorts – were kicking a football around in the alleyway. Harry had seen them before; he wasn't sure who they belonged to, but he had often wished that whoever their parents were would just give them both a damn good bath or at least show them a bar of soap for Chrissake. The boy caught the mud-spattered ball with an audible splat and stared fixedly at Harry as he locked the door, pocketed the keys and mounted his moped. Harry smiled at him and nodded, but the child merely stared back clasping the ball to his little chest, a trickle of muddy water running down his cardigan. The small girl stared on too. Slightly uneasy, Harry shrugged to himself and started Darren the moped, which, at a second attempt, sputtered into life.

As he turned into the alleyway and set off in the direction of the main road, Harry looked into his mirror to see the boy launch the football at him with venom. It struck him squarely in the back, sending him flying from his beloved bike, which scuttered into his neighbour's wall as Harry hit the cobbles. Shaking his shocked and helmeted head, Harry pushed himself up from the floor and on to his knees to look at the monstrous infants who had since run over to his inert motor scooter. The boy had collected his football and now stood with it raised above his head.

"TWAT!" shouted the child at the top of his shrill, young voice, and with that, he slammed the ball down on the moped saddle. The ball caromed up into the air and then splattered down in a puddle.

"TWAT!" echoed the girl, but instead of shouting it at Harry, she shouted it at Darren.

Harry himself then realised that the young boy had yelled in precisely the same direction.

"TWAT! TWAT, TWAT, TWAT!" they both chorused venomously at the prone and defenceless moped, leaning forwards and yelling with all their might.

Harry, breathless, staggered back to his feet and pushed the children aside wordlessly before heaving his cycle back onto its wheels. The infants fell silent and glowered at him.

Harry thought about this for a moment. "Stop that," he said, climbed back on and rode away. Nervously, he glanced at his mirror to see the children staring at his departure, the muddy ball at their feet.

***

Harry was out of town now, grumbling down a long country lane. As instructed, he was heading for the cement works, which seemed like an odd thing to do at the best of times. Growing up, his father and grandparents had warned him to keep away from the industrial site, with its dangerous machinery, dusty trucks and barbed-wire fences. Harry had lived all of his life on just the other side of the valley, towards the edge of the beautiful Derbyshire Peak District. As he pottered along, he reflected how nice it would be if this were his morning commute, heading into the countryside rather than out of it. Most of the jobs he'd applied for had been in the bigger towns in the county and beyond – Chesterfield, Sheffield, Derby and Stoke – all with their one-way systems and ring roads that clogged up during rush hour.

There was no rushing to be done here. Fields stretched away on either side of the hedged lane, and, occasionally, a lush, green tree would appear and whistle past. Apart from a singular walker replete with beard, gnarled walking stick, cagoule and inappropriately short shorts, Harry had encountered no one since turning into the lane four minutes or so before. He'd had time during his journey to ponder this mysterious job opportunity, and while he didn't want to get his hopes up and have them dashed, which had happened as recently as only a fortnight ago, something felt good about this one.

The lane had become more tree-lined the further down he went, although the trees cleared momentarily, and Harry finally glimpsed his target: the valley cement works. Constructed in 1929, it was a well-established part of the local landscape; a colony of factory-style buildings, the largest of which was home to a tall, white chimney from which smoke was drifting lazily into the morning air. The works were right in the centre of the valley floor, in the middle of this vast, green, patchwork basin. Surrounded on all sides by a thicket of dense woodland, the panorama opened out into a network of fields that then scooped upwards to form the hills that rose and fell like a frozen green wave on all sides.

The drizzle had become a heavier rain, and Harry could feel his trousers clinging heavily to his legs. He wiped his visor with a sodden woolly glove. Ahead, the lane grew more densely wooded, closing in on him. The trees arched overhead, protecting him from the majority of the rainfall, although one large drop managed to find its way down the back of his collar, running chillingly and uncomfortably down his back before plunging gleefully into the channel between his bum cheeks. The atmosphere within the copse was cold, and, consequently, the temperature of his entire body had dropped fast. This, coupled with the dampness of his clothes, caused Harry to shiver, and he took a deep breath to steady himself as he rode on. Either side of him towered warped and wet tree trunks, which were ancient, dark, silent and completely unsympathetic to Harry's wet and frustrated predicament as he then whizzed past his turning, shouted a swear word and drew to a halt before turning Darren round clumsily.

The entrance road to the cement works was unbelievably small: a tarmac-surfaced gap in the undergrowth barely big enough to let Harry and his moped through. This had to be wrong, surely, thought Harry to himself. There had to be another entrance for the huge cement lorries that went to and from the industrial site each day – either that or all their deliveries were handled by an army of tiny people pushing wheelbarrows.

Still, there it was. He girded his famished and sodden loins, kicked Darren back into life, trundled forwards before turning right into the gap, and then promptly let forth his second expletive of the morning. "Shitting Christ!"

The cement works had disappeared.

Where they *should* have been, a stunningly grand, baroque, English country mansion now stood resplendently among immaculately manicured lawns and gardens, facing Harry at the end of a long, statue-lined driveway. Harry drew his moped to a stop and stared, open-mouthed. He looked around the horizon to check where he was, and, yes, sure enough, there it all was – the familiar landscape of his childhood exactly as it should be, minus the huge cement works, chimney stack, steam and dusty trucks.

He turned his moped and rode back to the gap in the trees where he'd glimpsed the cement works over the hedgerow minutes before and there they were, steam still rising from the chimney and no sign of a huge country manor whatsoever. He took in the view for a moment, and he could even pick out a worker in a neon vest and orange work helmet clambering into the cab of a truck, slamming the door closed and driving it off. He could *hear the engine* on the breeze. He rode back to the gap in the thicket, and the cement works might as well never have existed at all.

Harry's brain raced. Just what in the name of giddy fuck was going on here? He had no need to pinch himself. He was there, right there in the moment, wide awake and fully aware of the gentle breeze on his cold, damp skin; the noise and vibration from his moped; and the golden sandstone palace standing proudly and blatantly where it wasn't supposed to be. He was exactly where he had been asked to be, precisely where he had been instructed to turn up, it was Monday morning, and the time on his wristwatch was 8.48am.

Tentatively, he edged the moped through the gap in the greenery and onto the long driveway, before speeding up a little to putter forwards towards the mystery house. It appeared solid enough against the brightening horizon; it was around five stories high with large windows across the façade, which in itself was dominated by an ornate, columned portico entrance. As he advanced towards it, weathered Romanesque statues gazed down at him from either side of the tarmac, with swords, discuses, spears and beards at the ready.

At the top of the drive was a small, crescent-shaped car park. The presence of regular cars in front of this odd, hitherto-unseen building – with their tax discs, number plates and Good Year branded rubber tyres – felt somehow ludicrous. A dose of normality where everything else felt quite literally out of place. There were a number of smaller spaces for motorbikes, and so Harry pulled up there, kicked down the bike stand and removed his helmet.

He breathed in deeply and listened. The rain had stopped, and the valley carried on as normal; skylarks twittered and danced above, the gentle breeze worked its way across the fields, and the sun crept out from behind the clouds to warm Harry's face and illuminate the enormous, golden building behind him.

If he was only slightly intrigued before, he was now positively (and nervously) captivated. Gripping his helmet underneath his arm, Harry turned to face the stately entrance and made to follow the sign that read "Reception".

Plunge

*U*p, and down. Up and down. Up, down, up, down.

The rise and fall of the orange-and-blue inflatable dinghy, as each wave rolled under it, was difficult to handle at first. The dinghy had felt more solid when on the beach, pumped up with a foot pump and ready to set sail.

In the shallows too, where the sun made the water gleam and the sea just about washed over your ankles, it felt reliable and safe. However, out in the deeper water, at the point when Dad clambered in after leading the boat out using a small length of cord tied to the bow, it felt like we weren't in control anymore.

Dad offered a smile of reassurance and a, "Hey, don't worry, sunshine!" at my worried look over the side.

I could see all the way to the rippled, golden sand below; it really wasn't that deep. But it was deep enough that Dad could no longer stand on the sea floor. The water was in control now.

Dad had taken the oar, wooden with a maroon, plastic fin at either end. He dipped it into the warm sea and pushed us out a little further. "Let's go up towards the pier!" he said enthusiastically.

I didn't want to. I put my hands to either side of the dinghy, and my legs either side of my dad as he propelled us forwards.

The pier jutted out from the promenade, over the beach and into the sea. As we neared it, it loomed high above us – a dark, wooden

Victorian structure pointing out towards the ocean and the rest of the world beyond. It had wooden supporting legs, cloaked lower down in slippery, bright-green seaweed, the tentacles of which rose and sank in perfect unison with the rise of the waves.

As we got closer, Dad started to hum the theme from Star Wars. "Let's go over to the Dark Side, shall we? Bom, bom, b-b-b-bom, bom, b-b-b-bom, bom... "

"I don't like it, Daddy... " I whispered.

The dinghy had two blue, plastic oar holders on either side of where I sat. Dad didn't use them. He never did. He paddled his own way, dipping the oar over one side, pulling against the water and then dipping the oar over the other side to do the same. I grabbed the oar holders and held tight as we bobbed towards the shadow cast by the pier above.

Sailing sideways meant that the waves, which felt enormous to me, were now washing under the sides of the dinghy, lifting us up from the left and then dropping us back. Lifting. Dropping. Lifting. Dropping.

"Dad—"

"Here we go," he said cheerfully over me, "It's Star Wars time!"

At that, the shadow of the pier swallowed us both, and the warmth of the sun was gone instantly, replaced with a damp coldness that made me shiver and become aware of the water on my skin.

"Dad, I don't like this... "

And then he turned to face me. He was different, somehow. Alert, agitated. He looked about, and then turned to face me again, the shadow from the underside of the pier darkening him and everything about us.

"Son, I can tell you now. There's something you have to know, about the accident, but I won't have long to tell you. I need you to listen to me. Okay? Son?"

I saw the wave coming towards us only seconds before it happened, but it was slightly bigger than the others, and there was a menacing dark shape in the middle of it, leading it. As Dad pulled the oar desperately through the water, the wave came under the boat, slammed into the bottom of it and tipped it, sliding me out and into the sea.

I took a full mouthful of salty water, which was horrible, but I was under the water. I panicked, my arms and legs flailing into nothing but sea around, under, over and above me. I couldn't make a sound, and yet – somewhere, somehow – I was aware of just how calm and serene everything was down here. I could see the sand far below me, away from the shadow of the pier, golden and glowing in the sunlight from far, far above.

The water flowed away forever, so clear; it was another world down here entirely. One I had never seen but that had always been here, waiting for me. It was beautiful. Enchanting. Enticing. Calling. You belong down here. Below the sea. Below the land.

Forever. Down here, this could be forever.

A hand tried desperately to hook itself under my armpit before sliding away. Another one, tried to grab my shoulder, but slid off, unable to find a grip.

And in the distance, swimming towards me from the shadows beneath the pier, came a large, black shape. Red eyes. Huge, sharp, white teeth – a menacing smirk speeding towards me. Something like a shark, but not. A dog. It wants me to stop. It wants me to focus on it. To focus on the dog, not the surface nor the world above. Closer now, closer My lungs are heaving. There is the rumble of bubbles as a body joins me in the water; harsh, strong hands grasp me and push me and pull me upwards towards the dinghy.

Dad.

The daylight sparkles beneath the surface of the water. I go up, further, back into the daylight, and a wall of sound and noise. I am coughing, struggling to get the warm and horribly salty water from my lungs, gasping, then struggling into the rubber dinghy. Coughing, heaving, but safe, up above. Here. Safe. Safe. Safe.

For now.

Awakening.

5. Newman

Harry was standing in one of the most impressive reception rooms he'd ever seen. The ceiling, far above his head, was painted intricately with scenes from some ancient, cataclysmic battle in the sky between one group of muscular sorts dressed in flowing, white cloaks with impressive grey beards, and another group of equally muscular and bearded boys (and beardless girls) dressed in exactly the same way. Here and there giant, white dogs gnashed and snarled; the occasional goblet was held aloft among the swords; and Harry noticed a huge, purple mountain far off in the distance.

Nervously, he looked away from the ceiling to a wide, richly carpeted staircase that swept down from a balcony running the length of the back wall. The walls either side were home to large, golden-framed portraits of people he didn't recognise, who were dressed and painted in styles from various periods of history, and who gazed down accusingly at him from all angles. Harry was aware of activity somewhere beyond this space, but right now, he couldn't quite pinpoint it.

If the idea of all this was to intimidate, then it was working very well indeed.

"Salt?" came a voice suddenly, breaking into Harry's wonderment.

"Yeeargh!" yelped Harry, spinning round to face the source.

"Salt!" came the voice again. It was sharp, clipped and almost militaristic in tone. It came from the vocal cords of an inscrutable and balding man in his sixties or thereabouts.

Harry took a sharp intake of breath as the man, who stood about level with his chin, frowned and peered up at him in a manner that had something oddly familiar about it. Before Harry had chance to even attempt to place it, the man then grinned at him intently from beneath his thin, brown moustache. Beneath that and the rest of his beetling face, he wore a navy-blue pinstripe suit and a red tie, and his forehead gleamed enthusiastically far below the painted ceiling that Harry still hadn't quite recovered from.

"Salt!" The man thrust his hand forwards eagerly to shake Harry's.

Harry took it and gingerly moved it up and down.

"Good, good. You must be Harry Salt, am I correct?"

"Er, yes. That's right. I have a meeting here at 9am; I'm here to see Mr Newman?"

"Who?" frowned the odd little man. "Oh – me! Ye gods and little fishes! Of course, yes you are, aren't you? And so am I. Well, here we are. You're Harry Salt, I'm Mr Newman, and that, my boy... that is the God's honest truth."

Mr Newman finally gave Harry his hand back after nearly having shaken it off entirely. "Welcome, Salt. Welcome to the MOP."

"Thank you, it's nice to be—"

"Would you care for a sandwich?" At this, Mr Newman reached into his blazer and pulled out a fresh, crusty, white baguette, the crumbs from which spilled out on to his blazer lapel. "Look. Ham."

"I'm sorry?"

Mr Newman continued to beam encouragingly up at Harry, pushing the ham sandwich towards Harry's nose.

"Er... no, thank you," replied Harry politely, hoping he'd said the right thing. He hadn't really been thinking about whether he was hungry or not, although the baguette did smell freshly baked and delicious.

"Good! Follow me, please." With that, Mr Newman placed the baguette gently onto a small, marble-topped table, patted it once as if it were a good boy, swivelled 180 degrees and strode off purposefully down a corridor that opened out beneath the right-hand side of the balcony.

Harry gaped, glanced a little longingly at the sandwich, and then took a deep breath and followed in Mr Newman's wake, striding as quickly as he could to catch him up.

As Harry pulled up alongside him, the intense little man continued. "You see, Salt? Corridors. And doors. Doors and corridors. That's what makes Britain great," he concluded proudly, almost with a patriotic tear in his eye.

"You think?" asked Harry.

Mr Newman stopped and pondered for a second, almost causing Harry to trip as he came to an abrupt halt. "Occasionally, yes," he mused. "Helps me put things in perspective. Anyway, into the lift. Quickly now."

They were standing by a warmly lit elevator, which stood invitingly open. The lift itself had an immaculate, art deco feel to it, and Harry felt momentarily as if he were being given a speedily-guided tour around a grand city hotel. In a flash, Mr Newman was already inside and beckoning to his guest with his finger. Harry stepped in, feeling the lift dip and correct very slightly as he did so.

As his brain scrambled to make some sense of what was going on, he saw a set of strange images that formed a pictorial border around the lift walls. The first picture, positioned to the right of the doors, featured a super-magnified image of a sperm fertilising an egg. The next one, if Harry remembered rightly from his school biology lessons was a zygote, the one next to that an embryo, followed by a foetus, a naked human baby, a child, a spotty teenager and then, finally, a full-grown man whom Harry recognised as, somewhat disturbingly, TV talent-show judge and pop impresario Stephen Sutch, all shiny teeth and immaculate hair. He was also naked and seemed very pleased with his generous and equally immaculate pubic mound.

Meanwhile, Mr Newman was standing, hands on hips, looking up at the ceiling. "Floor, floor. Who's got the floor?" he puzzled.

Harry, not wanting to overstep the mark, but also wishing to be helpful, pointed tentatively at the lift buttons, located to the left of the left lift door.

"Ah!" exclaimed Mr Newman with delight. "Of course. Very good, Salt. Incredibly good, in fact. A good start. Righto, risotto."

At that, Mr Newman stuck out his finger to press a button, which Harry saw featured – rather than a number – an image of Mr Newman's face looking out with an overly intense frown, as if studying a Bible the size of a stamp. With an accompanying ping, the doors slid shut, and the lift began to rise.

Harry stood with his back to the wall.

Mr Newman grinned back towards him somewhat mischievously. "Well, what do you think then, eh? Fit for a king, what what?" he asked Harry.

"I'm sorry?" answered Harry.

"This lift. Up as well as down! Good, eh?"

"That's... amazing."

"It is!" Mr Newman clapped his hands together enthusiastically. "Now watch this!"

At that, the lift stopped, pinged once more and the doors opened. A young lady – a brunette with bobbed hair who was wearing a white lab coat – entered, her head down as she prodded busily at a tablet screen. She looked up, examined them both briefly and smiled warmly as she registered Harry. Before the doors closed, he had just enough time to be aware of a clinical corridor of frosted-glass walls, behind which he could just discern moving shadows.

"Mr Newman," greeted the new passenger, nodding.

"Yes," he confirmed, unnecessarily. "Absolutely on the bloody nail. Reginald, isn't it?"

"Jade, sir," she replied, without looking up.

"Isn't it just. This is Harry. Say hello, Harry."

Harry smiled in return. She had a confident air about her and was pretty in a way that served to remind him all too quickly that his own appearance was, thanks in part to the soaking he had received on his moped, somewhere way off at the negative end of the sexy spectrum. "Good morning, Jade," he found himself saying suddenly, and the smile she flashed back was magic.

There followed an uncomfortable pause.

Mr Newman glowered at Harry from across the elevator. "A simple 'hello' would have sufficed, Salt."

"I'm sorry, Mr Newman, I, er... "

As Harry fumbled for an answer, Jade gave him a suspiciously knowing look, which Harry enjoyed all the more.

"Never mind; this is Jade, one of our new starters!" interrupted Mr Newman. "Last week, in fact! That's right, isn't it?"

"I've just finished my first year here, Mr Newman," she confirmed.

"Of course you have! Of course! Good Lord, time flies. Exit!"

The lift glided gently to a halt, and Harry returned Jade's wry smile with an embarrassed grin that was briefly acknowledged with, of all things, a wink. She then returned her attention to her tablet.

The doors pinged wide open, Mr Newman strode out, and Harry, his palms sweating and seeing no other option available to him at that moment in time, followed.

***

Mr Newman's office was oak-panelled, cosy and felt (or rather smelled) old. The thick, grass-green carpet was soft under Harry's shoes, and he was fighting a polite urge to ask if he should remove them or not. Each wall, lined with filing cabinets, featured framed pictures of all sizes. As Harry scanned across them, he realised with something akin to alarm that every one of those pictures was the same: a stern portrait of Mr Newman in his pinstripe suit. No, strike that – there were two landscape paintings: one of a stormy seascape and one of what appeared to be a gargantuan cave with a mountain in it. Harry had a compulsion to look more closely at the second one, but Mr Newman had stridden over to his large, oak desk and was settling himself into a sizeable, black, leather chair, humming in a satisfied manner. A laptop sat open on his desk, beside a jar of stationery and – Harry now saw – a couple of framed photos, including a silver-framed, black-and-white photograph of Mr Newman in exactly the same intense pose seen around the room. Newman picked up the frame, looked lovingly at it, made an approving sound and put it back on the desk. He then smiled expectantly at Harry, who stood staring back, unsure of what to do.

Without warning, Mr Newman reached down to press an intercom button, glowing red, protruding from a metal box on his desk. "Doris!"

"Yes, Mr Newman?" crackled a haughty reply.

"My secretary," said Mr Newman to Harry with fawning affection, before continuing, "Doris, we have arrived. I am sitting down in my chair. Harry is standing up, facing me." He winked knowingly at Harry.

Harry knew not what Mr Newman knew, so decided against winking back.

"We are about to conduct the internet," Mr Newman declared.

"The interview, Mr Newman?" corrected Doris.

"By jingo, you're good. Yes, the interview. That."

"Very good," came Doris's reply. There was a short pause and then, "Will there be anything else, Mr Newman?"

"That's all, Doris. That's all."

"Very good, Mr Newman. By the way, you left a ham baguette here yesterday."

"Ah." Mr Newman released his finger from the button, and the intercom clicked off.

He sighed from behind his desk and turned to Harry, who still stood there awkwardly. "She's a brilliant woman, Salt. Quite brilliant. Everything you could possibly want from a human being. A person if you will." He shook his head in wonder. "Righto. Risotto. Let's get down to it."

With intent, Mr Newman opened a drawer on the desk, pulled out a wet flannel, wiped his face with it and then replaced it in the drawer before slamming it closed. "Take a seat, Salt."

Harry, still standing, had already noticed a row of wooden chairs upholstered with comfortable-looking, green, velvet cushions lined up against the left wall of the office. He walked over to them, but as he did so, Mr Newman reopened his drawer to pull out a small, wire-bound notepad, which he flipped open. Studying Harry intently, with an inscrutable frown matching that seen in the multitude of photos and paintings around the walls, he took a yellow pencil from his jar of stationery. By now, Harry had picked up a chair and turned around with it, ready to take it over to face Mr Newman.

"Oh!" exclaimed Mr Newman slowly. "I see... " With that, he scribbled something into his notepad.

Harry paused. "Oh, was I meant to... ? Should I take... Wrong chair? Sorry, I'll... "

Harry turned, put the chair back in its original position and looked at the others. They were all identical: worn, carved, wooden frames and matching green, velvet cushioning. He picked another, and as he edged towards it, he looked back at Mr Newman to gauge his reaction.

Mr Newman's eyes narrowed. "Hmm... " he hmmed before writing something further in his notepad.

Harry was now sweating, and he cleared his throat. "Maybe not that one then, no."

Again, Harry turned to study the chairs, looking for a clue. Nothing presented itself. Going on what might have been instinct, he went to the last chair on the far end of the row, put his hands on it and lifted it. Yes. This one. At this, Mr Newman sucked through his teeth loudly, causing Harry to drop the chair noisily. Mr Newman returned to his notebook and scribbled further.

Harry sighed nervously. This was all getting a little too much. Exasperated, he took a seat from the line-up at random, carried it over to the desk and placed it opposite Mr Newman before clearing his throat and sitting in it.

At this, Mr Newman stared at Harry with a look of incredulity, frowned back at his notepad in puzzlement, shook his head, tore out the offending page and threw it into an empty metal wastepaper bin. As Harry watched, Mr Newman stared back at the pad for a second more before flipping it shut and throwing it into the bin, followed quickly by his yellow pencil. The pencil had only just clanked on the bottom of the wastepaper basket when Mr Newman stood up, pointed at the bin accusingly, his veins bulging at his temples, opened up the window behind his desk, and threw the entire bin and its contents out of it. With that, he slammed the window shut, span round and faced Harry.

"Oh. Now that's much better." He pulled his blazer snug, noticed the baguette crumbs on his lapel from earlier, flicked them off deftly and then sat back in his chair with a satisfied sigh.

"So... Young Harry Salt. First things first. Can you do magic? Spells and the like?" Mr Newman enquired.

"Beg pardon?" spluttered Harry.

"Magic. You know the sort of thing. Applied science, essentially. I think. I'm no longer sure. I can't remember, if I'm honest, but I think that's it."

"I'm sorry; no, I can't," Harry admitted, pondering why this was in any way relevant.

"Ah, pity," said Mr Newman, looking inwards. "Pity. But there we are. So, shall we get down to it? Shall we? You must have questions."

"Ah. Yes, I do as a matter of fact, thank you. Just a couple." The biggest one was with regards to the building itself, and why it wasn't a cement works. He decided to hold off on that for a moment.

"That's only natural," mused Mr Newman, leaning forwards, his hands clasped together and giving the now trademark stare. "Only natural. You must, of course, wonder what this place is. Who I am. What we do. What you can do for us. What we can do for you. The size of our canteen. The staff discounts. The biscuits."

"Well, yes" blustered Harry. "Yes. Yes, please. That would be great. You mentioned—"

"Do you work, Salt?"

Harry, feeling a little irked suddenly at the one-way direction of the questioning and the lack of answers, took a breath. "Work? Yes, at the moment I work for Chegwin and Blunt, a bus company in Chesterf—"

"Function. I phrased that one incorrectly. Forgive me, Salt. Do you work? Do you function? In one end and out the other, so to speak? Is the fettle in which you find yourself, fine?"

"Sorry? What—"

"Do you work?"

The pause. The scrutiny.

"I... I do, yes," Harry confirmed.

"Good! Then the job is yours!" announced Mr Newman; he clapped, stood up straight and offered his hand out to Harry, before frowning and staring doubtfully inward again. "No, not yet, Roy," he chuntered under his breath to himself. "Not that bit yet." He sat down again and shook his head before looking back at Harry.

"The question is, Salt," continued Mr Newman in a low, conspiratorial whisper, "would *you* like to work for *us*?"

Harry blinked, thinking his way quickly through a number of responses. "I don't know," was the one he settled on. "Honestly, I don't know. I am looking for a new job, yes, but maybe you could tell me... what the job actually is?" He smiled back, uncomfortably.

Mr Newman returned his stare with a puzzled frown. "The

what, now?"

"The job."

"Ah! That badger. Yes. The job. Well, look now, see," he said, raising an eyebrow and leaning in towards Harry, "are you aware of the shortage? The people shortage? The shortage of people?"

Harry thought fast, vaguely remembering something doom-laden he'd seen on the news about worldwide fertility rates being low, and how it would mean fewer people, and complicated problems for employment levels and pension pots. Not enough people being born. The people shortage. "Um, I think so, yes. Fewer people being born, and fewer people to do the important jobs. Too many pensioners and not enough people to work, or something like that?"

"By heavens, he's got it! You're exactly right. The job's yours. NOT YET, ROY!" he yelled at himself, with Harry involuntarily yelping in surprise back at him.

Mr Newman steadied himself before continuing, "You've hit the nail on the shin. We are an institute tasked with dealing with this particular and problematical problem. Our resources are vast, our technologies impressive and our hours agreeable. We're doing all we can to put things back on an even keel, to ensure a sense of order for the people. Or, at least, that's what it says in the brochure."

Harry opened his mouth to speak, paused and closed it again.

Mr Newman let forth a bellowing chuckle. "People, Salt. People! The success of this country, of the world at large, depends on its people, agreed?"

"Well, yes."

"All those people, helping one another, working hard to put this country – and by association, the world – back where it belongs! Do you remember the good times, Harry?"

Harry thought long and hard. "No."

Ignoring Harry's response, Mr Newman stood up, looking past Harry's head to some glorious distant vista. Spittle formed at the sides of his lips. "The wheels of industry turning. Everyone working together. The greater good! A Britain that is global-ly respected and ruddy prosperous. Making Great Britain great again. And then, the world. Which would be great, wouldn't it? Happy and hard-working people, here there and everywhere? Bloody hell."

He stopped, drew a ragged breath and then looked down at Harry, who (not for the first time that day) looked on suspi-ciously before fashioning his face into something resembling polite appreciation.

"We need people who share that vision," Mr Newman said, sitting down again, "people who care for other people. People people. Persons. That sort of thing. We have openings, and lots of them, but the people we choose have to be the right people."

"Right."

"Right you are. Right as a kipper, Salt. Now, listen... " He leaned forwards again to almost whisper, "It's non-disclosure time here, Harry. Everything I tell you today you must keep to yourself, close to your chest. Not a word to anyone. There will be papers for you to sign."

"That sounds serious." Harry himself was now leaning for-wards to match Mr Newman. "But, yes, of course, you have my word."

"What we do here, it's not for everyone to know about. There are some things better left not known by the people."

"But I thought you said this place was *for* the people?"

"Quite. Quite. But would you not agree that, sometimes, some things are best left unsaid? Nobody on this majestic isle needs to know *everything*, otherwise *nothing* gets done. Not one person. Certainly not those currently in power. Ignorance is bliss. The Change referendum is proof of that, *capisce*?"

Harry had wondered if this particularly thorny topic was go-ing to make an appearance at some point. He was about to com-ment, but, again, Mr Newman pressed on.

"Sorry, Salt. Italian. Possibly German. Sounds impressive, but I don't understand a bloody word of it myself. All Greek to me.

Let me put it to you this way... " (At which Mr Newman changed his seating position three times before settling with a satisfied nod at his faithful 'hands clasped together, leaning forwards' configuration.) "The people, Salt. The people. What the world has always loved about Britain is its people. Hard-working, never say die, always say 'crisps', positive, punctual and polite. Always working together. Getting results. Cheerfully and with cheer. Centuries of it. Centuries. I've seen it. It's to be encouraged! That's why we're here. We need to ensure we always have enough people to make the world go around. We're doing that. We're fixing things, and by the cut of Barry Manilow's enormous jib, we're bloody good at what we do. Now, would you call yourself a people person, Harry?"

"Yes, I think so," he answered hopefully.

"I knew you would. I knew it. I said to myself when you arrived, 'Roy, this lad is a man of the people,' I did. Now, you're sure you can't do magic?"

"Definitely not. Should I learn?"

"Doesn't matter. Look, if you feel you're up to the challenge, I'm certain we can give you the new direction you're seeking to point your little self towards. It'll be a trial run at first – a period of probing. Probation. That. Stick to what you're told, do as you're asked and everything will fall into place. You've applied for the role. There's no doubt about your application. Now apply yourself. Do your thing. If you like it, and you are sufficiently liked in return, then I think you'll be very happy here at the Ministry of People."

"The Ministry of People?"

"That's us! When can you start?"

6. Star

Harry flopped onto the sofa, and he slapped the envelope containing his signed contract onto the coffee table with satisfaction. It had arrived in the post as Mr Newman had promised; Harry had scanned through it and signed both copies before nipping out to pop the other in the post, confirming his acceptance.

He'd done it. He had a job. A new job. Something he felt genuinely excited about. He reached for the remote, clicked the TV into life as a matter of habit, and as this habit often dictated, he proceeded to give it little to no attention whatsoever. Besides, it was just the end of another pointless government advert, which concluded with the slogan "YOU CAN'T STOP THE CHANGE! CHANGE IS INEVITABLE!" in large, cheerful, white letters on a blue background.

This was it! This was his way out of Chegwin and Blunt! No more monotony. No more Alice. No more feeling like he'd settled for seventh best at best.

Instead, it was something to look forward to. Something good. Something with prospects. He sat and allowed his mind to drift a little. Mr Newman (strange, little man that he was) had made him feel wanted – *genuinely* wanted – and that he had something to offer.

He imagined riding up the immaculate drive to the building, only this time it was bathed in sunlight rather than rain, with the gilded edges of the windows twinkling in welcome, and the statues smiling down as he trundled past. The large chimney beyond was happily puffing away, a reminder of the strange technology at play, which disguised the mansion as a cement works. (He must ask about that sometime, he reminded himself.) After parking Darren in his own personal space, he strode confidently into the hall, where a string quartet was playing a whimsical tune, with a tuxedoed cellist nodding a knowing smile to Harry as he pulled his bow across the strings. Harry wished a good morning to the beaming Mr Newman, who stood there with a silver serving dish. "Welcome home, Harry!" he said, before lifting the lid to reveal a pyramid of stacked ham baguettes. Behind him was the lovely lady with the bobbed, brown hair whom he'd met in the lift. Jade. That was it. Jade. She was walking towards him, smiling, winking and applauding, sending his blood racing. This was where he was meant to be. This was it! This was where it was all going to happen, and everything was going to make sense! Soon, Mr Newman was applauding too, and then other workers appeared, entering from doors and corridors, corridors and doors, all applauding Harry's arrival, louder, louder still, the sound swelling until...

Harry sat up with a jolt. He'd been daydreaming, and the TV was still on, showing a brainless, production-line talent show at which the studio audience were rapturously applauding. It was one of those where people pretended to be someone else, someone famous. Once upon a time, the contestants used to dress up as their heroes, and the show's make-up and costume departments would do the rest. Nowadays, people went further, undergoing painful cosmetic surgery or a variety of medical enhancements to look the part. Harry blinked as the camera showed the judging panel. A memory of something – possibly someone – had been triggered, but his slightly fuzzy, post-nap head wouldn't quite allow him to grasp what or who it was.

As he pondered on it, the two bouncy and virtually identical hosts of the show jigged into view onscreen to introduce the next unfortunate to take to the stage.

"So, Kevin, where are you from?" chirruped one of the hosts with more ebullience than was strictly necessary.

"I'm from Pontefract, Zack," replied the contestant, a short, balding man with a neat moustache, who wore a pale-yellow t-shirt tucked into his jeans and whose forehead was beaded with sweat under the studio lights.

"Pontefract, in fact! Wow, amazing, Kevin! Amazing!" exploded Zack.

"That's right, yes," confirmed Kevin, winking in the direction of a solitary "Whoop!" from the studio audience.

"Yeah, but, Kevin, what we really want to know is how are you going to entertain us tonight? How are you going to show us that you're the *Star That You Are*?" enquired Zack's equally buoyant co-presenter.

"Well, tonight, Brack, I'm going to be... " Kevin from Pontefract paused, following the tried, tested and tired-out TV format to allow a ticking clock and menacing note of doom to be heard as the camera cut from the goggling and expectant faces of Zack and Brack (who seemed about to rupture themselves with the suspense) to the faces of the judges once again: two F-list popstars from the 1980s and former tabloid editor and TV's 'Mr Nasty' Stephen Sutch, presenting between them an immaculate wall of preened hair and glinting teeth.

Of course! Harry had seen Stephen Sutch in a picture on the wall of the lift at the Ministry of People. Stephen Sutch and his neatly maintained pubes.

Sutch looked on as Kevin finally broke the tension and announced, "I'm going to be considerably taller than I am now!"

"CONSIDERABLY TALLER THAN HE IS NOW!" yelled Zack as Brack's eyes widened to the point of no return. "Go Kevin!"

Mayhem. The audience erupted into a wild frenzy of cheering and applause, pyros flamed terrifyingly into the convulsive crowd while Zack and Brack leaped into the air and chest-bumped one another as the booming roar of an unseen choir sang the name of the TV show, *Star That You Are*, into the heavens.

As Harry watched dully, a set of doors opened at the centre of the stage to let through a plume of theatrical smoke from which Kevin now re-emerged, still in his jeans and yellow t-shirt. Only now his limbs were hideously elongated, unfurling slowly as he made his way through the portal like a giant, newborn spider. His face was now a false, cleaned-up, enhanced and warped version of what it once was, as if it had been transformed via an industrial version of a social media image filter. Once he was through, he extended himself to his full terrifying height, a good five or six times taller than both Zack and Brack, who by now were in danger of applauding and cheering themselves to death.

The crowd silenced, the note of doom returned, Zack and Brack held on to one another tightly, and the camera cut to the neat, raised eyebrow of one Stephen Sutch.

"Well, Kevin," he purred. "You're from Pontefract, I'll give you that. You've got feet. Two. You've got a t-shirt, and it's most certainly yellow. But are you tall? That's the question I'm asking myself here. And what's the answer? What's the answer, Kevin? Are you tall? Considerably tall?"

Brack fainted.

"Kevin," continued Sutch commandingly. "I've watched you here tonight and I'll admit that, when you first came out with your t-shirt – your yellow t-shirt – and your two feet, I said to myself, 'There's a man from Pontefract.' But can he be considerably taller than he already is? And you know what? You know what, Kevin? You can. You're a star, you are. You're the *Star That You Are*."

That audience roared with approval.

Harry, however, clicked off the TV and headed into the kitchen, his mood a little soured from the excitement he'd felt earlier when his contract had arrived in the mail. This wasn't Saturday night TV as he'd remembered it from his childhood. Steven Sutch and others like him had changed the landscape of TV and the viewing habits of millions in a way that Harry had never entirely been comfortable with. There was something darkly manufactured about it all, cheaply turning normal, average people into something they weren't, giving false and grotesque hopes and dreams to them and anyone impressionable enough to be sucked in. Some people would give anything – and undergo all kinds of terrifying measures to change themselves – to conform to some notion of perfection. But did they *really* want it? Or was it because Sutch and the media *told them* they wanted it? It all felt like a part of something bigger, something that swept people up before they had time to realise who or what was doing the sweeping, or what life would be like afterwards.

Harry was simply happy enough right now with his new job to look forward to. A way to improve himself and his prospects in his own way, a bit of extra money at the end of the month and new people to work with.

But people, lots of them, watched this stuff. They seemed to like it. Maybe he should just cut them some slack, he thought to himself as he boiled the kettle. Perhaps he was being a stick in the mud. Maybe he should just roll with it. Accept it. They were happy; they knew it. They clapped their hands. They voted. It was easy. It didn't require thought.

It wasn't *real life*, not really. Was it? In real life, the most recent vote had been for The Change referendum, and 51% of the country had voted to Change. After three years of painful, divisive campaigning, that was that, and The Change itself was coming in the next few months. Thinking about this made Harry feel a little sour again. It wasn't something he'd wanted or indeed voted for; it just seemed to have upset everyone one way or the other, and had irreparably damaged the UK's relations with some other countries. Harry sighed and stared out of the window. Somewhere outside, a dog was barking aggressively and doing its level best to distract him. Momentarily, Harry forgot what he'd come to the kitchen for. Damn dog. Give it a rest.

Tea. That was it. A cuppa.

Sometimes, he reflected, it was hard to tell when he'd started to wonder about this kind of thing. As the kettle boiled and he went to the fridge for a carton of milk, he pondered when and why his attitudes had formed, where his influences came from, and what difference he and his thoughts could ever make in the wider world anyway. He was just one guy, and to be fair, he could be out of touch sometimes. He admitted as much.

Milk. Tea. Focus.

Eventually, he settled back down on the sofa with his mug of tea, taking a moment to appreciate the silence and solitude around him. The dog had stopped barking. The rest of the world didn't matter right now. He thought about his new job. He was excited. It was the change he'd been after for a while, and he intended to make the most of it. It was enough. It was his role, his place in the world. He would quietly do his thing and do it well. It was something worthwhile. He'd make new friends. Jade. He'd get to know Jade. Well, he would definitely try to get to know Jade at least and, hopefully, not balls it up.

His dad drifted into his thoughts, which made sense. It was at moments like this that he wanted to share his news with him, to let him know what he'd achieved. To chat through the news of the day, that would be enough. Just ten minutes, a cup of tea shared and a hug from his dad. Despite the years that had passed, the pain of losing him could still hurt with a rawness unlike anything else.

Sudden tears stung at his eyes, and again Harry blinked. He reached for the remote and went in search of a different channel with something else to watch this time – something to cheer him back up. But every channel was showing the same thing: a blue screen emblazoned with "GET READY FOR THE CHANGE!" in reassuring, big, white letters. Harry waited for a moment, but, sure enough, no advice on how to get ready precisely was forth-coming. Instead, he turned off the TV again, wiped his eyes and returned to the kitchen in search of a biscuit, which failed spec-tacularly to be there.

7. First

So, his first day in the new job. It was finally here, and Harry, as much as the term could ever be applied to him, was pumped.

The cement-works thing gave him a jolt all over again. When the chance arose, he was going to ask someone about that. Right now, though, he was ready to take whatever came his way. He was here to learn, earn and, he hoped, unlock something of his so-far-untapped potential. This was the new start he'd craved for far too long. Whatever his new role was going to entail, it couldn't be any worse than hammering in bus-driver data that was likely to sit forever forgotten on an ancient computer server buried in an underground chamber God only knew where. That was history. The grand, classically beautiful, sandstone mansion standing impressively before him was the key to his future. This was the place where it was all set to change for him. He didn't just hope it. He knew it. This was where he was meant to be.

His moped parked on the tarmac by a riotously colourful and immaculately maintained flower bed, Harry walked to the towering entrance and stepped inside, in a manner that he hoped looked confident. This time, his ears picked up on the sound of chatter. A queue of twenty or so men and women of varying ages were standing in a gaggle on the black-and-white tiled floor, some talking, some gazing up at the ceiling in astonishment and some glued to their phones. One or two of them were fleetingly aware of Harry's presence, and they turned to smile at him, before returning to their conversations.

Suddenly, a thin, middle-aged woman in a dark-green, velvet blazer emerged from the crowd and elegantly but firmly made a bee-line for Harry. She wore a floral brooch attached to her collar, and her reddish-brown hair was fiercely pulled back. She wore angular spectacles to match the angles of her face, and she peered through the lenses inquisitively as she came up to him.

"Harry Salt, I believe?" she enquired.

"That's me, yes," Harry verified.

She proffered him a slender and well-manicured hand and smiled calmly. "I am Doris; I am Mr Newman's assistant and *you* are right on time for your first day here. Welcome to the Ministry of People," she purred proudly.

Harry smiled back, shaking her hand probably a tad too eagerly.

"Mr Newman will be speaking to you and the other new starters shortly. You'll all be assigned a guide each for the day, who will be there to answer any questions you might have. Yours will be with you shortly. It's delightful to have you here, it truly is."

"Fantastic, thank you."

"Good, gooooood," sang Doris, "Now, do join the rest of the cohort and prepare for your first day of training."

"Prepare?"

"Prepare, yes."

"Should I have read something? Brought something?"

"Join and prepare!" she trilled, before swiftly and efficiently gliding off and out of sight.

Harry swallowed and was just about to attempt to introduce himself to a group of four people in the queue ahead of him, when there was a firm tap on his shoulder.

"Are you Harry Salt?" came the cheerful voice of a young, brown-haired woman, her head down and checking details on a tablet.

"That's me, yes," he confirmed once more.

She looked up and smiled with recognition. "Oh, it's you! The chap from the lift."

"And you must be the lady from the lift, then. Jade, is it?" he asked, fully and excitedly aware of who she was.

"Crikey. Well remembered. Yes, I'm Jade; Jade Birch. Nice to meet you – again. I'm assigned as your guide for the day, so I'm afraid you're stuck with me." She punched him playfully on the arm, causing him to flinch and immediately feel embarrassed for having done so.

He cleared his throat. "Well, well done for remembering me too. It was all a bit hurried that day."

"Yeah, that's Newman's style. You'll get used to him. Or you'll learn to tolerate him at least. He's lovely really." She dropped her voice and looked about before addressing him conspiratorially, "Just absolutely fucking bonkers, if you'll pardon my French."

Harry laughed politely, a little taken aback by Jade's familiar approach. "Well, I'm glad it's not just me who thought that," he answered under his breath. "I'll be honest... I'm not 100% percent sure of what I'll be doing here. He gabbled a bit about me working with people because I'm a 'people person', apparently – does that sound about right?"

Jade stepped back and gave him a knowing smile, similar to the one she'd flashed in the lift when they'd first met. "Yeah. Pretty much. You know what, there's so much to learn about this place and what it is we do here. I've been here just over a year, and the only thing I'm certain about is that I've hardly scratched the surface. This place is nuts. There aren't many people out there that know about us, either."

"Well, I'd certainly never heard of the Ministry of People before."

"Neither had I, mate. Trust me, you'll be signing non-disclosure forms left, right and centre before the day is out. It's like Newman – a bit bizarre, but you'll get used to it soon enough.

Did he offer you a ham baguette at all?"

"Actually, yes... "

"Speak of the devil," interrupted Jade, looking up and past Harry's shoulder, causing him to turn and face the balcony.

Mr Newman, he of the beetled brow and pencil moustache, stood with his hands tightly gripping the brass rail of the balcony edge as he proudly surveyed the assembled crowd of chattering new recruits below. At his side stood Doris, the assistant who had startled Harry moments previously. With clipboard and papers under her arm, she too was beaming at the assembled newbies.

"PEOPLE!" he bellowed.

All conversation stopped, and everyone's attention flicked upwards in unison.

"New people! How lovely to see you all here! Here! Here for your first day. How pleasing that is!" Mr Newman declared.

Harry and Jade gazed upwards too.

Mr Newman continued, "Let me start by saying how pleased I am. How pleased I am that you, the people, have decided to join us here at the MOP. It is my solemn, no... my fervent, no, no... my sincere, erm, no, come on, Roy... "

"Your genuine?" suggested Doris, without breaking her smile.

"Yes! Good heavens, yes!" exclaimed Mr Newman, with a twitch of relief, "It is my fervently solemn and sincerely genuine wish that you all have a long, happy and fruity—"

"Fruitful."

"Thank you, Doris, yes – fruitful, ahahaha – period of employment; employment of the most gainful and successful kind for you and for the MOP itself. For the people of Britain. Starting today!"

Harry glanced quickly at Jade. She continued to gaze up at their CEO, smiling, her lips pursed as if fighting the urge to giggle.

"And starting in just a few minutes from now, on your starting day, the day you all start – a video, no less! Every first day must feature a video, and so we have a video feature for you all to introduce you to life here at the MOP on your first day. So, order yourselves into an orderly order, and follow your assigned guides, who have been assigned to you as guides. Quickly now," barked Mr Newman, reaching a little too far over the balcony to scoop the air below him, "Quickly! Video. Video now!" And with that, he hauled himself back from the precipice and disappeared from view.

Doris, bizarrely, curtseyed. She then smiled, fluttered her long eyelashes and straightened her already straight blazer before following him.

***

Harry, Jade and the assembled newbies had been ushered through a number of matching corridors and into a small lecture hall, with a screen and lectern at the far end. Harry was already lost. As other people filed in, they took their seats, rustled about with coats and bags, and threw in the occasional apology for the occasional elbow which served to break at least a smidgeon of the ice between them all. As Harry took his seat and stowed his helmet beneath it, Jade sidled into the chair to his left.

"Well, maybe I'll start to get some answers here," he suggested.

"You might, but I wouldn't bank on it," warned Jade with a grin.

A door opened to the left of the screen, a voice from behind said, "No, Roy. No... " and the door was promptly shut again.

A moment later, a door to the right of the screen and behind the lectern burst open, and in strode a beaming Mr Newman, his blue pinstripe suit looking as neat as ever. "Ah!" he exclaimed in satisfaction. "Ah. Here you all are. They're all here, Doris," he enthused to his assistant, who now stood at the back, her eyes to the floor, smiling and nodding gently with a clipboarded sheaf of papers still clutched to her chest.

"So, the video. The first day video for all of you here, on your first day," Mr Newman reminded his audience.

Jade turned to Harry, still grinning. Harry nodded back.

"People," said Mr Newman, with astonishing reverence, "I give you your Prime Minister, the Right Honourable Royds Spittoon."

There were a few oohs and ahs, along with audible grunts from the assembly, and a clear, "Oh, fuck off!" from a dissenting man sitting somewhere a few rows behind Harry.

As the lights dimmed, Mr Newman held out his hand in introduction to the screen, nodding sagely and stepping backwards as he did so, before tripping over a wire and falling into a potential heap, unseen but certainly heard, as the lights went out altogether, and the film began to roll.

The round face of Royds Spittoon, his blond hair awry, like a badly-maintained ministerial thatched roof, came into view. He stood before the MOP building, with an aqua-blue sky dotted with fluffy, pure-white clouds above. Staring into the lens with a curious smile and giving a thumbs-up, he addressed the audience (who sat facing the screen) using his own brand of boisterous pomp, for which he had become famous.

"Before The Change referendum, it became apparent that things needed to change," he began. "The people wanted change, so we had a responsibility to provide it for the people. We wanted to give people what they wanted, which was change. So, for a change, we handed over the big decision to you, because that's what we wanted and what we hoped you wanted too. We crunched some figures and decided that it was. It made good common sense."

"No," called the lone vocal dissenter in the dark behind Harry.

Royds continued, "Change for the better. Change for the good. Change that would make Britain a truly Great Britain again, just like it always was. Like it always used to be. Changed back. A good change. Backwards to go forwards. Huzzah!"

"If you say so," whispered Jade to Harry, who nodded grimly.

"Rich. Powerful. Plentiful. Strong. Unleashed, like a monstrously great big British tiger driving a tank. A place of change. A place where people could be given opportunities – opportunities to become the best people they could be. The best people possible. You voted for it, so we're going to deliver it like a big, padded envelope covered in stamps with the Queen's face on. Britain. A place where everyone counts, even if they haven't got access to a calculator."

"Not for me, no," came the voice from the back.

"A kingdom united. A United Kingdom, under one queen. That is why we're ruddy proud to work with the Ministry of People. A collection of the best minds working together for the good of the people. People unburdened by the worries and machinations of politics. Politics has tried and politics has let the people down. People wanted change, and so we had The Change referendum; you voted, we did things, and now everything will change and be better." The Prime Minster waggled his hands in the air and pulled a funny face, with his eyes and mouth as wide as possible, exposing at least four fillings. "The Ministry of People is solid, credible proof of that, let me make that abundantly clear." His face got even funnier as he peered into the lens as if looking down a well for a hidden refugee.

"He's so right because he's one of us!" yelped a gleeful lady in the audience, who didn't have a funny face at all.

At this point, the film cut to an interior shot of the MOP building where the Prime Minister bounded his way through, still addressing the camera and still giving a thumbs-up. "Because of the Ministry of People, we have improved employment levels for the people, and we have increased worker satisfaction," he continued. "Because of that, we are a more productive nation, a happier nation, and a nation free from persecution and worry. Crime levels have been reduced, productivity is up, our economy is strong, education is also a thing, and our people are working for our people. This is what the people wanted, and this is what we are going to provide. A change for the better. A change for the long term. A change the people wanted, because they said they wanted it. The Change is coming, and nothing and nobody is going to change that."

"Wazzock," barked the voice from the back of the room.

"Yes, but he's *our* wazzock. He's doing his best under difficult circumstances. He's one of us. End of," snapped back the gleeful lady, with a smidgeon of holier-than-thou malice on the side.

"Our people are the best people," said Royds Spittoon, now lolloping through what looked like a vast, pristine laboratory where people in white lab coats and surgical masks stood working at tables piled with computers, machines, Bunsen burners and row after row of test tubes filled with liquids of all colours. The scientists at work seemed barely aware that their Prime Minister was walking among them, such was the intent and focus they had upon their work.

He wasn't wearing a mask, however, and kept on talking fervently. "People all over the world have always admired the British people – our spirit, our willingness, our strength and our compassion. Our ties, our collars and cufflinks. With the Ministry of People, we are giving the best of ourselves to the world. Getting it right for our people, so that our people can get it right for everyone in these times of change.

"A strong world; a happier world. You wanted control, so we're going to take control, control you, and give you that control using our controls. You'll have control, we'll have control and Britain will be in control of what it controls. Bazinga."

"HUZZAH!" yelled someone somewhere, likely punching the air as they did so.

"Did you just hear what I just heard?" said Jade under her breath.

"I think I did, yes."

"What. The. Actual. Heck. Did you vote for The Change, if you don't mind me asking?"

"Erm... " Harry looked about nervously to see if anyone was listening in before answering, "No; no, I didn't. In fact, I don't really know many who did if I'm honest."

"Hmmm. Me neither. But here we are."

"We thank you, the people, for the work you do to and for our people," continued the Prime Minister, practically frothing at the mouth with excitement now. He was stood outside the MOP building, a glorious, red sunset filling the sky. "Your people. The people. The work you do is making our nation great again, and for that we thank you. Our people thank you. You are the people. We the people thank you people, and look forward to meeting the people you send out among the people to make our people great. People! Make The Change! The Change is coming! Prepare and rejoice!"

With that, the screen turned blue, fading out all evidence of the Prime Minister and the MOP before the words "WE'RE YOUR KIND OF PEOPLE" replaced them in happy, big, white letters.

The screen faded, and the lights came back up.

"No, no. Fuck right off. Not for me," came the disgruntled voice from the back again before a middle-aged man in a long, grey coat stood up, shook his head and walked out the back door, firing a final "No!" into the face of a shocked-yet-determined-looking Doris, who was trying to stand in his way.

Meanwhile, a woman in a blue suit stood up and said, "Clap for Royds!"

Two people did, twice, before promptly sitting down again.

Harry looked at Jade. "Well, that explained nothing."

Jade, however, was staring at Mr Newman, who himself was looking at the screen from which the Prime Minister had just spoken to the room. Something was wrong. His face was red with anger, his fists clenched, and his veins bulged at his temples. He was shaking his head, muttering something indecipherable under his breath. Quick as a flash, Doris strode from the back of the room and confronted him, whispering something sharply into his ear. Abruptly, Newman looked about, nodded and took a deep breath. He smiled, but seemed a little lost. Doris simpered.

"Your Prime Minister, ladies and gentlemen; your Prime Minister," said Mr Newman, nodding gravely. "As a ministry, we are duty-bound to our government who are duty-bound to the East—"

Doris cleared her throat noisily, elbowing Mr Newman as she did so.

"Duty-bound to you, the people. Our people. Of course. Just as it should be," finished Mr Newman, before adding, "Duty-bound. Duty. Yes." He stared inwardly, frowning, as Doris adjusted her clipboard awkwardly before addressing the room.

"Stay in your seats ladies and gentlemen while we reconfigure the room," she said cheerfully. "Tea, coffee and biscuits will follow. Thank you."

"Baguettes?" asked Mr Newman, hopefully.

"Not now, no."

The lights came back up, a number of identically dressed technicians entered, and an uneasy chatter began to fill the room.

Harry turned to Jade. "So... what exactly just happened there then? Is this normal?"

She shook her head. "You'll soon find that there are things here that don't exactly make sense. That's part of the fun of working here, but it can be a bit frustrating sometimes, between you and me. Newman's a fruit loop, no question, but he's the boss too. The rumour is that he's been here since anyone can remember and he was involved in setting this place up with a couple of other boffins, or something like that. Daft as he seems, he knows his shit and he really looks out for the staff here. He's been great with me, very protective and very encouraging. Silly, old bastard," she added fondly.

"But what was that just now? I got the feeling he's not a fan of the Prime Minister... "

"I dunno. There's a bit of a culture of 'do what you're told and don't ask questions' here. You'll see."

Harry raised an eyebrow, but Jade broke into a huge smile in response.

"Listen, I'm not trying to put you off," she explained, laughing noisily, "God, I'm a shitty guide, aren't I? Seriously, it's a great place to work. I love it here, more than anywhere I've worked prior to now. Things can be a bit baffling sometimes, in terms of the way things are done and so on. But that's the same with everything right? From the top downwards. Baffling."

"I guess," said Harry.

Visitor

When Dad fell into one of his dark days, it affected everything in the house and nearby.

Even the silence felt darker. It was as if the world outside was doing its best to ignore us; people elsewhere were cosy in their homes, and warm light shone from their windows. They had no reason to come out or even think about us.

But in our house, everything would stop dead. Dad would lock himself away in his study, which was up in the loft, and accessed from his bedroom by a hatch and pull-down ladder. When he was up there, he would pull the ladder back up, shut the hatch door behind him and lock himself in. Occasionally, I would hear bumps and clunks as he padded about, up in the roof above, moving things. There would be one-way conversations on the phone, but I could never really hear what was said. Only the occasional word.

I never wanted to feel his empty despair for myself. I felt afraid of it. I worried that it would drag me in and pull me under too, taking me somewhere I didn't understand and couldn't control.

No. On those days, I read, doing all I could to lose myself in books and the worlds that existed on the pages within. On the days that Grandma and Grandpa couldn't come, I would send myself off to school in the mornings. Sometimes, when I came home to the stillness of our house, there would be food left for me in the fridge, which was the only evidence that Dad had emerged at some point during the day to feed himself and ensure I was fed too. This was how he coped, and how I had to cope too. I don't think Grandma and Grandpa always knew when he was having a dark day. Sometimes they would spot it, but sometimes not. I think Dad hid things from them from time to time. But there was always something in the fridge.

On this particular day, a visitor came.

It was a day when Grandpa was looking after me. Grandma was out shopping, and there was a knock at the front door. It was a spring day, but the temperature had dropped. I was in my bedroom when the knock came. I had been sitting on my bed, reading, with a pillow behind my back. From where I sat, I could see out across the fields towards the motorway – a distant strip of lorries and cars whizzing along the horizon. I'd lost interest in my book, though, instead watching with fascination the foggy mist that had crept across the fields towards our house. The motorway was no longer visible, with the grey tendrils of mist snaking ever closer by the time the knock came.

Grandpa had been making lunch. I heard him open the back door and have a conversation with another man. It went on for a few minutes. Perhaps it was the pedlar who went door to door selling cleaning products from the big sports bag he hefted over his shoulder. Dad had once told me he was an ex-criminal, and he had bought a pack of dusters from the man. When I'd asked him why, he'd replied that everyone deserved a second chance at life. The trouble was that now he'd bought something from him, the man kept coming back every fortnight, even though we didn't need any more dusters.

Grandpa was coming up the stairs. I wondered if he needed to see me about something or if the man had gone.

He walked along the landing past my room, and into Dad's room. I heard him go into Dad's bedroom and knock on the loft door with the pole that opened the hatch door. There was no answer.

"Gregory?" Grandpa called.

I sat up to listen. It was very rare that Dad would answer a knock when his study door was locked shut. I couldn't even remember the last time he had.

"Gregory? Your friend from Carmarthen is here for you again. Greg?" Grandpa enquired.

I didn't know a man from Carmarthen. I didn't even know where Carmarthen was, not then.

I heard the study door open and the ladder being lowered. I couldn't tell what Dad was saying. His voice was low, quiet. Grandpa didn't say anything.

There was someone coming upstairs. I swung my legs off the edge of my bed and went to the doorway to see who it was. I had just enough time to catch a glimpse of a man coming up the stairs, staring intently at me as he did, before there was a large, blurred movement, with something big rushing up past the man to get at me. I leaped back to close the door, forcing it shut against a sudden heavy weight. It slammed into the closed door, pushing back at me.

Frantically, I braced myself against it, holding it shut with my back pressed against it. Whatever it was, it was doing its level best to get in. I looked desperately around my bedroom for something to jam against the door, but anything I could possibly have used was out of reach, and there was no way I could leave the door now and stay safe.

There was a low, menacing growl from the other side of the door, and then the pressure was suddenly gone. But I didn't move. I didn't dare. The cold feeling of fear was in my veins and coursing through me; my breath was coming out in gasps.

I looked out the window to see that the fog had enveloped everything. I could only just make out the pointed wooden roof of the garage.

I was aware of voices, however. My dad was arguing with someone. It couldn't have been my grandpa, who was one of the most placid and kind people you could wish to meet. It had to be the *man from Carmarthen.*

"I CAN'T STOP NOW!" yelled my dad.

"You have to. She was never part of it, Gregory," replied a voice I didn't recognise. "It's hard I know; by God, I know. I've seen it too often before, but you have to put the boy first and do right by him. He's the important one."

At this, the growling on the landing began again, and I pushed back again from my feet, holding the door tightly closed. It was threatening or warning somehow. The voices next door carried on, seemingly oblivious. I wanted to listen – I felt like I needed to – but I couldn't grasp all of the words. The animal outside wanted my attention.

"But... so close now! Almost... it's all I need to... back to how everything was," pleaded my dad.

The animal was barking now. A dog. A terrifying and angry dog that wanted me to pay attention to it.

"... too dangerous, Greg. Far too dangerous... I can't even go back down there anymore... for the sake of what remains of my sanity... I don't know what would happen to you if you tried... "

Scratches against the door. Frantic. A heavy thud. Another. Ferocious bark after ferocious bark, but it wasn't coming in unless I let it. Still my father and the other man carried on their conversation.

"... in the loft, after all this time... this moment, for God's sake..." continued my dad.

"That time is coming, but it's not now... ready when it does... everything I could for you and, by Jove, I will continue to do so but... listen. Don't go there... ruin you and centuries... "

"Get out!"

The barking had intensified, it was actually hurting inside my head now. It was too much.

"STOP IT!"

Before I even had time to realise that I'd yelled out, the door gave way, and I was thrown against the bed. I scrambled to my feet, turning to face the malevolent force that had burst in to fill my room, but there was nothing there.

Everything was still. The only sound was that of my breath, and my heart hammering in my chest.

I looked at the door as it slowly came to rest on its hinges, halfway open. There were no scratches to be seen in the paintwork. There was no conversation either. Outside, the mist was gone without a trace, and I could see across to the motorway once again.

I ventured out onto the landing. "Dad?"

No response.

"Dad? Grandpa?"

No answer. The landing was silent and empty, only it wasn't the landing anymore. It was a corridor, stretching off in both directions into the darkness. Along either side, countless doors – all closed – ran off into infinity. Somewhere in the distance, far away, a dog was barking. Look at me. Look at me!

8. Training

This was the life. At the MOP, every day was different because, frankly, Harry never quite knew what to expect. There were lectures, some of which had something of a sociological slant while some were more psychological. He was excitedly looking forward to meeting the people he would be training, if that was indeed what he and his fellow newbies were working towards. There were tests, in which Harry scored quite highly. Despite not exactly knowing where all this was heading just yet, Harry felt as if he was doing well. He enjoyed the rides in on his moped. He enjoyed working in this incredible ornament of a building. He still hadn't asked anyone about the cement factory thing, and he intended to get around to that as soon as he had a minute. There just never seemed to be time. Besides, whenever he felt he had a moment to catch his breath, Mr Newman would appear, as if on cue, and ask how he was getting on.

Mr Newman was every bit as curious as he'd been warned to expect. Most of the time, he seemed to be in his own little world, spouting what seemed like almost nonsensical ramblings, well-meant though they were. There were occasions on which he seemed much more lucid, offering Harry practical advice and solutions to work-based queries. It was a strange balance, a balance that he wasn't entirely sure how much Mr Newman had control of, but that was the way it was, and everyone else seemed fairly ambivalent about it. There was no doubt that Mr Newman was fond of Harry, however, sometimes to the point of it being a little embarrassing. Some of Harry's newly made friends seemed to have noted the fact that there were numerous times that their CEO would steer Harry off for a chat, his hand on Harry's shoulder in a fatherly fashion, just to see whether all was well and he was enjoying the canteen food. Nobody else seemed to get this treatment, as far as Harry could tell, but rather than make an issue of it, he kept his head down and focussed on the job in hand.

Jade had quickly become a good friend. Like Mr Newman, she checked in on Harry from time to time to see how he was getting on. Harry enjoyed her company and her brazen refusal to conform. She was edgy. She had a potty mouth. She was fun. She had mischief in her eyes, and it wasn't long before he wanted to take that mischief by the hand and run away with it, across fields and through forests. But Harry wasn't necessarily a 'spur of the moment, run away and get mischievous' kind of guy, so he generally tended towards chatting and sharing his prawn cocktail crisps with her at lunch in the canteen instead.

His days now followed a decent routine of riding in down Derbyshire's leafy country lanes with the spluttering Darren. He'd still see old Doreen Twigge, waving from exactly where she always stood on the pavement, regular as clockwork. Just very old and very wrinkly clockwork, stooped and with the odd prickly chin-hair. Breakfast from the staff canteen would follow upon arrival (subsidised – the bacon-and-egg muffins were something else), with coffee, and a catch up with Jade and one or two others, then into the working day: timetabled modules delivered in training rooms throughout the MOP buildings, which had been carefully scheduled, planned and plotted, and which delivered the right amount of variety to keep them interesting. That was split by an hour for lunch (Harry was now so organised as to bring in his own sandwiches that he'd prepped the night previously, despite the daily mountain of ham baguettes that seemed to be the canteen speciality), which was taken in the refectory or on picnic benches in the maintained grounds behind the hall, and not forgetting the occasional use of the staff gym (he never thought he'd hear himself say that) before Darrening himself home each evening. Things were good, and the dull feeling that had been a constant cloud over his time at Chegwin and Blunt was receding.

Of his old job, there had been the occasional text message from Alan, who always signed off with his name, even though his contact details appeared automatically at the top of each missive. "MISS U MATE. HOPE UR GUD. ALAN" had been the first one. "HOWS UR NEW JOB? ARE THE GIRLS THERE FIT? ALAN" was another a few days later, and "WISH U WERE HERE. IT'S FKIN SHITE. ALAN" was one of the more recent efforts. Although they hadn't spoken as such, a number of text message conversations had established that Alan had clearly had enough of bus-driver data and was actively looking for a way out too. He'd seemed quite interested in Mr Newman, however, and often asked about him. "HE SOUNDS LIKE A RIGHT BELLEND, MATE. ALAN" had been his opinion one afternoon, while it also emerged that Alice, Harry's former owl-like office manager with the large and unsettling eyes, had taken ill suddenly and been replaced with someone equally as odd. "ALL A BIT HUSH HUSH, MATE. SOMETHING NOT RITE. ALAN" was as much as his friend could offer on the matter, but thinking about Alice wasn't high on Harry's list of things to do these days.

Or at least it wasn't until late one afternoon towards the end of his training period. Harry had just been to the toilet and was returning to the lecture hall to complete a written test he had almost finished. It was taking him longer than usual as the nearest loo was out of action, so he'd wandered off to a wing of the building he'd not seen before (although it looked practically identical to the others, having warmly lit corridors with regularly spaced and unmarked doors, all closed) in an effort to find somewhere to relieve himself. He was just re-emerging from the gents when he almost bumped into someone heading down the corridor. "Sorry," he said automatically, stepping back before noting that it was, in fact, Alice, his previous boss. The juxtaposition of his old world and his new one, coupled with the fact that he was still zipping up his flies, caught him momentarily by surprise.

By the time he called her name, she was rounding the end of the corridor in which he stood. "Alice?"

She was gone. Harry, curious and slightly unnerved, nipped after her in a quasi-jog before rounding the corner just in time to see her join the end of a queue of people who were shuffling into a room, under the guidance of two identically dressed technicians who stood either side of the door. Harry stopped and watched, with the unnerving feeling that he'd blundered into something he shouldn't have. The people in the queue were silent, all dully shuffling forwards at the behest of the technicians, who appeared to be scanning each person in turn with a small handheld device that let forth a shrill beep as each one passed. There was something so oddly docile about them all, and it wasn't until he turned his attention back to Alice at the end of the queue that he realised what had been nagging him: everyone else in the queue was dressed exactly the same as her. In fact, they were all the same height too, and appeared to be sporting the same unimaginative hairstyle.

9. Alex

Harry was itching and ready to put his learning to use. But despite her one-year advantage over him, Jade had kept her cards close to her chest when it came to letting him know what exactly he was in for beyond training. He rather got the feeling that she enjoyed holding back on the details, as if she were purposefully teasing him.

They'd both retired to the cosy confines of the Pelican and Shrew, a charming and smoky country pub a mile further up the lane from the hall, to round off the week and celebrate Harry ending the training period in a pleasant hour of convivial conversation, cosy lighting, comfortable seating, cheese-and-onion crisps and a cheeky beer, as had become their end-of-week wont.

"I don't know exactly what to expect," mused Harry.

Jade listened, absentmindedly twirling the plastic cocktail stirrer and causing the ice to clink in her glass of gin and tonic as her friend spoke.

"I mean, I don't think I could have learned much more in terms of what they've crammed into my brain these last few weeks, but it's like everything here. Just do what's put in front of you and everything will be fabulous. Crack on and don't ask questions. I mean, I don't mind. I just feel a little unsure as to what's next." He was staring at a set of brass horseshoes on the wall, their shapes shivering with the reflected glow from the fireplace. "It's like I feel really ready to hit the ground running, to get going, but I'm not sure where to, exactly. I can't deny that I'm a little nervous too if I'm honest. There are things about this place that excite me, but there are other things that properly spook me out."

"Now you're getting it." Jade chuckled.

"You're no bloody help," declared Harry in return with a snort. "I've been asking you for guidance for weeks. You were my guide once way back when, remember?"

"Yes, and I was very fucking good at it too. You don't get my help that easily, though. I was new here once too, and spooked out as well sometimes. I had to start from the bottom and learn as I went along, so why should you be any different?"

"Because it would be helpful? And just generally nice?"

"Not my style, Saltalicious; not my style. But I will tell you one thing: don't be surprised by anything that's put your way over the next few weeks. There are things we do here that affect all levels of society, in one way or another. You'll start off small," she said, fixing Harry in the eye as she picked up and ate a single crisp from the open packet they'd been sharing, which was on the small, round table between them, "and then work up to something bigger." At this point, she grabbed a handful and noisily chomped down on it, crumbs shooting off in all directions as she did so.

Harry rolled his eyes to the ceiling. "You're such a classy bird," he pointed out.

"Meeehh," replied Jade, opening her mouth wide so that he got a good view of the mushy cheese-and-onion mass and her tongue within.

"Nice. Just, nice. Are you trying to seduce me? If I knew any better... "

"Which you don't," stated Jade sarcastically. "Neither of us do. We're both as clueless as the next person. I may have been here a year longer than you, but I'm still at a loss about what goes on deep inside the MOP. I intend to find out one day, though. Just you wait and see. I've got a plan, me. Anyway, I want to know all about your first day, once it's done."

"You will," Harry confirmed. He'd also pondered on just how Jade went about seducing people. He couldn't deny having experienced the occasional bout of loinal stirrage since he'd met her, and he wasn't sure exactly what to do in regard to that. There was something curiously attractive about her – curious in that it hit you the moment you looked at her, but it was difficult to say exactly what you'd just been hit by. She was pretty, but not in the way that usually floated his dinghy of thingy. Yet the more he looked at her, spoke to her and spent time in her company, the more his warmth towards her grew, and the more he found himself struggling to get the right words out. She was infectious, and Harry was bitten. He loved her company, and as recently as last Tuesday, he had awoken with a start from a dream involving the two of them, a picnic rug, a Black Forest gateau and several wheels of exquisite cheese.

"Anyway, what do you mean 'spooked'?" asked Jade, shaking Harry free from his dream memory. "What have you seen?"

"Oh, I dunno," said Harry, a little abashedly. "I thought I saw my old boss Alice here the other week."

"That's not spooky. It's a big place," suggested Jade nonchalantly, "Maybe she got a job here?"

"Yeah – no, it's not that," answered Harry, "at least I hope not; I wouldn't work with her again if you paid me to. It was just that she appeared to be in a line of people all dressed exactly like her, and they were being marched into a room together. It was just a little bit weird."

Jade took another crisp and shrugged. "Yeah, I wouldn't know about that."

"You're hiding something. I know it."

"Seriously. Maybe she's an Oompa Loompa or something. A queue of people isn't weird. Get over yourself."

"Oh, and what about the building itself? The cement-works

thing. What the hell is that about? I've lived around here since I was a kid, and it's always been a cement works. How the hell does it turn into a mansion when you get right up close to it? What is it, some kind of projection screen? Lights? Mirrors? What?"

Jade choked momentarily on the crisp she'd just taken, such was her excitement over the new topic.

"Oh, now, *that*," she said as soon as she was able, patting herself on the chest as the offending snack finally went stomachwards, "Yes, how cool is that? Mint, innit? I'll be honest though, Harry. I don't have a bloody clue how that works.

"Truly?"

"Seriously. Not a Scooby. The technology that powers that must be mind-boggling, and I've been desperate to find out about it since I got here a year ago. Nobody seems to know, though. I've asked maintenance guys, technicians, Dave on the gate, and even the girls in the canteen. Nobody has a bloody clue. None of them. Or if they do, they're not letting on. Trust me. There's more to this place than meets the eye, and I'm going to get right to the bottom of it one day."

***

The following Monday morning, Harry reflected on their conversation as he stood waiting by the door of the examination cubicle on what had been, on the ride in, a beautifully bright start. He allowed himself a brief smile and a bemused shake of his head before snapping his attention back to the present. His first subject, or subjects, awaited his arrival inside. The conditions were controlled: the steel door remained locked, and was to be opened only when the session was due to begin. He looked at his watch. There was a good couple of minutes to go yet. He'd hoped that the reading he'd put in at home this weekend was enough. He couldn't see into the cubicle; they were keeping him guessing until the last minute, almost as if they were toying with him. A small, round window in the door gave no indication of the interior, other than a blurry impression of a light source within, obscured as it was by thick, frosted glass and a wire mesh.

He was primed with a folder of documents, the most hefty and important of which had been vacuum-sealed in a large, blue, plastic envelope bearing his name that Doris (Newman's secretary) had presented him with when he arrived that morning. Underneath his name were the date and the instructions "Do Not Open Until 12pm" in forceful, large, black lettering.

Not for the first time in this new and perplexing vocation, he found himself wondering what to expect.

And as was often proving to be the case at such moments, Mr Newman appeared; he rounding the end of the corridor, spied Harry and motored towards him forehead first. "Salt!"

"Mr Newman," he answered, bracing himself.

"About to begin, I see! Excellent. They say the start is the best place to begin, and, begad, I see that's exactly where you are. All set, Salt?"

"I think so – I have all my materials," Harry answered cheerfully, indicating his precious printed bundle.

"Good, good! Now, Salt," Mr Newman's tone quietened, he quickly looked about the empty corridor and took Harry by the shoulder. "Come by, lad, come by." He edged his puzzled employee to the other side of the warmly lit, distinctly featureless (save for identical cubicle doors) and utterly deserted passageway. "Salt, what you are about to undertake is not for the faint-hearted. Nor for the fainted or, indeed, the asleep," he confided. "It takes guts, Salt. It takes steel, it takes wit, it takes patience and it takes it out of you, you can be sure of that."

"Really? I had no idea that—"

"Let it not trouble you, Salt. A man of your height and gait shouldn't struggle," said Mr Newman cheerfully, standing back to look him up and down, and to take his fill of Harry's countenance.

"I wish you all the luck in the world young Salt, I really do," declared a beaming Mr Newman, with more than just a hint of emotion, as Harry started to wonder once more what he had let himself in for. "And," announced Mr Newman, flicking up his left arm with a flourish so that his sleeve pulled back to reveal an elegant and smart golden timepiece attached to a blue-and-green striped leather strap about his wrist, "in four, three, two, one..."

At this, an alarm blared a short, violent note and a lock clicked. "There we are, Salt; there we are! In you go, and the best of British!"

The door to the cubicle stood ajar. Harry, feeling suddenly both nervous and excited, turned to Mr Newman, who gave him a swift thumbs-up. With that, Harry stepped in, shutting the door behind him.

Again came the short blare of the alarm and the click of a lock. He was sealed inside, and there appeared to be no lock on this side of the grey, steel door. Although that would normally have been something of a worry, Harry was instead focussed on what sat before him. All expectations and thoughts of what he was going to encounter had evaporated.

He was now standing in a small room with a concrete floor. Three of the four walls were white, one was mirrored, and the white ceiling was home to a solitary energy-saving lightbulb, which hung down underneath a grey, metal lampshade.

Immediately beneath it, the bulb illuminated one of only three pieces of furniture in the room – a stainless steel table. Against the back wall sat the other two: a cushioned, grey chair with arms; and a small cabinet, also made of stainless steel and featuring a number of drawers. A water fountain sat atop it, accompanied by a small stack of plastic drinking cups. To the side was a small, chrome pedal bin. Clinical.

However, it was what was on the table that had captured and was currently doing a splendid job of holding on to Harry's attention. In the middle, enjoying the lion's share of the bulb's illuminative powers, sat, or maybe lay, a creature. And it was looking at Harry. The electricity of an instant heightening of the senses immediately possessed Harry.

"YEEEARGH!" He leaped backwards upon meeting the gaze of the thing, dropped his paperwork to the floor, and promptly turned his attention to fleeing the scene, grasping the cold, smooth and round door handle with both hands and turning it. It was no use. The door remained resolutely locked.

He looked back and locked his gaze with that of the creature. "Let me out!" he called, banging the palm of his hand a number of times against the door to noisy effect. "Let me out! There's a bastard thing in here!" He pounded the door twice more and gave the handle a damn good turning again, but Mr Newman, or indeed anyone else, made no attempt to introduce themselves into the fray.

There was only one thing for it. Harry was going to have to confront the thing and take it on – alone. His hands released the inert door handle slowly, and as he brought his arms down to his side, he turned unhurriedly back to look at the table and the monstrosity upon it. *No quick moves, Harry; no quick moves*, he told himself.

Monstrosity was, however, harsh. As Harry took a deep breath and once again returned the creature's gaze, he made an attempt to study it in a little more detail. Completely covered in white fur and no bigger than a small Scottie dog, the animal had not yet moved at all. What Harry had immediately taken as a fixed stare from the big, dark eyes was actually something duller than that. It was lifeless. There was no life behind those eyes whatsoever.

It was now that Harry, rapidly calming the hell down, began to feel some sympathy towards the thing. He was reminded briefly of small seal pups in the Arctic, as the creature did indeed possess four small, pawed feet and a small, black snout above a tiny, closed and whiskered mouth. It was close to being a seal pup, but it most definitely wasn't that. The long, furry tail – which Harry now saw extended out, motionless, across the far end of the stainless steel surface of the table – was enough to confirm that.

Whatever it was, it was dead. And it was now that Harry noticed another feeling welling up in him: guilt. Whatever it was that he'd signed up for, it wasn't this. If he was standing in his cubicle, looking down upon an animal that had been killed purely for him to do his job (whatever that yet was), then how many of his fellow new starters now found themselves in the same position throughout the MOP building? And, besides, what had this to do with people, for the love of piss?

He stared at the poor, prostrate thing for a moment, as if waiting for someone to give him an answer. Feeling a little annoyed when nobody did, he saw his sheaf of paperwork, still scattered on the floor, poking out from which was the sealed envelope. He looked at his watch – it was 12.05pm.

Bending down to pull together the papers, he shuffled them into a straight-enough order and then knocked them together on the table, in the style of a newsreader getting ready to clock off for the night. Placing them down on the metal surface, next to the silent animal, he took the envelope from the top of the pile and ripped open the plastic covering.

Inside was a disappointingly concise white paper document of four pages, looking suspiciously like an instruction manual for the assembly of a Swedish coffee table. On the front cover was a line drawing of the thing that lay on the table, and a single word. "Alex," read Harry out loud.

At that, the creature twitched, and Harry froze. "Shit!"

The creature cocked its head to one side, and – as ridiculous as Harry found the whole thing – looked at him in what was most definitely a quizzical manner before opening its mouth and mewing quietly, then it gurgled from the opposite end, arched its back and lifted itself up onto its legs to excrete a small, shiny and brown gift onto the previously stainless steel surface.

Harry winced. Having never been a dog or cat owner (his parents were allergic to furry animals and therefore his childhood pet had been a tortoise called Gordon), he was not into the business of cleaning up turds, and he hadn't planned on signing up today.

Frowning at the animal in what he hoped was something of an authoritative and disgusted manner, Harry felt even more annoyed when the creature simply returned his stare with a look of vomit-inducing cuteness, blinked its big, dark eyes twice and mewed once again before smiling back at him.

No. It couldn't be. Surely not. But, yes, the infernally adorable, shitting furball was smiling back at Harry with a look of devotion that he wasn't quite sure what to do with.

"Off," commanded Harry. "Off."

Again, the table-top pup simply cocked its head to one side and blinked at him.

"Off. Fucking off."

Again came that smile. Harry rolled his eyes, sighed and opened the manual. Sure enough, there were more line drawings and very little else by way of an explanation. He looked pleadingly towards the mirrored wall. He felt uneasily that he was being watched and assessed from behind the reflective surface, that it was a two-way affair. Only his one-way exasperated reflection stared back at him, however, and so he returned his attention to the manual.

The first picture showed 'Alex' on a table, with a crude and basically drawn human smiling at him and letting forth a speech bubble containing the animal's name. Harry could work that one out for himself.

The second panel was a little more ambiguous and, rather bizarrely, featured the same smiling person with another speech bubble, only this time it contained a single musical note, and in this instance Alex was standing on two legs while sporting a top hat, holding a cane and winking at the reader with his left eye.

The panel after that showed Alex in what appeared to be a tiny bathtub while the smiling idiot who had also featured in panels one and two looked as if he was giving him a shoulder rub. Harry looked doubtfully at Alex. Alex peered back and sneezed in a dainty fashion.

The fourth panel was the hardest to decipher. The smiler and Alex were once again in attendance, only this time they had been joined by a wizened-looking visitor in a wheelchair. In this scene, Alex was being presented to the elderly caller, who was responding by smiling heartily and letting rip with a speech bubble filled with a solitary heart.

This time it was Harry who cocked his head in puzzlement.

"What are you, Alex?" he asked.

Alex let forth a noise that was far too close to a giggle for Harry's liking, at which he set his jaw and walked over to the cabinet on the opposite wall. After putting down the leaflet and opening the top drawer, Harry found a small roll of plastic monogrammed with a repeating pattern of purple bones, which he realised quickly was in fact a fresh roll of small bags for collecting dog shit.

"Ah, great. Task number one," grumbled Harry under his breath, pulling out a bag and tearing it away from the roll at the perforations. As he'd seen dog walkers do on the common near his house during his weekend constitutionals, Harry slipped his hand into the bag, making it into a glove, before turning his attention to Alex's steaming discharge.

With a look back at the mirrored wall before turning back to the poo with a lurching heave of his stomach, Harry confirmed to himself that this was not something he was particularly looking forward to or indeed ready for. He turned away from the table and took a deep breath, held it so as not to allow any noxious fumes to enter his delicate nasal passages, and scooped up Alex's deposit. Thankfully for Harry, it was a pretty solid affair and left no residue on the table. With no elegance whatsoever, he clasped the ejectamenta with as much pressure as he dare and, using his other hand, turned the bag inside out using his fingertips with an expression of pure disgust on his face.

But he'd done it. In his left hand, he now held a dangling and poo-heavy sack. Alex mewed in appreciation from the table, stretching his legs and neck out contentedly. Harry himself felt surprisingly proud about the whole affair, pressed his foot to the pedal on the chrome bin and dropped in the sack, faeces and all.

It was at that point that the alarm sounded once again, causing Harry to jump out of his skin. Once more, right on cue, the lock of the door clicked. But instead of the door opening to let Harry out, the smooth handle rattled a number of times before turning. The door then opened to let someone in.

"Hello?" came a confused sounding voice from the corridor. "Anybody in there?"

"Er, yes – that would be me," replied Harry.

"Ah. Right. Th-there we are then," declared the voice, and in came a shuffling old lady, stooped over a walking frame. As she clacked her way into the cubicle, she looked up to survey the situation.

"Oh no," she said. "Oh, no, no, no. That just w-w-won't do, now will it?" She stopped on the spot where she was standing and chomped on her dentures a couple of times in thought. "No," she concluded, looking to the floor sadly. "Bugger me, no, no, no, no, no. Not ever."

"Hello," ventured Harry. "I'm Harry, may I help you?"

The crone's head shot up and she looked about the ceiling, as if catching the scent of a burning Yorkshire pudding. "Wassat? Eh? What now?"

"Harry. My name is Harry. Here," he added, moving to collect the cushioned chair from where it stood and setting it out just behind where she wobbled on her frame, "have yourself a sit down." He patted the cushion of the chair invitingly while looking back towards the mirrored wall hopefully.

"Chair is it?" said the old woman, and she chuckled before shuffling over, taking hold of the chair arms and slowly sitting herself down. "I know your game. Sit me down, cup of tea, bun, then steal all my jewellery. I know."

"Well, no. That wasn't the plan." Harry laughed nervously.

"No, no, no. Never was," continued the old lady, staring at

Harry with rheumy eyes and shaking her head gently. "Never was. Oh Derek... "

"No," stated Harry. "Derek's not here. I'm Harry. Ha-reee."

"I know that, you blithering oik," she fired back in a moment of fierce lucidity. "Harry you are, and Mavis I am. I just want my Derek, but he's not here now is he." She said this more as a statement of fact than a question, and Harry felt the note of sadness in her voice as she did so.

"Tractor," she said softly, now staring both at Harry and at some distant memory she appeared to be conjuring up where he stood. "Always the bloody tractor. Loved it... I'll never know, I'm sure... Loved the dratted thing... " At this her voice broke, and her already runny eyes began to well up with tears.

"Oh, Derek, you silly old bugger... " By now, Mavis was sobbing noisily where she sat, her shoulders shaking. She made for a desperately sad and pitiful looking sight, and Harry suddenly felt uncomfortably far from his comfort zone. This wasn't just another day at work; this was another test, and right now – after having felt so triumphant on cleaning up after Alex moments before – he felt as if he were failing things miserably.

Alex. From the moment Mavis had blundered into the room, Harry had forgotten all about the white bundle of bathos on the metal table. He picked up the manual from where he'd left it, and turned to study the closing panel once more before turning to look at Alex, who was panting slightly on the table. Mavis sniffled from the chair.

"Mavis," said Harry loudly.

"Derek, is that you?" she asked hopefully.

"No, Mavis," responded Harry, wincing. "Mavis, I'm going to give you something to hold."

"AARGH!" screamed the old lady, "Filth! Perverted filth!"

Deciding not to answer but to instead just get on with it, he scooped up the creature from where it sat. It settled into his arms immediately, and felt warm and soft as he cradled it to his chest, much more so that he expected it to, somehow.

"Here you go, Mavis. This is Alex," he offered gently, and he delicately placed the creature in her lap.

"Aargh! Aargh... " Mavis sat bolt upright, stiff with nerves.

Alex, however, merely settled himself in her lap and looked up at her adoringly. As Mavis looked down at the creature and plucked up the courage to touch it, she began to settle and relax. Alex merely cooed back at her, never once taking his eyes from hers.

"Oh my. Oh I... oh I say," chuntered Mavis, a smile breaking out across her face. The more she stroked Alex, the more he mewed contentedly, his tail wagging slowly across her lap.

Harry felt himself sigh with relief, and found himself smiling too. It was a beautiful scene, save the godawful Cold War interrogation-room backdrop. Alex had settled into Mavis's lap by now, as if they were long-term friends, and any thoughts of Derek and his enigmatic tractor appeared to have faded altogether.

Harry sighed with satisfaction, taking a handkerchief from his pocket and wiping his hands because that felt like the right thing to do. "You're alright there, Mavis?" he asked, pocketing the hankie as he did so. "He's not bothering you?"

"Oh Lord, no," smiled Mavis, "Heavens, no. He's wonderful. Just wonderful! Where on earth did you find this little one?"

"Well, just there as a matter of fact," replied Harry a little awkwardly, pointing to the table.

But Mavis was too preoccupied with her new companion to notice his response, and she didn't even flinch when the alarm blared once more, the lock clicked and the door swung open to allow Mr Newman to enter, his hand already held out in front of him as he galloped purposefully towards Harry.

"Good work, Salt! Sensational!" He gripped Harry's hand firmly and shook it three times before withdrawing his own and placing it on the startled lad's shoulder. "You got it; by Gerald, I knew you would. Look at her. Just look at her. Go on."

Harry went on and just looked at her. She was utterly taken and infatuated with the creature, which continued to mew and look up her adoringly.

"What, erm... " began Harry as he looked on, "What is that thing actually? Is it real? A robot?"

Mr Newman's brow beetled in excitement, and he escorted Harry to the corner of the cubicle. "A real robot, yes," he whispered. "Part robot, part biological. Designed to keep the elderly company, to provide them with joy, happiness and... well, the other one, you know?"

"Not really, no."

"No matter. Alex is a prototype we're testing out here at the MOP. Our elder citizens, the senior citizens of our great nation, have been there, seen it all and eaten most of it. They've given for our country their whole lives, and, by Ernest, I'll be buggered if they're going to sit alone and windy for their final days. Loneliness is a killer, Salt," concluded Mr Newman, fixing Harry with a determined stare, "remember that."

"I see... " pondered Harry.

Mr Newman continued, "Alex and his ilk are designed to observe, learn and respond. They'll keep the old folk company, helping them out and boosting their levels of happiness exponentially. It's intuitive, see? Learning what their owners like and need, and making for the best of companions. The test you carried out here just now was proof of that. It hasn't been easy, Salt. These things rarely are. There've been plenty of malfunctions and botched tests, but you've joined us just as we're getting these little beggars right."

Mr Newman moved to where Mavis sat, and he leaned down to look up at her, a dozy smile firmly fixed on his shiny ball bearing of a head. "YOU CAN KEEP HIM YOU KNOW, MAVIS," he said slowly and far too loudly. "ALEX. HE'S ALL YOURS TO TAKE HOME, MAVIS. YES."

"Don't be preposterous, you silly, little man," admonished Mavis, "I couldn't possibly take this little laddie home."

"OF COURSE YOU CAN, MAVIS," confirmed a beaming Newman, rubbing his hands together tightly as he wandered over to the small unit of drawers at the far end of the room, and then returned holding a red, leather collar and lead, which he attached around Alex's neck.

"But what on earth shall I feed him with?" asked Mavis worriedly.

"JUST LOVE AND KINDNESS, MAVIS."

"Pah," spat Mavis, with such force that necessitated her to chomp her momentarily dislodged dentures back into position, "I couldn't possibly do that."

"NOW, NOW, MAVIS, DON'T BE MODEST," simpered Mr Newman.

"He'll starve! And for goodness sakes stop ruddy shouting, will you?"

"GOOD, GOOD! THERE WE ARE NOW," continued Mr Newman, oblivious.

Alex had leaped to the floor and stood waiting as Mr Newman began to help Mavis from her chair, motioning to Harry to assist.

"I don't think he needs food at all," spoke Harry into her ear as they lifted her upright.

"THAT'S GOOD, ISN'T IT? HERE WE ARE, OLD WOMAN!" he yelled, pressing the looped end of Alex's lead into her hand. Harry noticed that the creature had his name embossed in bright-red letters on a shiny, metal oval that dangled from his collar.

By now, Mavis was smiling at the creature on the floor as it looked back up at her playfully. As she shuffled to the door, aided by Harry and the grinning Mr Newman, Alex trotted along behind and into the corridor with her.

Harry stood and watched as she joined a procession of elderly citizens who were emerging, one by one, from the remaining cubicle doors that ran the length of the corridor. Each had their own Alex on identical red leads, all obediently and loyally following behind.

"Look at that, Salt. Marvellous!" Mr Newman was shaking his head in wonder. "With each Alex that heads out into the world, another geriatric finds themselves in good company. Intuitive company, begad. Serving, fetching and keeping those old minds sharp."

Harry found himself smiling again. "That's actually pretty fantastic," he said, watching the aged cavalcade as it slowly filed arthritically onwards. "But... without meaning to sound daft, what does this have to do with the Ministry of People, exactly?"

"Aha! Your inquisitive mind delivers right on point," enthused Mr Newman, eagerly spinning to face him. "People. This ministry is designed for the betterment of all people. Not just those who are out earning and taxing themselves with the returning of taxes. From the young to the old, the Ministry of People is doing all it can to make the world better for all people. You. Me. Him. Her. That one over there," he stated, pointing vigorously at an old chap at the back of the queue heading out with his new creature consort. "Alex and all his furry, little chums are taking the pressure off rest-home and hospital staff and caregivers, not to mention families up and down the country. Less pressure for them, and with these little blighters being so reliable and ruddy durable, they're money-savers too. Stick that in your pipe and inhale it rapidly, that's what I say. Britain. Britain. Britain!"

Mr Newman reached into his trouser pocket and produced a small tin, clicked it open and helped himself to a small, white sweet. "Mint," announced Mr Newman decisively, patting Harry hard on the back before setting off rapidly in the opposite direction to which they had been facing. He'd reached the far end of the corridor and was about to turn the corner when he stopped, turned and huffed back towards Harry, who stood watching his advancing, determined and increasingly shiny face with a perplexed expression.

"Don't forget to file your report, there's a boy," puffed Mr Newman at the point when he found himself nose to nose with Harry. "All details, including the shit." That done, he turned and motored off once again, spinning neatly on his heels at the corridor end and out of sight.

Idris

*D*ad never got over losing Mum.
  It never stopped affecting him. I guess now that it was a case of time. It's supposed to heal. I think it does heal some things, or at least it heals them temporarily, but it doesn't erase things or rub them out completely. What's done is done. No matter how well something heals, it can still leave scars. As a child, I didn't fully understand it, but I was always aware of this dark, black shadow that followed my dad around. Most of the time, he was able to keep it locked away, but when it surfaced and took hold of him, he changed.

  I know he didn't mean to let it surface and overwhelm him like that, but it did. He couldn't always lock it away, and couldn't always resist it, and when it burst free, it overwhelmed him and everything he did.

  When it happened, he would disappear. Grandma and Grandpa were ready to step in. They understood it. They knew the drill. Dad wouldn't say much. He would spend hours up in his study, surrounded by his books and papers, working frantically. His cabinets of papers. His fridge. His trunk. The things he locked away. It was his private place, but I'd seen enough to know the layout. He could have lived in there and survived alone if he'd wanted to. His work consumed him often enough, but when he had his dark spells, he would throw himself headlong into it. When he did emerge, he looked grey. Worn and tired. I remember his eyes, so often red and bloodshot from a lack of sleep. He'd smile, but there was no conviction behind it.

I'd go in to take him drinks, such as a cup of tea, and he would be so grateful. Too grateful, almost. He'd hold me by the shoulders and tell me how good I was. He'd apologise for being so busy, but would tell me he'd make everything right again and that we would go on holiday soon. To Wales.

This time he was crying. I had come upstairs to get something out of my room. My room sat at the other end of the landing to Dad's bedroom, which led up into his study.

I heard him before I saw him. Giant, snotty, shaking sobs. His door was ajar, and I peered through, my heart in my mouth and unable to speak. He was kneeling by the bed, with a box of photographs scattered across the blanket, and in one hand he held a colour picture. I couldn't see what it was, but I was too confused by the sight of my dad in such turmoil to worry about that.

"I'm so sorry, Helen! So, so sorry!" He apologised, over and over.

It wasn't his fault, though. He'd had nothing to do with Mum's death. It wasn't Dad's fault.

I'd backed away, about to leave, but he'd seen me. He looked at me, and there was something foreign in his eyes at first. I shouldn't have been there in his room. He grabbed me, and I froze, unsure of what would come next. But he held me; he held me close to him as his body shook with violent sobs.

"She should still be here. With us. Now," he declared.

I didn't say anything. I was still numb at seeing my dad so worked up and talking like this. I could only hug him back, and he held on tighter as I did. I looked about his room, the afternoon sunlight awash with dust – lazy dust, dust that had no right to be here, oblivious to the pain my dad felt.

The holiday to Wales did come eventually, a month or two later. We needed the break, the space. We needed to get out and remind ourselves that there was still a world outside of our house and the grief that filled it like a fog.

As it turned out, it was actually a beautiful summer, and we had a few lovely walks together around Dolgellau.

It was the happiest and most positive I'd seen Dad for a long time. During the drive there, he let me play some of my tapes on the car stereo, and we'd also listened to the tennis at Wimbledon on the radio. He'd brought some big, heavy, old books to read with him, things he said he was studying and would look at closer while we were on holiday. He had bought me a few new books too, including one about King Arthur.

Those stories had always appealed to me, and my dad did all he could to encourage my interest. I'd get lost in the myths and legends about how Arthur pulled the sword Excalibur from the stone, his battles with Mordred, the adventures of Merlin and the beautiful Guinevere. For the duration of the drive, I'd left the book well alone, though, to avoid the likely travel sickness I'd get from reading in the car.

But in Wales, we had a lovely time. We'd stayed in a small bed and breakfast in Dolgellau, owned by an old couple called Alf and Beryl. They would cook us a fry-up every morning, and Alf would tell us his theories as to why the moon landings were an out-and-out fake made by an American movie director. Dad thought it all pretty funny, and I'd chuckled too as Beryl gave us both a wink and shook her head in amusement as she'd poured tea from a cosied teapot.

One day was different, though. Dad woke up in something of a hyperactive mood, and said we were taking a drive to Machynlleth, a town about half an hour away by car. On the way there, he said little of why we were going, and I simply presumed it was a sightseeing trip.

When we arrived, we parked near a large clock tower in the middle of town, and Dad ushered me out of the car and towards a gloomy, little pub just off the square. Unusually, he had with him a large, black briefcase that he used to take projects to and from work. He kept checking his watch. We'd sat at a table in a back corner of the inn, near an empty fireplace. Dad had bought me a Coke, which I sipped through a straw. The bar was empty, and the barman had retreated wordlessly back into the kitchen after serving us.

As Dad looked at his watch again, a tall, broad man came through the doorway, looked about and then fixed his eyes on me before coming over to us. He had a good head of thick, white hair, but it was unkempt, and a very slight stubble showed on his square chin. His eyes were bright blue, however, and they had me transfixed in a way that I wasn't entirely comfortable with as he came in.

"Gregory?" he greeted my father soberly in a low, almost growling voice, thick with a heavy Welsh accent.

My dad had stood up to shake his hand enthusiastically and motioned him to sit down.

"Are you okay to nip out with your book for a bit, son?" asked Dad, indicating through the window at a small backyard patio with a few apologetic-looking benches and parasols. "I just need to have a word with Mr Owens," he added, by way of scant explanation.

Again, the man looked at me with his piercing, blue eyes, glinting like the clearest gemstones. Despite his stubble and messy hair, he had a very dignified air about him, and I felt I was in the presence of someone of some importance and someone who commanded respect. I smiled at him, and he nodded, smiling gravely back. I shrugged back at my dad, and took my King Arthur book outside as I'd been asked.

Sitting on the bench in the slightly chilly back yard, I began to lose myself in my book a little and was glad of the chance to read some more. Occasionally, however, I'd glance up to see my dad and Mr Owens inside, deep in conversation.

Dad had opened his briefcase and had something that looked like a map out on the table over which they were both hunched. He was very animated, pointing and nodding enthusiastically, while Mr Owens sat stock-still, nodding occasionally.

I went back into my book.

I don't know how long I'd been reading when, suddenly, I felt a feeling of dread crawling over me. The day was changing, and the light was being drained from it. I shivered and looked towards the far end of the patio area, where a wooden gate had swung open in a silent breeze.

Beyond the gate a large, black dog was staring at me, its tongue lolling as it panted, and its sharp, white fangs bared. Where it had come from, I didn't know, but the world seemed to stand still as it faced me.

I'd seen it before. I knew this dog. It knew me.

Despite the rising fear in my chest, something was telling me to face it. That I had survived it before, I could survive it again, and that, for some reason I couldn't fathom, it was vitally important that I didn't show the dog I was scared.

The dog growled, but I stayed by the patio bench, rising from it slowly. This time, I wouldn't run. This time, I would face it. As frightened as I was, I looked towards it.

The creature locked eyes with me. Terrible, red, angry eyes. Again, it thundered a low growl that seemed to come from its deep in its ribcage, before barking angrily. I gasped instinctively.

"You alright?" came my father's voice from the pub doorway behind me.

I glanced behind to see that he was standing at the edge of the patio, smiling at me. I turned again to face the dog.

It was gone.

"Come on, we're done here," said my father, smiling. He had his briefcase in one hand, and the man known as Mr Owens was nowhere to be seen. I looked back at where the dog had been. The wooden gate was closed, as before.

"How do you fancy camping tonight?" asked my dad, as I warily joined him to head back through the pub to our car on the road outside.

***

That afternoon, with some sausage rolls and apples to eat on the way, which Dad had bought from a local shop, we hiked our way up Cadair Idris. It was a beautifully sunny afternoon, with a light breeze that whipped through the lush, green grass as we made our way to the top. The beginning was tough, and it got tougher from there. Dad stopped a few times to pause and wipe his brow, while we drank from a water bottle. We spied a waterfall, which Dad eagerly pointed out to me, and when we eventually reached the top, a good couple of hours and more later, the view down into the still, blue-green waters of the lake below was breathtaking.

With a head full of Arthurian legend, I half expected a lady's arm to appear, clad in shimmering, white satin, with Excalibur held aloft. I told my dad this, and he gave me a long look before smiling and nodding.

After he'd found a suitably smooth patch, just shy of the summit, Dad and I got to work on pitching the tent together before settling down with a camping stove and a tin of baked beans and pork sausages. Dad had brought a small kettle too, and brewed enough tea for a couple of mugs each as the sun began to dip. Sitting on a thick, woollen blanket, I watched in wonder as one of the most spine-tingling and ethereal sunsets I would ever witness began to unfold before me.

As we'd drunk our tea and the summer sun began to fall, tendrils of mist had started to wend their way through the valley below until the lake, which my Dad told me was called Llyn Cau, was barely visible. By then, the sky that kissed the horizon was ablaze. The temperature was dropping noticeably, and I'd grabbed a thicker jumper from my rucksack in the tent as I'd joined my dad, who was now standing watching the sunset from a higher, rockier point fifty yards or so behind where we'd pitched the tent. He was a dark silhouette atop a misshapen pyramid, his hands on his hips, watching the light dissolve and confronting the darkness as it approached.

I touched him on his elbow – just a gentle touch to let him know I was there with him. He flinched almost imperceptibly, but didn't take his gaze away from the performance. It almost seemed instantaneous as a riot of flaming pink, purple and crimson shot across the landscape, tinged by a fiery orange as the yellow ball of flame sank lower. I looked up at my father to see he was sobbing, with glistening streams down his cheeks marking where tears had already fallen. He was saying something, no, chanting something through ragged breaths, and he grabbed my hand tightly as his lips continued to move with urgency.

"Dad?" I queried.

In response, he shook his head vigorously. I was not to interrupt, but he kept a tight hold of my hand, his focus still on the plateau of swirling mist and the burning sky. We watched it together in silence, saw the fading light turn into dark, with the stars and moon making their entrance onto the stage of clear night sky above.

When the sun had been gone for five minutes or so, I felt my dad squeeze my hand, and I looked up to see him glancing down at me, his features now illuminated by moonlight alone.

"It's all going to be alright," he stated.

"What is?"

But he didn't answer my question. "Come on, son. Time for bed."

And with that, he led me back to the tent, never once letting go of my hand until it was time to unzip the door so we could scrabble inside to where our sleeping bags lay on a couple of roll mats.

I don't recall falling asleep once I was snuggled warm, still fully clothed, minus my boots, which stood untied just behind the zipped flap. On a diet of sausage rolls, the freshest of air and a day of exercise, I can only imagine I was asleep in a matter of minutes once my head hit the pillow.

***

It was the middle of the night when I awoke and realised, with a jolt, that I was alone.

I reached out to where my dad should have been sleeping, but found only his sleeping bag, empty and cold to the touch.

"Dad?" I asked.

There was nothing. Only silence. But, no, there was **something**. I clamped my mouth shut to hear all the better – to hear what I realised quickly was breathing from outside the tent. Something was outside, circling our pitch. I could hear the breath, panting, working its way slowly past the tent wall to my left and towards the entrance, just beyond my feet.

I didn't dare make a sound.

Instead, the world outside did it for me. From somewhere beyond our camp, a bird screeched a long, lonely call into the night sky, and when all fell silent again, the panting breath was gone. I knelt there, rigid, my sleeping bag curled around my knees and feet, straining to hear anything, anything at all, but there was nothing. Not even the breeze.

As quietly as I could manage, I crept to my boots and lowered my socked and woolly feet into them slowly, before tying the laces hastily, crawling to the tent flap and slowly, slowly unzipping it. With a feeling of heavy dread, I poked my head out into the night and was immediately startled by what I saw.

Below and around our small plateau, the mist had solidified into thick cloud, which lay blanketed silently across everything below us and glowing blue in the moonlight. Above, the night sky was shatteringly clear, with every star gazing down at me, **into** me, with an awareness that I could almost touch and a whispering chorus of voices I could almost hear.

The valley was alive. I looked away behind our tent to the rocky peak where I'd seen the sun go down only hours before. I felt sluggish, the very act of turning my head a painful struggle, as if I were submerged in heavy waters.

My father was standing there as before, his figure so much harder to discern in the dark, but it was him. His hands were at his hips once more, but as I tried to walk towards him my steps became more and more laboured, as if my laced-up hiking boots were weighed down with rocks. I had to get to him.

As I watched, struggling desperately to reach him, he turned sharply to look over his shoulder at me, accusingly, with glowing, white eyes that pierced the thick night air around us like beams from a torch.

I wanted to scream, but the only sound I could make was a weird, useless swallowing sound at the back of my throat.

At that moment, another figure appeared from beyond the summit where my dad stood, again with terrifyingly blank and glowing eyes, only this time they burned with a cold, aquamarine shade of blue. The figure rose sickeningly, climbing, reaching, grasping for my father. He turned back to face this unknown figure, their hands came together, and all at once, the voices at the edge of my consciousness were freed, like 1,000 brass bands sounding one violent, terrible blare into the heavens from the valley below us. As the awful noise swelled, a thousand pairs of red eyes punctured the clouds and slowly turned their burning gazes to the peak of Cadair Idris.

10. Teacher

For Harry, the first few weeks at the MOP had been full of energy.

Full of learning. Full of new experiences. Full of terrific fresh bacon-and-egg rolls enjoyed at breakfast in the staff canteen (twice a week as a treat to himself, with a sizeable blob of ketchup and brown sauce combined).

It had been fun. Mysterious, but fun. The one word Harry had not expected to use when talking about his new job was 'monotonous', but, unexpectedly, a twinge of that very same feeling had crept in over the last couple of days. It had been six weeks since he'd first locked upon the doe-eyed gaze of an Alex, and he felt he had now arrived at the point of knowing pretty much all there was to know about the furry little blighters after working with them daily since. It unnerved him at how such an amazing piece of technology had so quickly become something ordinary – something he now took for granted.

There had been some great revelations in the hours spent in the cubicle following each morning's manual deciphering exercise, some of them heart-warming and some of them just downright peculiar. One particular elderly test subject – a tall, gentle fellow by the name of Graham – left the room in tears and hugging Harry closely to his fusty, cardiganed chest after the Alex's large, dark eyes had merged together during the exercise to form a small viewing screen. Within seconds, the face of Graham's daughter Giselle, who had moved to live in Australia a year previously, had appeared on Alex's face in razor-sharp high definition, and they'd enjoyed a half-hour conversation in which Graham had also seen his new grand-daughter for the very first time.

The Alex creatures had demonstrated a further range of impressively neat tricks besides that. From the basic task of fetching slippers, or getting medicines from the fridge, to more complex assignments, including heating and serving food packs. A loudspeaker from within the creature could call out trivia quizzes to engage veteran brain cells, and gentle calisthenics routines to exercise the aged muscles. It could play music from a seemingly infinite library of tunes from yesteryear. There seemed to be little limit to what the Alex creatures were capable of. Harry had to admit that the small robots were as useful to their new owners as they were charming.

So, it was something of a surprise when Harry received no paperwork from Doris upon arrival for work one Monday (he hadn't seen her all morning, in fact), and he found himself startled further when he then entered his cubicle immediately following the familiar alarm blast to find someone already sitting in the space.

"Oh, sorry. Wrong room; my mistake. Do excuse me," said the ever-polite Harry, excusing himself from his own room.

"No, not at all," replied the gentleman in what sounded to Harry like a friendly Scottish burr. "Harry, isn't it?"

Harry turned from the door he'd been about to exit through. "That's right, yes. Harry. Harry Salt," he explained, now holding out his hand.

The fellow in the chair stood up to return the gesture. Harry reckoned him to be around six feet tall, and quickly noted his smart, grey suit, lemon-yellow tie and classic brown brogues. His slightly-greying-but-thick head of hair was neatly cut, and his spicy aftershave wafted its way around and into Harry's nostrils. In contrast, Harry now felt somewhat underdressed in his regular Marks & Spencer shirt and tie, the suit jacket of which he'd left in the cloakroom. His 'Chisel' body spray, bought in haste from his local supermarket on Saturday, wasn't exactly cutting the mustard either.

"Jason McDonald," smiled the fragrantly tall gentleman, "It's a pleasure to meet you, Harry."

He took off his jacket – which Harry found himself a little pleased about – to reveal an immaculately ironed, lemon-yellow shirt, which emphasised that Jason was a very well-built fellow underneath – which pleased Harry slightly less. Placing it on the back of his chair, Jason stood there respectfully, smiling as he waited for Harry to take his own seat opposite. The stainless steel table gleamed beneath the ceiling lamp, completely free of any evidence of an Alex ever having sat or, indeed, shat there.

"I'm sorry, Mr McDonald; I wasn't expecting anyone this morning," admitted Harry as he settled into his seat.

"Oh gosh, sorry," apologised Jason, who immediately reached down beside his seat to produce a small, black briefcase, which he placed on the table and clicked open. He withdrew a familiar-looking sealed envelope and pushed it across to Harry.

"I'm supposed to give you this," said Jason, smiling a clean, white smile again as he put his briefcase back on the floor.

"Ah. Thank you," responded Harry, taking the envelope and tearing it open.

A series of documents sat inside, stapled together. The front cover bore the legend "APPLICANT INTERVIEW – JASON MCDONALD". Behind it in the pack sat a neatly presented curriculum vitae, packed tightly with Mr McDonald's vital curriculums.

"Ah, okay. Gotcha. Thank you, Mr McDonald," said Harry. "Just give me a second and we'll get things rolling."

"Smashing, thank you," replied the recent arrival, pushing his chair back slightly to enable him to cross one sharply trousered leg over the other.

Harry got a brief view of an exceptionally hairy leg before Jason smoothed his trousers down, and he noted again the exceptional brogues, reminding himself internally that it was high time he bought himself some decent shoes.

Scanning through the document, Harry saw that it was a series of questions aimed at ascertaining Jason's suitability for a role as a science teacher. There were no diagrams to be seen anywhere, just text, as with a normal job interview. There was seemingly no need to collect and dispose of excreta, which was a plus.

This seemed odd though, despite the fact that Harry was getting used to that kind of thing here. Was this actually a job interview with a real person? There were no wires to be seen. Just a smartly dressed, smiling chap who wanted to be a science teacher. Surely, the MOP wasn't pumping out science teachers as well as cute robodogs? What was the sense in that?

Well, thought Harry to himself, if variety was the spice of life then the corridors of the MOP fair reeked with it to the point that it seemed prudent to open a window.

Jason smiled back, waiting.

"So, Mr McDonald... " began Harry, working his eyes back to the top of the form, "you're here in regard to a role as a science teacher?"

"Jason, please," he replied with a smile, "and, yes, exactly. That's me to a tee."

Harry remembered his manners and pointed at the kettle at the back of the room. "Sorry. Speaking of which, would you care for a cup of tea or a refreshment of some sort?"

"No thank you. Refreshed myself thoroughly just before I got here, haha!" followed up Jason, smiling and nodding encouragingly.

Harry, caught a little off-guard, nodded and smiled back, clicking his biro into action and writing carefully, "Early unexpected joke concerning wee" in his report, then returning to the crib sheet. "So, you're new to the area then?" enquired Harry.

"Oh yes, that's right. I was teaching further down the motorway until recently. Milton Keynes; do you know it?"

Harry wasn't certain that he did. "Ah. No. Not really. Concrete? Roundabouts?"

"That's it, yes." Jason smiled charmingly. "Yes, most people tend to know that stuff. Not a bad old place, though; there's some lovely countryside round and about. I taught at a smashing wee school there for six years, four as head of sciences."

"So I see," said Harry, finding himself smiling as he glanced again at Jason's résumé. A good, pleasant start to proceedings, despite the wee and concrete thing.

"Yes," continued Jason keenly. "A great, little place actually. We had two Ofsted inspections while I was there, and we sailed through them. I mean, it's never as easy as that, though, is it? I had plenty of late nights prepping course materials. Nightmare."

Harry returned his chuckle. "Yes. Always so much pressure. But I can assume you handle pressure fairly well, having run your own department for four years. How many staff were under you?"

"Seven, or nine if you include the lab assistants. It was a fairly big and busy department, but that kept things fun."

"I bet," offered Harry encouragingly. He returned his attention to the CV, raising his eyebrows in amusement as he read. "It says here that you were quite involved in extracurricular activities too, running an after-school ukulele society for the staff?"

"Oh aye, that's right; I did!" Jason nodded, giving a briefly puzzled look before flashing his remarkably pearly whites in a winning smile. "Yes, I'd picked one up for my wee lad, but he was never really bothered with the thing. I found myself playing it one weekend, watched a few videos online and gradually got the hang of it. It turned out that a few of the others at work played too, so we formed a small class and encouraged others to join it. Great fun."

"I bet," said Harry again. "Nice to have something fun to wind down with at the end of the day." Harry realised he'd jumped ahead from the order of questions on the sheet he'd been given.

"Oh, absolutely; great fun, yes," concurred Jason with a smile.

"So, to go back to the classroom for a bit," continued Harry, "was teaching a profession you'd always wanted to get into? I mean, when did you first realise you wanted to be a teacher? As a child?"

"Ah... " Jason grinned with a nostalgic look in his sparkling eye. "This is not anus."

Harry did the thing. That thing where someone says something unexpected to you, at which point you doubt yourself in terms of what you thought you heard that person say, and say it over again in your mind – just to check – while they smile as if everything is normal. You smile back in return while trying not to widen or narrow your eyes, realise that they did in fact say what you thought you heard them say in the first place, decide that you have absolutely no idea how to respond, and simply smile back and nod. All in the space of a millionth of a second.

Jason grinned immaculately back. Harry squirmed slightly before saying, "I'm sorry...?"

"Oh no, I'm sorry," apologised Jason with a laugh, realising his mistake. "This is not anus." Clarification delivered, Jason nodded knowingly.

Harry fixed his smile and held it in place while his brain whirred speedily through several calculations once more, shuddering to precisely the same unsatisfactory conclusion. It was now pretty apparent that Jason had gone from discussing teaching to something more private and biological, and Harry was decidedly unsure as to what to with such a segue. Prickles of sweat formed on his brow. "Mmm? I... I beg your pardon, Mr... McDonald?"

Jason's smile fell. He looked as if Harry had just asked him to perform the entire works of Shakespeare on yellow roller skates. "I... this... er... this is not anus?"

"I... what? I don't understand what you mean, Mr McDonald."

Now Jason looked panicked. He shook his head, looking inward, trying desperately to figure things out. "Anus. This. This is not anus." He gasped in shock. "This is not anus!"

"Erm... we were discussing teaching, Mr McDonald. Perhaps if you... " But Harry had no idea what to suggest.

As he watched, the increasingly alarmed interviewee leaped up, edging away from the table, looking around the room wildly as if to find a way out. "This is not anus! This is not anus!" Edging ever backwards in frightened confusion, he backed into the mirrored wall with a loud slam. Harry, facing him, quickly and without thinking was on his feet in seconds, leaping to his aid.

"Mr McDonald! Jason, what's wrong?" Harry looked quickly past him at the mirrored wall, where his own worried face looked back at him. He hoped he was right, that there was indeed someone on the other side watching the scene unfold. But right now, he was very much on his own.

Meanwhile, Jason responded with an agitated gasp of surprise the moment Harry grabbed his arms. He looked down at him, his eyes filled with horror. "This is not anus." He wrestled his hands free and shoved Harry hard in the chest, sending him tumbling to the floor, sickeningly whacking his chin on the table edge on the way down. Stunned and edging himself to the wall, Harry saw a splash of his own blood on the floor. Putting his hand to his chin and feeling the warm ooze in his palm, he looked up in fear as Jason loomed powerfully above him, fixing him with a deeply disturbing stare. Harry could only freeze and look back agog as he did so.

"This. Is Not. Anus."

Then, at that very moment, with Harry scrabbling around desperately in his mind for a suitable response, Jason's expression changed and he stared into Harry's eyes with wonder. "This is not anus?"

"Wh-what?"

Jason gasped, reached down to drag Harry strongly and unceremoniously to his feet before turning the startled lad around ninety degrees for a better look underneath the light, and then transferred his hands gently to Harry's cheeks, tenderly cradling his petrified face.

"This is not... anus! Oh! This is not anus!" Once again, Jason laughed, shook his head in disbelief, and looked again into Harry's eyes as if joyously seeing another fellow human being for the very first time.

"It... it's probably not, no. I can't imagine it would be. I mean, I know some people say I talk out of my arse, but that's really a little unfair... ahahaha!" Harry declared.

Without responding, Jason continued to gaze into Harry's eyes with astonished wonderment as a couple of drips of Harry's blood fell to the floor. Harry smiled awkwardly back, and moved his own hands to Jason's large paws, which still cradled his cranium.

"Er, Mr McDonald – Jason – I don't suppose you'd mind awfully if you, er, let go of my face? Let me have it back, perhaps? My face?"

Harry, among other things, was aware that Jason hadn't blinked at all since he'd last spoken. In fact, he hadn't moved at all. He'd just, well, stopped. He was rooted to the spot, unmoving and staring with an indefatigable gaze that was more than a little unsettling. It reminded Harry of something he'd been thinking about recently, but he couldn't quite grasp what it was and, besides, he had more pressing concerns. It was fast becoming clear that Jason was not about to relax his grip on Harry's sweaty chops anytime soon, and so Harry tried to wriggle himself free.

Thankfully, sufficient amounts of sweat had accumulated in Jason's palms to act as a lubricant, meaning that Harry could – albeit slowly, a little painfully and rather clumsily – slide his head downwards and out. As he did so, he noticed his reflection in the mirrored surface of the wall, his cheeks and mouth stretching upwards slowly, with a smudge of blood on each, until they met his eyes and forced them shut.

With a disappointing lack of an audible pop, Harry's head was clear of Jason's hands, and he pulled himself free, gasping for air and shaking the vision back into his head as he did so. He dabbed at his sore chin and looked again at Jason, who simply stood there motionless, frozen in a tableau of wonder, reaching out into thin air.

"Jason?"

No response.

"Mr McDonald?"

Harry moved to peer into Jason's eyes once again, which simply continued to stare through and past him. He poked him in the ribs, feeling the skin squish and return into place as he did so, warm and obviously still alive but with not the slightest hint of movement – not even the rise and fall of his chest from breathing. Just stopped.

11. Fridge

As Harry stared, the alarm blast sounded, and the door clanked and swung open. Two orderlies, dressed in the blue uniform he'd seen being worn by various utility workers around the buildings and grounds, entered with their heads down, pushing a gurney. Without acknowledging Harry whatsoever, they scuttled over to where Jason stood and pulled back the white sheet that was draped over the bed atop the trolley.

"Ah, Salt. Young Salt." It was Newman, who had just entered the lab and was standing behind Harry, who turned to face him. With a grave look, Newman held out his arms. "Come, Salt. Let me envelop you."

Harry frowned. "This... is not anus?"

Newman frowned back, his arms still held out to the unwavering Harry. "Beg pardon?"

"It doesn't matter."

"Oh, I see. Well, anyway, I thought the customary move here was to provide a comforting hug to my staff member, but, yes, that's possibly a little too far into your personal bubble right now. Inappropriate. I apologise, Salt. Forgive me." He dropped his arms to his sides and stood for a moment, sighing and pondering morosely.

"It's fine, honestly, Mr Newman. But, er, thanks... " he tailed off, his attention back upon the gurney, where the orderlies had managed to get the rigid form of Jason onto the mattress and underneath the sheet, which now poked out at all angles. Anyone seeing this strange scene could have been forgiven for guessing that they were wheeling away a dead stag, antlers and all. He also noticed that his blood had been cleaned from the floor and that it was back to its regular, clinically spotless form.

"Is he going to be okay? What the hell just happened?" blurted Harry.

Newman, his face grave, furrowed his brow and sucked at the corner of his moustache before speaking. "He'll be fine; you needn't worry. He'll get the best care and attention. It... happens sometimes. It wasn't your fault."

"I never thought it was," answered Harry, slightly affronted, "I was just worried. I had no idea what to do." His voice faded as he thought back to what had just happened. "I mean, what was wrong with him?"

Newman was facing the mirrored wall, and he paused once again before speaking. "I wish I could say more right now, I really do." He put his hand into his inside blazer pocket and produced a blue sticking plaster, peeled the backing off, turned sharply and placed it gently on Harry's reddened chin. "There, there, Salty Salt." He squeezed Harry's shoulder, stepped back and gave Harry another sober look. "Listen, get your report written up and take the rest of the day off. I insist. Rest up, eat, sit down, stand up and sit down again. But do yourself a favour, young Salt... " Newman winked and made that clicking noise that some people do when they wink. "Keep this brief afternoon sojourn to yourself, what? Can't have people thinking old Newman's gone all soft in his old, ancient, old age! Ha! Non-disclosure."

And with that, he span on his meticulously polished black shoes and was out of the door at speed, leaving Harry standing alone, facing the mirror. Harry let out a frustrated sigh and set to work tidying up the spilled paperwork. As he bent down, there was a tentative knock on the open door.

"Harry? Everything alright?" came the equally tentative voice of Jade, as she stepped into the cubicle.

Harry turned and smiled, placing the now organised paperwork on the table.

"I saw the trolley go past just as I was coming out of my room – and you've got a cute, little, blue plaster on your chin... " she observed.

"Ah. Yeah... a bit of a weird one, to be honest. I'm not sure what to make of it... " he explained.

"You don't look so good. D'you want to get some air and tell me all about it?"

"Yeah... that sounds like a plan," answered Harry. "In fact, Newman's given me the afternoon off. Let me just grab my papers," he added, distractedly.

Jade clicked her fingers and smiled back at him. "Well, bingo. I'm only doing a half day today anyway. Let's walk, and you can tell me all about it."

Minutes later, the two shining examples of the People Resources Unit's finest were walking together through the maze of ministry corridors.

"That's freaking weird," said Jade after Harry had run through the events of the previous hour, "'This is not anus?' What the jiggery fuck?"

"Bizarre, right? And then with that he just froze to the spot. Like he'd been switched off, like a sodding robot. Yet I was convinced he was a real bloke. I still am. He just seemed too... normal," explained Harry.

Jade stopped and gave him a sideways look. "You don't really think...?"

"No, I mean, that'd be ridiculous, right? He was warm and he was alive; he was just... frozen. It was more like hypnosis; you know, when somebody says a certain word, and it just flips a switch and causes people to freak out? Maybe it was something I said... "

"Wouldn't be the first time."

"Piss off. Seriously, though. This job. This place. I was okay settling in and getting paid to begin with, but some of the stuff around here just doesn't add up. When he started speaking gibberish... the poor sod looked frightened and then, seconds later, it was as if he'd come to some kind of realisation, like he wanted to tell me something. But he couldn't say anything other than—"

"Anus."

"Exactly that."

"Well, be sure to stick his anus in your report, and don't get it the other way around."

"Oh Christ! Yep, I forgot. The report," said Harry, looking at the paperwork still clutched in his hand. "Are you okay to hold on for a minute while I do this, so I can hand it in on the way out?" He looked about for somewhere to write, but the corridor – like all the others – was furniture-free.

"How about in there?" Jade was pointing to a door halfway down the passageway, which stood slightly ajar.

"Brill." Harry followed behind as Jade scampered ahead.

"Hello? Anybody home?" she called into the cubicle. A second later, she smiled back at Harry and beckoned him in with her.

Inside, he found a cubicle exactly like his own, and he headed straight for the stainless steel table in the centre, arranged his paperwork upon it and started writing.

"It's not often you see doors left open like that around here," said Jade, staring at the mirror and pulling faces in it.

"Hmmmm?" enquired Harry.

"The doors. You don't often see them open like that. Not very secure, is it? Speaking of which, does your cubicle have a second door?"

Harry was halfway through his top sheet, and that was taking up the majority of his mental abilities at this moment. "Door?"

"A second door."

"Nope, not me. I don't imagine anyone does, do they?"

"Well, no, I don't. Not in my cubicle," explained Jade, "but whoever has this one struck lucky."

"Eh?" Harry looked up from his papers. Sure enough, a second steel door stood in the wall, in the corner near to the sink. "Well, bugger me, so they did."

Jade was already standing by it, and she shot Harry a mischievous look over her shoulder. "What do you reckon? Shall I?" She reached for the dull, metal doorknob.

"Hey, hang about; you shouldn't. You don't know what's on the other side."

"Course I don't. That's exactly why I should."

"Oi, no, wait... " Harry sighed as Jade worked at the doorknob. It clicked a couple of times, but wouldn't budge.

"Naaw... well, you needn't stress your pretty, little chops, Salty. It's locked anyhow," said Jade, disappointed. She tried once more. This time the click was more of a thunk, and the door opened. "Saying that, however... "

"It's open?" asked Harry, his interest now piqued and his paperwork momentarily forgotten about.

"Sure is. You coming?" Jade fixed him with a look that confirmed that he was, whether he wanted to or not.

He looked back to the entrance door, gritted his teeth, got an even more expectant look from Jade, and shrugged slowly. "I'll have a quick look, but that's your lot. There's a beer in the fridge at home with my name on it. You've no idea how much I want that beer right now." Harry realised he was doing a very bad stage whisper all of a sudden.

"And here was me thinking you were so adventurous. Come on, we've been looking at the same four walls for weeks. It'll be fun."

And with that, she cautiously stepped through the doorway and was in. Harry edged over stiffly and followed her.

They found themselves in what looked like a small laboratory, which was not much larger than Harry's cubicle. It was deserted. There were no windows anywhere, just like the cubicles; all the light came from the sensor-driven ceiling lights that had blinked on automatically as they'd entered. A number of machines were arranged against one wall, with their lights blinking away in a sequence that could only be guessed at. In the centre of the room was a piece of furniture that looked unnervingly similar to a dentist's chair, which was only made all the more unnerving thanks to the addition of wrist and ankle restraints. Jade wandered over and bent down to look closer.

"Bit kinky," she declared.

"Don't be touching anything, for God's sake; you don't know what might happen," interjected Harry, touching his chin gingerly.

"Why are you whispering, you silly sod?" asked Jade, "there's nobody here."

Harry looked about uneasily and shrugged, shaking his head. On the counter immediately in front of the bank of winking machines sat a large, white mug bearing the words "YOUR TEXT HERE" underneath a lipstick stain on the rim. As Harry stared thoughtlessly at it, he noticed steam rising from the coffee within. "Jade, we probably shouldn't hang around here too long," he said uneasily, indicating the mug.

Jade wasn't paying attention to him, however; she was studying a circular piece of apparatus above the central chair, a ring at head height covered in switches, wires and plug ports. "What the actual dickens is this?"

Harry stood and stared at the chair to which she was referring, taking it in properly for the first time. "It's a bit torturey... "

"Are you alright, Harry? Sadism and masochism not your deal? You're looking a bit on the pasty side."

Harry stood staring at the chair and swayed slightly. His vision wobbled for a minute, he took a deep breath and shook his head. "I'm... I'm okay. Just a little dizzy. I think that knock on the chin back in the cubicle with the anus chap took the wind out of me."

Jade peered back at him. "Yeah, that'll be it. Too much anus and not enough vitamin D, that's your trouble. Hey, what's this?" Her attention was back on the chair and the device above it, and she'd taken hold of a long, dangling wire.

"Jade. Seriously. We're not meant to be in here. Let's leave it, eh?"

"Shush yourself. Look. This is just weird. See where it goes?"

Jade was holding up the long, black USB wire that had caught her interest moments before, and she was now tugging on it in a way that made Harry feel queasier still. Nevertheless, his eyes followed the lead from the circular device above the chair, through her hands and downwards towards the far end of the room where, curiously, it disappeared through the seal around the edge of a closed fridge door. The fridge stood, or rather lurked, beneath a counter next to another steel door.

"What do you reckon? Last night's Chinese?" Jade was following the wire hand over hand towards the fridge.

"Bloody hell, Jade; I swear I'm off."

Blissfully ignoring him, she put her fingers around the door into which the wire disappeared and opened it. A dull light emanated from within, accompanied by the tired and clunky whirr of the internal fan. The fridge was stuffed with all kinds of things; Harry could only make out dull shapes from where he stood tentatively by the door.

With a rustle, Jade pulled out a carrier bag. "*Oh my God.*"

The hairs instantly went up along Harry's arms and the back of his neck. "What? What is it?"

Jade turned back to Harry with a look of terror. "Piccalilli," she said with disgust, still crouching and now holding up a homemade sandwich with luminous, yellow edges, wrapped in clingfilm. "Seriously, who eats this stuff anymore? Bleeuurrrgh... What? What is it?"

It was Harry who now looked terrified. Any remaining colour had drained from his face as he stared wordlessly past Jade's shoulder and into the murky glow of the fridge. Following Harry's frightened gaze, she turned slowly without getting up and saw for herself where the wire ended up.

Beyond where she'd removed the sandwiches and to the left of a twin-pack of raspberry yoghurt, the wire terminated in a thin, black frame that featured a solitary, winking, green light and a small, white switch. That was no worse than anything they'd encountered in the small laboratory so far. It was the fact that the frame was nightmarishly attached to a glistening brain, positioned on the centre of a metal tray, that was making Harry fight to avoid bringing back his lunch all over the floor.

Jade leaped up and backwards from her crouched position, and clattered noisily into the chair in the middle of the lab. Her eyes were wide open in terror as she straightened herself, staring open-jawed at the monstrous organ in the cooler. "Oh my God! Oh my God!"

Harry realised that Jade was now affecting the stage whisper too. At that moment, his back went rigid once again as he simultaneously both heard a fumble at the door latch through which they'd entered and noticed that, in the panic, Jade had tossed the sandwiches in the air and onto the chair, where the impact had caused them to unload their sticky, neon-yellow contents onto the shiny, blue leather. The door handle clicked and was fumbled once again, but the door remained closed.

"Someone's coming in," hissed Harry.

At this bit of news, Jade regained at least a degree of her composure and pushed the fridge door shut quickly before seeing the huge pile of cheese, pickle and disintegrating granary bread on the chair.

"Shit. Shit, shit, shit." She fumbled at the soft mound of luncheon and succeeded in getting most of it into her cradled hands before turning automatically towards the door through which they'd entered and colliding with Harry.

Fixing her with a panicked stare of admonishment, Harry rapidly shook his head in the negative and pointed instead to the second door by the fridge behind her. Whether she realised what he meant in that split second or not was moot – there was no time to tell as he opened the new door and bundled her through it, closing it as quietly as he could behind them.

Kite

I'd awoken with a start.

It was a bright, sunny summer morning, but the feeling of fear lay heavy on my chest. It felt like only moments since all those piercing, burning, red eyes had opened simultaneously across the moonlit landscape, looking towards the rocky summit where Dad...

Dad.

I could hear him outside the tent. I sat up to see that the tent flap was tied open, and the green grass outside was decorated with lusciously gleaming dew, which sparkled in the sunshine, while hilltops loomed as grey shadows beyond. Somewhere nearby, a bird tweeted and chirruped into the morning freshness.

Tentatively, and with a dull ache that seemed to permeate all my joints, I crawled forwards to peek out of the tent flap and into the morning warmth.

Sure enough, there was my dad with his back to me, stirring at whatever he had on the go over the camping stove. As I looked about, the cloud cover from the previous night was nowhere to be seen, with the beautiful, aquamarine expanse of Llyn Cau sparkling below.

As I turned my attention back to my father, he turned sharply to look over his shoulder at me. "Ah, there he is. Sleepy von Sleepington. Wakey wakey, eggs and bakey!"

I stared at him.

He stared hard for a moment, but smiled back. "Well, it's beans and sausages again. I hope you don't mind? I'll pick up something more substantial for us both on the way home." And with that, he turned back to the stove.

I blinked, my eyes still adjusting to the sunshine. "Dad, are you... is everything okay?" I stammered, my thoughts in a whirl.

"Hmmm?" he muttered, without turning back to me. Instead, he started to pour the beans and sausages into two blue, plastic bowls, which he had laid out ready for us both, and once filled, he licked bean juice off his fingers noisily and handed me mine.

"Sorry, what did you say?" he asked, sitting cross-legged on the woollen blanket facing me.

"Erm... just... " I floundered, looking away from him and down into my beans while taking a fork from the carrier bag of utensils. "Did you... did you hear anything strange last night?"

"Mmm? Me?" he replied, already part way through his first mouthful, "No, not a thing. Why, did you?"

Again, I could only look on in astonishment. It had all felt so real. In fact, I hardly felt like touching my breakfast, as my stomach was still in knots. "I, erm, maybe. I'm not sure. I don't know."

A dog barked urgently somewhere in the valley below. Dad chuckled, spooning another mouthful of beans out of his bowl as he did so. "That's what comes of sleeping in the wild; there's all kinds of things out here at night-time!" He chuckled again before putting the beans into his mouth, and then pointed to my legs with his empty spoon, "Sleeping in your boots won't help either; no wonder you were uncomfortable, you daft sausage."

I looked at where he pointed, and sure enough, not only was I fully clothed but I was wearing my hiking boots, with the laces tied.

***

On the way home, Dad had told me that I would be staying with Grandma and Grandpa for the next week or so of the summer holidays, as he had a huge project to undertake at work and would be spending some days away from home.

It wasn't that unusual. There were often occasions when I'd needed to stay with them both due to his work projects, but even I could tell that it was also sometimes their way to take the load off Dad emotionally, as a widowed single parent. I didn't mind either. I loved Grandma's cooking, and although there wasn't much to do at their house, I could always take my Walkman and a few tapes, along with a stack of books, and they'd happily leave me alone to do my own thing.

That was about as much conversation as we'd had, or that I can recall anyway. For large parts of the journey home, despite being sat in the front next to him, I'd hardly been able to look at my dad in the face, so shaken and confused was I by the things I'd seen – awake or otherwise – the night before. I kept replaying things over and over. The tendrils of mist creeping into the valley like the breath of a giant as the sun went down in a riot of fire. The blanket of cloud in the moonlight, my father's eerie silhouette and, with a clarity that made my stomach drop, his glowing, white eyes turning towards me, arrowing into my mind.

We'd stopped at a garage near the Welsh–English border. I'd watched the beauty of the landscape as we'd driven along, but I'd kept myself to myself. It didn't feel right, but I was afraid. Afraid of my dad. Here in the daylight, with bright sunshine streaming down from clear, blue skies and warming my skin, he was himself. A livelier, more animated version of himself, admittedly, but he was him.

And yet, he wasn't. He wasn't because I could picture, all too clearly, his face from the night before, every time I looked at him. He'd gone into the small shop to get us both a sandwich and pay for the petrol he'd just fed into the car, and I'd walked to the edge of the forecourt to watch the cars and lorries powering up the in-cline towards England.

High above, a hawk was floating lazily in the summer heat, its majestic wings opened to their full span. It wheeled above once, then twice, and I found myself captivated by it, shielding my eyes from the sun. I felt myself wondering what its view was like from up there, of the wide landscape of the world below, with the fields, roads and villages all spread out like an immense tablecloth. The sheep on the hillsides. Me.

"Red kite."

I was startled and looked to see my dad standing next to me, also watching the beautiful bird high above.

"The bird. It's a red kite. Gorgeous, isn't it?" he continued, a touch of awe in his voice, "I think they're extinct in Scotland and England now, sadly, but you'll still find them out here in Wales. Look at that. Wings of fire. Like a dragon!" He was pointing to the bird, and sure enough, the sunlight was hitting its outstretched wings in such a way that the feathers looked to be alight.

I shivered, despite the heat, and followed Dad back to the car. Moments later, we were back on the road and heading off again towards home. We were flanked either side by trees, through which the golden sun flickered and flashed.

"Nearly at the border now, son," said my father as the car worked its way up the hillside, "another two and half hours or so and we'll be home."

I nodded.

"Listen... " he began.

I could already feel my hackles rising.

"You don't mind having to go stay with Grandma and Grandpa for a few weeks, do you? On and off?"

I shrugged. "No, it's fine. It won't be for too long, though, will it?"

My father smiled. "No, not too long. I hope not anyway. It's a big project, but we're nearly there with it now."

He paused, with his attention on the road ahead. He sighed, and his voice wavered as he began to talk again. "Look, I have to tell you that it's been horrible at times since Helen – since your mum – died."

I was looking at the road ahead too. I didn't answer; I only nodded my head. The car was quickly gathering pace again now. Having mounted the crest of the hill, we were descending into a valley, among trees again.

"I know I've been dreadful to be around at times, and I'm sorry for that. I didn't mean to make things more difficult than they already are, and I've not been much of a dad to you," he apologised.

I found my voice then. "No, Dad, you couldn't help it; I know—"

"It's alright, son," he interrupted, and he looked at me with a sad smile, which was more than I could really bear at that point. "You're such a good lad, but you don't have to defend me. I've not given you the attention and love you deserve during your life so far. You'll be a teenager next year, for God's sake. I should be around for you more; I should be more... more present. More of a parent; more of a dad."

"Dad, no, I understand. I know it's been horrible for you too," I persisted. I could feel tears welling in my eyes. I wanted him to know that, at least as far as his sadness was concerned, I understood. I loved him no matter what.

"Son, just know this," he announced, cutting me off once more, "just know that everything, and I mean everything, is going to be alright. There are... there are things I can't tell you just now, but you, me... your mum... It's going to be okay, and life is going to be better than it's ever been. Better than ever. You'll see." He was nodding fervently, and his eyes were glassing over too.

I had frozen. Staring at him from the passenger seat, I suddenly felt ice cold.

Mum? Mum had died when I was born. What was he talking about?

He turned to me again, and there was something else there in his eyes, something that drained the car of all air and noise, and seemed to freeze the world altogether. "You'll see, Harry, it's all going to be okay!" he said with fervour, nodding and grinning in a way I didn't like. "I can't wait to tell you – to show you, even!"

Then, all of a sudden, the noise of the car and everything in *that moment became sharp, became present, with a hot clarity. I saw the black blur ahead of us first: large, busy, bulky and fast. My father saw my expression change and followed my gaze, but it was too late.*

He yelled, and pulled the steering wheel to the right to avoid the huge, black dog in the road ahead of us, but in doing so he sent the car – our car – up the kerbside and into the metal barrier of the central reservation.

There was a horrible noise and then the world turned.

The sky was below us.

Everything turned black.

12. Sandwich

In the pitch darkness, Harry leaned there panting, his back against the door. Jade was somewhere nearby, her breath also coming out in gasps that she was making an effort to control.

"Oh my God," she whispered between breaths, "Oh my God."

From the other side of the door, they were just able to hear somebody finally succeeding in gaining access to the laboratory. They'd escaped with only seconds to spare.

"We can't stay here," whispered Harry. "Whoever that is will discover their sandwiches are missing soon and might come this way."

"Oh my God. Yeah, do you want some?" came Jade's hushed reply.

Harry's nose and ears told him that she had just lifted her handful of mashed sandwiches up towards his face with an audible squelch.

"No. Come on... " He was feeling unsteady enough as it was. "There has to be a light in here somewhere." He'd turned and was sliding his hand, palm downwards, across the wall behind him. There was a click as he made contact with a switch pad, and the lights came on.

"Oh my good night," said Jade out loud.

This prompted Harry to first give her one of his rarely accessed admonishing looks, before turning the full half circle and jumping when he saw exactly what she was exclaiming at.

This time, the room was much bigger, both lengthways and in terms of height. Harry squinted and blinked as his eyes began to readjust to the light. It was a room of four brick walls, with a concrete floor and ceiling. In the middle of the room stood a giant, glass box on four metal legs. Surrounding it were four video cameras on tripods, all focussed on the empty cube.

Once again, they were alone.

They edged forwards, and it was then they noticed that the glass cubicle wasn't empty at all. Bizarrely, the floor area was covered in lush, neatly mown, green turf with a layer of soil beneath. Wedged into that soil were twelve irregular and weathered large stones, each about chest high and arranged in what looked to be a perfect circle that took up most of the cube. Harry would never confess to being a geologist, which was precisely due to the fact that he wasn't one, but he suspected that the rocks were hewn from limestone.

There was also a comfy-looking sofa facing the glass box, with an accompanying table and an attractive pot plant.

"I... well, I... what?" exclaimed Harry, his stage whisper back in force. "An indoor stone circle?"

Jade didn't reply. She simply stared and shook her head slowly, which was fair enough.

A muffled noise from the room behind them came as a reminder that they could be sprung upon at any moment. A further steel door stood at the far end of the room, separated from them both by the twelve standing stones.

"We should move, Jade. Come on," declared Harry.

Though neither of them could explain why later, they both felt queasy as they dashed forwards, past the cameras all pointing at the box containing the stones. It was only at this point that they both noticed that the room itself was just as circular as the ring of stones itself. Jade spotted this and, rather than speaking, gave Harry a quizzical look, which he returned.

Jade reached the door first, went to open it, remembered her hands were full of what was once a cheese-and-piccalilli sandwich, and looked about. "Never a blasted bin around when you want one, is there?" she hissed.

As Harry watched in horror, she mounted a small set of steps up to the glass cube, opened a door on the side and crouched down to wipe her hands on the turf. "It's okay; it's grass. The birds'll have it." She winked at Harry who could only smile thinly back. Her hands cleaned, she closed the door to rejoin him by the circular brick wall.

"Allow me," he said, reaching for and turning the dull, metal doorknob. This time it opened smoothly, and with one last, bewildered look at the stone circle, both he and Jade piled through, this time into a thankfully familiar and well-lit corridor, not once looking behind.

13. Shrew

"Look, I know how much you hate it when I swear, but that place is fucking crackers." Jade took a long gulp on her cold pint of fizzing cider, sitting back with a loud breath against the faded fabric of the booth in which they were sitting. The Pelican and Shrew public house was a cosy, fire-lit place into which they had retreated after a swift exit from the MOP. Harry, stony-faced, sat across from Jade and munched on a mouthful of dry-roasted peanuts.

"I mean, a brain. A sodding brain in a fridge." Jade shook her head slowly, reliving the encounter. "Scared the absolute biscuits out of me. I could have touched it. Smelled it. An actual brain, for God's sake."

Harry continued to stare into space, shaking his head slowly, just as Jade had. "I don't get it, Jade," he said. "None of it seems to mean anything. And why was there a stone circle in a glass box?" His eyes were desperate for anything even close to an answer as he turned them back to Jade.

"You know what you need?"

Harry blinked out of his trance, to look back into Jade's eyes hopefully.

"You need a decent meal in you, Salt," she chided, folding her arms. "You're not putting enough in those sandwiches of yours.

Big doorstoppers is what you want, and stacks of fruit in your lunchbox. Huge packet of crisps. Penguin. You've got to look after yourself, man."

"A penguin?"

"The chocolate biscuit."

"Oh, right. Yeah."

"Seriously, Harry. You've not been looking after yourself of late."

He'd have been lying if he didn't agree with her on that point. His recent self-examinations in the bathroom mirror first thing every morning had reflected back a version of himself that was a little tired, a little lacking in colour and, well, a little shagged out around the edges. It was true that he probably needed more sleep, but then sleep had proved to be a darker place than he would have cared for of late.

"Yeah... " he mused, momentarily off somewhere else. He cleared his throat and forced himself to refocus. "Yeah, sorry. I've just been feeling a little tired, that's all. I just need a little more sleep. A Penguin. You're right."

"I often am. So, what the frig do we do with this?"

"With what?"

"With this knowledge? I mean, what the dickens is going on when someone keeps a brain in the fridge with their lunch? Or their lunch in the fridge with a brain, more to the point? What the hell is this... this operation we're working for?"

Harry nodded, shuddering at the thought of that lumpen thing menacing him from inside a kitchen appliance. In his pocket, he felt his phone vibrate. "I don't know, Jade. You've been here a year longer than me. You know full well that we shouldn't have been in there, but we were and we saw what we did. Do you think anyone else knows about it?"

"Well, the poor prick with the piccalilli sandwiches will be in for a nasty shock when his lunch hour comes around."

"No. I mean among us – the proles like you and me who turn up – day in, day out – to work in this place. I mean, what about

Newman?"

"Newman doesn't know what day of the week it is at the best of times," scoffed Jade.

"Yeah, but... There's no arguing that our beetle-browed head of operations seems to be several pebbles short of a beach, but a man in his lofty position has to know more than he's letting on? Surely?"

"You want to know what I think?" said Jade, and of course, he did.

As she leaned in conspiratorially, he noticed she was wearing some kind of delicate, fruity fragrance. He also noticed that he liked it. His phone vibrated again, but now wasn't the time. "Go on."

"I say we keep schtum. I say we're on to something big here. And while I'm at it... " She looked about before continuing. "I say we pop back soon for another sneaky peek. I want to know what else lurks in the fridges at work. This place has puzzled me senseless for the last twelve months, and now I feel like we're on to something. Maybe someone's having liver and onions tomorrow. Onions, Harry, and a massive, juicy liver."

Jade was delightfully close to Harry's face. He could smell her perfume stronger now and feel the warmth of her breath in his ear.

"I say we go back in there. Tomorrow. After we finish," she concluded.

Harry grimaced at the thought of liver and onions, and the idea of going back. The fire popped. He could still smell her.

"Come on, you've been wanting to know more about what the hell goes on here. We're on to something! There's no harm; besides, what else do you have planned tomorrow evening?" she questioned.

Knowing full well that his diary was emptier than the glass Jade had just plopped back onto the table, Harry paused and pondered to keep up appearances.

Jade knew better, and arched her left eyebrow to prove it. "Seriously?"

"Well, okay, nothing," he conceded. "But... we should be careful, right? We weren't meant to be in there, and I'm not sure I entirely liked it if I'm perfectly honest with you."

"Ah, get over yourself," teased Jade, making Harry blush. "If it gets too crazy, we can head back the way we came. Come on," she added, squeezing his thigh and sending a pulse of electricity groinwards as his phone once again picked entirely the wrong time to vibrate once more, "it'll be just the two of us. We'll have each other's backs."

Despite his uneasiness, Harry did feel a pang of curiosity. And a pang of something else entirely, as Jade's eyes widened in encouragement. He was about to respond, but Jade got back in first.

"Besides, this is the best fun I've had in ages. I mean it."

And he could tell she did. *Those eyes; those sodding eyes.*

"I liked having an adventure with you today. You're good company, you know that? Great to hang around with," she confirmed.

And with that, she kissed him. Not on the cheeks, but on the lips. Not a lingering kiss, just a quick one, but one with intention. On the lips.

On the ruddy lips. Soft and warm, and again with the faint smell of her perfume.

"So that settles it then, yeah? Oh, and it's your round," she added, indicating her drained pint pot and getting up to head to the toilet.

Harry was reeling. Good company. Great to hang around with. *On the ruddy lips!*

Harry sighed a sigh that covered a multitude of meanings, picked up their empty glasses and headed, slightly dazed, to the bar.

Functional

*I*dreamed a lot during that time in the hospital. Sometimes, the dreams were deep, or at least they felt that way. Deep as in I felt like I was far down, a long way from the surface. A long way from waking up. Sometimes, I would fall deeper, scared I would fall too deep and not be able to get back up again. At other times, I felt myself rising euphorically.

Mostly, I would float there. It was warm. It was all around me. Things moved slowly. I felt safe enough, but there were things that haunted me down there. My father's face, concerned and worried, would swim in front of me and around me. Sometimes close; sometimes far, far away in the distance.

The black dog was always with me. Again, it would be close, snarling directly into my face. At other times, it would be distant, warning me and keeping me from looking too hard at what it was guarding. Sometimes, I was just too tired and had to give in to it. It barked loudly, commanding my full attention and setting my nerves on edge. Constant and angry. Look away! Stay away! Don't touch! At other times, I could yell at it, and it would retreat, but it was always there.

There were other things too. Occasionally, a tiny bird would call to me. It was a wren. I don't know how I knew that, but I did. Perhaps my dad had told me once; he had a thing for wildlife.

Maybe we'd seen one on our walks or bike rides together. I don't know. It would sing to me – a long, beautiful song. It wanted to let me know that everything was going to be okay, and as I listened, I knew that it was. Of course it was. Eventually, it flew away and never came back.

At other times, I was nearer to the surface. Really close. I could hear different sounds. Voices talking and machines pumping. Changes. Doors opening. Doors closing.

"HIYA! HIYA! HIGHER! HIGHER! FUN! FUN!"

Hello! I'm here. I can hear you!

"HIGHER FUNCTION!"

Can you hear me?

"RAIN FUNCTION SUN!"

You can't hear me, can you?

"RAIN! SUN! SON!"

It was no use, so I went deeper when that happened. I could always come back and try again another time. So I swam. I swam down to my safe place and floated.

"GO BACK, ROY."

"FETCH! FETCH! ANN MOON!"

Was the dog called Roy? Who on earth would call their dog Roy? Was Ann Moon his owner? That was animal cruelty, giving it a name like that. I threw a stick for the dog. It was a really good throw; my dad would have been really proud of me. It flew upwards in a high arc, spinning slowly over and over and then down, and on downwards. Stop, stick! Stop!

Downwards, downwards. The dog, its tongue lolling, swam downwards for the stick. The deeper the dog swam, the darker the world became. I stopped following it. It was too deep for me. Too deep. But Roy kept going, even though it wasn't going to be good for him. I didn't know why, but there would be consequences for him. It was something to do with going below and coming back, over and over again, over time.

I couldn't see the dog anymore, but it could see me. It was always watching.

I waited. It might have been hours. It might have been days. I wasn't counting. Until then, I just floated in the warm, and I felt safe. Safe and warm. Warm and safe.

Here he comes. But he's changed. He's even bigger now, but he's white. Pure, brilliant white like the brightest lightning. A splash of red on each ear. He's swimming hard; he's so strong. Swimming up from far below.

Good boy. Good boy, Roy.

But wait. What happened to the stick, Roy?

There was something else in his mouth. The stick was gone, but he was carrying something else up from the depths for me. Just for me. Something really important. It was really important that I have it. It is really important that I have it.

He opened his jaws wide, and there was something in there. In his throat. Something there in his throat for me, behind his razor-sharp fangs. But it was okay, as he wouldn't hurt a fly. This wasn't the black dog anymore. Shucks!

A purple glow, something shining from in his throat on a pedestal. A velvet cushion. A blue, velvet cushion, with smart, white pinstripes. Wait. I'm climbing in.

Say AAAAAAAARRRRRGGGGGHHHHH.

It was really hot in there, but that was okay because this thing, this thing just for me, is what makes everything work. Everything. Just a little, purple sliver – a little, purple slice. The slice of life! Piece of cake!

I don't remember taking it or being given it. But when I swam back out, the dog was ill. It didn't work properly anymore. Poor boy. Poor Roy. Poor Roy's poorly head. He had gone a long way to get my slice and now he had paid the price. It was Ann Moon's fault.

The dog had a headache; the dog couldn't remember how to think straight. It couldn't do tricks anymore. Magic tricks. It was okay, though. There were more beds here. Roy could still be a good boy, a useful boy. A guard dog. That was what Dad wanted. Dad wanted Roy to be on guard. Roy had been a faithful servant to our family and had never let us down. Good boy, Roy.

But David...

David wanted the slice, but the slice was mine and mine alone. In fact, David didn't even know he wanted the slice.

He didn't know I had the slice, so that was okay. But if he did, he would want me, and he would want the slice for himself.

He didn't know he wanted the slice because Roy was a good boy, and Dad was going now. But David was probably going to look for it anyway, even though David didn't know what it was. Dad was going now. He had to make the choice, and the choice was that I would have the slice, and he would go away now.

"I LOVE YOU."

I love you too, Dad.

"I'LL MISS YOU. I'VE BEEN A BAD DAD, BUT ROY IS A GOOD BOY.

"I'LL MISS YOU, MY SON."

You haven't been a bad dad. I told you that. You don't have to go.

But he went. His face floated away, and I never saw it again.

Then it was time. It was time, so I started to cough. The cough was horrible; it came from the deep. From far down below. There was so much down there. It was time, and so the cough came from the depth of my lungs. I couldn't stop coughing; in fact, I coughed so hard that my oesophagus turned inside out and ended up on the floor where I stood looking at it for a while, puzzled. It was full of warm fluid, which spilled out all over the hospital floor. I wasn't swimming anymore.

But I wasn't standing up either.

I was on a bed, flat on my back. Coughing. There were bright lights over me. Someone was flashing those bright lights into my eyes.

Higher brain functions normal.

The black dog was telling me to look away, to stay away and to not go back there. Away! Away! Look at me! Look at me!

14. Second

The next day dragged by, as Harry had a sneaking suspicion it might. There was nothing remarkable to report; his trip to work in the morning was marred only by the two grubby children with their football yelling, "TWAT!" and chasing him down the cobbled alleyway behind his house. He hadn't seen them for a day or two, and had been more than fine with that, but they were back, and he'd only just managed to evade them. There was also a dose of heavy traffic in the town centre. Doreen Twigge had been there as per usual, waving like mad and grinning her gleaming dentures at him in a display of genuine and heartfelt affection that could toast even the coldest cockles of his heart. He'd felt his phone, which was in his trouser pocket and pressed up against his leg, vibrating and demanding his attention as Darren the moped spluttered along.

However, sometime later when he went to look through his accumulated messages at work, Harry discovered his phone was dead. He cursed himself internally for not charging it overnight, before cursing himself a little harder for not bringing his charger either. The likelihood was that all the missed messages and accompanying vibrations had worn the battery out, so he'd just have to wait until he got home in the evening to see what was so important. Most likely it was Alan with another moan about life at the Chegwin and Blunt office. That seemed such a long time ago now. So much had changed in such a short time.

That morning, Harry tested an Alex robot, which performed all necessary tasks without a hitch, and then he interviewed a thirty-two-year-old lady named Lindsey who wanted to be a school crossing warden. Bizarrely, and in the spirit of trying perhaps a little too hard, she'd turned up fully dressed in the regulation neon uniform and carried a "Stop – Children" lollipop sign to finish off the look. She'd been doing well until she yelped suddenly and ran out of the cubicle when Harry had asked her about her childhood, just as his instruction sheet had asked him to. She'd muttered something cryptic about how, "people shouldn't be allowed pets in the workplace" as she'd made a swift run for the exit, which Harry thought was quite ridiculous. He'd checked to make sure he hadn't accidentally left the Alex robot from the previous job in his room, but it was nowhere to be seen.

Lunch was a reheated rehash of a Chinese takeaway from a couple of nights before (house special chow mein, in a moment of exuberance), and he'd had a brief chat with Jade while eating it, during which time he noticed that the black turtleneck sweater she was wearing highlighted her impressive boobs, despite how desperately hard he tried *not* to notice this and then felt uncomfortably guilty for having done so in the first place. She'd checked if he was still up for a session of exploring after work, and – given the fervour with which she talked about it and *kissed him on the ruddy lips* the night before, Harry was not in a mood to decline.

Part of him was massively looking forward to it. Jade had been impressed with their little adventure and impressed with him, or so it seemed. It was something different, but just a bit of fun and an excuse to hang out together. He longed for another kiss. Another part of him told that part of him off, and made a point of reminding him that he shouldn't be meddling in things he didn't quite understand and that might get him into some kind of trouble. Besides, she was a woman – an incredibly delicious, fun and intelligent woman – and he was getting way above his station and punching above his weight, so he should just jolly well stop it.

A third part of him was thinking about ham for some reason.

Harry was sitting at the central table in his cubicle, signing off his reports for the day, when his door opened and Jade's glorious visage popped through. Behind her, a row of seven crossing ladies – again all dressed from head to toe in the famous neon uniform – were marching up the corridor towards the exit.

"Saltychops! Get those reports done, and let's go. What's up?" she enquired.

"Crossing ladies," he said, indicating behind her, "Did you interview one today as well?"

"Oh, yeah. A couple of them, in fact: Lucy and Deborah. Bonkers, the two of them. One tried to bribe me with a yo-yo. They'll be great."

"Bonkers is about right. Robot dogs for old people one minute, teachers and crossing ladies the next. This place is nuts."

"Oh, just you wait," declared Jade with gusto, "it'll be milkmen next, postal workers a week on Wednesday and female pool lifeguards throughout June. Anyway, let's skedaddle. The coast is clear!"

"You sure?" He signed his final document before shuffling his papers in a way in which he hoped looked cool. It didn't.

"Course. I checked. It's a Friday, so everybody who actually has a life has buggered off early. I think you're the only one still here, give or take the odd crossing lady. And that's a big 'odd' by the way. Come on, grab your rucksack, gird your nutsack, and let's get cracking."

Minutes later, with the lights flicked off and his darkened cubicle locked behind him, the two of them were off in the direction of the previous day's excitement.

"Did you ever read any Enid Blytons when you were younger? Fantastic Five? Secret Seven?" asked Jade.

"Famous," he corrected.

"What?"

"Famous. It was the Famous Five," said Harry, pretty certain he was right, but not wanting to press the nerd button too hard at this point.

"Oh yeah... but what were they famous for, really?" questioned Jade, hitting her stride. "Bit too far up their own arses if you ask me. I mean, who declares themselves famous at the age of twelve or whatever for causing mischief in 1953? One of them was a dog, for God's sake."

Harry couldn't find a response to that.

"It's all a bit... I don't know... " She waved her hand in the air, searching for the correct word. "Cunty."

This time his response was to cough and nearly trip over himself. "Jade. Wash your mouth out."

"Oh come off it, Harry," she scoffed, "Bloody Famous Five. You can just imagine a film version; it'd be Jemima Whatsherface and that other one she's always in films with. What's her stupid name? Squelchy?"

Harry shrugged.

"Anyway, the thing is that we're a bit like the Famous Five, only there's two of us," explained Jade as they continued down the corridor.

"So, what? We're the Terrible Two?"

"No. I mean yes, something like that. Now you're getting it! Not terrible though. Twatty, maybe. The Perfect Pair?"

Harry coughed again.

"Nope. Something else."

"The Curious Couple?" piped up Harry, before immediately blushing.

Jade stopped in her tracks, a delightful smile crossing her face slowly. "Curious Couple! I like that."

"Well, I wasn't... " stuttered Harry, trying to backpedal and contain his sudden embarrassment. Couple. Kiss. *Oh God*!

"No, it's good! The Curious Couple. Solving mysteries, eating enormous amounts of crisps, throwing handfuls of piccalilli at our enemies, and rounding it all off with a well-earned cider. Brilliant."

Harry smiled.

"Definitely less cunty."

Cough.

Jade had stopped still again and was looking at the cubicle door they'd ventured through roughly twenty-four hours before. This time, the door was shut, and that meant it needed a specific code or card to open it, personalised only to the assigned room user.

"Oh, now, that's a shame," sighed Harry, but Jade had already pushed past him to give it a shove. Miraculously, the heavy metal door swung slowly open.

"Have I got the touch or what?" purred Jade, one eyebrow raised invitingly.

Harry stared at her momentarily before peering into the empty room. "There's something wrong with the door. That shouldn't happen," he said, shaking his head.

However, Jade already had a hold of his sleeve and tugged him in. Harry closed the door behind them both with his trailing arm.

"The Curious Couple strikes again," declared Jade once they were inside and the light was on, elbowing Harry in the ribs.

Harry was starting to feel that his time with Jade was something of a difficult balancing act this afternoon; on the one hand, he was really enjoying her cheeky, carefree and – dare he think it – flirtatious attitude, but on the other, he was aware again of a feeling that things could tip over the edge any second, and they could find themselves in trouble.

There was no time to dwell on his apprehension; Jade was already striding across the room and opening the door into the small office at the back. Again, she was in with ease, and once more they were into the testing laboratory with the mysterious chair, face to face with the terrifying fridge lurking at the far end. Jade gave Harry a mischievous look and pointed towards a second door in the room, which was situated across from the one they'd gone through the previous day. Neither of them recalled seeing it before. It was ajar.

"Another day, another door. What do you reckon?" Jade enquired.

Harry took a deep breath and smiled. Bugger it. She was in her element, she was enjoying being with him and – despite the fact that they were standing near a fridge with a brain in it – life felt good.

Seizing the moment, Harry strode forwards, stepped past Jade and pushed at the door, which opened obligingly for them both. "After you," he said, and he bowed slightly.

Jade's eyes lit up in a way that made his underwear move. "Well, Mr Salt. I don't mind if I do."

With that, they were through, and Harry, ever the gentleman, closed the door behind them both with a click.

They were in another cubicle office almost identical to the one they had just emerged from, again deserted.

"Aw, rubbish," was Jade's considered opinion, "I was hoping for another indoor stone circle. Bah." She immediately headed for the door at the opposite end, before Harry even had a moment to share his thoughts on the matter.

This time, they found themselves in a long corridor, identical to all the rest that connected the MOP. For the moment, it was completely silent and deserted. However, set into the wall opposite them was a small door, which – as was becoming something of a pattern – stood slightly ajar.

"Okay, this is getting silly," said Harry, his stage whisper once again in full effect.

"It really is," replied Jade, "It's like someone wants us to follow a treasure hunt. Utterly marvellous! This door should definitely not be open either; look at it." She pointed at the join around the edge of the door, which was almost seamless. Were it not for the fact that the door was open, it would have blended in completely with the rest of the wall, and they would never have noticed it.

"Still up for it? Come on; if it's crap, we go to the pub."

Harry pulled the tiny door open wider to reveal a dimly lit, narrow and winding metal staircase, which went both up and down from their point of entry.

"Now this is more like it," declared Jade with unhidden glee before grabbing Harry's sweaty hand and dragging him in with her.

In an uncomfortable and decidedly awkward few seconds, they both discovered simultaneously that the staircase was much too narrow to accommodate them both abreast of one another. That didn't stop them from trying, however, and after a few fumbling touches and grunts, along with a quick round of, "Sorry," "No, I'm sorry," they arranged themselves with Harry two steps down from Jade, clinging on to the narrow handrail for dear life and shamefacedly contemplating the soft mounds of heaven he may or may not have made contact with seconds prior. Jade carefully closed the small panel they had squeezed through by pulling on a small doorknob, and it clicked gently into place in the wall. Again, were it not for the small, round, wooden handle, the panel would have been invisible.

They both stood in silence for a moment, savouring the cool, damp draught of air that seemed to float up past them from below. It was impossible to see what lay above or beneath them, as the winding staircase pretty much filled the shaft in which they stood.

"Okay," said Jade quietly, "now we're really somewhere we're not supposed to be. This is the shit, the absolute shit!"

"Shush!" Harry frowned, standing immediately behind her and bringing his finger to his lips.

"Oh, come on, Sensible Sally," retorted Jade, turning to face him, "The only way we're going to get to find out all about this place is if we explore, and you—"

"No, shush. Listen," said Harry, straining to hear something.

Jade blinked and then did as she was told. Sure enough, there was a noise. A voice came from somewhere far above them, but as soon as they tried to focus on it, it was gone. Jade was about to speak, and then the voice returned.

"Phone call," whispered Harry, "one-sided conversation. Listen... "

"Get you, Sherlock," murmured Jade, putting her head to Harry's chest and causing him to gasp slightly as she listened. Although it was annoyingly impossible (and only just) to hear what was being said, there was something familiar in the cadence of the voice...

"It's Newman!" exclaimed Jade as loud as she dared.

Harry listened on for a second before nodding in agreement. They appeared to be standing in a hidden staircase that, for whatever reason, led up to (and down from) Newman's office.

"So that's how he gets about this place so quickly," muttered Jade. "Maybe he's got a whole network of these things throughout the building. The sly sod. Do you think he spies in the ladies' loos? I always had him down as an underwear sniffer," she mused, before doing her best Hannibal Lecter / fava beans / nice chianti impression.

"Come on, he's weird, but he's not *that* weird," protested Harry, despite being unable to hide a smile, "but anyway, what are we doing here? Are we done now? Pub?"

"No! For God's sake, we've only just—"

This time it was Jade who stopped and motioned for a break in the conversation. There was another noise. Newman was no longer speaking, but another noise was coming from above them, a dull thumping that was growing louder to the point that they could feel the vibrations of the sound reverberating through the handrail.

"Down!" whispered Jade, pushing Harry roughly in the back, "someone's coming!"

Without a second's thought, Harry was heading downwards as fast as he could manage, with a complete lack of elegance, courtesy of the twisting confines down which he was squirrelling himself while simultaneously trying not to make a sound with his feet. These problems dovetailed perfectly with the fact that, with each step they took together, they were no longer able to hear or feel the steps from above. And – to make their hurried panic all the more intense – it was also impossible to see who was coming or how close they were, due to the swirling mass of twisting metal staircase above them.

Harry had just taken a moment to figure out that this possibly wasn't the best time to admit to occasional bouts of claustrophobia when, suddenly, he ran out of stairs.

As he squeezed down the last few, he noted that the floor of the shaft in which they were standing was, in fact, a metal grate through which the draught (decidedly colder and more intense down here) was gusting upwards. Not only that but set in the wall was an ancient and dust-encrusted elevator, with a hand-operated and criss-cross mesh door. It was the only exit available to them, and as Jade stepped onto the platform with him, they both became aware that the footsteps above were still coming. Whether their pursuer had passed the small panel door or not was impossible to tell.

Without hesitation, Jade reached past Harry to yank on the mesh door, which – after a moment of persuasion – concertinaed open to reveal a polished, wooden chamber, which was dimly lit and barely big enough for the two of them. Immediately, Jade scrambled in, leaving Harry on the periphery, looking desperately upwards to where the clank of descending footsteps was growing louder.

"Harry!" spat Jade in a whispered hiss.

Harry screwed his eyes tightly shut, muttered, "Fuck it," and piled in after her, drawing the concertina door shut behind them until it clicked into place. Harry looked to the wall panel that housed only three buttons in a row, one above one another. The top button was embossed with Newman's beetled face, furrowing its brow back at him judgementally. The bottom two buttons were made of a plain, unmarked, maroon plastic, and the very lowest one clicked loudly as Jade stabbed her index finger at it.

With a jolt, the lift began a jittery, spluttering descent into darkness.

15. Down

In the dim light that glowed from the ceiling of the old and cramped lift car, Jade managed to shuffle herself round enough to face Harry.

"That worked out alright in the end then, didn't it?" She grinned.

Harry, slightly out of breath from their hurried escape, pressed a button on the side of his watch to illuminate the digital screen. "Well, it's just gone 6pm, and I'm dropping towards God knows where in the centre of the earth in a death-cage of a lift, which feels like it might fall apart any second, plunging me to my doom. I don't know, but I just pictured my evening being a little more dinner, beer and televisiony somehow."

"Oh, come off it, soft lad. We'll just wait at the bottom for a bit once the lift stops, then ride it back up and get the hell out of the MOP. Piece of cake." She sounded convinced.

Actually, she didn't at all, but Harry felt a bit bad about what he'd just said and wanted to convince her that she was right. The trouble was that he couldn't, as the dim light had just gone out, they'd both yelped in terror, and Jade was now repeating the word 'shit' over and over again.

In the pitch dark, the lift continued noisily and haphazardly down the cold, windy shaft. Although neither of them were able to realise it in the blackness, they had both pressed themselves tightly against opposite sides of the cramped cabin.

Harry yelped out in alarm as Jade fumbled for him in the void. "*Yeeeeeeaarrrrrgh!*"

"It's me, Harry. Who the hell did you expect?" she chided in a low voice.

"Why are you whispering?" Harry whispered back.

"I don't know. I think I'm just trying to take control of the situation."

"Oh. Is it working?"

"No. Shit, shit, shit, shit, shit."

Harry reached back out for Jade in an effort to comfort her. "*Yeeeeeeaarrrrgh!*"

"Sorry. I just thought—"

"No, it's fine; it's fine."

Jade grabbed hold of Harry's retreating hand and clasped it tightly. He returned the favour. The warmth was welcome, as the temperature had dropped to a damp chill. It was hard to tell exactly, but in the darkness, it felt like the lift had gathered speed.

"You're certain this thing is going to stop, right?" questioned Jade.

"The lift?" responded Harry uncertainly.

"No, us holding hands, Harry. Yes, of course the lift."

"It has to, surely." They were still whispering. "Every lift has a bottom. You pressed a button and sent it on its way, and we'll eventually get... somewhere. It's probably just a warehouse or something. Storage."

"Yeah. Storage. Sounds good. Storage. Okay."

"Well, at least we're having an adventure together, right?" offered Harry in his best attempt to brighten the situation, which was ambitious.

However, Jade chuckled and, to Harry's surprise, she hugged him tightly. "Definitely that," she said with her head on his shoulder, "We'll be alright in a minute, right? I'm just not brilliant with the dark or confined spaces."

"Me neither."

"And you were going to tell me this when?"

"Well, I... " started Harry, pulling back.

"Don't let go of me."

Harry did as he was told, and as he put his arms around Jade, she held him all the tighter. The descending lift lurched, clumsily jolting each of them into the other and before Harry knew it, he felt the warmth of Jade's mouth colliding against his. Even more clumsily and in genuine embarrassment, he started to say the word 'sorry', but was completely unable to do so thanks to Jade's lips being on his, followed swiftly by the wet hotness of her exploring tongue.

In a split second, he wondered exactly what the gentlemanly response to this development should be. He reflected that it was Jade who had made a move on *him*, reflected further on the thought that he really liked her and *just what was happening in his mouth?* He began to kiss her in return – this time, with genuine meaning and intent – just at the moment when the lift shuddered to a halt and the light came back on.

They pulled back from one another immediately, blinking in the light before both staring wide-eyed in shock.

"I do weird things when I get scared," blurted Jade.

"Oh. Yes. Me too," answered Harry, clearing his throat.

They stood looking at each other – eyes like saucers, red of cheek, and both wishing that something would happen to divert from their sudden speechlessness. Duly obliging, the doors of the lift opened judderingly.

"Oh thank fuck," said Jade in a fast outward breath. "Ooh, a tunnel."

Sure enough, the doors had opened to reveal – as much as the dim light from the lift was capable of showing – an unlit tunnel. Harry, seizing the opportunity far too quickly for Jade's unspoken liking, leaped from the lift. As he did so, a number of lights suspended from the tunnel roof clicked into life to reveal...

A lit tunnel.

"What do you reckon, a quick scout down here, and then head back up and home?" asked Harry.

He was trying his best to sound like the intrepid adventurer he assumed Jade wanted him to be. However, still reeling from the kiss and with an intensely nice sensation in his chest, he would have preferred to talk about that instead. He looked down the tunnel. It was circular and had been dug out impeccably – without even the tiniest visible scratch – from a smooth, black stone. The tunnel curved away to the left about fifty yards from the lift doors, and apart from the cable carrying the electric lamps along the roof ceiling, there was no other sign of, well, anything.

Jade was just about to say something when, without warning, she and the lift fell swiftly from view.

"HARRY!" she screamed from the depths of the lift shaft, her voice plummeting into silence with a horrible quickness that set all of his senses to high alert.

"JADE!"

Harry ran to the lift entrance – now merely an upright, rectangular, black hole in the wall- and stopped himself at the edge before he could fall to his doom. There was nothing: no sound and not even a sign of the lift cable. Just damp, musty, cold air and a blackness that hung dankly where Jade had been only seconds before.

"JADE!" he bellowed down the shaft, the sickness of panic turning his brain to fire. "*Jade!* Can you hear me? Jade!"

Again, there was nothing. He pressed the single button by the doors, but nothing happened. He pressed again. Again. Again.

"Come on, you fucker. JADE!" Harry hammered the button now, but to no avail.

He stared into the abyss once more, tears prickling at his eyes, but there was nothing to see. Nothing to cling to. He had no idea how deep the shaft ran or where it ended. From here, it looked like it could run forever to the centre of the earth. The small amount of light from the overhead lamps provided just enough of a view into the eternal pit to show that the sides were just as smooth and featureless as the tunnel he was standing in. There was nothing to hold on to. No way down. No way out.

She was gone.

And he was trapped.

Salad

*M*y grandparents had always been so, so good to me.
They were from the old school. The old school where manners, compassion, gentleness and patience were the most important lessons on the curriculum. They had their routine, and I fell into line with it without really realising I had.

Mealtimes were built in around Grandma's baking and washing schedules, with clothes neatly hung to dry on the wooden clothes horse Grandpa had made her years before. Grandpa would be out in the morning, running errands, picking up shopping and checking in on old friends, as sprightly as ever. He'd pop back for lunch (1pm, always) and then spend the afternoon working in the garden before tea (6pm, to coincide with the news). Tea was always triangular sandwiches, with a cucumber, tomato and lettuce salad (from the garden and greenhouse), and a bowl of crisps that we all shared from, set out on the tablecloth on their fold-out, wooden living-room table in front of the TV.

It was simple and it was quiet, but it was exactly what I needed to get me back on some kind of track. Other kids my age would have found it stifling, I know that. But for me, it was something I could hang on to now that I had lost both my parents. I never thought of myself as an orphan. It sounded a bit Charles Dickens, and a bit like someone who had nothing and no one.

That was never the case with Grandma and Grandpa. They were the ledge on to which I held to stop myself from falling further downwards, and they held me tight, held me close, pulled me up, and gave me what I needed to steady myself and step forwards instead.

I missed my dad. Of course I did. My old life had been pretty much perfect. It was a warm, hazy place that I liked to think back to at night before I fell asleep. My grandparents felt the loss too – Mum had been their only child, and since her death (and my birth), they had become ever fonder of my dad and very sad to lose him so suddenly. Grandpa had been especially close to him, and had cried a little when he had brought home the remains of our old life to store in the loft. All my dad's work, his files, his endless books, his research and his notes. All packed away, stored and gathering dust ready for when I was older.

But Grandma and Grandpa never tried to take Dad's place. They were my grandparents, and that was how they stayed. The love was unconditional, and I knew I was safe with them and that life could be happy. I had friends over, and we'd go for long rides on our bikes, often with packed lunches that Grandma made for us. Life eventually **was** *happy and a level of normal. Once the grief was less immediate. When I started to get back into school.*

I'd had my mum's old room. It was small, but it looked over the garden, and I could see out beyond the greenhouse to the fields and hills beyond. It caught the sun in the morning, illuminating all the colourful spines of the books that adorned my shelves there, with the gold lettering. Books my dad had bought me. Books my grandparents had bought for my mum when she was a girl. My Arthurian legends. My atlas. My Guinness Book of World Records. My maps and walking books, and my photo albums packed with holiday memories.

One morning a few years later, while Grandma and Grandpa were in town getting the weekly shop, I decided to venture into the loft. I'd remembered that Grandpa had stored some things belonging to my parents up there, my dad's work and things from my early childhood, and – due to a sudden sense of curiosity – I wanted to see what was on the other side of the hatch door.

After pulling the hatch down from the ceiling using a long, wooden rod with a hook on the end, and then extending the metal ladder, I clambered up and in. As I'd expected, everything up there was arranged neatly and filed away. That was my grandpa's style. He ran a neat and tidy ship. There were folders filled with accounts and sales records from the craft shop they used to own. Some of my mum's old dolls sat on a shelf, looking out at me. They were sweet, but a bit eerie too.

And then, in a far corner, underneath a plastic tub of Christmas decorations, sat an arrangement of huge cardboard boxes, each labelled either "Gregory" or "Helen". I wanted to go over and look at them, but the huge, black dog was sitting there, panting and blocking my way, its pink tongue hanging from its mouth and its wild eyes locked on my every move.

No.

Wait.

That wasn't right.

Grandma and Grandpa had never owned a dog, so why was there a black dog in the roof now? There hadn't been. There shouldn't have been. So why was it there?

The dog barked angrily. I jumped back at first, but looked at it. I stared at it.

It was only a dog.

What harm could a dog do? I knew it wanted me to stop and to not go further. To not get past it. But it was only a dog and it shouldn't be here, and I was tired of running from it. It wore me out. It gave me headaches.

The dog gulped and made a strange, sad sound. It looked about, before looking back at me, but it wasn't happy. It barked again, but it cowered back as if it had made a mistake.

"Let me look in the box," I commanded.

There was a noise from outside: a crackle and a crunch. Grandpa's car was pulling onto the drive, meaning he and Grandma were home with the shopping. I heard the boot open, and the driver's and passenger's doors open too.

I turned to look back at the dog, but it was gone. However, there was no time now to look in the boxes; I had to get back downstairs before my grandparents caught me snooping in the loft.

But the dog was gone. It shouldn't ever have been there in the first place.

16. Glass

There was no way for Harry to tell how long he had been sitting slumped against the cold smoothness of the jet-black tunnel wall. Five, ten or twenty minutes? Half an hour, maybe? He'd yelled down the lift shaft to Jade for a while, but he hadn't been able to discern even the slightest sound. Just the faint breeze coming from far below. All he'd been able to do was sit. At first, he'd attempted to rid his mind of the millisecond look of shock in Jade's eyes before she disappeared, but the more he tried to push the image out of his head, the clearer it became.

He tried to think of a way down to her, but without a cable to hold on to or anything to grasp on the walls, that was impossible. Tears evaded him, despite the horror he felt. Not to mention the helpless frustration. After a while, the lights clicked off, and he was plunged into a darkness unlike any he'd ever experienced before. It was absolute, complete. He could no longer discern anything, not even his hand in front of his face. For a moment, he sat there, letting the blackness consume him until the he wasn't sure if he could feel the wall against his back anymore, if the floor was still beneath him or...

He waved his hand in the dark, and the motion sensor reactivated the lights. The lift doors stood open, inert. The tunnel curved away to his left. There was no point in staying here, he knew that, but Harry felt an unease at leaving the lift behind. The only thing that felt in any way positive to him was the hope that he might be able to find a way to her from the tunnel, or at least a way to find help for them both. Above (how far was that?), the day would be darkening to evening. The MOP building would be as good as deserted, with people heading home to dinner, to families, to the gym and to the cinema – to normality. And here he was, stuck in a tunnel underground, in a place that made zero sense to him. A dark, cold place that was as far away from normality as he could feel.

And then there was Jade. Again, the image of her shocked and terrified face filled his mind.

He shuddered, heaved himself up off the ground, looked forlornly to the lift doors one final time and set off down the corridor.

The curvature of the corridor was definite, and Harry worked out quickly that he was unlikely to be plunged back into darkness for now, so long as he kept moving. There was no sound apart from his footsteps, but there was something odd about those, something he couldn't place, due partly to the fact that his mind was still racing from the events of the day so far.

Echo.

That was it. His footsteps didn't echo. Although he could hear each footstep as it made contact with the smooth stone underfoot, the sound was dulled, as if the rock were absorbing the noise. It made the atmosphere a little more stifling and a little more unsettling. Harry's pace quickened, but that in itself only served to heighten his awareness of the muffled acoustics and the sense that any call for help would be unheard.

His thoughts on that were cut short as he rounded the bend to discover a pair of closed steel doors in the wall to his right. For some reason, it felt odd seeing something man-made down here, despite the functional and industrial nature of the cabled lamps above his head that continued on around the bend. It felt to him like the doors shouldn't be there, but there they were, and doors had a habit of leading to somewhere else. Jade – he suppressed the thought – would have been all for opening them and seeing what was on the other side.

There were no handles, nor any other sign of how to open them. There wasn't even a pad of any kind on the wall. There was a tiny gap between the doors, however, where the rubber seal appeared to be worn. Harry got his fingers into the gap and tried his best to prise the doors open. He was able to get a little purchase, and, gradually, the more he strained, the more the doors staggered open.

He was able to make a small gap that was wide enough to squeeze himself through, and without a thought for any possible consequence, he leaped forwards to avoid the doors forcing themselves shut and squishing him. With a dull thump, they closed behind his heels, and he was inside.

The doors were as featureless in here as on the other side. He wasn't sure if he could get his fingers in between them again to get out, but – for now – Harry took a moment to compose himself as much as he could and look around. He was in a cavernous-but-darkened chamber, with the only source of illumination a faint, blue glow from somewhere ahead of him. It was cool here, artificially so. The softened chill of the air conditioning had raised the hairs on his arms, despite it having already been cold in the tunnel. He allowed himself a minute or so to get his breathing back to normal and to give his eyes time to adjust.

Before him, he could make out only shadows from beyond where the blue glow emanated. He was also aware of a faint hum, although whether or not that was due to the air conditioning he couldn't tell. As with the tunnel, he seemed alone. He didn't dwell on the thought, but moved carefully and quietly, regardless. For now, he simply hoped he could find a way out of this place.

Carefully, he stepped forwards, towards the light source. His feelings of shock and panic had levelled out from what he felt earlier, but the lack of light in here kept him wary. He edged himself forwards with one of his arms in front of him, careful not to trip or walk into something suddenly.

The blue light, he could now see, was pulsing slowly. He could also now tell that it was throbbing from behind a section of the room where it branched off to the right. Continuing to play it safe, he backed into the wall and skulked along until he reached the edge, took a deep breath and peeped around.

Immediately to his right, at waist height, a console protruded from the wall. The blue glow spilled down onto it courtesy of a row of six computer screens, which were in operation and which also illuminated a row of six office chairs that were standing before the console, all empty. Harry wasn't able to see any further than this little oasis of dim light, but he looked and listened for any signs of company.

Satisfied he was still alone, he came out fully from behind the wall to look at the closest screen. The information on the screen was updating, sometimes scrolling up and sometimes changing altogether to a different set of data entirely. His eyes fixed on the screen, he lowered himself slowly into the accompanying chair to get a better look for any clues as to where he was and how he could get out or get help.

He saw numbers and occasional words that he recognised, but nothing that seemed to form any kind of familiar pattern. They scrolled up and faded out, and then a new set of figures emerged and proceeded to scroll. Again, there was nothing familiar. He looked about for a notepad and a pen – anything that would enable him to jot down the figures before the screen changed- but there was nothing where he was sitting. Above the terminal was a printed sticker, the edge of which was curling off, but that was labelled "S6"; he looked at the adjacent screen to the left to see that it was labelled "S5".

Other than that, there was nothing he could hang anything on. He could feel his palms getting clammy again, and he glanced back towards the closed steel doors in a moment of panic. There was no movement there.

He got up and took the seat at the adjacent computer, hoping to at least see something different, something that made sense. Again, there was nothing but lines of data, scrolling hesitantly upwards, fading out to be replaced with...

Something different this time. The screen had divided into six individual segments, which were views from what appeared to be a set of security cameras, focussed on what or where he couldn't quite tell. There – "S1", "S2" and "S3"; each camera view carried a legend to match the labels he'd just seen. Harry sat forwards and squinted at his screen, but all he could make out in each section was, again, a dark and barely illuminated shadow.

All of a sudden his eye caught movement. On camera S4, something altered, and the light level changed as a result of...

A human figure. Jade? Or someone else? Where or what was S4?

At that moment, the screen reverted back to the juddering and scrolling reel of faceless data, but Harry's stomach and chest had both dropped, his breath frozen on the intake. He'd seen a dark, fuzzy shape that was most definitely a human figure and that had most definitely moved. Swallowing hard, Harry looked down the row to see if any of the other terminals were showing the camera screen, but they simply scrolled line after line of pixellated data back at him.

All of a sudden, there was a dramatic and metallic thump to Harry's right. As he poked his head around the edge of the wall, he was able to see the steel doors buckle slightly as something thumped against them once again. He had a moment to consider that he'd opened the doors himself easily enough, but decided to hold that thought and move. Something hefty was whacking that door, and a hefty whack of any kind was the last thing he needed right now.

"Bollocks," muttered Harry under his breath, a powerful and affecting choice for the first word he'd spoken in what felt like an age. He'd felt he was on the edge of finding out something important that could lead him to Jade. Unfortunately, he also felt there was a strong possibility that he was about to suffer some-thing extremely unpleasant. He took one last frustrated glance at the screen – which showed annoying, senseless data still – and decided to keep hunting for an exit and hide by edging back into the darkness behind the row of chairs at the console.

It turned out to be a very interesting move. As he walked backwards, Harry had zero expectation of the giant, glass wall that he thumped into, which subsequently announced the con-tact between them both with a deeply resonating hum. Harry bounced off the wall and fell to the concrete floor, offering a far less impressive splat in return.

Momentarily confused, Harry scrambled up onto his feet and looked behind him to see what he had made contact with. Again, it was just too damned dark to tell. He ran his finger up the smooth, glass wall, and noticed it was slightly curved, warm and vibrating gently under his touch. Try as he might, he couldn't quite see through the wall, and so instead felt his way along it as best he could. It merely reflected the blue glow back at him from the computer screens, although as the wall curved round into the darkness, he realised it wasn't a wall at all, but the exterior of some kind of large, glass cylinder, which he estimated to be several yards in diameter and goodness only knows how high. Whatever. It was something behind which he could hide, which was ideal given that the steel doors had just taken another blow.

Harry continued to what he estimated was halfway round the cylinder from where he'd begun, and he was now facing into the darkness beyond. He was just about to stop and plan his next move when his hip connected with something jutting out from the glass. His hand shot down instinctively, and he discovered it was a metal box, which was cold to the touch. As he ran his hand over it, he caught something underneath his palm, felt it move and abruptly everything around him changed.

Harry had flicked a switch, and that switch was connected to a light behind him. This light was situated inside the cylinder itself, and its sole purpose in life was to cast its glow upon the contents contained inside. It was doing a very creditable job of this, illuminating the vast quantity of liquid that filled it (the slightly yellowish hue of which reminded Harry of something lavatorial) and the lifeless human being floating upright within.

Harry shouted in terror at this, and pressed the button once more in an attempt to turn off the light. Nothing happened, not even when he frantically pressed it a third time. He looked once more to the steel doors. Nothing was happening there, but they were looking battered, and Harry didn't want to guess at how long they would hold.

Swallowing and trying to refocus, he looked back to the figure he was now confronted with, which was floating above and in front of him. It was male, youngish, of average build and clad in a pair of tight swimming trunks, which Harry noticed were made by Speedo. As if a floating, lifeless body in a giant cylinder full of wee were not enough, this struck him as odd, and he half expected to find a sewn-on badge commemorating a swim of twenty-five yards.

The creature's eyes were shut, and his mouth and nose were covered by a dark mask connected to a long tube, which undulated very slowly in the water and was connected to something unseen in the base of the cylinder. While Harry stared wide-eyed at the figure above him, he then became aware that, by switching on the light, he had thrown a pool of illumination into some of the gloom beyond, where it was now clear that more of the macabre capsules stood – at least four of them in total.

Driven by the kind of curiosity that was well known to be a risk to those of a feline disposition, Harry swallowed once more and moved towards the next capsule. He located the small, metal control box and pressed the light switch.

This time, he really wished he hadn't. Again, a figure floated in what appeared to be a capsule full of urine. Again, it was a male complete with a mask and Speedos, but this time he was clearly older, sporting a grey beard, shaggy hair and a small forest of the same on his chest. But something was wrong. Despite a number of similarities to the occupant of the previous cylinder, this unfortunate chap was in possession of a misshapen head almost twice the size of his twin, his spine was twisted, and his shoulders curved in a horrible and miserable fashion. Where his left arm should have been, something akin to a fleshy tail with a series of small stumps at the end floated uneasily in the liquid, and the left leg was withered and useless.

Harry stared in terror at this sad creature, preserved and trapped for whatever unthinkably sinister reason in a giant jar. Despite the horror of his recent discoveries, *there was something else*. He couldn't place it (his mind was busy performing somersaults as it was), but it was strong enough to send the hairs on the back of his neck in an upward trajectory.

Another water tank stood to the right of this one. Harry's compulsion to find out more – to find at least some tiny element of an explanation for this aquatic chamber of horrors – had overtaken him, and he was already on his way to the corresponding metal box that was attached seamlessly to the glass surface. This time, he hesitated momentarily before pressing the button, holding his breath as he did so.

Once more it contained a masked, floating body. Male. Young, as with the first one he'd encountered. This time, however, the body was thinner, emaciated almost. Despite the mask that almost covered the lower half of the occupant's face, Harry was able to read something from the countenance of this wretched being. The eyes were scrunched tightly shut and – yes – he noticed now that the hands too were clenched together as fists. This one had died in pain. But why? What was this place? Moving forwards towards and illuminating this cylinder had exposed another two behind it. There were now at least six in this ghastly warehouse and Harry was willing to bet his last pound that they contained further versions of this tragic urchin.

Harry thought to himself, was that it? Was the inexplicable sensation the fact that these were all somehow different versions *of the same person?* That couldn't be right, surely? He looked back at the previously illuminated glass cases, snapping his gaze from one to the next and then back again. He had to be imagining it, but the more he looked, the more he saw it. Differences in ages and aberrations in form, yes, but more similarities than diversifications. As he looked again, circling the cases with a sense of unsettling awe, there they were. Even the explosion of sun freckles and moles across the shoulder blades of each seemed to match exactly...

It all happened at once. With an alarming thump and a crunch, the doors at the far end of the cavern were now being pummelled repeatedly, and they began to work their way open slowly. But worse than that – far worse than that – was the writhing movement that happened around him. As the thump at the doors had shaken Harry out of his rumination, so too had it affected each body within the cases.

They were alive, and they were awake. With a sickening jolt, each one opened his eyes wide, vividly and immediately alert and aware. As Harry gasped in horror, they each snapped their gaze downwards to stare at and scrutinise him.

The eyes. The eyes of all three of them matched perfectly, and as a sickening fear rose in the back of his throat, Harry knew.

The eyes of the three of them matched his own.

17. Underground

It was at that point that an alarm sounded, and it was also at that point when Harry nearly passed out.

It wasn't just the fact that these wretched creatures in their liquid suspensions had the eyes to match his, it was the fear he saw behind them. The moment they had awoken, it was as if they'd been torn from a terrifying nightmare, only to be plunged into an even more monstrous reality, which – given their current state – was not hard to appreciate.

However, there was no time to dwell on the situation. Harry had to get out of there, for both the sake of his sanity and his safety – and potentially that of Jade too, if she'd even survived the fall.

He staggered back into the cold, glass wall of the huge tank behind him and tried to collect his thoughts. He noticed that the creature facing him was watching him with a puzzled look. Again, something was all too sickeningly familiar, and it sent Harry cold. But the creature was trying to tell him something. He looked about, as if scanning the area from his higher vantage point, then focussed back on Harry before, with his left arm, he jabbed through the liquid in which he was suspended, causing a multitude of bubbles to rise haphazardly upwards.

Harry stood up, and looked about too. He glanced frantically back at the creature, who repeated the movement, this time with more of an imploring look. He was pointing at something he wanted Harry to see.

Harry could see only darkness beyond, and so he moved towards the cylinder for fear of missing something important. As he did so, he became aware of movement from behind him too. He looked back to see that the unfortunate suspended behind him was doing exactly the same: pointing desperately in the same direction, into the darkness. It was the opposite way from which Harry had entered the chamber earlier, and from that direction came the sound of a scuffling movement. He was no longer alone with the inhabitants of the cabinets of horror. He had company, and it was headed his way.

He looked desperately back up at the creature in front of him. "What's over there? What do I do?"

The person in the case floated towards him and then – in one terrifying, bubbling movement – the unfortunate reached up to tear the mask away from his face, revealing a contorted version of Harry's own.

"RUN," he mouthed at Harry.

The rest of him took a moment, but Harry's legs were already on the case.

***

He could sense rather than see the additional enormous cylinders around him as he plunged into the darkness. He had no wish to see into them and was glad for the blackness around him as he ran, his arms in front of him. Despite himself, he was also able to notice that the temperature was dropping, and that there was a stale dampness to the air he was gulping in.

He stopped for a moment, his head still aching. He looked behind him to where he had been and where the rows of terrifying cylinders stood. They were pale and distant, and he could just make out the figures floating in them when, suddenly, all illumination disappeared, the alarm ceased and everywhere was plunged into darkness.

But he had no time to utter "Shit," the word that was in the process of escaping into the silence from between his clenched teeth, as from the darkened chamber, four torch beams flicked suddenly into life, their long shafts of illumination abruptly sweeping this way and that, searching.

For him.

However, the torches had also revealed something at the end of the chamber, the point to which the figures trapped in the glass cylinders had been directing Harry, and which was far closer than he had thought. He ran as the torch beams flickered about him, heading towards a small archway in the wall with a winding, metal staircase within. A way out.

Whether those who held the torches had seen it or not, he was unaware and didn't care. As he reached the steps, he saw that they only went in one direction: upwards. He grabbed the handrail and used it to haul himself up and out of the range of the torch beams. It was a tight staircase, and the shaft into which it was bolted was stale and clammy, but as he ascended the first few rattling steps, he was glad to be on the move and away from the horrors below.

Minutes later and still ascending, once more in the pitch black, he paused. Grasping tightly on to the rail and holding his ragged breath, he listened carefully and waited to see if the staircase moved. There was nothing. No torch beams. No noise. He had evaded his pursuers for now, and – physically, at least – the only way was up.

However, there was no way of seeing how far that was. Down and up were immaterial here in the dank darkness – there was just the staircase and his grip upon it. He felt suddenly sick, as if he were about to throw up. But he daren't even cough – he was still listening intently for any sound that might indicate his pursuers were closing on him. Instead, he pushed on, now taking each step carefully. One at a time. Up and up and up.

Stones

A stuffy afternoon on a sunny summer weekend. I'd cycled nearly fifteen miles, my rucksack filled with the sandwiches I'd made in the morning and bottles of isotonic drinks. I'd been slogging up hills and whizzing down winding roads, climbing up and down every one of the gears on my bike. It had been a glorious day. I felt free. This was my last summer before I left for university, and I intended to make the most of my days in between and after my A-level exams.

As the afternoon meandered lazily along, the skies began to darken. A storm was coming in from the west. I was a long ride from home, but I didn't mind the wet weather, especially in the summer. Days like this still felt like an adventure, a risk.

Grey, stone cottages began to fringe the road as I pedalled into and through the village. I passed an unmanned, wooden stand laden with fresh eggs and an honesty box. A man in a flat cap shuffling along the pavement, the morning newspaper rolled up in his hand. I passed the old market hall and the Shoulder of Mutton. The people sitting on benches outside were getting up and taking their pints inside, looking towards the horizon as they did so. There was a definite crackle in the air and a build-up of static.

The storm was closing in, but it didn't matter.

On I pedalled, through the next village and up, powering away from the houses and leaving them behind, standing on the pedals and climbing my way up Cliff Lane, grunting, sweating, straining and pushing myself on.

Fields. Farms. A green patchwork that stretched and undulated on to the horizon and down the other side. The single track tarmac road weaved its way through them all as I raced along. Huge and ancient trees stood like sentinels, whistling past and joining together overhead occasionally to form a tunnel of green.

A rumble.

Reaching the entrance to one of the farms, a long drive that ran between the fields to a distant farmhouse, I pulled to a stop, snapping my shoes from the cleats before propping my bike against the gate. On the edge of the moor to my right stood a tall oak tree, and in the field beneath it stood the Grey Ladies, a circle of four Neolithic standing stones rising from the ground like giant, limestone arrowheads. It had been the feature of various local tall tales when I was younger. The place where the faeries from the underworld came to dance. To the right, as I looked across the grass and the well-trodden path of the Limestone Way, the strange castle-like edifice of Robin Hood's Stride loomed against the sky, surveying the scene.

I took a gulp from my water bottle, reflecting on whether the rumble I'd heard was a distant lorry or thunder.

It was dead still. The world was waiting.

Then. There.

A flicker, and the landscape turned white briefly. My eyes darted towards a distant hill, from where I'd managed to glimpse a fork of lightning.

Then came the rumble; slow at first – exactly like a rumbling lorry in the distance – but sustained, growing, growing, fading, gone.

I waited, my breath now steadying after my ride, but excited. The hairs on my arms were standing up, and it was exhilarating.

Nothing. And then it came.

The entire world around me turned blindingly bright white

for a split second, and it felt like all the air was sucked instantly upwards and into the sky. Tearing through the afternoon, a bolt of pure, white energy ripped downwards and split into four jagged rods, each connecting with the tip of one of the four standing stones.

Then came the almighty boom. I was thrown to the road, my hands instinctively going for my helmeted head as the sound slammed into me with full force.

Moments later, I opened my eyes again; the blinding light had gone and the malevolent greyness back in place.

"Jesus Christ." I'd said it out loud. I was back on my feet and staring over to the Grey Ladies. Each stone was glowing and pulsing in an ethereal shade of purple. Small tendrils of golden light were coiling their way skywards, undulating as if alive. Tentatively, I edged to the drystone wall to get a better look into the field.

Only, it wasn't there.

The field had vanished and been replaced with a perfectly smooth and clear sheet of glass, or so it seemed. I could see far, far down into the earth below the glowing stones, which now appeared as the jagged tip of a subterranean mountain that descended far below. Almost as if it were topped with a glowing crown. Deeper still, at the mountain's foot, far below, as if I were looking out from the window of a cruising aeroplane, I could make out a patchwork of green and yellow fields, and a river winding its way through them.

I blinked in confusion. It looked too real. It was crystal clear, at first. Yet my brain was screaming at me that it couldn't be. It shouldn't be. I blinked again. The light was fading, and the green of the grass was returning and blurring all that I could see. In less than a minute, it was all gone, almost as if it had never been there in the first place. The stones, no longer a mountain top but jagged rocks in a field once more, ceased to glow.

There were no smartphones back then, but even if there had been I doubt I would've thought to have taken a photo. Instead, I just stared at the stones before another fork of lightning shot down *from the sky, this time further ahead and in the distance.*

Eventually, I pedalled my way homewards. I don't know how long I stood there staring, questioning myself and what I thought I'd seen. The storm faded out, and the sun made an attempt to poke through the grey clouds. It looked to be winning, and as though I would have some hot sunshine once again to see me through the final miles.

But then, as I reached the top of Harper Hill, a gust of cold wind swept its way past me towards Chesterfield in the east. In moments, the sky darkened again, with the clouds swirling once more to pack together tightly with unnatural speed. I stopped suddenly.

As I watched in the sudden gloom, a bright, white bolt of lightning seared downwards from the sky a few miles ahead, connecting instantly and flowing into the iconic twisted spire of Chesterfield church. The thundering boom that followed milliseconds later was no less powerful than before, to the point that I felt it in my ribcage as it reverberated across the landscape. This time it was brief, being only seconds long, but I saw it again. The famous spire of the church, warped and twisted by time, glowed with a purple luminescence against the grey backdrop of the sky. It was there. It was most definitely there.

But then it was gone.

This time, the dark clouds parted once again. They dissolved and evaporated, and the blue sky and sunlight returned.

18. Daylight

Harry had lost all track of time. But when he eventually emerged – sweating, utterly exhausted, dehydrated, hungry and desperate for the loo – it appeared to be early morning.

He'd been underground for at least twelve hours.

At the top of the never-ending, cramped and winding staircase to the surface was a rusted and heavy steel door, which had groaned in a way that Harry was able to empathise with all too easily. After much persuasion from his shoulder underneath it, Harry had been able to expel what energy remained in his drained body to force the door open. Pale-but-nonetheless-blinding light had nearly knocked him back down the staircase. He'd gasped and hauled himself out before flopping into long grass, his M&S shirt a stained, sweat-drenched and grubby mess, and his trousers all too similar. He was just glad for the light, for fresh air. To be out. Morning mist hung over the field, and although there was an autumnal chill to everything, Harry was just glad to let it seep in and cool his aching, overworked body for the time being.

Somewhere in his consciousness, he remembered that, luckily, he had an alternative set of clothes in his work locker, which he'd brought with him a fortnight prior for an evening game of squash he hadn't played.

What the hell was the time? He noticed with despair that at some point he'd smashed the face of his watch. He fumbled instead in his pocket for his phone to check, and after a few seconds of uselessly pressing the button on the side, he remembered that it was drained of all energy and dead.

For now, he was alone, as far as he could tell. Upon repocketing his phone and raising his head, he saw the MOP building and the surrounding trees in the distance, a good quarter of a mile away. The car park looked empty, save for a vehicle or two. Darren, his faithful and decrepit moped, would still be parked over there somewhere, rusting in the morning dew. Jade's car would be there too.

Jade.

There was her face again, front and centre in his mind, falling and frightened in the dark. And there was the hollow blow to his empty stomach once more.

He had to do something. There would be no one in work yet, but there was always someone on security. He'd have to admit to what they'd done. Well, he'd admit to some of it. Everything up until the lift. Jade was his priority.

The glass cylinders. The creatures submerged inside them that looked like him. Being chased out by torchlight and escaping up a metal staircase to emerge in a field. Harry felt it probably prudent to not talk so much about those things, if at all. They could and would have to wait for now. Jade.

Jade. Jade. Jade.

He began to trudge back towards the MOP building across the field, in a weird state of confusion combined with exhaustion and determination, and he tripped full-length over something in the grass.

"Bollocks!" he cursed under his breath, clutching and rubbing his already throbbing shin.

It'd been partly obscured by the grass, but a grey and weathered stone, approximately the size and shape of one of his grandma's garden gnomes and equally as annoying, was submerged in the earth and was the culprit behind Harry's tumble.

He got back to his feet, gave his leg a rub and a shake before gingerly putting his weight back on it, and was about to continue walking when he noticed that the offending boulder was part of a group of around ten, as far as he could make out, all in a circle of around twenty yards or so in diameter.

"Chuffing druids," he muttered, and he continued, wincing, towards the MOP.

***

When Harry reached the entrance, the grand foyer was cold and empty, save for Darryl, who was one of four security guards who rotated their duties every week, each sitting in overnight until their shift ended. They were all minor celebrities in their own right, or at least they liked to think they were.

As Harry entered, he noticed that there was a faint reek of fresh paint in the air. Harry raised his hand towards Darryl in a sheepish greeting.

"Morning, Harry. Bit early for you, isn't it?" Darryl enquired.

"Er, yeah. Something like that. Actually, what time is it?" Harry countered.

"Oh, I see. Been burning the midnight oil again, have you?" chided Darryl, looking at his watch. "It's 5.30am. You dirty stopout. Look at the state of you." He chuckled. "Seriously though, Harry, I can't let you in looking like that, today of all days. You'll have to get yourself changed into something a little less scruffbag."

Harry scowled. "Yeah, I was going to use the showers if that's okay? I've got a fresh set of clothes in my locker as well. Look Darryl," he said, leaning into the desk conspiratorially, even though there was nobody else there, "um, I've had a bit of an accident."

Darryl nodded and shrugged. "Don't worry, mate. Happens to the best of us. You get in that shower and nobody need ever know about it."

"No, that's not quite what I meant. This is a bit more drastic. It involves Jade. Jade Birch."

Darryl eyed Harry up thoughtfully. "I see. Not sure I can help you there, Harry. I'm no expert, but you should consider speaking to a family planning clinic about that kind of thing. There are some leaflets in the bathrooms—"

"Sorry, no, it's not like that either. Jade's in trouble. She's had an accident, and she's stuck at the bottom of a lift shaft."

"She's what?"

"She got in the lift, it malfunctioned, and now she's at the bottom of a lift shaft and needs getting out. It's kind of my fault. Sort of."

Darryl stared long, hard and suspiciously at Harry. "Have you put it in the accident book?"

"What?"

"The accident book. If there's an accident on the premises, you have to put it in the accident book. Then we can look into it."

"Well, I've only just got here, Darryl. From the lift shaft. Sort of."

"You left her down there?"

"No! Well, kind of, but no. Look, somebody needs to go down there and get her out. She might even have broken something and she could be in a lot of pain. She should get to a hospital."

Darryl nodded sagely. "Right. Yes. Get it in the accident book, and then I can sort something out." He rummaged under the desk for a moment before producing a blue, leather-bound book with the gold-embossed word "Guests" scribbled out on the cover and replaced with "Accidents" in black pen. He proffered a lidless biro to Harry. "Go on. Pop it in, there's a chap."

Harry gawped at Darryl. "Can you not just, I dunno, get a few lads together and go down now? Like, right now this minute?"

Darryl shook his head with his eyes shut. "No, Harry. Sorry. There's a process. The accident goes in the book, I read it, I assess it and I act accordingly."

"But I just told you about it. The lift down from Newman's office, in the east wing. It broke while Jade was in it, and now she's stuck at the bottom of the fucking shaft."

Darryl gave Harry a quizzical look, nodded and sucked his teeth. "Hey. Language. No need for that. Any road, here's the thing: you'll have to write that all down here. It's the process. And there's no lift in that part of the building anyhow. There's only the big lift over yonder." He indicated over his shoulder towards the main corridor. "Newman uses that one like anyone else; he hasn't got owt special for himself, like."

Harry looked in that direction and swallowed in frustration. Time was ticking.

"Well, okay. I see how this works. So, let's say there was another lift in the building then, one I'm *not supposed to know about*, but that I may have accidentally stumbled upon, with Jade," proceeded Harry, winking, "and that may have malfunctioned with Jade in it, right? That is the lift to which I'm referring, although, of course, *I know nothing about it*. Not a thing."

"Not a blessed thing!"

"That's right. So, will you now look into it, Darryl?"

Darryl, caught up in the moment, nodded enthusiastically. "No."

"What?"

"Not until you've written in the book."

"Christ on his throne!"

"Rules is rules, Harry. Go on, pop it in, and we'll have a look."

With a sigh of frustration, he glared at Darryl (who responded with his well-practised 'not my fault' shrug), turned the book towards himself on the reception desk and began to write. When done, he span the book about so that Darryl could read it.

"I'll get my reading glasses." Darryl nodded, satisfied that all relevant procedures had been observed. "Just a minute."

***

Harry hadn't waited. Instead, he headed into the main part of the building and made for the staff lockers. As quick as he could, he was out of his sweaty and stained attire, and into his clean shirt and trousers. He figured he had to act as fast as he could, but also figured it wasn't wise to have everyone's attention focussed on his dishevelled, sweaty and muck-encrusted appearance, especially if he were going to try to sneak his way back to Newman's secret staircase as the staff arrived.

Then there was the fact that he had been followed down below. Whoever was after him would have worked out the route he would have taken, and it was likely they would come looking. It wasn't much by way of a disguise, but by slipping into different clothes, at least he felt like he was doing something.

Changing into clean kit wasn't easy going, however, as he could feel his limbs and joints starting to ache more and more from his endeavours of the last few hours. What the hell had he and Jade uncovered? And what state was Jade going to be in? These two questions were buzzing around his tired and addled brain as he made his way back towards the reception area.

By the time Harry got back, Darryl was mid-conversation on the phone and had a grave look on his face. One or two staff members were starting to enter, heading briskly to their offices or cubicles.

Darryl caught sight of Harry and motioned him to wait. "Yes, sir, of course. I'll make sure everything is ready once he arrives. Absolutely. Yes. You can count on us, sir. Thank you."

Darryl placed the receiver back on the phone and sucked his lip once again.

"Everything alright?" asked Harry.

"Yes, yes. Bang on," replied Darryl, his eyes momentarily off somewhere else with his thoughts. He snapped back to look at Harry and smiled grimly. "The lift. Sorry, yes. I've got a couple of maintenance crew coming over to take a look at it shortly. We'll have her sorted. Your Jade'll be alright. She'll just be stuck in the carriage, that's all; no doubt a little frightened, but alright.

The maintenance lads assured me that the lift system has a hydraulic failsafe that cushions any falls, no matter how fast or far."

"Oh, good. That's good. Thank you," said Harry, the relief washing through him. "Will you need me to lend a hand at all?" he asked, not sure exactly what more he could do apart from point into the shaft in a downwards direction to show where the lift had gone. He just felt that he should at least do *something*.

"Ha. No, no. We'll have to leave them to it. Qualified experts, see. Insurance and all that. You look smarter, by the way; that's much better."

"What?" Harry was temporarily phased by the question, his mind still elsewhere. "Oh, these clothes? Oh, yes. Thank you. Look, do you know when Newman – sorry, Mr Newman – is due in? I could do with making an appointment to speak to him."

Darryl nodded and brought up a calendar on his computer. "He'll be busy most of today, of course," said Darryl as he picked his fingers over the keyboard, "but you're in luck. He's due in at 7am, and he should be free for just over an hour. Mind you, that mad sod sometimes works overnight and stays in, so you never know your luck. But, regardless, if I were you, I'd go up and grab him as early as you can, before he gets busy."

"That's great; thank you, Darryl."

"No sweat," replied the security guard amiably.

***

Harry felt a little better, but the cloud of panic still swirled around him, and he wouldn't be happy until he locked his eyes on hers. Soon, Jade would be back at the surface, and he could make sure she was okay. But, first, it was time to go see Newman and ask a few questions. Like why the building in which they all worked sat on top of an underground cavern filled with terrifying creatures in giant, glass jars that looked like him, and why Newman himself had a secret lift that took him directly to the said lair. He also felt he should point out that the lair itself would most likely need new doors, but, again, he thought he'd leave that fact until last.

As Harry made his way along a corridor towards his cubicle, it was clear that something was different. Despite the early hour, staff members were buzzing hurriedly up and down the corridor. At this time of the morning, there was normally hardly anyone about, yet there was an excited hustle and bustle today, with more people in and around the place than was usual, each seemingly in a hurry.

As he reached his cubicle, he caught sight of Gupinder, a colleague he'd been paired up with a week or so previously in a slightly underwhelming team-building task involving baked beans and a protractor. A polite, incredibly neat and painfully shy young man, Harry had a soft spot for him. But even he seemed to be keeping to the frantic pace of the others, keen to get somewhere, with a sheaf of folders clutched to his chest.

"Gupinder!" greeted Harry.

"Oh, hi Harry! Didn't see you there, sorry," the lad replied.

Harry looked behind himself into his empty cubicle, and up and down the momentarily deserted corridor. "There's nobody else here."

"Oh. I know. Sorry."

They stood there awkwardly, with Gupinder looking at the ceiling, as if searching for an escape.

Harry felt it only fair to break the silence, seeing as he'd stopped him and inadvertently terrified him. "So," he said in his best cool, approachable manner, "what's going on? Why's everybody in such a rush?"

Gupinder looked at Harry in shock, and then apologised for having done so. "Sorry, but didn't you hear the announcement yesterday afternoon?"

Ah.

"Er, no," said Harry, feeling suddenly more lukewarm than cool, "I must've been in the toilet or something... Why?"

"Oh, right. Sorry. Well, government visit! They're coming to take a look at the facilities later this afternoon. Got to tidy up, like. 'Get the place ship-shape and like all the fashions of Bristol' is how Mr Newman described it!" Gupinder added, doing a pretty good impression of Newman in the process and then apologising for it. "Sorry."

"No, no, that's quite alright," answered Harry, "I'd best get to it, then. See you around."

***

Harry had occasionally pondered on just how much of an interest the government actually took in the MOP, and thought it was about time someone from the top brass paid a visit. Not that he paid a huge amount of attention to politics these days. Staying off social media as much as he could had helped him avoid all the cross-party fighting, point-scoring, scandals and 'fake news' that had annoyed him while firing up and dividing so many people since The Change referendum four years ago.

It was good to see that what the people of the MOP were doing day in, day out had registered somewhere in Westminster. Harry took a moment to make sure he looked a little more presentable than he had a few hours previously (he did, which wasn't difficult) and was about to head out to confront Newman when a knock came at his door. Was it news about Jade?

Excitedly, he went to open it and was more than a little disappointed to see Karen, his line manager, standing in the doorway.

"Well, don't look so pleased to see me, will you?" she said.

"Sorry," fumbled Harry, "Everything alright?"

"Give or take a visit from a government delegation this afternoon, everything is tickety-boo, Harry," she replied, drizzling her words with the sarcasm for which she was well known throughout the MOP. "It's ridiculous," she continued, with a soupçon more anger thrown in for good measure, "an overblown photo opportunity for the government that's made our lives hell. Do you realise they've made us repaint the walls of the foyer?"

"Um, I smelled that as I came in, yes. I wondered what that was all about."

"Hmm," she hummed, "not our idea, though. Some heavies from the government decreed it, and that's that, so it's happening. Nobody here really wants to meet them, not after the way they've shafted us into accepting the result of The Change referendum. Besides, we're all busy as hell and just don't have the time, but that's nothing to them. It's all so bloody artificial, but it sells papers, doesn't it? Poor old Newman will have to be the one doing the hand-shaking, although he's a mine-field himself. Speaking of which, you all set? Ships to Bristol or whatever it was that he wittered on about yesterday?"

"Yeah, pretty much," said Harry, stretching and yawning as he did so.

"Burning the midnight oil at both ends, were we?" enquired Karen, repeating Darryl's accusation with more sauce than Harry was comfortable with, and arching an eyebrow. "Actually, speaking of which, have you seen Jade this morning?"

Harry coughed and then straightened himself. "Jade? No. Why?" he asked with none of the nonchalance he was hoping for.

"Oh, not to worry," responded Karen. "She's just not in her cubicle this morning, and her phone is going to voicemail. It's not like her," she mused, flicking her tightly permed, long, black hair as she did so, "A very organised and conscientious girl, Jade. You could learn a lot from her, Harry. That's if you weren't so busy staring at her boobs."

"I'm sorry?" spluttered Harry, his mind suddenly elsewhere.

"Oh, come off it," Karen remonstrated cheekily. "It's as obvious as the day is long! You fancy the pants off her! Not that I blame you," she mused again, flushing slightly, "she's a heck of a girl. Exciting. Tenacious. Gregarious. Voluptuous. Anyway... " She turned her suddenly fervent focus back to Harry, who had gone very pale. "We'd best get ready for all these bloody bigwig

MPs. Tell her to pop in and see me when she gets in, there's a dear."

With that, Karen swept off up the corridor, Harry's door slowly swinging shut behind her.

Shit. Jade.

Harry had simply assumed that she'd be back up in the MOP now, the lift drama done with, sitting in the medical unit with a blanket and a cup of tea. In fact, he'd simply assumed that Karen would be aware of the lift issue and Jade's situation as a result. Had Darryl forgotten to get the maintenance crew on to the task? No. That couldn't be right. He said he'd already spoken to them. So maybe she simply wasn't aware yet? He wanted to brush aside the worries that were firing their way through his synapses.

Shit.

Just how fucked up were things? It wasn't supposed to have ended up like this. This wasn't part of the plan. Was this on him? He'd been trying to impress her by going along with the adventure she wanted. He'd kind of enjoyed it to begin with, seeing her excited and being part of it. But Jade wasn't out of the lift. She was in trouble, and it was his fault. Harry felt that uncomfortable, hot rise of heightened fear squirming up his spine, and not for the first time in the last twenty-four hours.

Shit. He had to speak to Newman and get Jade rescued. Now.

***

Harry's throat was a little dry when he knocked on Newman's door, which was far from ideal, given that it had some serious talking to be an active part of.

"Come!" came Newman's voice from within.

Only it wasn't his voice at all.

When Harry entered, he found someone else sat in Newman's office. In Newman's chair. In a thin, black suit with a white shirt and dark-red tie. He was staring through small, round, wire-framed spectacles at a picture on Newman's desk (no doubt of Newman's beetling little face), which – as he looked up to see Harry – he turned and carefully placed flat on the table, face-side down.

"May I help you?" said the stranger slowly, without smiling.

"I, er... sorry. I was hoping to speak to Mr Newman."

The stranger paused momentarily, staring at Harry. "I see. Well, sorry, he's not in today. He's taking time off. I'm... " He paused again, before smiling thinly, then continuing, "Covering for him."

"Oh. Oh, right," said Harry, not sure what to add.

"Was it something important?"

"Um. No," Harry lied, "not really. I mean, yes, but... " He fumbled, caught off-guard by this pale, cleanly cut man of indeterminate age who was now eyeing him with something like a look of disgust.

"Well, it either is or it isn't. Which is it to be? I have quite a day ahead."

"It's the lifts," Harry blurted.

"The lifts?"

"Well, a lift, specifically. Here in the east wing, down from Mr Newman's... well, this office, actually. Via a flight of stairs? It's broken, there's someone trapped in it, and she needs hauling up as a matter of urgency, really." Harry clenched his teeth and nodded quickly, confirming simultaneously his slight embarrassment and the awkwardness he felt admitting such things to this severe and unsettling stranger.

The stranger merely raised an eyebrow. "There's no lift down from this office. You must be mistaken."

"Perhaps you haven't been made aware of it yet," said Harry, curtly but politely, "there's a staircase that leads down from—"

"There's no staircase, and there's no lift. *You* are mistaken. Now, if there's anything else?"

Harry stared at this man, who merely stared back with the faintest glint of a thin, almost triumphant smile that failed to bring light to his gaunt, pallid face.

"Erm, no. No, nothing else. Only... when will Mr Newman be back?" asked Harry.

"Eventually."

At this, the stranger picked up a document from Newman's desk and began to study it closely, with no sign of any awareness that Harry had ever been there.

"Right. Okay then. I'll, erm... "

"If you would." The stranger continued to study the paper, never once looking up from it.

Harry let himself out.

***

The government visit turned out to be a blur of pomp, flashing cameras, bright lights and blue suits. Harry had eventually been called from his cubicle, where he'd spent an hour stewing in fervent anguish and getting no work done whatsoever. He'd attempted to get out on two occasions, with the intention of trying to sneak off to the corridor where he and Jade had found the hidden door a day previously, but the building was simply too busy, with sections closed off for security reasons. Now he, along with the rest of a carefully arranged crowd, were forced to stand in the newly painted and media-friendly reception hall.

Unfortunately, the day was to be more disrupted than everyone had initially thought and planned for. The expectation was that the Minister for Something Tradey, Vivienne Harris, or maybe Harness, would be dropping in, meeting a few workers, shaking hands, posing for some photos and then getting away.

No one had expected the Prime Minister himself.

To everyone's visible, audible and – in some quarters – intestinal shock, he had stomped out of his car and into the entrance hall, a blur of badly fitting blue suit and a thatch of messy, blond hair. Taking the microphone and waving the assembled crowd to silence, he'd then waffled on about what a great job everybody here was doing for the British economy, how The Change would be delivered turbo-charged and on time (despite this being the sixth attempt, although he hadn't mentioned that) and how the future was looking very exciting and microwavable indeed, or something like that.

He seemed to be doing his very best job of trying to make everyone feel that they were a part of something very big and important, and that everything was going to change in a very big, noticeable way very soon. This was something he'd repeated *ad nauseam* throughout his three years in office, and the only real perceptible change had been that people who were marginally pissed off about things before were now constantly outraged, and had developed a habit of taking it out on one another. That and the fact that things generally felt a little more damp than before. Despite this, though, something very exciting was about to happen in the next few days. The Prime Minister couldn't say what exactly, and he just encouraged patience.

Despite his initial surprise at seeing the Prime Minister up close, along with the general buzz and hubbub that lingered throughout the MOP, Harry was more worried about the present than the near future. He'd watched the Prime Minister waffling on, as if from behind smoked glass, while all he could think of was Jade and how the hell he could get her out. She'd been down there for hours now. In fact, throughout the afternoon, a couple of people had already asked him if he'd seen her. If he'd seen Jade.

Jade.

Just thinking about her made him feel sick. Minute by minute, second by second, the fear was growing inside him. He was sure other people must've noticed he was sweating and that he wasn't himself. Nothing about the last two days made any sense. The fear, coupled with the exhaustion that felt like it penetrated all the way to his bones, had him wondering if he had a firm grip on reality anymore. It was dizzying, nauseous. There was nothing else for it. As soon as the chance presented itself, Harry was going back down underground to find her.

He looked towards the lectern on the raised stage where the Prime Minister stood. He was still waffling, but also motioning to a crowd of five or so people who were standing in line to the left of the stage. As Harry stared, he became aware that people around him were looking at one another in shock and confusion. A nervous hush had suddenly fallen across everyone.

"And I have no doubt, absolutely no doubt whatsoever, that you are going to love your new head of operations – your new boss!" blustered the Prime Minister, smiling despite the muted response from everyone gathered in the hall. "Ladies and gentlemen, it gives me a huge amount of pleasure to introduce you all to a very good friend and colleague of mine, Mr David Simeon! Come on up, David, you old rascal!"

From out of the crowd of five stepped a tall, thin man in a black suit. A pair of round, wire-framed glasses rested on his nose, above a smile that turned Harry's already churning stomach a few revolutions further.

So the stranger had a name. David Simeon. And it appeared that he now had Newman's job at the top of the MOP too. He turned his sinister face to the crowd – nodding in recognition of the slow, unenthusiastic round of applause that was struggling to rattle out – right into the eyes of Harry. When their eyes locked, it was as if Simeon's were ablaze, locking on to prey.

Harry had to get out and away from here. He felt as if he were about to faint. He began edging his way through the crowd, feeling cold and clammy and afraid. Jade was trapped, and nobody was getting her out. And something was very wrong here in the MOP. Where the hell was Newman? He elbowed his way through, apologising every other breath as he fought his way from the hall and towards the toilets.

"Well, look at that!" exclaimed the Prime Minister from the stage, where he stood clasping Simeon's hand, "Sorry, are we boring you? Guess you can't please 'em all, eh? Don't take it personally, David!"

Harry was gone.

Moments later, he was in a toilet cubicle, kneeling over the bowl with fresh vomit dripping from his mouth and tears streaming from his eyes. He stood up groggily, wiping them with the back of his sleeve before unlatching the door and peering out. He was still alone. Gingerly, he stepped out and washed his face twice with cold water, before drying himself off with paper towels. He stared at himself in the mirrored wall before him, his hands either side of the sink and his breath ragged. He took a good, long, hard look.

He felt he hardly recognised himself now. Staring back was a man-boy, someone who had left someone special down at the bottom of a lift shaft. That someone special was a person who he had grown to care for more than he was able to say out loud. He couldn't even do that. He couldn't even get this one thing right. He'd slipped from one job to another, living a safe-but-utterly-unremarkable life, doing as he was told until – *bang* – out of nowhere, Jade had come and given him something to get out of bed for in the morning.

They'd even kissed! *Kissed!* And now he'd lost her, abandoning her while snooping around the MOP, sticking their noses in where they shouldn't. It wasn't all true, he knew. He'd reported it straight away, but as with so much in life recently, nothing had made sense since. Why wasn't she being rescued? Why were people denying that the lift shaft even existed?

Shit, it seemed, had become rather real lately, and Harry felt far from being in any form of control.

So he did the only thing he could. Giving himself one last glance, he blew out a ragged blast of air from his lungs before heading back towards the corridor where he and Jade had begun their descent the day before.

19. Simeon

With most of his fellow staff held as a captive-yet-decided-ly-uninterested audience to their immediate and national leaders, Harry was able to sneak his way unhindered through the rooms in which he'd dodged with Jade the day previously, and in doing so, he was able to dodge the security teams on the main corridors. Eventually, he was back opposite the small door to the staircase.

Only there was no door. The wall was as smooth as any other in the building, painted from top to bottom in pale pink with a runner of white skirting board extending the entire length of the corridor.

He needed to look harder, he told himself. He was rushing and needed to compose himself. There had to be some sign of the tiny door – a pair of minuscule vertical cracks in the skirting, or a bump in the paintwork above.

Harry began walking along the wall, feeling with the palms of his hands as he went. He was completely certain that this was where the small door had been ajar the day before, yet there was nothing.

This was ridiculous. Stop. Think.

Harry heard a clinking noise further down the corridor to his left. It was Darryl the security guard, wandering towards him with a set of keys in his hand.

"Harry! Ey up," called Darryl as he approached, causing Harry to look about in alarm at first. "About this bloody lift of yours. Now, don't think I'm daft or anything, but I can't find it. I've even had the schematic whatsits out from the archives, but there's bugger all in there that mentions a lift shaft, not even in the plans of the most recent renovations back in the 1980s. Not a sausage, mate."

"It makes no sense, though!" Harry exclaimed. Darryl was now standing at Harry's shoulder, his hands on his hips, watching as Harry continued to feel his way up and down the wall. "There was a small door. Here. Jade and I went through it, down a flight of stairs and into a lift. It has to be here! She's trapped, Darryl!"

Darryl looked on sympathetically as Harry palmed the paintwork fruitlessly. "Look, wherever she is, I'm sure she's all right. The maintenance team tested the main lift for faults and it's fine—"

"We didn't use the main lift, Darryl!" said Harry, turning to him.

"But there is no lift here, Harry!" continued Darryl, unabashed, "Never has been, youth. Look, I get it, you were both out late last night, you had a few sherbets, did a bit of the old wacky 'baccy and – *blam* – Jade has gone home, and you're staggering round a field in the Peak District talking to a cow about nuclear physics. We've all done it."

Harry gaped at Darryl, who patted him on the shoulder. "It'll be alright on the night, kiddo. Jade'll be back in tomorrow once the headache wears off. Just you wait and see. Any road, my shift is up and my dinner is waiting. Do yourself a favour and get home too. Oh, before I shoot off, I've been meaning to tell you something."

"What?"

"Yesterday afternoon, there was someone here looking for you. Said he needed to talk to you about something important;

right pain in the arse he was. Hang on, I've got his name here somewhere," added the security guard, reaching into his pocket and producing a notebook.

Harry looked about in exasperation as Darryl flipped through it.

"Yeah, right nuisance he was. Said he had to let you know something urgently, but he wouldn't leave any details other than that. The most awful wig he had on too. Ginger, it was. Ah, he we go... "

"Alan."

"Alan – yes, that was him. Yeah, Alan. Right panicked he was, flapping about like a total turnip, but as I couldn't get hold of you in your cubicle, he just swore at me and tore off; he said he'd try to find you another way." With that, Darryl continued up the corridor and was gone.

Harry shook his head in bemusement. What on earth did Alan want with him, and why was it so important that he'd come all the way out here? He couldn't think of a single thing, but he didn't dwell on it as he turned back to the wall, which was still no closer to giving up any secrets than it had been a moment ago, and he sighed heavily. In terms of getting to Jade, there was only one other option that he could think of.

***

Thankfully, the presentation in the main reception hall was still in full swing. This gave Harry the time and freedom he needed to head back to Newman's – or Simeon's – office.

Harry reached the top of the stairs and lingered, looking back and forth along the landing to see if he had been followed or had attracted the attention of anyone. There was no one but him, and only the faint, mechanical hum of air conditioning accompanied the sound of his own heart thumping gently in his ears.

He knocked lightly on the large, wooden door and waited. No response.

Again, he took a furtive look along the corridor. Another knock. Another lack of acknowledgement.

It was time to push his luck. Slowly, in an effort to make as little sound as possible, Harry turned the door handle, which creaked in exactly the way he'd hoped it wouldn't, and opened the door enough to poke his head inside.

In the office, all was dim, thanks to the blind having been rolled down over the large window to block out the view of the outside world. The only light was a small pool of warmth created by the glow of a desk lamp.

The room was as deserted as he'd hoped – as deserted as many of the rooms he'd snuck into over the last few days. He scanned about quickly, noting that there were no other exit doors that he could see. If there was one (there had to be, surely?) then it would likely be in the small chamber that opened up to the left of the large desk.

Easing himself in through the door without opening it fully, he closed it gently behind him.

As his eyes started to adjust to the gloom, he saw that things were pretty much as they had been when he'd sat in this office, a little more green about the gills, when Newman had blustered into his life for the first time. The chairs against the wall, the endless portraits and the desk. Harry had been too preoccupied by the appearance of Simeon last time he was in here to notice a half-eaten ham baguette that was sitting in among crumbs on a china plate, next to a roughly stacked pile of documents that had recently been rifled through. One of which, he figured, was most likely the one he'd seen Simeon looking at.

Harry made his way to the desk, noticing also that the framed photo that Simeon had been looking at was still face-down. With a prickle of curiosity, Harry picked it up to see it for himself. The frame was old, wooden, hand-carved and neatly varnished. It sat heavily in his hand as he took in the picture behind the glass. It was a black-and-white photograph of three men cheerfully standing together in celebration, their champagne glasses raised in a toast. Judging by the hairstyles of two of them (the third hadn't much hair to speak of) and their attire, Harry guessed the snap had been taken in the late 1970s or early 1980s.

But that wasn't what had grabbed his attention. The big deal for Harry was that he immediately recognised all three of the smiling subjects in the frame: a younger-but-eternally-pinstriped Newman, a less-severe-but-still-thin David Simeon and... Gregory Salt, his own father, smiling at the camera. A smile he knew so well and still saw so often in his dreams. Dad.

Part of him wanted to cry. Part of him wanted to swear. Another part of him simply couldn't comprehend what he was looking at.

Newman and Simeon knew one another already. Well, okay, that wasn't beyond the realms of possibility. *But Newman knew his dad. His dad knew Newman.* Why? How? And who the hell was Simeon in all of this?

Suddenly, Harry was hit by a hot, blinding white pain in his head. At the same moment, there was a noise and a large, dark blur of movement to his left.

Reeling, and not seeing any other viable alternative, Harry dropped to his knees and crouched under the desk as quietly as he could. As soon as the searing pain had come, it had receded, but Harry was left shaken and with the strangely familiar and uncomfortable feeling that he'd just seen a large, black dog in the room with him.

From beneath the desk, there was just enough room to sit with his knees pulled up to his chest and his head bowed uncomfortably. As he hid, he heard the noise again, but realised with relief that it was the mewling of a small Alex robot, just as it came into view in the small pool of light cast onto the carpet of the office.

Harry breathed out slowly to steady himself and was just getting ready to unfold himself, origami style, from underneath the desk when the cute and furry little white sprite sniffed the air, sensing something. Finding the fragrance and locking on to it, the Alex stopped suddenly and turned its head slowly to look directly at Harry.

Something was very wrong.

Gone was the trademark tender and lovesick gaze of the nation's favourite friend of the fogey. There was no mistaking what it had been replaced with now, as the big, dark eyes narrowed and burned red with malevolent threat. In an instant, the Alex raised itself onto its legs and emitted a long and terrifying high-pitched screech.

Harry, now horribly trapped under the desk, pulled his arms in front of his face as best as he could to defend himself. In a split second, the Alex leaped at him, and then everything seemed to move in slow motion.

The motion was slow enough for Harry to notice that the creature was in possession of an indeterminate number of razor-sharp, chromium teeth, which were frighteningly bared and ready to bite. But in the micro-second that it took to register that fact, a silver blur swept violently into view and made contact with the Alex by way of a loud, metallic clang, leaving the carpeted gangway between Harry and the door momentarily clear.

With that, Harry pushed himself up and out from underneath the desk, bringing him face to face with a sweat-drenched Newman who stood there sporting a nasty cut to his domed head, sans blazer and with his sleeves rolled up, holding a golf club.

They started at each other in disbelief for a second, before Newman yelled, "SALT! OUT OF THE WAY!"

Feeling it would be prudent not to disobey, Harry leaped in the direction of the door before turning to see Newman raise the golf club above his head, in the style of an executioner, before slamming it down to the floor with a roar.

There was a crunch followed by a screech that was every bit as horrific as it was short.

Harry, breathing heavier than he'd realised, came to stand by Newman, who stood there shaking and looking at the floor with an expression of wide-eyed terror. Where his golf club had struck, there now lay a slightly mangled, smoky and twitching

Alex, with two of its legs bent the wrong way; a gash ripped in the 'stomach', which revealed a mess of wiring; and a now sad and forlorn look in its big dark eyes, which stared, no longer blinking, towards the door.

With a start, Newman dropped his club noisily and turned to look at Harry with a look of confusion. "Salt? What are you doing here?"

"I-I... " Harry spluttered, "I'm looking for your secret exit!"

"Beg pardon?" Newman creased his sweaty brow.

"The exit to the lift... Jade! I've got to get to Jade! But Simeon – *who the hell is he?* And my dad! And have you been in a fight?"

"Good gardening stuff, Salt," spluttered Newman, "don't worry about me. We're past that! Now listen to me, you tinker. You wonderful, wonderful tinker. You've got to get out. Get away from this damned place. Heaven forgive me, but I've gone about this all the wrong way! Despite everything I've seen, by trousers!"

Newman was lucid in a way Harry was sure he'd never seen him before, and he now grabbed Harry by the ears, which – despite current events – Harry thought was a bit much.

"Get away and warn everyone," he wheezed, sending salty spittle into Harry's startled face, "Get as far away from here as you can and tell everyone the truth. The MOP is doomed. Everyone is. We all are! We've been sold up the river. Lies. All of it lies, Salt!"

No longer holding Harry's head like the FA Cup, he let go with a gasp and scrabbled around on the floor to rearm himself with his faithful driver.

"But what—" started Harry, bewildered, "What do you mean? What the hell got into that Alex? Those sodding teeth!"

"Spies!" blurted Newman, brandishing his golf club over his shoulder, his eyes darting around the darkened office frantically as he did so. "Blasted spies! Watching our every move, evaluating and learning! Listening! Listening! Compiling, begad! Oh, very clever. Very ruddy clever!" With this, Newman cackled maniacally, still looking around in fear for the next foe. "They'll know this one has gone missing; it'll have registered already. There'll be another one of these little swine along to follow up and finish off the job! Get out, Salt! Get out now, for the love of all fish! Oh, look!"

Harry gawped about in fear. "What? What?"

"Ham!" declared Newman with delight, having spied the half-eaten baguette on the table. As if he'd forgotten the current situation, he dropped the golf club before snatching up the baguette and taking a huge bite from it.

"Ah, that's good ham," he sighed in relief, crumbs falling from his face, before swallowing, turning to Harry once more and doing the scarily lucid thing from before. "Now you really must get out. There's so much you need to know, Harry. In hindsight, I should have told you before now, but hindsight, as we know, is a massive swan with anger-management issues."

Harry only had four milliseconds to squint in confusion at Newman before the door to the office started to open.

"Cactus flaps!" panicked Newman. "Quickly, this way!"

Without waiting for a response from Harry, Newman bundled him into the chamber room where they both pressed up against a wall behind a grandfather clock. Desperately trying to silence their panting breaths, they listened attentively as the door was closed and floorboards creaked as someone padded over the carpet towards the desk.

"Been practising your swing again, Roy?" came the voice of Simeon from the office. "You could have at least shouted 'fore' before you took aim, and given this poor little bastard a chance to get out of the way."

Harry looked desperately up at Newman, who was sweating profusely and trying to think, the latter of which seemed to be making the former even worse.

"It's no good, Roy," continued Simeon calmly, "you should have stayed put, if you'll pardon the pun."

Newman dug Harry in the ribs, and pointed to the wall at the far end of the chamber. Next to a tall wardrobe made from a dark mahogany there it was a small, nondescript and roundish door set in the wall. Harry understood, and nodded this to Newman in return.

As Harry tiptoed over to the door, he checked behind to make sure Newman was following. He wasn't. Instead, he was walking back into the main office – distracting Simeon and covering Harry's escape as he did so.

"David, you can't expect me to just let you waltz back into the MOP and hand you the keys, you lugubrious baboon," said a weary Newman from behind Harry, as he quietly opened the door and ducked through, pulling it gently shut behind him.

He was back on the metal staircase down which he and Jade had scampered the day before, only this time he found himself alone and at the top. He felt terrible leaving Newman at the mercy of Simeon while something drastically wrong was clearly unfolding. Newman had obviously taken a beating, there was the rogue Alex, and handing Simeon the keys to the MOP? He pressed his ear to the door, listening.

"... governmental appointment, Roy. You can't seriously have been thinking that this was all for the benefit of the old and vulnerable in society, surely? Besides, a third of all this is mine, Roy. Mine. You've had your chance, and you failed."

Newman spluttered something in return, but Harry couldn't make it out. He'd given Harry a chance to escape, and he had to take it. Now. He took hold of the winding stair rail and began to make his way down. He'd get to the bottom and work things out from there. If the lift cable was still in place then he might be able to climb down it to the bottom of the shaft. He couldn't think of any other way to get down there. It would have to work, otherwise...

Well, it didn't bear thinking about.

But he was on his way.

Having said that, five steps later, he was on his way back.

"Stop where you are!"

The voice came from just below him, and as he stared, startled, down through the metal steps underneath him, he saw it had come from one of two black-suited security guards who were looking at him and heading upwards.

"We've located the staircase, sir. And there's someone here. Intercepting."

***

Having been duly intercepted by two tall, clean-cut, blond and virtually identical men in matching black suits, Harry found himself in a studded, green, leather armchair back in Newman's office, sitting next to the man himself. Both of them were facing Simeon, who sat behind the large desk, his elbows on the surface, and his fingers interlocked and resting on his chin.

He stared at them. They stared back. The two identical black suits stood either side of Simeon against the wall, looking dead ahead.

Finally, Simeon broke the silence. "I'll come to you in a minute," he said, looking disinterestedly at Harry before turning to Newman, "however, you, Roy, I shall address now."

"You'll never take me alive!" said Newman with gusto.

Simeon continued to stare back. "We've already got you, Roy. It would probably be in your best interests that you keep quiet for now and listen."

"You'll never take me—"

"Stop it," said Simeon dully, cutting in. "Your time as chief operating officer of the MOP is over. You have defied Her Majesty's government on various occasions over the last four years, continually blocking access to vital inspections of projects that you were tasked with, which, may I add, have cost considerable sums of treasury funds. This is a situation that cannot continue, and so – in light of the forthcoming Change and carrying out the wishes of the people – the Prime Minister has put me in charge."

"Wishes of the people! Pah!" spat Newman defiantly. Har-

ry noticed that the cut on his head had started to ooze slightly again as Newman's all-encompassing forehead furrowed in
disgust. "That's dishwater, and you know it, David. Dishwater
filled with bits of carrot, pea and ephemera. The truth about
what they were all voting for was never made clear, was it? It was
hidden far from view while your minions whipped everyone up
into a blind frenzy against one another. Admit it!"

Simeon smiled his thin smile back at Roy, steepling his fingers once again as he did so. He seemed to be enjoying watching
Newman losing his rag, while Harry could only feel that this
wasn't going to end well for his former boss (recently deposed).
"Not for the first time, I have no idea what you're talking about,
Roy. You know what? I think time away from this place will actually do you the world of good. You're so far from the Roy New-
ton – sorry – Newman I once knew."

"That's good coming from you, you reptilian monk!" Newman laughed. "You of all people! We trusted you, David. Trusted
you to only ever use our combined science for good! For the
good of the people! Not for profit, not for ill will, but for good!
You worked so hard with us to unlock all those discoveries back
then. Don't you remember? We all worked so hard together, and
we swore never to bow to outside pressure or influence."

Harry thought he saw a momentary change in Simeon's cool
exterior. His smile was fading.

Newman continued, "You swore, David. You knew that things
would only ever have got out of hand to the detriment of us all,
and yet, here we are, you bespectacled wart. For the love of all
cakes, your greed has done this. You should have listened to me!
We made a pact – you, Gregory and I!"

"Yeah, about that," said Harry, raising his hand and seizing
the moment. "Why is there a picture of you both with my dad
on your desk?"

The silence that followed this question was a heavy one. All
attention was instantly focussed upon him, changing the mood
in the room completely. Even the two guards had softened their

rigidity a little to both incline their heads simultaneously and stare at him where he sat, in the leather armchair.

"Revolving breasts," said Newman fearfully and slowly under his breath, "dear, sweet, pendulous-yet-revolving breasts." He was staring wide-eyed at Harry, a look of terror completing his terrible countenance.

Simeon was looking at Harry as if he were a rare, long-lost Egyptian treasure, uncovered and shining in the sunlight for the first time in over 2,000 years.

"You're... you're Harry Salt?" he said in a whisper, faltering over each syllable of his name. "Good God. So it's true. You... are. You're Harry Salt. Of course, I can see it now. Christ, you look just like him." Simeon was salivating, rising slowly from his chair, but all the while staring at Harry in wide-eyed wonder.

"What? Yes... I'm Harry Salt... " he confirmed, unsure if it was a wise move to do so.

Newman grasped Harry's hand in both of his own. They were sweaty and clammy. He looked him dead centre in his eyes, his fear growing visibly by the second as Simeon came to them both slowly from behind his desk.

"Harry, I'm so, so sorry. I've let you down. I've let both you and your dad down. And the rest. Please forgive me! Believe me, I tried absolutely everything to keep you safe and hidden."

"You have no idea *what* you are, do you?" enquired Simeon, still in a state of awe, but with a hungry look in his eyes that Harry disliked immensely. "You never told him, did you, Roy?"

Newman simply looked to the floor, his head and shoulders drooped.

"How did you do it, Roy? How did you keep this... " He indicated towards Harry with an outstretched palm. "A secret from us? There's been no trace, and yet it's true. It lives."

"What do you mean, 'it'?" demanded Harry, "What the hell are you talking about? Look, I don't know who you are, but you need to get the lift up from the bottom of the shaft. One of your employees is trapped down there!"

Simeon started to laugh, a slow and nasty chuckle that grew in intensity. "Well, I'm afraid that would be quite pointless," he stated suddenly. "No one has ever survived a descent past the tunnel network. Not one human or animal. Believe me, we've tried. We've even sent down five Alex prototypes. Did you know that, Roy? They all came back completely inert and with their circuitry melted. So, I'm afraid your Jade Birch is now simply one less burden on the payroll."

"NO!" shouted Harry, shooting up from his chair as he did so, causing the smirking Simeon to lean back.

The two suits moved in tandem from their position, but Simeon waved them back.

"You get her out of there! Get that lift back up!" Harry ordered.

"Oh, we will in due course. Her death will likely be attributed to a workplace accident, we'll get public relations on to it. We'll ensure a generous wreath gets sent to the funeral. I might go along too, if I'm free."

"*You fucker!*" Harry raged, tears prickling at his eyes, at which point the suits lurched past Simeon, gripped Harry's shoulders and forced him back into the chair. Harry writhed and struggled beneath them, but their conjoined grip was vice-like and their fingers dug in painfully. "No! No! You bastards, you can't just leave her there!"

"Oh, I'm very much afraid we can. Besides, it's not us that killed her. We're not the ones who lie in wait down there. Anyway," said Simeon, retaking his seat behind the heavy desk and picking up the wooden photograph frame to look at it, "I never did answer your question. Shall we fill him in, Roy?"

Newman let out a wail, a sound that Harry found horrible to endure.

"No, David," Newman pleaded, "he doesn't need this. Let the boy be. You don't need him. You have this all wrong, David. All wrong!"

"Wait. No!" interrupted Harry, angry and frustrated. "What?

What don't I need? I don't understand any of this you're... " He pointed accusingly at Simeon for as long as half a second before one of the suits behind him shoved his arm back down by his side. "You've just told me Jade is somehow dead, and as far as I can see, everything here – in this room and beyond – is just batshit crazy. So, you just fill me in, you fucker. Go on."

"You've got your father's temper, I see," mused Simeon before continuing. "Really impressive. Okay then. I want you to think back, Harry. Back to your childhood. Think back to the day you were both driving back from Wales. The day everything changed for you, and your father was killed in that car crash. Go on, Harry. Think about it. You were there. Put yourself back in that car with him."

Harry stared at Simeon in disbelief. "Why should I do that?"

"Stop it, David. You don't need to do this to the boy. Aargh!" Newman's protests were halted quickly by a swift backhanded strike to the face from one of the suits. He winced in pain but held his silence.

"Just take your time, Harry. See how much you can recall. That's right. I should imagine you can pull out quite a lot of detail if you try hard enough."

Harry was staring off into the distance, the scowl on his face fading a little as painful memories resurfaced in his mind. All of a sudden, there was a blur of movement in the chamber to his left again. A black shadow was lurking, but making its way slowly towards where he sat. Harry began to feel cold and clammy, with a sweat that prickled from his skin breaking out all over.

"What's wrong, Harry?" asked Simeon, his eyes narrowing. "Go on, focus on that fateful day. What can you remember? What can you see?"

To his side, Newman grunted in anguish, but Harry wasn't aware of it. Instead, he was now focussed on the fact that two more dark shadows were looming either side of where Simeon sat, rising from behind the desk, red-eyed, and coalescing into the solid forms of two giant, slavering, black dogs. They mirrored the one that now panted and watched them all from the chamber where the grandfather clock still ticked solemnly.

"What's the matter, Harry? Has the cat – sorry, has the *dog* – got your tongue?" queried Simeon.

Harry felt like he was struggling to breathe, and he could feel an acute headache coming on, making it difficult to focus – to see, even. And yet the dogs remained clear as crystal – the slickness of their jet-black fur, and the ham-like pinkness of their tongues that shook as they panted hungrily – with the three of them now circling him where he sat, staring up at him with malevolent, glowing, red eyes.

"Stop it, David! You'll kill him!" commanded Newman.

"Oh, you think so, Roy? Kill him? Or will he just... stop?" Simeon suggested.

Harry was blinking and panting, his eyes glassy and glazed, lost now, and aware only of the dogs and his memories. "Red kite... it's a red kite... huge bird... watching above... "

"That's it, Harry. Tell me what you see," encouraged Simeon with unbridled glee.

One of the dogs stopped at Harry's feet, never once tearing its eyes from his. Panting. Watching.

"Dad... he's driving... we're going home. Mum... he wants to tell me something about Mum... but... she's dead. She's dead," explained Harry.

As the tears started to well and then fall from Harry's eyes, the dog at his feet slowly raised its enormous paws to his knees. Harry edged back in his seat in terror, but the dog simply kept on coming, bringing his ruby eyes and dripping maw slowly to within inches of Harry's face. It pushed down on his chest, with the heat and weight of the giant beast gradually crushing him where he sat, its rancid breath flooding into Harry's lungs as he fought to breathe.

"Yes, Harry!" exclaimed Simeon from somewhere beyond where he was now, his voice distorted, "Yes! Tell me what you see from that day, Harry."

"Red kite," mumbled Harry, struggling to force his words out and only managing a faint whisper as the dog crushed into him, "Red kite... the car... the sky... "

"Take me there, Harry! Take me back to the day you and your father died!"

Harry almost fell out of his seat, as suddenly all the pressure upon him disappeared. Gasping for air, he looked about him. The terrible dogs were gone, and nowhere to be seen. It was impossible. The biggest of the three had been right in his face. He could still sense the smell of its vile breath.

Getting his own breath back, he reattuned himself to his surroundings. The dimness of the office. Simeon, fixated on Harry. He sensed Newman before he turned to look at him. His former boss returned his stare with a horrified expression.

"So it's true... " stated Simeon slowly. "It was you all along. You're the one that kept going. The one with the mystery ingredient. The one that worked."

"What... what the hell just happened? And what do you mean?" questioned Harry.

"You've beaten the flaws in the protocol. I don't know how, but you've done it."

"What do you mean about the day me and my dad died? Clearly," Harry tapped his own chest, "clearly, I didn't die! My dad was killed, yes. But I'm here. Sitting here. Right now. Not dead. Very clearly alive. Utterly in the dark as to what the hell is going on, but alive. I haven't beaten any system."

"You're the key." Simeon had stood up again and was slowly walking to where he and Newman sat, staring at Harry in awe. "That's to say, the key is very much inside you, somewhere." He thought for a second, before looking to the suits stood behind the two armchairs. "Take them down to a holding room. I need to make some calls before we decide on our next move. Hurry."

Despite initial protests from both Harry and Newman, the suits were simply too strong and weren't about to take anything negative for an answer. They were hauled from their seats and marched unceremoniously from the office as Simeon returned to his leather chair and picked up the phone.

Rama

At university, I felt that things were coming back together. I was surrounded by people whom I felt connected to, I had a great social life, and I was learning.

I worked in the university cafe to get a bit of cash in to support my council grant, and my grandparents had generously given me an allowance to help with buying books, food and other essentials.

I was happy. I enjoyed living in the halls of residence during my first year, then moving into a house with some of the friends I'd made for years two and three. When I look back now, it feels as if it all went past in a rush, but while I was there, it felt like it would never end, this new and exciting life I was living.

I made so many memories there. So many friends. But I didn't connect with anyone as much as I connected with Jon Taylor. Jon was still reeling from the death of his mother when he arrived in our halls of residence to start his course. He arrived a couple of weeks after the rest of us, who had survived freshers' week and done all the registration together. We'd all started our courses and learned the ins and outs of the uni bar and nightclub.

I felt sorry for Jon when he arrived with his dad, with a couple of suitcases, a rucksack, and a box packed full of pots and pans, rice and pasta. I was ironing a shirt in the hall corridor when they both arrived on an overcast Sunday morning. Loud music was blaring from a couple of rooms along the landing. "Welcome to the mad house," I'd said in greeting, and once Jon and his dad had started to unpack, I stuck my head in to his room to see if I could offer any help.

After he and his dad had shared a tearful farewell (I never told him that I'd noticed him hastily wiping away the tears as I'd popped back in with a couple of cans of lager), we sat down and introduced ourselves properly to one another.

It was to be the start of a lifelong friendship. Jon wanted to know all about my life, and so I filled him in. Another can of beer each came and went as we spent a few hours in excited conversation. Jon was to study communications, and he was hugely sympathetic when I told him about my mum and dad, and how I'd lost them both.

This time, the tears had come again for him as he recounted the loss of his own mother to cancer just months before. We had embraced as he'd sobbed, but he sniffed it up quickly and thanked me for listening. Jon had a thick Welsh accent, and I was intrigued to know whereabouts he hailed from, so I changed the subject quickly, and we talked about that instead. Eventually, I could see Jon was getting tired, and I offered to leave him alone to relax in his new room. But we had rapidly bonded over those two beers, and it was a friendship that was to endure.

It was a few months later when Jon had joined me in my room and we'd shared a Chinese takeaway and talked through our love of science fiction. It was a particularly cold night, and our dorms were taking something of a battering in the wind, standing as they were on the side of the steep hill on which the university had been built. Jon gave me some books to read by Arthur C. Clarke, something about humans encountering a giant alien tube in space, big enough to house forests, cities and oceans and all kinds of life forms, while no one had any idea of where it came from or where it was going. I swapped him Tales of the Knights of the Round Table, as he'd never read any fantasy books and was keen to try.

Once we'd devoured our food and cleared away the greasy foil *trays and plastic forks into the kitchen bin, we cracked open an-other couple of cans and settled down to chat further. We never seemed to run out of things to talk about. Jon picked up a photo album that was sitting next to a pile of lecture folders. We had a look through it together; he wanted to see my friends from home, my old school and my family. It was fun telling him all about this first part of my life, even the darker bits. It felt good to share them.*

"Bugger me, that's Llyn Cau!" he said as he flipped over one photo. Sure enough, it was a photo my dad had taken of me when I was younger and we had climbed Cadair Idris together. "Been up Idris, have you? That's a decent climb, mind."

"Yeah, we camped up there one night," I explained, and I felt a sense of unease as I thought back to that strange trip, just before the car crash that had turned everything upside down. I hadn't revisited that night for so, so long.

"You camped?" Jon burst into laughter. "Who the hell camps up there? You bloody nutters! No disrespect to your old man, like."

"Why?" I asked, part amused and a little defensive. "What's so weird about that?"

"Oh, man! Really? Bloody hell, you English haven't a clue, have you?"

"Seriously, what?"

"You've never heard the stories about Cadair Idris?"

"Something to do with a giant, right?"

"Well, alright, partly. But you've never heard the legends about sleeping the night up there? I tell you now, it's not especially good for you. I'm surprised you're sitting here alive, to be honest with you."

I shook my head bemusedly, waiting for a dollop of Welsh leg-end.

"Alright then. The old story goes that if you sleep on the slopes of Cadair Idris, you get a dose of magic. One of three things can happen: either you wake up a poet, you wake up a madman or – worst of all – you don't wake up again. Ever. I'm not putting money on you being a poet, and you're sat here with me, so... " He

broke out into his raucous Welsh laugh.

I laughed along too, but I felt cold. It was all coming back.

Jon didn't stay in my little room for long after that. That night, I felt I wanted to sleep with the light on. I couldn't get the images of that forgotten trip up the mountain out of my head. From far beyond, as the wind moaned across the hillside, I was certain I could hear the howls of dogs, baying at the moon. I pulled the duvet over my head, my eyes scrunched tightly together. At some point, I must have fallen asleep.

20. Guards

Harry and Newman were sitting next to one another in chairs that were far less comfortable than the armchairs in Simeon's office, although the discomfort was exacerbated by the orange cable ties that now attached their wrists and feet to the furniture. The suits had been very swift and clinical in their efforts to make their captives as motionless as possible, before one had stood guard outside the holding room, with the other standing beside the closed door, watching over them both. Aside from his initial encounter with them both on the metal staircase, Harry had not heard a single word from either of them, and he'd also noticed that they didn't just look similar, they were *exactly* alike. Identical twins in every respect, including dress sense and levels of unprompted viciousness.

Newman was the first to speak, wincing as he did so. "Not exactly your average Thursday this, is it?"

Up close, it was now obvious that Newman was weary and in more pain that Harry had first suspected. A nasty bruise was forming around the cut on his forehead, and as he caught sight of the menacing suit in his own peripheral vision, Harry had a fair idea where it might have come from. "Mr Newman, are you alright?"

Newman looked to Harry, winced harder, and then gave what

was his best attempt at a smile. "Ah, Salt, begad. I could've sworn I told you to make a run for it."

"Well, yes, but I wasn't expecting him and his mate to come up the stairs I was attempting to run down."

Newman gave his best wince so far, shaking his head as he did so. "No, Harry, I didn't expect them either. I'm sorry. We find ourselves in the middle of a really awful mess, like solemn cabbages caught in a wild, effluent stream."

Harry was weary too. He ached physically and mentally, and was feeling a strange mix of fear, confusion, anger and resignation. "So then, Mr Newman."

"You can call me Roy, if that helps."

"Not really."

"Righto."

"How about you tell me just what the dickens is going on, please? You said something about wishing you'd told me before now?"

"Erm. That's true, I did. Yes."

"Well, better late than never."

"There are a few elements to this, however, young Salt. There's, well, quite a lot you don't know and," continued Newman, "as your overall manager with something of a care of duty to uphold, I'm a little worried about the impact this might have on you and your, um, mental health, so to speak."

Harry stared dead ahead at the expressionless, motionless guard by the door. "Well, it appears we have a bit of time on our hands. As for my mental health, well, I've had quite an interesting few days as it is, and as for you being my manager, well, you're not are you? Not any more."

Newman looked to the floor and chuntered a little.

"I'm sorry?"

"You're right, Salt. You're right. I may not be your boss right now, but I'll be damned if that overprivileged fruit fly in glasses is going to take my place. You deserve to know."

"Why did he – Simeon, that is – why did he seem so convinced that I'd been killed in the car crash with my dad when I was sitting there right in front of him? And why was he so keen for me to relive it all?"

Newman sighed, thought about speaking twice and stopped himself on each occasion. On his third effort, he pushed through. "Harry, that car crash you – he – mentioned. He was right. You... you died that day."

"Bollocks."

"Testicles?"

"STOP IT."

"Stop what?"

"Talking such bloody nonsense. For once. For God's sake. Please." Harry was desperate.

Newman stared back at him, unsure. "So... not testicles then?"

"What the hell were you both talking about? How could I have died? I remember everything after the crash, recovering in the hospital, moving in and living with Grandma and Grandpa, and—" He stopped mid-sentence, with an all-too-familiar dark blur dashing suddenly through his vision to his left. He took a deep breath. There was no dog, he told himself. *There was no dog.*

"Besides," he continued through gritted teeth, "I'm here. Breathing. Alive. I can see you. Hear you. Feel myself tied to this stupid chair!"

"Of course you do, Harry. You're here; you're just alive as I am, as anyone else is. It's just that... well, when you were twelve years old and you lost your dad, you died."

"You mean like, my heart stopped for a while? Like those people who die on the operating table but are shocked back to life with electric pads or whatever? I mean, okay, I can get with that, it's just—"

"No, Harry. Not like that. I'm afraid you were well beyond that by the time our ambulances arrived."

"Well, then, what the—"

"Harry." This time it was Newman who interrupted to call

Harry to silence. "You died. You were dead. Your life was over. But you were *cloned*!" At this, Newman attempted to raise something of a determined smile. "Cloned, Harry! Recreated just as you were, and allowed to continue living your life from that point onwards."

Harry began to laugh, but he stopped the moment he turned to look at Newman again. He meant it.

"Mr Newman," said Harry with sympathy masking something deeper, "you're wrong. I'm sorry, but you're wrong. It's not possible. I have a lifetime of memories that bring me right to this spot. Besides, the kind of technology you're talking about doesn't exist. It couldn't."

"Harry, what have you been doing here for the last few months? What have you been testing out and reporting on?"

"Robots! Robots for old people and teachers! Crossing ladies! People who were looking for new jobs! Are you trying to tell me that the people were robots too? These clones you're talking about?" Harry laughed bitterly and would probably have thrown his hands ceilingwards were they not tied down. "Don't be so ridiculous," he continued, "they were people! Simply that! Okay, they were a little stranger than the average. There was that teacher and the whole anus thing, and then he just... well, just... stopped... but he was Scottish! Whoever heard of a Scottish robot, for God's sake! And that traffic-crossing lady who thought there was an animal in the room? She was just nuts! Clones? Robots? They were nothing like me! Nothing!" Harry spat out another laugh. "Robots are like computers, preprogrammed; they follow routines based on what they see and hear. They don't *feel*, for God's sake! They don't have memories; they've been given them. Programs, algorithms or whatever. I mean, mine...my memories, they're real. Right? They're real, aren't they?"

For once, Newman stayed silent.

"This is ridiculous. Let's talk about something else please, Mr Newman."

Although he had turned his attention back to the seemingly

inert guard standing by the door, Harry was all too aware that Newman continued to stare at him from his matching confinement.

"Have you ever seen the black dog, Harry?"

Harry felt a tightness in his chest, a coldness in his stomach. "What? What do you mean?"

"A great big, black dog; terrifyingly big," continued Newman, gravely. "Have you seen it? At various points in your life since childhood, sometimes clear as day, other times less so, to the point at which you were never even really sure if it was there in the first instance?"

"I... I—"

"You saw one in my office with Simeon just now, didn't you?"

"How did you know? How *do* you know about the black dog?" Harry's mouth had gone dry.

"The Black Dog Protocol, Harry. It's a computer program. An algorithm. I should know; I helped design the damned thing." Newman took in a deep, ragged breath. "Designed to keep the clones – the People we engineered – from accessing thoughts and memories that would occasionally surface from their former lives. The Black Dog Protocol automatically acts to frighten the Person away from remembering, so that they can carry on, unaware that they'd existed before. Unaware of how they came to be. Only remembering the past we'd designed for them, not that of their actual former selves. It works mostly, although in a lot of cases recently, it's malfunctioned. People have been able to get around it, accessing small parts of their former lives, which has just been too much for them to cope with, sort of like an overload or a short circuit, if you will."

"Their former lives? What the hell are you on about? Robots don't have... I don't get you... " Harry was staring at the floor, and he noticed that, as he shook his head, fat beads of sweat were splashing to the floor.

"This is all so, so complex, Harry. I'm sorry. They're not robots, they're People. Yes, they have one or two hugely advanced electrical components in there, but they're almost entirely organic. Organs grown on demand, a few tweaks here and there, but only electronic where they need to be. That was the original idea anyhow, but now it's all something else, Harry. Far, far from what you are. Far, far from all our original ideas and hopes. We knew the dangers, but we swore together, the three of us; by gad, we swore, Harry."

"Far from what *I am?* What am I, Mr Newman? Just tell me that. Forget all that stuff about organs and components for now. What am I? Me? Harry Salt? What the hell are you saying?"

"That you're a marvel! You're everything your dad hoped you would grow up to be! You're a bright, capable young man living a life. You got a second chance. His research and his life's work saved you."

Newman, as much as a recently beaten arthritic man who was secretly prone to loose stools and had been roughly tied to a chair could do, was staring at Harry with genuine hope in his eyes.

Harry took a good, long look at them. A good, long look. He studied the sincerity there, and blinked. "You're mad," was his conclusion; one that wasn't considered to be especially ground-breaking within a five-mile radius of where they currently sat.

Newman let out a crestfallen sigh. "Well, yes. That's partly true. I have your dad to thank for that too."

"Absolutely mad," continued Harry, oblivious. "I've lived my entire life up to this point. Me. I've lived it. Not anyone else. I go to the toilet. I throw up if I get ill. I fart if I eat too much rich food. I can't fly, I can't leap tall buildings in a single bound and I sure as hell bleed when things cut me. Why the hell would anyone design... " He struggled to indicate his body using only his head, and gave himself a number of extra chins for effect instead. "This? Why would anyone design me as an example of cutting-edge British technology? It's like nobody tried hard enough."

"Cutting edge was never the point! That was never what it was about!" spat Newman angrily. "We were looking to give parents of lost children a second chance with their loved ones. It was as simple as that. It was an innocent premise, but things, well, things span out of control. But when you died, an opportunity presented itself, you see."

Somewhere inside Harry – whether it was in his head, his heart, his stomach or all three at once, he couldn't tell – something shifted. As he looked to the floor again, a huge, black dog was forming, rising up to the height of his lap, then his chest. Panting; staring. The red eyes sending an all-too-familiar fear coursing through him once again.

"How are you doing this?" questioned Harry breathily, recoiling as much as his confines would allow him to.

"Ah, the black dog again, see?" said Newman. "Right on cue, yes? You're starting to consider it – the fact that you might not be quite who you thought you were. And as soon as you do, the protocol starts to kick in. You're not supposed to think about it, so the dog tries to stop you. Distract you. Only you – yes, you Harry – you're able to circumvent the program somehow. You're the *only one*. Every other Person: bang, fizz, nothing. They stop every time the dog first appears, go completely inert, and have to be brought back for repairs and analysis. *But not you.* That's why they – Simeon and the others – are so interested in you."

The dog watched Harry, almost at eye-level now.

"It's still here. It's... it's looking at me. It's huge," moaned Harry, fear punctuating his every word.

"Don't be afraid of it, Harry. The best thing is to accept it. Accept that it's there. Even though, well, er, it's not."

Harry took a long, deep breath in an attempt to calm himself. As he did so, the dog cocked its head to one side, raised itself to put its paws on Harry's lap and then proceeded to playfully lick his face with its hot, slavering tongue.

Harry scrunched his face up as it did so, closing his eyes tightly and feeling warm, wet spittle on his cheeks. "Gah! Get it off me! *Get off!*"

As soon as he opened his eyes, the huge dog was gone again. Newman was looking at him with an almost amused look on his face, while Harry spluttered, "It was real. I could feel it. I could feel it! Claws on my legs and drool all over my face. I need to wipe my damn face. It's still there on my face; I can feel it! Urrgh! Gaaah!"

"Harry, I'd give you my handkerchief and wipe your poor, terrified face down if I could. But if it's any consolation, your face remains just as clean and slightly tired-looking as it was before. There is a distinct lack of dog residue. That dog is not going to hurt you. It can't. There is no dog, but *you* are still here."

The coldness was still in Harry's stomach too, however. He was momentarily elsewhere, recycling the words Newman had used earlier in his head: *You died. Cloned. Former lives. Have you ever seen the black dog? His research saved you!*

"The actual me," said Harry slowly, almost to himself as he thought through what Newman had been telling him and what the dog had been showing him, "the *real* me, died years ago, and I'm some kind of... *replacement*." He felt every syllable of the last word as he said it – a word that disgusted and repulsed him.

Newman continued to look at him, and Harry saw it. Behind his eyes. There it was: a shift, a breaking down of a wall that had stood firm for a long, long time.

"And you knew? All the time? Before Simeon got involved?" demanded Harry.

"I'm sorry Harry, but yes. And... I... I knew. I always knew," Newman capitulated.

Harry found himself nodding. Smiling even. A bitter chuckle burst upwards from his chest and out into the room. "All those memories," Harry shook his head as he spoke, suddenly remembering and seeing in his mind's eye a millisecond snapshot of an afternoon in the sunshine with his dad, on a beach somewhere: the heat, the sounds of seagulls, waves on the shore and children playing. A black blur. "All these memories. I can *feel* them, almost touch the damn things. But they're not mine?"

"Harry, I—"

"They're not mine!"

Harry shot his gaze back to the floor. "They belong to someone else. Someone dead. Because I'm not me. *I'm some freak creation grown in a goddamn laboratory!* Admit it!"

"Of course you're *you*, Harry," pleaded Newman. "Who else could you be? Those memories... " Newman sighed before continuing, "Those *are* yours, Harry. All those things you remember. *You* did them, and they make you who you are today; it's just... "

"I'm not me. I'm some pretend, false version of who I was. Created in a chuffing laboratory. The real me is dead!"

"Harry—"

"DEAD! DEAD!"

Silence fell between them. The suited guard stared on expressionlessly, having never flinched once throughout the whole revelation.

Harry felt tears prickling at the corners of his eyes. "Why the hell didn't you tell me before now? Who else knows?"

"Just me, Harry. Until now. I promise you that. That was the idea. Harry, you are a very complicated, and may I say, quite wonderful reproduction of the original Harry Salt who died in 1999, aged twelve."

"In 1999? Twelve years old...?"

"Yes... "

"Jesus Christ... So, since then, I've been this... this thing?"

"A beautiful thing, though, Harry... "

Harry scowled. "Don't." He paused, swallowing and remembering how desperate he was for a glass of water. "So that's it then. Nothing of me, none of what I am, is real. All the things I've done since I was twelve and all of the things before. Who—"

"Now, that's not strictly true," chided Newman, adopting the tone of a geography teacher.

"What?"

"You said that no part of you was real. That's not entirely true, you see. For the cloning process to work, we had to at least use a healthy part of your... your former self's, erm, remains."

Harry looked horrified. "What, so part of me is... the original me...?"

"Yes, although—"

"Which bit?"

"I'm not sure I should—"

"WHICH BIT?"

"Your... oh Lord. It's your anal sphincter."

"I'm sorry, what?"

"Trust me, it made sense at the time."

"Oh great. Well, that's just wonderful. Hey, your thoughts were designed on a laptop, but relax, at least your bowel movements are the real deal!"

"Now, now—"

"Good God!"

"It's to do with muscle memory, and—"

At that, there was a loud thump on the door. The guard moved to open it and let in his identical and – Harry now surmised – manufactured twin. He pushed a wheelchair in front of him, and once he was inside the room, he smiled a wide grin at Harry that was nothing short of demonic.

Holding the grin but letting go of the wheelchair, he then produced a long syringe from inside his blazer, held it up to the light and tapped it to knock any air bubbles to the top.

"Leave him alone, you repugnant whelp!" cried Newman.

But it was no use. The guard, grinning manically, advanced on where Harry was restrained.

Harry struggled uselessly against his bonds as the guard drew close. He could feel blood from where his wrists had rubbed against the plastic cable ties, hot and running into his clenched hands.

"THINK BACK!" yelled Newman at the guard turned anaesthetist. "Yes, you, you horrendous unit! Remember... remember your first bicycle! The one your father taught you how to ride! Yes? Remember the sound that the bell made, and how you felt when you rode on two wheels for the first time!"

At this, the guard paused while looming over Harry with the needle still primed in his hands. He frowned at Newman and then took a sharp breath. Harry looked on in shock, realising that, at that moment when he looked to the floor, the guard was staring in terror at a black dog that only he could see, which was looming up towards him from out of the ground.

"How you loved that bike! That wonderful bicycle of yours!" continued Newman, his eyes wide.

The guard edged back towards the door, fear now occupying his previously blank features.

And then he stopped. Still staring out in front of him and still with the loaded syringe in his hand, but with a sad smile frozen on his lips. Completely inert and dead to the world.

"Ha! You see? The Black Dog Protocol!" exclaimed Newman, turning his head towards Harry.

Harry, however, was too busy looking wide-eyed at the immobile guard. "So, it's true then...?" was all he could say.

Everything else then happened in a flash. The other guard, the one who had been standing by the door, snatched the syringe from where his decommissioned brother stood and plunged it into Harry's left shoulder, piercing his shirt along the way.

"*Aargh!*" he yelped, but there was nothing he or Newman could do.

As he watched the clear liquid within disappearing as the plunger sent it into his veins, Harry had just enough time to mutter that all he'd wanted to do really was to get Jade back and make sure she was okay, before darkness enveloped him and everything he was aware of disappeared.

***

There was no way out.

Not now. Not ever.

All I could do was float. Float and accept.

This is how it was, and this is how it was going to be.

Newman had decided.

But Newman was somewhere else, somewhere beyond the cylinders.

The cylinders were where I belonged, because the cylinders were where I'd come from.

This was cunty.

Urgh. It felt horrible to use a word like that.

Cunty.

It was hard to say it.

Anything was hard to say when you had a breathing mask on.

Besides, it was Jade's word.

Jade. Jade, Jade, Jade, Jade.

I let her down. I let her down so badly.

Like a pin.

Pin. Something to do with a pin.

The naughty schoolboy and the inflatable headmaster.

The inflatable naughty schoolboy with a pin at the inflatable school.

You've let me down, you've let yourself down and you've let the whole school down.

That was my dad's favourite joke.

When he was alive. It was his favourite joke.

But he's dead now and so was I.

This was Dad's joke now. This was all a sick joke.

This is not anus.

Was the answer in the box? In the loft?

Dad never let me in the loft.

The dog never let me look in the box.

The dog pushed me away, but now I could push the dog back.

This is not anus.

Stuck underground. Floating underground.

But not alone. There's someone else down here.
There are others down here.
So many others. Some for the surface.
Ready. Oven-ready and ready to go.
Ready to go and Change everything.
But further below.
More. Underneath. Far below.
So many things to understand. So many things to learn.
A lifetime of things.
So many things.
Just one more thing.
There are so many other cylinders here.
Miles and miles of cylinders, all underground.
Giant, glass eggs, hatching.
Hatching one by one.
The yellow water runs away. Splashes against the tyres.
Shoppa Boppa buses. There are Shoppa Boppa buses.
Clean now. Polished. Waiting.
Chugging and waiting for all the clones to board.
Nurses in blue.
Teachers in immaculately ironed, lemon-yellow shirts.
Crossing wardens in neon yellow.
Milkmen in white.
Soldiers in olive green.
TV presenters in sparkly jackets.
Talent-show judges in tight jeans.
Alice in brown.
Alices in brown.
All marching, filing, one by one.
Oven-ready.
The Shoppa Boppa buses, all full now.
Rising, rising, slowly floating to the surface.
Who's that tapping at the glass?
It's Jade. Jade and Newman and Alan.
Outside, looking in.

They're not in a cylinder. Not like me.
I'm the only one left.
I'm the one.
Pickled in a jar.
Pickles in a jar.
Piccalilli. Piccalilli sandwich.
They're not like me.
But they are like me. Only not like me.
Ridiculous.
Their lips don't move. They watch me solemnly.
Their lips don't move, but I hear their voices in my head.
"This is all in your head," say their voices in my head.
All I had wanted was to get Jade back.
All I had wanted was for Jade to be okay and be happy.
All I wanted was to be happy.
Jade is gone now. Newman and Alan too.
My dad is far away from here. Gone.
I'm the only one left.
Deep underground. Under the world.
Lights out!
The lights. Go. Out.
Only me down here now.
Only not me. Not anymore.
Only me.
The dog barks.
Change it! Change it now!
Change!
Changed!
You changed!
You changed me!
Change!

21. Fuzzy

There were things that almost made sense. There were things that really didn't.

The Change was coming. No, no, The Change was *here*. Finally. This was it. People were lining the streets behind temporary barriers, but whether in celebration or commiseration it was difficult to say. It had been raining, and the roads were wet, reflecting brightly in the morning light. There were banners and placards along Whitehall and up towards the Houses of Parliament. "*You're dead!*" read one. "*We choose your memories!*" read another. "*Who are you? Don't ever Change!*"

A procession was marching up past the Cenotaph as the crowds continued to cheer and wave enthusiastically. At the front of the procession marched a solemn-faced twelve-year-old boy, carrying a fresh ham baguette on a pinstriped, blue, velvet cushion.

Abruptly, the masses fell silent. From the direction of Big Ben, behind which a bright, white sun dazzled, the outline of a boy on a bicycle came into view, pedalling slowly up Whitehall to meet the procession. As he came closer, the procession stopped. London – England, even – was silent, transfixed upon the young cyclist. As he reached the awaiting procession, he stopped and put his feet to the ground, standing with his twelve-year-old hands resting on the handlebars.

He was identical in every respect to the boy with the baguette, and their eyes locked. He stepped over his saddle and carefully laid his bike down in the road, before walking the final few yards to his doppelgänger. As he did so, he noticed that everyone in the crowd had frozen still with confused, introspective looks on their faces. They had all stopped with their heads turned towards where his bicycle lay.

He reached to touch the face of the child in front of him, and as he did so, he noticed his hand was bigger and chunkier than he remembered. The child looked up at him. He had to, because Harry was older now, looking down at the younger version of himself.

From behind the child, a man had walked from the ranks of the procession. He had a gentle, loving smile. From somewhere within the crowd, a large, dark blur was moving rapidly backwards and forwards, struggling to find a way through the people and the barriers. But it was of no importance any more.

He turned his attention back to his father, and noticed now that his eyes were glowing bright white, like LED torch beams. His smile was full of love, and there was someone else moving to join him from the procession. Two people. Both joining his father to stand behind his younger self: Mum, smiling lovingly also, and as the sun continued to rise from behind them, Jade.

***

There was an intravenous drip in his arm. He could feel the material of the bandage around his hand, pressing the canular in just below his knuckles. There was a blind-covered window to his left, where sunlight fought to get in. A TV on the wall in front of him was tuned to a twenty-four-hour news channel, with a burgundy ticker tape of information scrolling endlessly from right to left across the bottom of the screen. He felt sick, and he obliged this sensation by grabbing a kidney-shaped cardboard dish that lay on the bed and filling it with a bitter vomit that stung the back of his throat as it emerged. Somewhere within himself, he noticed that he'd managed to keep it all in the dish.

Well done, me.

He fell back to sleep.

***

Now Simeon was looming over him, asking if it was ready and if it knew what had happened. As he watched, Simeon's eyes turned ruby red and began to glow menacingly. Simeon melted into the form of a giant, panting, black dog. It cocked its head to one side before leaning in to lick Harry's face slowly from his chin upwards. He scrunched his eyes tightly shut, and felt the dog stop mid-lick.

WHERE IS IT?

Daring himself, he opened one eye a little to see the tongue still engaged on his nose, only now it was hanging and slavering from Simeon's face. Harry was frozen and could do nothing as Simeon's tongue worked from his nose to his mouth, snake-like, pushing against his lips and trying to find a way in.

***

The TV was proclaiming the arrival of The Change. A field reporter was doing her best to interview the occupants of a noisy pub while the camera tried semi-successfully to keep up with her and her handheld microphone. A countdown clock in the top left-hand corner of the screen was working its way backwards from seventeen hours, twenty-three minutes and fifteen seconds. Fourteen, thirteen, twelve...

"So, what will The Change bring you personally?" asked the reporter, who had dragged into frame a man in a grey hoodie who was holding a half-empty pint of beer.

"Well, you see, it's like this," he slurred. "When I was a kid, right, things were much different. We didn't have any of this kind of level of employment, you get me? Unemployment. Jobs, yeah? We didn't have these kinds of jobs and people from Poland, right? Uzbeks. But now we have them. We won. We won, so they need to get over it and move on back to Lithuania."

"Right," said the reporter, "so the job situation will change, yes?"

"Exactly."

"But what will change for you personally? What will you get that you haven't had before?"

The interviewee, having taken a sneaky slurp of beer during the reporter's question, let it go down with a thoughtful look on his face. "Tables."

"So, you'll get tables?"

"Not tables. No. Platforms. A platform. That's what we're going to get, see. A platform to stand on and have our say, about what we want and when we want it. Now."

"You don't think you were able to have your say before?"

"No. No because there were people in charge who didn't understand what I wanted. We. They couldn't relate to us, you see; they were out of touch. But that's going to change now. Because of The Change."

"I see. I take it you voted for The Change then?"

"No, I didn't vote at all. But I would have. You get me? There's no way I would have voted to Not Change. Not me, because since my dad was a boy there's been too much of.. of.. erm... hospitals, NHS and the miners, right? Sovereignty. Coins. Not enough respect for fish, yeah?"

At that moment, a door at the end of the room opened and in came a masked male orderly in blue scrubs. Harry felt tired and a little dizzy. He didn't feel like himself. He also didn't feel like saying hello, and that was great because the orderly didn't either. He held Harry's wrist to compare his pulse with the time on a watch pinned to his chest, before moving to the end of the bed, making notes on a clipboard there, and leaving. He would have shut the door behind him but for the arrival of Simeon in his place.

Harry scowled and awkwardly pulled himself up the bed into a sitting position.

Simeon loomed by the bed, staring down at Harry with a smirk on his narrow lips. "So I take it Newman has filled you in on what you are, then?"

Harry winced as a number of fuzzy memories came back to him. *"You were cloned, Harry! You died, but your father... the Black Dog Protocol..."*

Right at that moment, there was a black movement in the corridor behind Simeon, but Harry took a deep breath and ignored it.

"Yes, he might have said something. Where is he? Is he alright?" Harry enquired.

"Roy?" said Simeon, drawing up a chair and sitting down thoughtfully. "Oh, Roy will be fine. He's back in his own little world, doing as he's told once more. No doubt he enjoyed his little break back in reality, but he'll be a little better behaved from now on."

"So, is Newman a clone like me?"

Simeon chuckled. "No. Far from it. He's one unto his own is old Roy Newman. Anyway, you needn't concern yourself with him anymore."

Harry didn't like the sound of that, but then there wasn't much he'd particularly enjoyed over this last few days. He steeled himself for his next question, and looked his captor directly in the spectacles. "What about Jade? The lift? Did you get her out?"

Simeon clicked his tongue impatiently. "We brought the lift back up, and no."

"No what?"

"It was empty. We didn't get her out because she wasn't in there. As soon as we can solve the mystery of how to send someone or something down safely, we will, and we'll get to the bottom of what on earth is down there, but we've more important things to be doing now," he said to himself, before turning back to Harry, "So, anyway, yes, you can stop worrying about her too. She's gone."

Harry's brain raced momentarily. That made no sense. Where the hell could she be? He could have understood if they'd got the lift back with her in it, but gone *altogether*?

"However," said Simeon, interrupting Harry's thoughts momentarily, "time is pressing."

Harry didn't care much for Simeon's time or lack of it. He'd got an update on Jade, which was all he'd really wanted. It hadn't amounted to a great deal anyway. Like Simeon said, she was gone. She was the best thing that had happened in his life for a long time, and the only thing that had made any kind of sense to him recently, but now she was gone. He was staring absently into the middle distance, now thinking over the fact that he wasn't *him* anymore. Wondering where his own memories ended and the real ones began, or whether any of them were, in fact, real in the first place. How was he even pondering and fretting over this? With his brain? Or through a processor? Too much. It was too much.

Simeon was oblivious to Harry's inner battles, and was looking at the TV instead. It was continuing with wall-to-wall coverage of The Change, now seventeen hours and sixteen minutes away and counting. "You, Salt," he declared, his focus still on the TV, "you have an important part to play in all of this. Did Roy tell you that?"

Harry looked up miserably.

"Yes," continued Simeon, now turning his way, "yes, you're actually going to prove very useful to us, to The Change and to the country as a whole. Does that surprise you?"

"No. What? Oh, I don't know. I don't care."

Simeon looked long at Harry. "The technology is absolutely wasted on the likes of you. No matter. Once we understand what it is that enables you to function fully and normally, without malfunctioning as all other clones inevitably do or will, then we'll be able to upgrade all our assets. Once we've extracted just whatever it is that makes you so different from all the others, we'll know. From top to bottom, from John O' Groats to Land's End. Fully functional and our remit fulfilled."

"Remit? What do you mean, remit?"

Simeon turned to look back at the screen. "'Take back control.'" He shook his head and chuckled to himself. "Nobody ever knew who they were really handing over control to in the first place, did they?" he muttered. "Well, they'll know soon enough. The Change is just the start. It's the green light we needed. All clones throughout the UK will switch to their new directives in seventeen hours, and once we know what your secret is, we'll replicate it countrywide. Our little island, serving as the ultimate testing ground." He turned back to Harry, a wild look in his eyes. "Thanks to you and your dear old dad. Poetry, Salt. It's pure poetry when you look at it."

"*Clones?* You mean there are more?"

"Ho ho! Of course! Hundreds of thousands of the things, all equally as oblivious as you. Filling in all kinds of roles across the UK right now, as a matter of fact, each one blissfully unaware of their true purpose. And you? You're the key to making sure they fulfil that without hindrance."

"Stop saying that," said Harry under his breath.

"Say again?"

"I said stop saying that!" repeated Harry, his voice rising in ferocity with each word, "Stop it! This has nothing to do with me! None of this! I don't want a part in it, any of it. You can't keep me here."

As a show of defiance, Harry made an effort to swing his legs over the edge of the bed and then stand on them. They gave way almost as soon as he was upright, causing him to swing his hand out to steady himself. This connected with the IV stand and sent it toppling. He tried to catch it with his free hand, missed and then threw himself to the floor after it, for fear of the canular being ripped from the back of his hand.

All in all, it was not his finest moment. Once the clattering caused by his limbs and the IV stand had subsided, Harry decided it would be better to stay face-down and motionless on the cold floor for a bit rather than look Simeon in the eye.

"I'm afraid to say that the evidence presented here is very much to the contrary," explained Simeon, standing over him. "We shall be keeping you here, and we shall be getting what we need. You're to be operated on this afternoon at 4pm. In the meantime, I must insist that you get back into bed and relax."

"Relax?" mumbled Harry from the floor.

"Yes. There's really no pressure on you whatsoever. Your purpose is done. You won't be needed any longer once we have what we need."

With that, Simeon left, and two orderlies entered to wrench Harry's body back into bed. He didn't struggle. He didn't fight. When the covers were pulled back over him, and the head of the bed raised at a forty-five degree angle, he simply slumped there facing the TV, watching the news as the seconds counted down one by one.

22. Spittoon

So this was the day it would all happen. The nation sat by their TVs, glued to their phones, their loins collectively girded and their breath held in readiness for one almighty gasp. The day when the country would finally take back control, get back on its bike and enjoy the oven-ready future that the people had been promised for the last five years. The Change was at hand!

Harry thought this a little too ironic as he lay in the centre of an operating theatre, stripped down to a surgical gown and strapped down to a bed, about to go under one if not several knives. He hadn't fought or argued as he'd been taken from his bed, put into a wheelchair, and taken through a number of hospital lifts and corridors to his now final destination. Given all the changes his life had borne in recent weeks, all he wished now was that everything could be changed back to how it was. A time before the MOP: before the job interview, before the discoveries underground and before he'd lost Jade. Before he'd learned that his life was, in fact, not his own and never had been. Before he'd learned that this miserable, made-up life of his was of significant interest to the government, one of whom was about to pull him apart at any moment to get what they'd been looking for.

Before. Before had been dull – a little uneventful, maybe. But Harry had recently developed a bit of a soft spot for his before.

He sighed, which was not easy given that he now had some kind of gag in his mouth.

"Everything okay, sweetie?"

Harry, as much as his bonds would allow him, turned his head to see an utterly matronly matron stood at his bedside, replete with blue uniform, white hat and cuffs, plus an upside-down and breast-mounted watch ticking away what he now had accepted were his final seconds. Her head loomed its way down towards him until it blocked out much of his view.

"Yes, everything okay, lovie?" she enquired.

What view he did have left to enjoy was then swallowed immediately by the appearance of a second matron, dressed exactly as the first. In fact, she was *exactly the same* as the first. The voice, the face, the lot. Right down to the mole on her cheek with three small hairs poking out, and the stale scent of last night's bolognese on her breath.

Those scarily clever bunch of bastards, Harry bitterly thought.

"Burglemumfenumph," he croaked, pointlessly.

The first matron flicked a puzzled look back to her mirror twin. "Didn't quite get that, Muriel, did you?"

"No. Loosen his gag a little will you, Joan? Let the poor wretch speak," suggested Muriel.

Joan, as she had apparently been named, leaned over him without breaking her huge smile as Muriel made way. In the process, her titanic bosom got to work on suffocating Harry a full five minutes before he was officially due to meet his maker.

As she leaned back, her task complete, Harry gratefully gulped in a lungful of air, and waggled his chin until the loosened and sodden gag rested upon it.

"So, young man," declared a beaming Muriel, "is everything okay? May we get you anything?"

"I suppose an axe is out of the question?" quipped Harry, despite himself.

The sinister sisters looked on in silence at Harry, never once dropping their terrifying smiles, before bursting into high-pitched laughter as if he'd just dropped the Edinburgh Festival Fringe Joke of the Year.

"Oh, he is a one, isn't he?" cried Muriel through the tears.

"A ONE! HE REALLY IS!" bellowed Joan, "Such spirit in the young pup! In fact, I was only just saying to—"

Joan's anecdote was cut short as the swing doors of the operating theatre burst open. In marched a male surgeon in a blur of blue, followed by three further young attendants – two of them women and one a man. The flurry of activity appeared not to phase Muriel or Joan, who both slunk back from Harry's bed to stand in quiet, respectful and smile-free attendance.

It wasn't until the surgeon spoke that Harry realised, with a jolt, who it was.

"Who took the gag off its mouth?" asked David Simeon. "No matter," he continued, without waiting for a reply, "One of you, get that screen on. Now." He stood with his back to Harry, busying himself in his notes.

One of the attendees had gone to a giant, dormant TV screen that hung on the wall facing Harry, something he'd not noticed until now.

However, his attention was now focussed on the hot feeling of anger that was suddenly surging up and spreading throughout his body, all directed at the thin minister-cum-surgeon hunched over his paperwork. In Simeon's case, it was rather fortunate that Harry was unable to move right at this moment.

"You bastard," breathed Harry.

Simeon stiffened at his voice, before looking briefly over his shoulder to where Harry lay. Without a word he smirked the leanest of smirks, nodded and went back to his paperwork.

It was enough.

"You bastard! You absolute shitting bastard!" Harry wriggled and writhed at the straps that held him down.

"Simeon, are you there?" came an all-too-familiar voice from the TV screen.

Three bastards, one of them shitting, was all Harry had managed before the TV screen came to life. There were plenty more where those came from, he thought to himself, although he wasn't likely to have long left to use them.

"Simeon?" the voice came again.

"Ah, yes Prime Minister, I'm here, sorry," Simeon apologised.

Harry looked on incredulously between his bare feet to where the giant TV screen glowed. Staring back at him from beneath a thatched mop of unruly, blond hair was the Prime Minister. Harry had a sneaky feeling he wasn't about to be treated to a party political broadcast courtesy of the BBC.

"You finally got it then, did you? Is that it?" Spittoon enquired.

The Prime Minister pointed by poking a blue-and-gold fountain pen into the camera, before peering in for a closer look, his pale, globular face filling the screen.

Harry's fury remained undiminished.

"Bloody hell," remarked the Prime Minister, sitting back with a look of disdain, "bit unremarkable, isn't it? Are you sure that's the right one?"

"Er, yes, Prime Minister, this is definitely the one," grovelled Simeon, "we've checked."

"I DIDN'T VOTE FOR YOU, YOU FAT, USELESS BASTARD!" yelled Harry, letting forth his fourth. If he was going down, which he certainly was, he was going down fighting.

However, at this, Muriel the matron's plump hand slammed down onto his mouth in a move of clinical efficiency, while the other propped up his head, forcing him to watch. From behind him, she smiled sweetly at Britain's *numero uno*. "Sorry about that, petal. He is a one, this rascal!"

The Prime Minister both flinched and scowled simultaneously. "Ruddy Christ," he frothed, "bloody clones and bloody hospitals. Can't stand either of them."

Muriel, still holding Harry's head mute and rock steady in her vice-like grip, winked appreciatively back at the Prime Minister.

"Anyway, Simeon," continued the Prime Minister, keen to wrap things up, "I don't think I need to impress on you any more how bloody vital it is that you get this sorted. You've had the best part of five years for heaven's sake, and our relationship with the entire Eastern Coalition is at stake, not to mention my bloody reputation."

"Yes, Prime Minister. Fully understood," answered Simeon. "You can rely on us," he added, in a voice that Harry noticed lacked its usual conviction.

"Well, get on to it then," barked the Prime Minister, "because The Change happens tonight come hell or high water. Probably both, as it happens. I don't care if you need to rip its head off and shake it until all its brains fall out, just find out what has kept this one going when all the others have failed. And Simeon, while you're at it... "

The TV signal was lost suddenly, the screen and loudspeaker filled with static.

Harry lay there, rigid with fear. The matron had now let go of his mouth and returned to her corner, but Harry couldn't find a single word to say right now. Panic had consumed him.

This was it. The end.

And there was absolutely nothing he could do about it. Within the hour, his life would be over, his unknown secret gouged from his discarded corpse, and the nation on its knees as the clones awoke to carry out whatever their dastardly mission was. Unstoppable. And all because of him, the clone that kept going.

It was hideous, and yet, somewhere in the recesses of Harry's mind, a sardonic voice told him that at least he wasn't so unremarkable after all.

"Get it under," commanded Simeon, gesturing in Harry's direction.

As Harry watched, the three young assistants busied themselves by laying out a set of gleaming chromium knives and other evil implements of dissection – long, hooked tools, pliers and more – on a steel trolley, which they then wheeled silently to his side. Simeon held up his hands as Muriel the matron dressed him, tying up his blue gown at the back and pulling his surgical mask over his face.

Harry was about to cry out, but Joan swiftly put the gag back across his mouth and tightened it once more. So. That was that, then. He'd not even get a final word.

As Joan then brought a plastic mask over his face, connected to the gas that would send him to sleep and onwards to oblivion, Harry noticed a shadow in the static of the TV screen before him. Desperately holding his breath to avoid inhaling, hot tears now streaming down the side of face, his lungs finally gave in, forcing him to gulp in the anaesthetic.

As he did so, two things happened at once. From somewhere beside him, the shrill and nerve-shredding sound of a surgical drill split the air and filled Harry with a woozy terror. As that happened, the static on the screen cleared momentarily, and a certain TV detective shambled into view, clad in an all-too-familiar and all-too-battered raincoat.

Above the roar of the drill, "Just one more thing," was the last thing that Harry heard.

23. Unleashed

There were fireworks.

Across Derbyshire, across the UK as a whole, people celebrated. They'd won and, finally, after five long years of waiting, this was their moment in the sun. Or in the dark, more accurately, as The Change officially began at midnight.

Victory was sweet, but victory came at a cost.

The Referendum on whether the UK should Change or Not was a difficult one. The consensus among many people, politicians and the more moderate sections of the media was, at the time, that people would generally see sense, that they would carry on with things as they were and that there was no real need for any upheaval of any kind. Things were pretty balanced. Unemployment levels weren't perfect, just average. Britain was doing its bit in the world markets, beaches were clean, and people were just generally getting on with things. In football terms, the UK had been looking at a steady top-half finish to the season, with maybe a decent run in the cup. As for The Change, well, the whole thing had come about, seemingly, as some kind of drunken and mean-spirited dare conjured up by some of the more rebellious celebrity politicians, one that sounded like fun, but had maybe gone just a bit too far.

There were some who saw The Referendum as an opportunity

to shake an angry fist at the establishment, and that was fine as well. These were, broadly and in the main, people who had never really cared that much for politics until newspapers plastered themselves with Union flags, told them they could have Control again and that although things might be difficult for a while, they would overall be better off because of Control and Sovereignty and Our Laws and Rights. After all, in a democratic society – especially a nice and steady one like the British one – people could share their views like that. In the pub, or over a cup of tea and, quite likely, a scone.

There were also some who had lots of money already and stood to make even more money if things swung in their direction. As is the way, they spent some of that money to try to get the result they wanted, so that they could soon get their money back and then some. They told certain groups of potential voters exactly the kind of things that they wanted to hear, making promises they may or may not have intended to keep. This was fun for them.

In fact, lots of things were said and promised by both sides, and these often changed depending on what day of the week it happened to be, or whether or not it was raining. A lot of these things sounded very nice indeed. Some were quite fanciful, some sounded a bit expensive and others sounded remarkably similar to everything everybody already had anyway.

Finally, the day of The Referendum came. The eyes of the world wandered lazily over to Britain that sunny summer Thursday, when folk young, old and even older followed the arrows on photocopied paper signs to former libraries and decrepit halls normally only used for coffee mornings or pilates classes for cats and their owners. In these places, the nation took hold of and considered smaller pieces of paper that had kindly gone to the trouble of narrowing the entire insanely complicated debate down to two simple outcomes. There they were presented with pencils, some of which even contained lead, and asked to make their mark before posting their papers into a plastic box, never to see it again. It all seemed so simple. So secure. So incorrupt-ibly failsafe.

Nobody, including many of the fist-shaking persuasion, really expected a majority vote for The Change to come in.

But it did.

And when it did, people got upset. Strangely, some of those who got most upset were those who'd won. They enjoyed telling people that they'd won at first, and they started to look forward to The Change happening in a month or two. This was fun for them. The trouble was that there were those who'd voted to Not Change. To them, it just wasn't right. It wasn't right at all, and it should never have happened. The politicians themselves had been lying to get The Change through for their own benefit and for that of the elite, they said. It was all a massive scam fuelled by misinformation and the great British people had been royally conned, they added. So, those who had voted to Not Change started to find ways to make everyone see sense and reverse the result of The Referendum. This spoiled the winners' fun some-what. They'd won and they didn't want any of these whining rotters telling them otherwise, regardless of facts, evidence or the opinions of experts.

This in turn caused a lot of bother between friends and even within families, and it saw the emergence of two factions: the Changers, who had voted for and wanted to see The Change happen, and the Strangers, who were christened thus by the for-mer group and the journalists from the type of newspapers they read. Politicians were quick to back one side or the other, even sometimes against the wishes of their party, which caused a lot of bother in Parliament too.

As such, the drafts of The Change struggled to get through Parliament, which dragged the whole affair out over five in-terminable years. This in turn caused a great deal more angst between Changers and Strangers, which would dominate the news every day and often got nasty. As this happened, many – including one Harry Salt – gave up on social media altogether in search of some peace and quiet away from the anger, silliness, mean behaviour and general dragging of knuckles.

This meant that he was blissfully unaware of the rumours that were circulating at the time, some of which involved voting skulduggery, supposedly influenced by the Eastern Coalition, a mysterious alliance of far-away superpowers and not-so-super powers. Whether skulls had been duggered or not was never clear, but it was reported that – maybe, just maybe – corrupt influence from afar with promises of financial benefits for the UK government had altered the result of The Referendum. Rumours were spun, investigations were promised, and yet nobody seemed any the wiser. Strangely, this coincided with a period in which journalists seemed uninterested in writing explosive, revelatory stories anymore unless it involved celebrities punching each other in the face or wearing the wrong type of shoe.

Prime ministers came and went until, astoundingly, one of the formerly rebellious politicians who initially suggested The Change for a bit of fun to his closest chums five years previously was voted into the hot seat. Once again, nobody in their right, left or centrist mind had really expected that to ever happen either. But now The Change seemed inevitable, and thus it proved to be. There was to be no turning back, and with a government powered into place by its readiness to "Make The Change For Good", as their one of their election slogans ran, nobody really pushed them to explain what plans they had in place for all the other necessaries of running a country, such as the economy, international relations, environment, health, education and the removal of dog shit from public spaces.

So, there were fireworks. There was merriment, there was lots of beer, and for those referred to as Strangers, there was another thing to be annoyed about as they attempted to sleep that night amid the noise and infernal frivolity.

Even at this point, there was still a lack of information as to what people had actually voted for and what The Change itself would tangibly bring. How *would* things be different? What would actually change, and how would anyone (and who, for that matter) really benefit? The answer came swiftly the following morning, as the country woke up, got out of bed and then collectively wished it hadn't.

The first wave were called Assistants. They'd come to 'help boost the British economy', and were an answer to the unfilled gaps in the job market – the roles that nobody seemingly wanted to do anyway. As people went to work that morning, they found themselves in the company of overly helpful and very efficient colleagues who hadn't been there the day before. One by one, the niggling jobs were completed, and productivity began to improve as a whole. Streets were cleaner. Roadworks were suddenly completed faster, and even waiting times for telephone services were slashed.

The second wave were called Attendants. These were brought in to boost numbers in the police, fire and health services, all of which had been the victims of drastic spending cuts over the last decade or so. Again, these new workers were boundlessly enthusiastic and keen to help; overnight, crime rates were reduced, hospital waiting times were cut, and people were generally very impressed and left feeling optimistic about the future that The Change appeared to be rapidly making into a present reality.

However, not everything was rosy in the newly trimmed and now clinically manicured garden of the UK. Very quickly, large swathes of the public took umbrage at these new, overly efficient and seemingly tireless colleagues who had appeared in their offices and canteens. They were 'taking their jobs' as many saw it, despite the fact that most of the jobs they were doing were ones that nobody ever seemed to get round to doing in the first place, or had been fulfilled by foreigners who had fled terrified of The Change and the fury that came with it. There was a definite sense of workers feeling threatened by these new individuals, who were very – almost annoyingly – good at what they did. They needed to calm the hell down and focus more on office gossip and last night's TV once in a while. How very dare they.

In fact, rumours were already filtering throughout society that these new workers were 'something other'; possibly immigrant types working for peanuts, possibly interns on some new-fangled government scheme or even, as some of the more excitable conspiracy theorists liked to speculate, scientifically manufactured androids that had been preprogrammed to disgustingly high levels of competence in specific workplace tasks. Androids that would become so efficient at stapling and cleaning as to one day be a threat to the British workforce and quite possibly the rest of humanity as a whole.

Protests, riots and, unfortunately, violence against these keen, new entrants into the job market were swift to follow.

That's when the third wave came crashing in: known collectively as the Aegis, these were highly skilled individuals brought in to support the military. Described by the government as "gentle and highly trained protectors of the country, of our democracy and all that we hold dear," these new soldiers were in fact quite efficient and ruthless. The riots and protests were quelled immediately. Many people were angry about this, and wanted to riot and protest about it, but didn't dare now take to the streets for fear of what would happen to them.

In a matter of days, Aegis members of the armed forces were placed in almost every town and village across the country as 'Wardens', a move that coincided with tighter government rulings on riots and public gatherings, which also included the introduction of curfews in all cities.

All of a sudden, in the space of a week, The Referendum – The Change even – were all, by and large, swiftly forgotten. The new government was now able to implement what the heck it wanted to, and if anyone had a problem, they could speak to a member of the Aegis about it and then get the hell back indoors. Besides, they now had nice, clean streets that were free of potholes to look at from out of their living-room windows, so what were they moaning at for heaven's sake?

The Prime Minister, looking very pleased with himself, appeared on TV in a party political broadcast at the end of that week to tell everyone that their new friends, the People, were here to help and make life for everyone in Britain great. That, "we Brits, as an accepting and welcoming bunch, should treat Assistants, Attendants and the Aegis with respect, and be grateful for their contributions to the new, sunlit uplands of a stronger United Kingdom." At the end of his broadcast, live from St Kitts, he raised a colourful cocktail to the camera and winked a jolly wink at his watching citizens. And as it was 10pm, the TVs and street lights across the country collectively winked out in a show of glorious, government-controlled energy efficiency, to be marvelled at nightly from now onwards.

The surface of the world that Harry had departed from seven days previously was, if Harry had been around to see it, barely recognisable from the one that existed now. People had wanted The Change, and they'd got it. It may not have been The Change they'd voted for, but no one could deny that they'd got it and that they'd got it very, very quickly.

24. Basset

Death, as it turned out, wasn't actually all that bad. It was warm. Nicely warm, not sweatily hot or anything like that. And it was dark. Now, it's fair to say that darkness sometimes gets a bad rap. The whole eternal-blackness thing. But this was a welcome dark. It was restful, and it made the cosy warmth more enjoyable and easy to snuggle into. There was no tunnel of light, which Harry had often wondered about. Just a warm, velvety blackness. Fine.

It smelled alright too. There was something homely about it. A faint note of fustiness that reminded him of his grandparents. That much he could just pick out from underneath the stronger waft of baking. Not fresh baking. It was more like someone had been baking a couple of hours prior, and the delightful, golden fragrance was still in the air. It was just so nice to float here. To lose yourself in it.

Being dead was also very, very Welsh. Harry wasn't sure why, it just was.

***

Later, death was lighter. Not in an existential way. More in a 'not dark anymore' way. It also felt hard under the head, round the area where the skull ended and the neck began. And speaking of / thinking of / remembering the neck, it ached like hell. Maybe that was it. Hell. Shit. But did robots go to hell? And why was he thinking about robots? Did robots get neck ache? Did robots even think about having neck ache?

He prised open his eyes and looked about for the first time. It was now light enough to see that the light itself was coming from a chandelier of candles hanging from the ceiling of the window-less, small sitting room in which he was currently lying down. The afterlife had provided him with a long, green, velvet sofa; a couple of cushions under his head; and a large, tartan blanket, which he had wriggled one leg out of and that still had a sock on. The afterlife had also done him the courtesy of a banging headache that, now that he'd acknowledged it, was getting rapidly worse.

Slowly and with great unsteadiness, Harry sat himself up. He felt like a miserable evacuee, recently arrived in a train station he didn't understand. The afterlife had a wooden coffee table on a darkened Indian rug. There was a mug of tea to welcome him to eternity, and as he clutched it in both hands, he noticed it was warm but cooling down. He shivered, his eyes staring in resigned bewilderment at the large, flat-screen TV set that sat dormant across the room from him.

He heard noise. Beyond the room, in what he assumed was hell's kitchen or the astral canteen, someone was busying them-selves by clanking around, opening and closing drawers, stir-ring, chopping, and doing – it seemed – everything in their power to make a racket. They were whistling. A smell of onions and garlic drifted nostrilwards.

"Be with you in a minute bud," came a thick, heavy accent from the kitchen.

The clanking resumed.

So, the afterlife. Thinking about it, death was actually a bit odd and not what he'd expected at all. It had felt nice at first, but on further inspection it was actually a bit shit around the edges.

Harry warily took a sip of his tea, and he allowed his eyes to wander around the room. The dark rug beneath his feet was a little threadbare, as were parts of the settee, but a worn pattern and a number of faded colours were still visible. A couple of paintings in intricately carved, wooden frames adorned the walls, both displaying landscapes – one of which was of a beach at sunset, with a stretch of coastline jutting out into and under the sea, before emerging again as a crop of rocks nearer the horizon, almost like a serpent's head.

Bookcases were packed tightly with countless leather-bound and well-worn tomes, and Harry noticed a couple of them on the coffee table in front of him, which was as impressively carved as the picture frames. A fire crackled and flickered in a blackened, stone-walled hearth, and the wooden chandelier, holding a half-dozen or so candles, burned cosily below the ceiling from which it hung. Harry was aware that further lights glowed warmly from unseen light sources in nooks and crannies around the room, and, unexpectedly, an NHS-issue wheelchair stood folded up in a corner.

Keeping him company while his host prepared something in the kitchen, a haggard-looking and completely white basset hound lay half-awake beside the coffee table; his ears drooped either side of his head, which sat resting on his paws. He looked up mournfully at Harry for a moment as their gazes met, blinked slowly, and then decided that was quite enough and fell back to sleep.

Despite the timeworn nature of so much in this sitting room, Harry noted that it was cosy, well kept and fairly tidy. He just wasn't sure what the heck he was doing there.

"Okay then," came the voice from the kitchen. (Welsh. Definitely Welsh, Harry decided.) Through the door came an old man in a long, grey cloak. He carefully carried a wooden tray in front of him, on which sat a steaming bowl of soup filled with all kinds of goodies.

"*Cawl*," he said through his wispy, ginger beard, as he set the tray down in front of Harry.

"*Gesundheit*," replied Harry, surprising himself.

The man eyed him suspiciously for a moment, then pointed to elements of the soup one by one.

"Lamb. Potato. Leek. Cabbage. Bit of bacon. Onion. All in my special broth. If you're veggie, you'll just have to pick the meat out with your spoon. You must be ready for it. Get it down you, *bachgen*."

The tray, lined with a layer of thin, green baize, also held a big, silver spoon, the metal of which was tarnished and showed a rainbow of colours whenever it hit the light. Harry looked from the soup and suspiciously back up at the man.

"Go on, please don't wait for me," the man replied, working his way over to an old armchair underneath a corner formed by two of the bookcases, "I've already eaten today." He sat with a satisfied sigh and looked back at Harry expectantly.

Harry took a spoonful of the soup, blew on it to cool it down, and slurped it clumsily into his mouth. A chunk of lamb fell apart and melted almost as soon as it hit his grateful tongue, and the broth was wondrously full of flavour. Immediately, he felt a portion of tension drain away as the hot mush worked its way downwards.

The man sat opposite smiled in response. "Not bad, eh? Mind you, it should be good. I've had long enough to get the hang of the bloody recipe! My mam taught it me a while back, see." He chuckled to himself and shuffled in his chair a little to get comfortable.

Harry found himself forcing a small smile before tackling another mouthful of soup. And then another. Before he knew it, he'd worked his way through the entire bowl, and the spoon was scraping the last traces of warming soup from the side of the dish.

"Easy now, you'll take the pattern off," said the man, taking the bowl and spoon from Harry's hands. He'd wandered over to him as he ate, although Harry hadn't noticed.

In fact, as Harry looked up, he felt his chin start to tremble, and in an instant, it all came out. He clenched his teeth together, shaking his head and determined not to cry, but it was all in vain as tears began to run down his cheeks, no matter how hard he tried to blink them back.

"Whoa, whoa, whoa. There, there, kiddo. Take a deep breath." Gently putting the bowl and spoon back down on the tray, he crouched down in front of Harry with remarkable ease and took Harry's hand in his own. It was rough, and the skin was old, but there was strength there. "Go on, lad, let it out. Go on. There's no shame in it."

Harry sobbed heavily, wiped his eyes on his back of his hand and looked back into the eyes of the man, who proffered him a soft, white handkerchief from the depths of his sleeve. He took it gratefully, wiped his eyes again and blew his nose with a trumpet call that caused the white basset hound to lazily open one eye briefly before closing it again.

"I'm sorry," choked Harry, attempting to regain his composure. "I just don't understand. I don't get any of it. I mean, what the hell? What was I? I lost someone. Someone important and now this... "

"It's alright; it's alright," continued the man, who looked at him with a little more sadness than Harry was comfortable with. "Ah, bugger me. You haven't got a bloody clue, have you, you poor lad?" He shook his head, sighed and then stood up again before taking Harry's empty mug from the table. "Let me get you another brew. There's a few things you should hear. You alright for soup or do you want some more?"

Harry pondered for a second, before shaking his head wordlessly.

***

Harry sat there, his second mug of tea of the afterlife in hand.

The man also sat, his basset hound curled up at his feet, with the two of them sombrely looking across at their guest. Somewhere, a clock ticked slowly.

"So," said the man eventually. "I guess you must have a question or two then."

Harry took a slurp of his tea and swallowed, staring into the old rug on the floor beneath his feet. "Erm, yes. One or two."

The man nodded. "Well, go ahead, boyo. I can't promise I'll be able to answer everything, but ask, and I'll see if I can help."

Harry took a breath and met the man's gaze. "Okay. So... Who are you? And do you need me to sign anything before I can pass on to the next bit? Is there a task or something?"

The man took a moment to hold his gaze, before nodding. "Good a start as any; fair play." He cleared his throat, and then stood up from his chair, suddenly looking at Harry with a strange and powerful gaze.

"I am the blessed and holy guardian of Annwn," he said, his voice suddenly booming as if he was talking through a bank of giant amplifiers, "eternal protector of the spoils within, everlasting loyal servant of Gwynn ap Nudd, and the most fair and courageous Tylwyth Teg, and master of the Cwn Annwn, the beasts of whom mortal men tremble and live perpetually in fear – never sleeping, always ready and indefatigable."

He stepped back, his voice still echoing around them. He had his hand clenched into a fist on his chest, his eyes were closed, and he was breathing in deeply and with pride. Seconds passed before he finally opened his sparkling eyes to see Harry still staring back at him.

He cleared his throat again. "Clive," he said, in a much less impressive manner, "my name's Clive, and this is my dog, Little Stevie."

Harry looked from the man and down to the crumpled white hound at his feet. "I'm sorry? What?"

"Which bit?"

"No. I mean... " Harry started to talk, but quickly gave up. He'd had enough nonsense to last him a lifetime recently, and now that he was a few hours into his death, he was in no mood for any more. "I'm sorry, Clive, and thank you for the soup and everything," he continued, standing up as he did so, "but is this it? You, me and the dog in here for all eternity? Oh... "

Upon standing, Harry was hit with a wave of nausea, and he slumped back into the armchair. His head still pounded from before, and dying had clearly knocked the stuffing out of him. He felt exhausted.

"Well, before you ask," stated Clive, "no, I didn't put anything dodgy in your *cawl*. You're just shagged out."

Harry let out a sigh.

"Now what was that about me and Stevie? Eternity you said, right?"

"I... I'm sorry about that. Yes. I'm exhausted. But Jade... " He started to try to get up again. "I need to help Jade. Is there any way, from here? Now that I'm dead and everything?"

"Dead?" Clive looked at him with concern, before his face creased into uproarious laughter. "Dead? You think you're dead? That's brilliant. Of course you do; I should've thought of that. Bugger, I could have kept that going for a bit; it would've been hilarious."

"But Simeon. The operating theatre," said Harry belligerently, "he was cutting me up to find something, a processor or something."

"*Ach y fi*, Harry! You're no more dead than Little Stevie here. Wake up, Stevie." Clive nudged the sleeping dog with his foot, who licked it in return. "You're alive and kicking, *bachgen*. Just a little knackered, but we'll soon sort that out with some rest and decent food."

Harry thought for a second before nodding wearily. Clive came over to him with a blanket, and just as he draped it over him, Harry looked up.

"So, what's this then? Cardiff?" Harry questioned.

Clive chuckled warmly. "I told you that already. This is Annwn, Harry. You wouldn't want to be up in Cardiff right now at this particular moment in history, trust me. Get some kip, and we'll all go through everything later, together. It can wait. Just about, anyhow."

This didn't please Harry at all, along with the fact that the beardy, ginger weirdo knew his name. He was pretty sure he hadn't told him. Dead or alive, however, he'd had enough and was struggling to keep his eyes open. With a frown on his exhausted face, he was soon deeply asleep.

***

Harry blinked once, twice and a third time as he emerged from his sleep. He had no idea how long he'd been out. The fire still crackled, and the light levels were much as before. Because of the lack of any windows, it was difficult to gauge whether or not it was daytime or the middle of the night. A steaming mug of tea sat on a side table beside his chair, along with a bonsai tree in a small, rectangular, red pot.

He didn't feel as if he were being held captive, but he did feel that he didn't want to linger here any longer than necessary if he could help it, wherever or whatever here was. Cabin fever was just as real whether he was dead or not.

"Aye aye, Rip van Winkle. There he is," came a thick Welsh accent from across the room, and there on the sofa sat Clive, a mischievous grin shining from within his ginger beard.

Harry took another look at his surroundings. "You never did tell me where I was," he said, sitting himself up slowly and stretching out his neck with a noisily drawn-out sigh.

"That's because you never asked," replied Clive, before following up quickly with, "Oh hang about, no, actually you did."

The unseen clock ticked on.

"Well, as you might gather," Clive began, "you're deep underground."

Harry nodded as he rubbed his eyes. "So, this is hell then, is it? It's not especially warm, shouldn't there be more lava or something?" He felt much, much better for his sleep, but was beginning to remember just how puzzling his situation was.

"No, you wazzock, you're not dead. I told you. I thought you'd be more pleased about that. It's not every day you get rescued from a messy and premature end, and taken into safe hiding."

"Rescued? Was I?"

Without answering Harry's question, Clive stood up, wandered over and proffered his hand. "Fancy a little wander? Just a quickish one, I promise you. Stretch the legs, see. Get a bit of strength back into them."

Harry took a slurp of his tea. "Is it safe?"

"Very. Bring the mug with you," suggested Clive, lighting a brass lantern containing a candle, "You can drink that on the way."

***

From the small, cosy comforts of Clive's mysterious apartment, Harry was led by torchlight up a small, unlit corridor to a set of steps, which he managed to make his way up by holding on tightly to a rope in the wall that served as a bannister. At the top was a door, which Clive opened before leading Harry out into somewhat familiar surroundings. Clive had put on a battered raincoat for their walk, and Harry felt there was something awfully familiar about that too. He turned his attention back to the walls.

"These tunnels, I was down here just recently," Harry declared.

"Not this far you weren't," answered Clive brightly, "Nope, not this far. But, yes, it's the same set of tunnels, give or take."

"Are we underneath the MOP here?"

"Oh yes. But a good five miles underneath."

Harry stopped still. "What?"

Clive chuckled and stopped too before turning back to Harry. "Yeah, we're a way down here. Far out of sight of you buggers up top. That's how we like to keep it."

"Yeah, but five miles? That's utterly insane. There aren't any mines on earth as deep as that."

"True, but if you're looking to measure things on a scale of mental derangement, then I'm afraid I'm only just getting going. That was the hors d'oeuvres, so to speak."

Little Stevie the white basset hound, who had come along for the walk, trotted to Clive's side and sniffed at his feet.

"The ceiling and the walls. They're so smooth," said Harry, taking in what little he could make out of the tunnel from the light of Clive's lantern, "I noticed that before. Not a scratch. How the hell did you tunnel all this out?"

"I didn't. We didn't." Clive stared at him in the flickering light of the candle, his ginger beard taking on a golden glow. "We don't know who did, either. These tunnels are ridiculously ancient, Harry; they were here long before me, you, man, woman, dinosaurs, geraniums, bacteria, you name it. Whoever made them had some cracking skills, but I'll be buggered if I know *why* they built them. Mind you, we've made good use of them, so they're not going to waste."

Harry stared wordlessly back at Clive, and then took another look around him. He shivered. There was something eerily unnatural about it all. It was too perfect.

Clive shrugged. "Ah, well. Come on. If you think this is interesting, what I'll show you next will blow your ruddy socks off."

He turned to continue along the tunnel, with Little Stevie alongside. Harry took a sip of tea and followed.

"Now then," said Clive as he walked, "you probably heard me mention a few things before you slept that you might have struggled with."

"Well, yes."

"Ha! Well, don't worry, *bachgen*. I know Welsh is a tricky language at the best of times," replied Clive.

"No, I didn't mean that," offered Harry apologetically, but Clive was quick to cut him off.

"Annwn. I mentioned Annwn to you, you remember?"

"You may have done."

"S'alright, lad. Truly. You were practically asleep when I did. Annwn... " Clive called over his shoulder, "Annwn is the place I've been charged to protect. That's my job, see?"

"So, this is Annwn?"

"Ha! No," replied Clive, who seemed to be having far too much fun right now, "No, this is just a tunnel. Annwn is a bit further down, see."

Harry was aware of a light source ahead. It was faint, but strong enough to reveal that the gradually descending passageway curved round sharply to the left further ahead. He was pleased to see light down here, but slightly unnerved as to the source. Clive, however, was bounding along keenly like an enthusiastic scout leader on his favourite hike, and Harry and Little Stevie found themselves struggling to keep up.

"See now, Annwn. It's a special place. Most people have forgotten about it," explained Clive, his rich voice clear and crisp.

It was a gorgeous voice that would have been a credit to any Welsh male voice choir, Harry noted, but despite its power, something was missing. There had been something unusual with regards to all the noises he'd heard since entering the tunnel – a dullness.

A lack of echo.

That was it. Whatever the material was that these unnaturally smooth tunnels were carved from, it didn't bounce any sound back. It swallowed it. Harry shivered and drank the remains of his tea.

"Forgotten about it?" asked Harry, "I'm not entirely sure I was aware of it in the first place. What is it? A cave?"

"Ha ha! You'll see soon enough. And there you are, see. The fact you didn't even know about it," continued Clive, "it's long forgotten. Nobody even really knows about the place any more."

The light source was getting stronger, and it was a soft but somehow delicate glow – a peaceful radiance as opposed to a stark burst of luminescence.

Clive stopped suddenly and turned to face Harry, his lantern casting a warm glow upwards to give his face a spooky countenance. He put his hand on Harry's chest to stop him. "Okay, *bachgen*, I'll level with you," he said gravely. "You're going to see some stuff in a minute. Some seriously crazy stuff. Proper scrotum-shrivelling weird, like. I hope you're going to be okay with this."

Harry sighed. "To be honest, Clive, I've seen my fair share lately," he said with more exasperation than he expected to, "I'm currently five miles deep into the earth with a Welshman in a raincoat and his knackered dog. No offence, Little Stevie. I thought I was dead, but, apparently, I'm not; I'm a living, breathing version of myself with robot bits, on the run from the government."

Stevie sniffed.

"So, what I'm essentially saying is go for it, Clive. Whatever you've got, go for it, because frankly it can't get any weirder than this," Harry declared.

They paused together in an awkward silence, with the glow of Clive's lantern flickering onto his face as he pondered his response.

"Fair dos. I think this will probably top it, though," concluded Clive eventually. Harry opened his mouth to speak, but Clive was quick to cut him off dramatically. "Alright then, let's get this done. This way."

***

If someone had taken the best parts of Snowdonia, mixed it with the Peak District, turned off the rain and encased it all in the world's biggest cave while simultaneously providing champagne, caviar and entertainment from The Beatles, welcomed onto the stage by Mother Theresa juggling onions on a unicycle, then even that wouldn't quite match the effect of seeing Annwn for the first time.

As they'd rounded the corner of the tunnel, and Harry's eyes had begun to adjust to the glare of daylight five miles under the surface of the planet, his brain simply shrugged and gave up for a few minutes.

First, there was the sun. Naturally, there wasn't one, and yet, somehow, there was.

From somewhere, cheerful, warming spring sunshine shone downwards to bathe the entire vista in a delightful brilliance that made all the colours across the landscape sing. Lush, green fields as neat as English summer lawns stretched off into the distance. A river lazily wound and sparkled its way through them, and a dense wood stood at the base of a mighty mountain that soared to a snowy peak atop the huge, almost purple edifice. And, yes, as thin as they were, those were definitely wispy, white clouds working their way past the summit.

Where the tunnel ended and this mind-bending sight began, Harry, Clive and Stevie stood on a black-and-white tiled terrace fringed by an ornate, marble balcony that looked out across this impossible sight, buried deep under the surface of the earth.

"Jesus," was the best Harry could manage.

"Didn't have anything to do with it, far as I can tell," muttered Clive, walking over to the balcony.

Harry followed, breathless. "It's... it's unbelievable. Surely someone built... all this?" he said, shaking his head in wonder.

Clive chuckled. "Well, if they did, they'd likely have done the same up top, as well. Annwn just is, same as England is or Scotland is and Wales forever shall be. When the countries formed above, so too Annwn formed deep below. Or so they reckon, anyhow."

Harry continued to stare on, trying his hardest to comprehend the scale of it all. Far above, three birds flew across the cave ceiling. In shock, he turned to look where they'd come from to see that the ceiling of this world continued on and curved *behind* them, beyond the tunnel entrance and the rocky wall in which it stood.

Then, as if his mind hadn't already been bent enough, Harry looked downwards over the balcony to see the sheerest of drops to the ground below, far more distant than he cared to imagine. As his stomach came up to make friends with his larynx, he thought he could discern tiny figures moving and going about their business down on that distant deck, although his look was only a brief one for fear of being sick on them.

"Not bad, eh? I must admit, even after all this time, it is ruddy brilliant. There's no place like home, right? Oh, mind out," Clive finished, pulling an oblivious Harry back from where Little Stevie had been sniffing around his feet seconds before.

"What the fuck is happening to Little Stevie?" Harry exclaimed.

"Language." Clive gave him a scolding look, but Harry was no longer staring at him.

Instead, he was looking down at the knackered basset hound who, unexpectedly, was staring up at him with more intent. At first, it was hard to tell, but he was certain that the tips of the dog's ears were now shot through with red fur. But the most disturbing thing by far was that Little Stevie was *growing and changing shape*. As they watched in the sunlight, the dog continued to develop in size, looking stronger, leaner and more athletic with each passing moment. At no point did the hound take its eyes from Harry's, staring at him with an intelligence that seemed all too human. In a matter of seconds, it stood level with Harry's waist, tall and powerful, and stopped growing.

Harry gaped in shock. The huge, white dog simply shook itself as if it had just come in from the rain before stretching lazily, yawning and trotting nonchalantly to Clive's side.

"Looks like someone wanted to put on his own little show, eh Stevie?" Clive stated warmly, patting the transformed dog on the head as he did so.

"What? What the hell just happened?" queried Harry.

"It's like I said," explained Clive calmly, "Little Stevie here is a long-standing member of the Cwn Annwn. The Hounds of Annwn. He's my boy, my *bachgen*. And whenever he heads home, like we're doing now, he takes on his normal form. I also think he just thought he'd try to help you get your head around the fact that what's going on down here *is* real." He took a breath and moved towards Harry. "And that this silly, old Welsh bugger in a detective's raincoat isn't making it all up. He won't hurt you." He motioned towards the no-longer-Little Stevie.

Harry stepped tentatively towards them both and nervously held out the back of his hand. The huge dog trotted over and gave it a warm, gloopy lick before tenderly nuzzling his giant head against Harry's leg, almost knocking him over in the process.

"See. Told you."

"That was... that was weird," panted Harry, still shocked. "But he's – Little Stevie, I mean – he's beautiful."

The hound looked up at Harry with mesmerising, golden eyes before trotting back to his master.

"Yeah, he's not bad for an old boy," the Welshman said, tickling under the dog's chin with his free hand. "Big birthday coming up as it happens." He looked up at Harry again. "Ten."

"Oh really?" said Harry, glad to be talking about something a little more mundane.

"Yeah. Ten centuries. Not looking bad for it, eh?"

Harry stared at the giant dog with a whole new sense of incomprehension. "Ten? Ten centuries? A thousand years?"

"Good maths, Stephen Hawking."

Harry continued to stare at the creature before another, even more disconcerting thought struck him. "So, if you don't mind me asking, how old are you, Clive?"

Clive took Harry's mug, which he'd completely forgotten he was still holding tightly on to, and put it on the floor along with the lantern. "Ha! And I had you down as a gentleman," he added, straightening up. "Well, I first got him when he was a newborn puppy, and I was just a kid in nappies at the time, so you work it out."

"Jesus Christ. So you're saying *you're over 900 years old?*"

"Give or take. I've lost count, to be honest with you, but I reckon around 951. Again, not looking too shabby, eh?"

Harry shook his head in disbelief. "But... but... you've got a TV," was all he could manage.

"Oh *that* thing," said Clive nonchalantly, "yeah, it's to keep me from getting bored during my duties, apparently. Lovely idea that, not sure where they got it from, mind. Sick sense of humour, though, those buggers. I had to wait the best part of 900 years 'til your lot up there started making programmes for me to watch on it."

Harry gaped.

"Bloody waste of space until the signals finally started coming through. Some of the elders reckoned they could make out messages in the static during the first few decades down here, but they gave up eventually. Worth the wait though, mind; well, just about, for the police dramas. Cop shows are my absolute favourite."

"Cop shows?"

"Yeah. *Kojak, CHiPs,* and *Starsky and Hutch.* All that crowd. I love them all. Even *The Bill* is pretty good. But the best of the lot, well— "

"Oh my God," said Harry, realising, "*Columbo?*"

Clive hitched his raincoat at the shoulders, stooped a little, mimed a cigarette in his hand and said, "And just one more thing... " before winking, clearly hoping Harry would be impressed.

"But... why are you dressed like him?"

"Well, it gets boring down here with just me and Little Stevie," Clive replied, a touch indignant. "And, well, I like dressing up, see."

"You should be careful who you say that to," responded Harry, with one eyebrow raised, "but what about the wheelchair back in your living room, then? *Ironside?*"

"What? Oh that," Clive said before clarifying, "no, that's

because I'm over 900 years old. Sciatica. Today's a good day, though."

With that, he turned back towards the incredible sight of Annwn, laid out before them. "So, you ready?"

"Ready?" asked Harry, bewildered.

"Annwn. Ready to take a look? We've got a few things to do, you and I."

Harry, deep underground in the company of an approximately 1,000-year-old man with a thing for *Columbo*, shrugged. "Might as well."

"That's the spirit."

***

There was an elevator ride down to the ground far below, which Harry was relieved about, as he hadn't fancied making his way down on foot. The mode of transport, given recent events, had still kept him on edge, however.

At the surface level, the lift doors opened onto a wide plaza, soaked in the rays of whatever was producing the light far above. A few people wandered about, chatting and going from one place to another. They were dressed in brightly coloured garments, not quite like those of Harry's world above, but not far off. A horse and carriage rattled by, clattering across the flagstones as the driver encouraged his animal on down a wide side street and out of sight.

Around the square stood a number of handsome, sandstone buildings, some of which were clearly for trading, as they had wooden boxes full of colourful fruit and vegetables or flowers laid outside on display. A scent of fresh bread hung in the air and a shorter, longer building had seats and tables outside, where one or two couples sat eating and talking under the shade of a row of fulsome apple trees. At the centre of the plaza, a gracefully carved, marble fountain – complete with cherubs and leaping dolphins – splashed and twinkled in the gentle breeze, adding to the lazy, peaceful air of where they now stood. A tall man with long, dark, tousled hair, dressed in a smartly cut, blue, velvet three-piece suit, walked by the three of them, nodding in acknowledgement of Clive and smiling towards Little Stevie as he passed.

"Nice, eh?" said Clive, taking a deep lungful of the air.

"It's lovely. I can't quite get my head around all this," Harry stated.

"Well, we've a few things to discuss. Fancy a drink?"

"To be honest, I'm okay after that cup of tea."

"No, seriously, come for a drink," insisted Clive, indicating towards the cafe by the apple trees. Without warning, Little Stevie the 900-year-old-yet-sprightly wonder-dog leaped off in that direction, his tail wagging like an aeroplane propeller.

"There you are. Stevie's made the decision for you. You're coming for a drink." Clive nodded, looking over at his huge hound, who had found a friend to fuss and stroke him.

Harry nodded and followed Clive. As he approached the cafe, he felt the hairs on his arms start to rise and a strange, fuzzy sensation begin in his chest. Little Stevie had left his new friend standing by her table, and she watched him run off at full pelt as he came bounding enthusiastically back to both Harry and his master with the full force of a motorised shire horse.

She waved to them. It was Jade.

Harry stared. There was no mistaking her. She grinned back at him. It was all he needed. Without worrying about Little Stevie, he bounded past the enormous hound with equal excitement, across to where Jade stood. Looking at him. Alive. Happiness on her face, and her arms outstretched. He ran into them, throwing his around her in return, feeling the warmth and the beautiful reality of her shoulders, her back and her hair, and he kissed her deeply on the lips, picking her up, spinning her round, stopping and pulling back to stare. Drinking her in. Jade. Alive. Beautiful. Here. With him.

Alive.

"I'm sorry," said Harry, blinking back tears, "I do weird things when I'm scared."

25. Stupid

"It's fucking crackers down here. And I love it," Jade declared. In the half-hour that Harry had sat with Jade and Clive, she'd hardly been able to stop talking, and Harry had spent much of that time staring, either with his mouth hanging open or with a wide smile plastered across his chops. It was just too good to be with her when he'd been starting to think he'd never see her again. Certainly worth dying-but-not-dying for.

Her story was a manic one. She'd survived the lift plunge, but it had knocked her unconscious. She still carried a pearler of a black eye, but apart from some bruised ribs and knuckles, plus a few scratches, she was otherwise miraculously unhurt. The lift didn't come out of the adventure too well though, apparently.

Clive had found her, taken her back to his apartment and treated her with warming bowls of his delicious *cawl*, the occasional bacon sandwich and continual mugs of tea, all washed down with plenty of rest and an episode or two of *The Rockford Files*. During her few days in Annwn, she'd also been exploring in the company of Clive and Little Stevie. The dog had clearly taken to her, and he was now curled up by her feet as she recounted her tale.

"This place goes on for miles, Harry," she bubbled, "and it's all so beautiful. There's so much to explore. You're going to have to come with me and check out some of the scenery; there's an amazing waterfall I found with Little Stevie only yesterday. Seriously. You'd love it!"

"I'd love to, yep!" Harry smiled, just happy to get a word in.

Clive was grinning, clearly enjoying the emotional reunion he'd been waiting for, but he cleared his throat too, flashing Jade what Harry took to be a polite-but-warning look.

"Oh yeah, that," replied Jade, nodding.

Harry, still smiling too, shook his head, not understanding. "What?"

"Oh, I'll tell you in a bit. Don't worry. Anyway, did you know that they never run out of food down here? That's what this guy told me anyway," she said, nodding at Clive, who gave an abashed shrug, "along with the fact that nobody gets ill. Ever. Cancer? Diabetes? Dicky tummies? None of that, thank you very much. Seriously, this place is amazing. I'd spent all my life thinking an underworld was supposed to be a hideous place with devils poking spears up your arse, and somewhere to avoid. Turns out it's like Disneyworld on acid."

Harry grinned and nodded, looking about at the breathtaking and quite impossible scenery. Behind the cafe where they sat, a range of lush, green hills provided a delightful backdrop. Harry spied a number of walkers, tiny dots of colour against the green, strolling their way along a pathway and enjoying the sunshine. He could even make out little, stone cottages tucked away here and there on the slopes. Closer to home, Little Stevie had got up to wander to a nearby table where a young couple sat with an equally huge, white dog, who was now standing and receiving a meticulous examination of his rear end courtesy of Stevie's nose.

Harry turned to Clive. "Do you get many of us down here? From the real world? Up top, I mean?"

"Not if we can help it," Clive responded.

Harry and Jade paused uncomfortably.

Clive frowned, then burst into uncontrollable laughter. "Only kidding. No seriously, we don't. But that's more to do with the nature of this place than anything. It's protected, see, and not just by the fact that it's buried five miles down. No human can set foot down here and live. It's impossible. There's a tricky enchantment of sorts to get through, and even if you do make it this far, then mere mortals – if you'll excuse the clunky terminology – have to remain. They can't go back."

Harry continued with his uncomfortable pause. Jade wriggled in her seat a little and looked to the floor.

"So are you saying we're stuck down here?" Harry looked first at Clive, then at Jade, who was still studying the finer elements of the flagstones beneath her feet. "I mean, thank you for rescuing me and everything, but I kind of have a life up there, and now that I'm actually alive to live it, there's a few things I have to do. Tell the world about Simeon and what he's up to, for starters! Plus Jade can't stay down here. She has more of a life than I do."

"Are you going to tell him?" said Clive quickly.

Jade's head snapped back up. "Sod that, you tell him! This is your crazy town, not mine."

"What? Tell me what?" queried Harry.

Clive had been tugging on his beard thoughtfully for a moment. He sighed, let go and span his chair towards Harry with a noisy scrape against the flagstone beneath. "See now, there's a little more to you being down here than we've let on. It wasn't just your government that was after you, it was us too. That's why we rescued you; although, to be fair, that would never have happened were it not for Jade thundering down the lift shaft and making her grand entrance last week."

"Hiya!" said Jade, making jazz hands to her audience of two.

"After a bit of questioning, we were able to ascertain that she knew you, and we were able to work out the rest. It was then a question of who could get to you first. It was very nearly them, not us, Harry. We know who and what you really are, bud."

"Oh Christ, not you as well," groaned Harry, rolling his eyes to the impossible sky-blue ceiling above. "Should I be worried about you too? Are you about to cut me open and pull out my diodes, or whatever it is you need to do?"

"Did they feed you *cawl*, Harry?" asked Clive, "Make you tea? Show you wonders? Introduce you to their dog, and let it lick you?"

Harry looked thoughtfully at Little Stevie, who had wandered off from his canine companion and was now dry-humping a lamp-post.

"Don't mention the dogs," he said, "definitely don't mention those. But, no, I can't imagine Simeon is in the habit of making soup unless it was to poison or drown someone with. And when you say you know what I am and who I am, do you *really* know?"

Clive and Jade exchanged looks again.

"You have nothing to be ashamed of," said Clive, "absolutely nothing. You're not the only one, of course. But you are pretty bloody special, as it goes."

"So *you* know about..." Harry shot Jade a worried look.

She responded with a hopeful look. "You were cloned," she confirmed, stealing Clive's thunder, much to his relief.

"Hang on. You know about it?" Harry asked nervously.

She nodded back. "It's okay, truly. It's like Clive said, you've nowt to be ashamed of." She smiled warmly, grabbing Harry's hand and taking it in hers across the round table.

He felt dizzy. "But I'm not normal. I'm, well, I don't know what I am. I feel and remember so much and yet, apparently, I didn't actually do half of those things. A former, dead version of me did. I'm not really real, Jade. I'm part of some hideous experiment, and I need to get back up there and let people know, so that we can stop it."

"You were never normal, you helmet," said Jade, squeezing his hand. "That's why I like you so bloody much. I don't care if you're a robot, a human or even if you're from Nottingham. I think you're fab. And it just so happens these guys down here do too. As soon as I mentioned you, it was like I'd told this one that I was going to introduce him to Columbo himself."

"Bloody hell. Peter Falk. If only," interjected Clive.

"There's a few things you need to know about, Harry," continued Jade, ignoring Clive, "A few things I've learned while down here. For starters, if you want to stop what's happening with all your clone brothers and sisters up in our world, then I'm afraid you're too late. It's already started."

Harry looked in shock at them both, taking his hand from Jade's as he did so.

Clive nodded gravely. "The clone army is already on the move, Harry. Your British government signed a deal with the Eastern Coalition a few years back to help itself out of a financial fix from the last recession. Basically, the Eastern Coalition was interested in the secrets of the cloning technology that your dad had started years ago with Newman and Simeon. It had a view on the practical implications of using clones as a force of control in its own countries, as a way of speeding up those societies in terms of efficiency, productivity and all that jazz. Dreadful stuff. David Simeon sold you lot up the river, quite literally. Once he'd handed over the technical specifications and industry secrets – very much behind Roy Newman's back, I might add – he also worked with a few unruly government ministers to hand over rights to use the UK as a testing ground for clone technology."

"What the hell?" asked Harry, but Clive was in his flow.

Standing up with a flourish, his raincoat billowed out behind him momentarily, like a cape, adding a note of drama to proceedings. "Oh, yep, he sold you alright. Your current Prime Minister was one of those Simeon was working closely with from the outset. He needed influence and support from those at the very top, and your man with the bad blond hair and no scruples totally fitted the bill. All he needed was a campaign that could be used to get him in power, and The Change was the perfect cover to make sure he got the votes he needed. As soon as he was in, the whole thing was green-lit, as I believe you people like to say. Something to do with traffic lights, I think. I'm not sure. Anyhow," added Clive, building up to a crescendo, "there's just one more thing... "

He stood, slightly stooped, about to drop the bombshell in the style of the great TV detective himself, give or take a ginger beard. Harry and Jade waited, breathless with anticipation.

"Ah, tits. There *was* something else, but I've forgotten what it was," Clive grumbled.

Jade coughed and appeared to say that Clive had an impressive vagina.

"What's that?" asked Clive.

"Great Hunt," she replied, under her breath.

"Ah yes! That's the chappie; that's the chappie," Clive chuntered, putting Harry momentarily in mind of his former boss far above, before turning to where he sat, "Harry, if you want to get back up there and do your bit in putting a halt to the ghastliness that your government is hell-bent on dropping upon the population, then you're not going to be much use on your own. No offence, like."

"Well, none taken I suppose. But—" began Harry.

"See, we've actually got previous when it comes to helping you lot out," continued Clive, "and we've been well aware of this impending doom. Officially, our people were last up top during The Battle of Britain in the Second World War, believe it or not. We only lent a little support, but the threat of Nazi invasion was very real, so we gave your troops a bit of back-up."

"You what?"

"Oh yes, the Second World War. Then there was Fishguard back in 1797. Dear Jessica, bloody hero that one, frightening off the French like that. The English Civil War. All the way back to when Julius Caesar came knocking and a good deal further back, even as far as the days of Trevor the Ridiculous."

"You fought?"

The ancient Clive sucked at his teeth before replying. "Not as such, no. We tend to intervene more than anything, using what skills and talents we have to just give things a kick and set them back on the right path, if you like. The Great Hunt is something we undertake when things are in a mess. All our strongest and wisest – our most valiant – we all ride together across the land with the full force of the Cwn Annwn at our side, and we set things straight. I have to say though, this time is utterly, utterly different to anything we've ever encountered before."

"How so? A bit more electronic and gadgety? Men against machines?" Harry winced while saying it, not sure under which term he should file himself anymore.

"No, not that. This is more of a hunt against idiocy this time around," said Clive, as if it were the most obvious thing ever, "against a country determined to roger itself into oblivion. Never in the past has Britain been so keen to self-destruct at the cost of all that is sensible. Stupidity is a difficult beast to tame. We may even be too late as it is. The Great Hunt can only do so much, but we have to do something. We always have, and your lot need us now more than ever."

Harry was a little overwhelmed, and he didn't quite like the way that both Clive and Jade were staring at him right now. "So you're saying the country is stuffed right now? And that even all your magic and whatever isn't going to be any use? Is it really that bad? I mean, can't we just confuse the clones with a bit of their childhood? A memory of their first goldfish or something? I've seen it. It screws their brains over. They think they can see a massive, black dog, which stops them from thinking about their former lives, and then all of a sudden they're rendered useless. Can't we just do that?"

"That'd be great if there was just four or five of them, and we could sit them down in a circle and play a bit of show and tell over a few photo albums, *bachgen*," said Clive flatly, "but, the thing is, there are thousands of them, all across the country. Not just the newly released additions of Assistants, Attendants and the Aegis, but all the clones who were dotted throughout society already from the early test runs. Teachers, doctors, nurses, bus drivers, ice-cream sellers. You name it. All now working to their new programs. All apart from you, Harry Salt."

Harry's shoulders dropped. He sighed and held his arms out in a shrug. "Why do I get the feeling I'm not going to like this? Do you want my brain or not? Clearly you need me for something to get this sorted."

Clive gave Harry a frank look, his beard bristling as he did so. "We don't need your brain, Harry."

"My anus then? My sphincter? How does this work? Go on, take what you need."

"Harry, chill the fuck out," chastised Jade, "he doesn't want to take anything from you. Keep your hair on."

"I don't need that either," added Clive, "although it is quite the lustrous bouffant. A credit to your barber. No, Harry, the reason you're of such interest to your government and the reason you were able to make your way down into Annwn without falling foul of any blocking enchantments is because you carry a piece of Annwn within you."

"Oh, stop it," scoffed Harry. "I'm sure your heart and soul will remain forever Welsh, too. But I've never set foot here before."

"No, truly, you do," said Clive, ignoring Harry's rebuff and pointing towards the great mountain in the distance, "a shard of crystal from within that mountain over yonder. The tiniest sliver, but it's there, and it's what makes you different from all the other clones and your regular humans up there. It's what keeps you going, and it means you can travel between this world and the one above with no bother. In the same way that all your wrist-worn timepieces of which you are so fond use quartz to accurately tell the time, you too carry a crystal within you that gives you abilities above and beyond those of your peers."

Harry paused. "Did you just compare me to a wristwatch?"

"I think he did, yeah," answered Jade. "You'd look nice in a strap too. Bit more Mickey Mouse than Rolex, though," she added, before winking at him with her blackened eye and then wishing immediately that she'd used the other one.

Harry flushed briefly, before pursuing Clive's line of thought. "So go on then. Great Hunt across the land; lots of wise and strong types; horses; huge, white dogs; and no doubt lots of cheering and flags of some kind. You want me to tell them the time whenever someone asks? Beep when it's time for them all to wake up?"

"I wish I hadn't mentioned the watch. Sorry," apologised Clive. "No, that's not really it. We need you to get more of the crystal to the surface so that we can get as many of the clones on side to work with us rather than against us during the Great Hunt."

"To convert them? So they can bypass the program Simeon is feeding them, like I do with the black dogs?"

"Essentially, yes! You've got it." Clive was brimming with enthusiasm.

Jade was nodding too. She'd obviously learned a great deal about Harry and what he was supposed to do in her few days down here, which he found left him feeling a little inferior.

"So what on earth do I have to do with anything? Can't you just do that yourselves? And I hate to remind you, but didn't you mention that there's thousands of the buggers roaming around up there, all doing nasty clone stuff? You'd never be able to perform the surgery to convert them all one by one, surely? I might not be a watch, but even I can tell you that kind of thing takes time."

"No, Harry. We have a way around such things. However, if we're going to be able to get more of the crystal, we're going to need you to fetch and use it," Clive confirmed.

"Me? Why? Again, can't you do it?"

Clive shook his head sorrowfully. "Sorry, Harry, but it absolutely has to be you. Anyone who touches the crystal slowly loses their mind and goes insane, such is its awesome power. Neither I, nor any of the rest of the Tylwyth Teg, nor any human from your part of the world can get within but a few feet of it before it starts to degrade their brain. You, however, you carry it within you already. It's part of who you are. You can touch it, lick it, exfoliate with it as part of a grooming regime, whatever the dickens you want. Nevertheless, for the purposes of this mission, we need you to get it up top to your neck of the woods, to a truly mystical place – one of tremendous wonder and enchantment where, we believe, we can turn things around and guide Britain away from the horrors it is currently languishing in and back to times of freedom, hope and safety."

Harry breathed in deeply, processing all he'd just heard. "And this mystical place. Does it have a name?"

"It does." Clive nodded, a sparkle in his eyes as he rose to his feet, his heart thumping. He looked to the sky, and as two giant black ravens flew high above, floating majestically on the breeze, he nodded determinedly and spoke with deep pride and reverence in his voice.

"Chesterfield."

26. Mountain

"Chesterfield? Really, though?"

The process of collecting the crystal had been much easier than either of them had expected. Now Harry and Jade were making their way back across the plain towards Vandwy, the stronghold town that stood between this world and the one above, and where a nervous Clive awaited their return.

"Yeah, I've got the feeling that Clive probably hasn't been to Chesterfield in a long, long time," answered Harry to Jade's outburst.

This particular late afternoon in Annwn was a warm one, and the 'sun' was slowly working its way downwards behind the mountain they were walking back from. A gentle breeze kept them both nicely cool and whispered its way through the long grass fields that stretched out either side of the worn path they walked along.

Harry continued, "Although, saying that, there are a couple of nice coffee shops near the church. Crooked Spires does lovely home-cooked soups. Old Clive would be in his element."

It had been a lovely walk there and back, and for the first time in goodness only knows how long, Harry had felt his shoulders drop in relaxation as he took in the world of Annwn with Jade. It was as beautiful as any national park, quiet but for the singing of birds and the soft wind that would sometimes blow through the valley to tease the trees and tousle Jade's hair.

Clive had packed them both off a few hours before with a canvas rucksack filled with treats: huge apples, a few Welsh cakes, a flask of sugared coffee and a cheese-and-tomato sandwich each. The entrance to the cavern where the crystal was kept had been easy enough to reach, located as it was around 250 yards from the valley floor, and accessible via a footworn path and, finally, a set of steps up the mountainside.

Above the entrance, chiselled into the rockface, was a piece of writing in an alphabet and language that neither of them had recognised. Two equally chiselled and handsome guards – one male, one female and both tall – stood to attention at either side of the lair's opening. Both were smartly dressed in maroon velvet and armed with a long, bronze spear each. Their eyes flicked immediately to them both as they arrived, and as neither Harry nor Jade were expecting to encounter them, they both were taken aback as they ascended the last few steps. Their fears were quickly allayed, however, as the guards simply smiled back and nodded in recognition.

The female guard rested her spear against the rockface and stepped forwards, her hand outstretched. "Harry, Jade. Welcome to the Cave of the Blessed Crow. My name is Nia. We've been expecting you."

Harry shook her hand first, then Jade. Nia's hand was slender but strong, her skin smooth to the touch.

Harry cleared his throat, smiling back. "Clive said you might be ready for us. Nice to meet you."

"How is Clive, the old coot?" asked the other guard, also coming forwards to meet them both and shake hands, "Sorry, my name's Hedd," he added, his accent a lighter version of the Welsh that they'd both encountered so far, his hand a chunky and equally strong version of Nia's.

They'd exchanged a quick and pleasant conversation, during which Harry and Jade were both made to feel very welcome, almost to the point of embarrassment. Nia and Hedd had taken them both into the cavern, which was huge and candlelit. Multicoloured stalagmites and stalactites sparkled in the flickering light, growing upwards and descending downwards from the shiny, wet rockface. A set of ancient, carved steps led down to a shallow pit, in the middle of which stood a giant cauldron.

Neither of them had ever seen anything like it, and Jade was quick to point this out.

"What the fuck is that?" she said slowly, marvelling at the sight before her. "I mean, pardon my Spanish, I can see it's a cauldron and everything, but that is something else."

And so it was. Standing at about chest height, the giant, black pot was about twenty yards in diameter, and despite the glow emanating from the many candles arranged around the cavern, it appeared to have no bottom, only a deep, black space within that seemed to suck in any and all available light, crumple it all up and then sit on it belligerently.

The rim of the cauldron was finished with a wide and beautiful band of aquamarine marble, interlaced with a gilded inscription in a language that appeared to match that which they'd both seen above the cavern entrance. Upon closer inspection, it was clear that the cauldron had at some point, likely long ago, been repaired after one almighty shattering. Long cracks in the outer surface were only just visible, running from top to bottom or veering off in different directions like forks of lightning or giant veins, all sealed back together as part of some fantastic, ancient welding job.

"So, erm, where's the crystal?" Harry had asked, still impressed by the cauldron, but not seeing anything that fit the bill.

"We are to summon it," said Nia pleasantly, "just give us a sec, and we'll get things going, alright, love?"

"Ah. Right. Of course. Please, don't let us stop you."

They didn't, not that they could have anyway, given the size of them. Instead, Harry and Jade had stood to one side while Nia and Hedd joined hands by the cauldron; the guards remained in silence for a moment before beginning to chant hauntingly in a strange dialect that had an alluring, almost soothing cadence to it.

There was no telling how long the guards stood chanting. It could have been minutes or it could have been as long as an hour. At one point, Jade coughed involuntarily. Nia started and stared at them both, without breaking hands from Hedd, who continued to chant. But the stare was enough to silence them both, as her eyes glowed a blank, shocking and burning pale-blue until she snapped them shut again.

Although neither Harry nor Jade was sure how long it took when they reflected back upon the moment, they were both eventually able to discern a faint light shining from within the gargantuan pot. As they watched in astonishment, a fragment of translucent, purple crystal began to rise from the light, pulsing as it rose before solidifying in front of them. It continued this way until a complete shard – about as thick and long as Harry's arm – had emerged, floating just above the marbled rim.

As Nia and Hedd drew their chanting to a close, Harry and Jade stared on in wonder at the hovering crystal. It was a beautiful, impossible sight, reflecting and refracting the candlelight into wondrous shades of sparkling purple, the likes of which...

"You need to grab it quick, like," said Hedd, his eyes tightly closed and still holding hands with Nia. "Go on, we can't touch it. It'll melt our brains. Hop to it, will you?"

"Oh! Right. Yes, sorry," apologised Harry, making his way awkwardly to the cauldron. "Like this?" He reached out his arms until his finger ends were almost able to make contact.

Nia, beads of sweat on her brow and clearly in some discomfort, opened one eye and nodded quickly. Disturbingly, it still glowed blue.

Harry grabbed at it and managed to catch a lump on the surface, causing it to spin slowly away from his grasp in mid-air. "Shit, come on you bastard," he said between his teeth, straining against the side of the cauldron with his fingers fully extended.

"Hang on, Harry. Dangle over the edge, and I'll grab your legs," offered Jade, coming to his assistance.

The two guards continued their vigil with strained looks upon their faces, groaning slightly as Harry hefted himself onto the rim.

All at once, he overbalanced, and he experienced a sickening feeling as his head and torso swung into the blackness of the cauldron.

"DON'T FALL IN, FOR GOD'S SAKE; YOU CLUMSY SOD," yelled Hedd in panic, despite the fact he still had his eyes shut.

Fortunately, the next thing Harry felt was Jade's arms locking around his legs, pulling him back and steadying him. With his heaving stomach resting on the cauldron rim, Harry was able to reach out haphazardly, gasping, as his fingers clasped around the cold, purple mineral. Moments later, he was back on the ground, panting and clasping the crystal tightly to his chest.

Hedd and Nia breathed a huge sigh of relief together, blinked and turned to look at the dishevelled pair who had recently descended from five miles above. The guards eyes were normal once more.

"Well, you made a bloody meal of that didn't you?" scolded Nia. "Thought you were a goner there. You alright?"

Harry breathed noisily and looked down at the heavy shard in his hands, nodding. "Yeah, I think so. God, look at the colours in this thing," he said, holding up the crystal to the light.

Hedd and Nia jumped back instinctively as he did so.

"Be careful with that, yeah?" chided Hedd, "Remember that you're the only one to touch it, and it's got some bloody important work to do. It'll be at least another fifty years before anyone can summon a crystal even a third the size of that, so look after it."

"Of course, sorry." Harry nodded, gingerly easing it inside his rucksack and gritting his teeth in silent embarrassment as he felt a half-eaten cheese-and-tomato sandwich squelching underneath it.

So, they were now heading back, and as they neared the outskirts of Vandwy, they passed a couple of carefree walkers – a young couple enjoying the sunshine and holding hands, who smiled and acknowledged them both. Beyond, the huge expanse of rockface loomed menacingly, reminding them just how deeply underground they were, which was something that was easy to forget when it felt like they were outdoors on a spring afternoon. Harry hefted the rucksack onto his shoulder, as it had grown steadily heavier the longer they'd walked. Its weight alone was a constant reminder that there was work to do, and that an important and potentially dangerous task lay ahead.

They'd been walking in silence for a while now, and Harry had the sense that Jade was priming herself to ask an awkward question. Given recent events, Harry reflected, it could be one of a number that were waiting to be asked.

"Harry, we've not really talked about it, and I guess you haven't really had chance to talk to anyone about it either," she fluffed.

"Go on," he prompted.

"Well, with you now being, erm... You know. Different."

"A cloned version of me, yes."

"That. Yes, that. Well, how is it making you feel? Clive was able to explain some things about it before he went up with some others and rescued you, but he was only guessing at how you might be dealing with it. I just wanted to make sure you're okay. Tell me to bugger off if I'm prying." She grabbed his hand and held on to it as they walked, which felt good.

He gave it a squeeze back by way of a thank you before answering. "It's... it's odd. Honestly, I don't really feel all that different. At first, I was like, well, so I'm not real. I felt almost like I'd been lied to. The idea of dying and then being brought back? It's crackers, isn't it?"

Jade nodded sympathetically.

He went on, "When I've pondered about it, it feels so odd to think that what I perceive as memories aren't that at all, but they're just lines of code or whatever, being sent from a processor and fired down pathways in my brain to convince me that I actually did them. Everything I was, my memories, and the way I feel about and react to things, it's all in that chip, and the rest of me is, well, a body that was grown in a laboratory."

"That must be so weird to deal with. I'm sorry, Harry. I feel like you've been to hell and back recently, and that it's partly been my fault."

"Don't be daft. How so?"

"Well," mused Jade, "if it weren't for me and my daft urge to explore the MOP for a bit of fun, then you would never have ended up going through all the things you went through. You might still be blissfully unaware about everything."

"I'd have found out eventually. The government was going to get to me one way or the other. God, don't be blaming yourself!" He squeezed her hand again. "Don't get me wrong, this whole thing is crazy. I mean, look around us. It's insane. We're five miles underground with a bunch of immortal Welsh people who have a thing for velvet. And as far as my view of myself goes – what I am and how I feel about it – well, that changes by the second. I'm just trying not to think about it too much at the moment, to be honest."

"I'm sorry, I shouldn't have mentioned it."

"No. Jade, please, don't be silly. I will talk about it eventually, but right now I'm more concerned about my role in all of this – everything that's happening at home. It's because of me – or at least the technology that Dad and the others set in motion by creating me – that things are going the way they are. People are suffering and are in danger because of this technology and the way it's being used. I feel responsible. I want to do something about it, something that's going to make a difference. And because of who or what I am, I can. I need this. It's, well, validating somehow. It gives me purpose."

Jade stopped, but kept a tight hold of Harry's hand, causing him to spin around and face her.

"What?" he asked.

Jade held her silence, staring into his eyes, a small grin spreading its way across her face. Harry took it in. The mountain and the setting sun behind her.

"You know, Harry, it's not just about the memories you already have, the ones from your former life. It's the ones that you're still making. The life you're living now. There's no black dog here. You're living as much a life as anyone else. I don't care if you were made in a womb or a microwave oven. It makes no difference to me whatsoever. You're just as Salty as the other Harry Salt," she announced.

And with that, she pulled him to her, her hands grabbing him beneath his rucksack to draw him closer still. Harry let her, never once thinking of resisting, his hands snaking round to the base of her spine and feeling the beautiful curve of her back beneath her t-shirt. They held each other, as two swallows sung nearby before darting past and away towards the mountain in their own sunlit dance, celebrating the afternoon and the evening to come.

"That means the world," Harry said, smiling deeply before kissing Jade deeper still, absorbing every tender feeling that was pulsing through him – every last second of it.

***

Before they even reached the plaza, hand in hand, it was clear that the mood of the town was a different one to that which they had left in the morning. A team of horses clattered towards and across the square, each with a rider, as a couple of stable hands ran alongside and shouted them on. The fruit-and-vegetable traders whom Harry had glimpsed the day before were busily carrying wooden crates full of food, hurrying in the direction in which the horses had just been ridden. A number of carts were being loaded with boxes of something that the two of them couldn't quite discern, while a young girl with a checklist noted and counted each one as it was hauled aboard.

Voices filled the air, and everybody around them seemed engaged in one task or another. As they headed towards where the elevator stood shut, at the base of the rockface, the twin doors rumbled open and out stepped Clive with big Little Stevie at his side. Clive's face was grave with worry, but brightened a little as he caught sight of Harry and Jade, noting briefly with a raised eyebrow that they were holding hands.

"You're back. Good-o. Get the crystal alright, did you?" Clive enquired.

Harry swung the heavy pack off his back and opened it up. Clive took a look gingerly before recoiling as if he'd taken a lungful of steaming, fresh horse manure. "Bugger me, so you have. Right. Brilliant. Well done."

Jade looked about as a group of athletic men and women, looking to all intents and purposes like a squad of Roman soldiers, jogged past in a small group of around ten or twelve, each carrying a spear. "What's the craic?" she asked, "I thought we weren't due to start preparations until the weekend?"

"Bit of a change of plan," said Clive, ruffling Little Stevie's hair as he spoke. "This morning, about twenty minutes or so after you set off, the lift from your part of the world – from the MOP, that is – came clattering back down."

"I thought it was knackered," replied Jade.

"So did we. All of a sudden, it was hauled back up and seemingly replaced. When it came back down, it had four of those furry, white Alex creatures inside of it. Alive."

"That can't be right, though, surely?" queried Harry as another team of horses made their way past, with a rider shouting across the plaza at someone. "Everything electronic that gets sent down gets fried, doesn't it? That old enchantment you were telling us about?"

"Well, that was always normally the case, but not this time. The four of them were able to wriggle their way out of the lift and managed to keep going for about ten yards before they short-circuited and their eyes went dark. One of them managed to sink his teeth into my mate Pete's foot, which caused a helluva fuss. God only knows how, but your lot are clearly on to something up there, and they're getting more and more interested in what's down here. Those Alex robots are fitted with cameras, and we can only hope that they didn't manage to film anything and transmit it back before the sparks flew and they copped it. And that's not all," he continued with a shake of his head, "Our source from your world has gone dark this last few days too. We've no way of knowing how things are above us now or what this latest delivery in the lift is all about. So we're getting things moving. The decision's been made. The Great Hunt rides tonight."

***

That night, in a large, high-ceilinged hall a short walk away from the main square, hundreds of people had gathered, including Harry and Jade. They sat on one of a number of long benches, which – with accompanying tables that were stacked high with food – appeared to run the length of the hall. It was warm with so many bodies in there, and the lighted torches that burned from the walls gave the place a cosy, yellow glow.

Clive was sat at their side, standing out a mile in his crumpled raincoat (which seemed to bother nobody), while Little Stevie curled up under the table giving them virtually no legroom whatsoever. As various chieftains, leaders and other important folk stood to talk tactics regarding the Great Hunt, Clive translated parts of what was said for them, as everything that was spoken was done so in Welsh from a high stage at the far end of the hall. Apart from the salutary, "*Iechyd da*," every time tankards brimming with beer were raised (which was often – these people could really drink!), Harry hadn't recognised a single word and was willing to bet Jade was in the same position.

Around them sat women and men of all shapes and sizes, and of all ages. There appeared to be no one younger than twenty, as far as Harry could make out, but given that Clive himself was the best part of ten centuries old and looked a lot like he'd only just taken early retirement from the civil service, he wasn't about to make any judgements. Everyone looked healthy. Strong. Their eyes all burned brightly and with intention, and there was a sense of excited anticipation in the air. There were other large, white dogs in the room too, all of a size similar to Little Stevie and with flashes of red on their ears.

At the centre of the raised stage sat a white-haired man in a dark-red cloak, who had the appearance of someone in his forties. He was well-built and muscular, but had a kind air about him that Harry warmed to without quite knowing why. The man was sitting listening intently to a slender lady with long, blonde hair that spilled down across the shoulders of her dark-blue cloak. She was sitting at his left shoulder, talking earnestly, while he occasionally nodded as she spoke. At their feet was a white dog that was slightly bigger than Little Stevie, and who appeared to be short of one ear.

"That chap is Gwynn," said Clive in a hushed tone, noticing where Harry's attention was, "and that's his dog, Dormarch. They'll be leading the Great Hunt tonight. They've both seen a lot of action between them, so they've got tonnes of experience on their side, but I think Gwynn would've been happier if he'd had an extra day or two to get everyone ready. Still, there we are."

"Is Gwynn in charge?" asked Jade.

"Oh yes. Gwynn, son of Nudd, is king of the Tylwyth Teg, and so Annwn is his kingdom so to speak. The beautiful lady to his left will be in charge while he's away. She's the Lady Creiddylad."

"Easy for you to say," muttered Harry before being met with a sharp look from Clive.

Jade rolled her eyes and looked to her feet.

"Don't get cocky, *bachgen Saesneg*. Those two are very much aware of who you both are, and while you may have an important job to do – and thank you very much for all that, by the way – you're very much honoured guests down here. And we're doing your lot upstairs a favour seeing as it was them who mucked everything up in the first place," Clive elucidated.

At that moment, Gwynn's gaze and that of Lady Creiddylad (and Dormarch, unsettlingly) *fell* upon Harry and Jade. It was a stare that they both felt as much as saw. Jade nudged Harry, and they both smiled weakly back at their royal hosts, who in return smiled broadly and nodded back at them from where they sat.

"Did we just get a nod and a wink from a king and queen?" asked Jade.

"I think so, yeah," mumbled Harry "We'd really best not fuck this up, had we?"

"I think it would be wise not to." Jade nodded, still grinning. "Just wait 'til I tell my mum, though."

"There you are," said Clive, smiling enthusiastically at their royal approval, "You'll be fine so long as you do what you're told."

The king and queen had now turned their attention to other matters, and were busily held up in conversation with two others on the stage.

"But we don't speak Welsh!" groaned Harry.

"Buddha on a bicycle, Harry!" exclaimed Clive, "We can do bilingual when we need to. Trilingual, quadrilingual and, well, whatever five lingual is. We've been around a lot longer than the English language, and a lot longer than the English, come to that. In fact, if I were to... Oh, bugger here we go."

Clive was halted from his tribal diatribe as a reverent hush descended, and the king and queen stood together to speak. With Clive translating for Harry and Jade, the two royal figureheads of the Tylwyth Teg calmly put forward their plans for the Great Hunt, in impressive voices that called everyone together to listen, cutting a silence so quiet that you could hear an atom drop, bounce and roll around on the floor, never mind anything else.

All participants of the Great Hunt were to ride forth and make their appearance almost directly above, taking advantage of Derbyshire's central position in the country, to ride out to all corners until the objective was achieved, the 'dead were brought alive once more' and Britain was freed from the tyranny of dangerous fools. It was expected that the Great Hunt would be completed before the sun rose, which Clive explained was the standard for this type of thing; at this point, Harry glanced at his watch and attempted to do some maths, before giving up quickly.

According to the final update from Annwn's source above, prior to winking out into silence, the government's plan was to install Aegis forces in every large town and city to enforce curfews and quash any forms of resistance or uprising. These particular clones were known to be strong, resolute and indefatigable by design, and it was likely that they would have already stamped their muddy boot-mark of authority upon the populace. On top of that, they were likely to be armed too.

In a sober voice, Clive translated that it was also likely that most, if not all of the remaining clones across Britain were now working under the orders of the government, thanks to a burst of electronic code broadcast from a source on or near to "the White Hill of *Llundain* where Brân forever watches" (at which point Clive corrected himself by adding, "The Tower of London to you folk"). The final part of the Great Hunt would see the king lead all remaining riders to destroy the mast and ensure that it could never be rebuilt, before returning to Annwn "as the wren announces the morning".

It was further disclosed that, prior to the final task in London, the riders were to divide into separate teams to take the Great Hunt to all areas of the land before regrouping and descending upon the sleeping capital. The first task for the Great Hunt centred on Chesterfield, however (or 'Caer Maes', which Harry noticed the king called it, as it was referenced a number of times). Harry's ears pricked up as he heard both his and Clive's names mentioned, before the entire crowd gathered in the hall turned to get a better look at them both, following the pointing finger of their king.

With no time to translate, Clive nudged Harry in the ribs. "Stand up, man. King's orders." Harry did as he was told, blood rushing to blush his face, and faced everyone. Slowly, following a clap from the king's huge hands, the assembled warriors and riders that made up the congregation broke out in heartfelt applause, grinning and nodding, and then standing in salutation one by one until everyone was on their feet. It was a magical feeling – a heady mix of pride and bashfulness unlike any he'd ever experienced – bettered only by the kiss and hug that came from a proud and grinning Jade a second later.

When the applause was over and Harry, red as a balloon, had sat back down, Clive turned to him and stated, "So, no pressure whatsoever, but the reason everyone applauded you is partially down to the enormity and importance of the task you're specifically riding to complete, which the remainder of the Great Hunt is depending on you for."

"I thought you said, 'no pressure'?" Harry queried.

"Okay, well, some pressure. A bit. I might as well be honest. A lot of pressure. Enough to squash a small child or a rock perhaps. Anyhow, the crystal has to be taken, by you, to the Church of St Mary and All Saints. Specifically, the font in the south transept. Once you place it there, it will work to transmit its power across the land, returning all clones back to an unaffected state, and thus reducing the amount of opposition we're likely to face for the remainder of the Great Hunt, especially once it reaches London. As the tiny shard of crystal works within you, it's hoped that the burst of energy we send out will work to affect all clones similarly."

"Hoped?"

"Well, when was the last time you heard of Britain being overrun by cloned people with electrical bits and bobs sewn in? It's not like anyone has done this before, and while our best and brightest are very hopeful that this will sort things out, there's no way of knowing for sure. But it's the best and only shot we've got. The Great Hunt is only able to ride out once every fifty years. Stuff this up and you've got at least another half-century under Royds Spittoon and his creatures. And I'm not just talking about his Cabinet, either."

Harry shuddered. "And what's likely to happen to me, given that I'm cloned too? Will I be okay?"

Clive sucked at his beard and gritted his teeth before answering. "Well, we're not entirely sure to be honest," he began, continuing quickly as a shocked Jade attempted to speak, "but we're fairly certain that – because you already carry the crystal and you've been doing so since you were, well... erm... reborn, like – you should be alright. Yeah, you'll be alright. Most likely."

Neither Harry, Jade nor even Clive himself looked reassured by this.

"Just one more thing, however," said Clive, a twinkle in his eye as he changed the subject, "we drink. Right now, we drink."

Three huge tankards of beer were placed onto the table before them, froth sloshing over the sides as they made contact with the heavy, wooden surface.

"Drinking before the Great Hunt?" asked Jade uncertainly. "Is that really a good idea?"

"Drinking is always a good idea," answered Clive mischievously, "doubly so in Annwn. There's no illness down here, so no hangovers. Get those down you; you can enjoy the buzz, but feel as fresh as a daisy before you head out. Shandy sharpener. *Iechyd da!* Bottoms up!"

And with that, Clive swept his pot from the table and glugged at it, foam decorating his beard. With everyone else in the hall doing likewise, Harry and Jade picked up their mugs and raised them unsteadily.

"Down the hatch, Saltychops," commanded Jade to her soon-to-be riding companion, who shrugged back and started to drink.

Moments later, Harry threw up. The entire hall erupted in an almighty cheer.

27. Hunt

Harry had never ridden a horse before. Neither, it quickly turned out, had Jade. They stood together in the gloaming as the dark rose, in a large field surrounded by the active hustle and bustle as riders mounted their giant chargers, some with swords across their backs, others with spears, and yet others with quivers full of arrows. As the excitement rose palpably, they both looked fearfully at the entire scene unfolding inexorably around them.

"May I just say that I feel hideously out of place right now?" said Jade.

Harry nodded glumly, his backpack now feeling heavier than ever.

"I mean, how the hell are we supposed to even get up on one of those things, never mind stay on it?"

They stepped back swiftly as a massive and muscular white horse, its rider carrying a huge, white flag emblazoned with a raven in flight, galloped past to join the team of horses to the west of them.

"Fuck knows," answered Harry, "and to be honest, I feel utterly pants right now. That beer turned my stomach. I thought people weren't supposed to get ill down here?"

"That's because you tried to drink it too quickly, plus the

fact you're a lightweight. Standard physics. Nothing to do with illness. The feeling you're experiencing right now is more likely fear."

"Hmmm. And where's Clive? I like having him around; I feel like he helps everything make sense, even when I don't want him to because the truth is actually just too horrendous."

"I haven't seen him since we joined the stampede out of the hall."

Beyond the field, Harry could spy an orange glow emanating from the windows of the stone-built hillside cottages either side of the valley. He wanted that warmth right now, that security away from all of this. He thought back to his grandparents' living room far above, remembering in an instant sitting in his favourite armchair, the one he always fell asleep in by the fireplace on weekends. He remembered how Grandma used to tease him lovingly about it before putting out triangular ham sandwiches that she had made for him and Grandpa, and how Grandpa used to cut his into smaller, bite-sized triangles with his butter knife, as a dark blur bounded enthusiastically past the conservatory window...

"Harry, Jade," spoke a rich, deep, friendly voice.

Harry blinked back to the here and now to see a tall, handsome, white-haired man in a deep-red cloak approaching them both, accompanied by a beautiful, blonde-haired woman dressed in deep blue. He carried a flaming torch and the hilt of an ornate sword could be seen over his left shoulder. As King Gwynn held out his hand to Harry, Jade found herself curtseying, an act which elicited a delighted smile from Lady Creiddylad.

"Your Highness," said Harry reverently, shaking his hand, his head bowed.

King Gwynn chuckled. "Not really, given as we all live so far beneath the earth, but I'll take it. I'll be high enough, soon enough. You can call me that then. Until then, Gwynn is fine, truly. This is my wife, the Lady Creiddylad."

Again, Harry shook her hand and bowed.

"It really is a pleasure to meet you both," she said, the pleasant smile on her face every bit a part of the warmth in her voice, "and I'm so glad that you can join the Great Hunt with us. It's been a very, very long time since anyone from your world has ridden with the pack, and we are honoured to have you with us."

Harry hefted his rucksack onto both shoulders in an effort to spread the weight a little. "I hope I don't let you down," was all he could find to say, awestruck as he still was.

Immediately, Gwynn set his heavy hand to Harry's shoulder. "You won't, I'm certain of it. You come from good stock, and Annwn has been long beating in your heart, even when you weren't aware of it. It gives you real strength within, more than you can possibly know of. Besides, I'll be right with you during the first part of the Great Hunt, to guide and protect you as far as the church of Caer Maes – my apologies – Chesterfield. From there, we'll ride on to London, but you will need to stay to guard the crystal. It must stay in place in the church until we've destroyed the mast on the White Hill."

Harry nodded. He didn't dare show his fear, but as he searched for it, he found it had waned at King Gwynn's touch. He stared up at the leader of the Great Hunt, who looked down at him with warm eyes filled with encouragement, his torch flaming above them and creating a hot, temporary grotto in which the four of them now stood together.

Gwynn continued, "I'm not going to say it will be easy, Harry. This will be a Great Hunt unlike any other – beyond imagining, almost. It will be fraught with danger, and yet I trust and believe in every one of my men and women. We're experienced, we are strong and we have the light on our side. I come from battle and conflict, and we have cheered the Cwn Annwn over the chair of Idris many times over centuries past. We will do it again tonight, and you will be an important part of it all, brave Harry Salt. That goes for you too, Jade Birch."

And with that, he shook Harry's hand once again before following the Lady Creiddylad, with Harry and Jade watching the royal couple as the glow from the torch followed them both into the crowd.

"We're still not going to be able to get up on one of those chuffing horses," sighed Harry.

Jade took his hand in hers and gave it a squeeze. All of a sudden, there was a discernible change in the air. As they watched, the mounted horses were ridden to form into ranks on a high slope at the far end of the field. The noise generated by hundreds of hooves and the shouting warriors encouraging their steeds was enormous and infectious, like the roar of a football crowd. Within seconds, they stood waiting impressively, poised. Harry estimated that somewhere between eighty to a hundred mounted horses were arranged on the hillside. A hush descended. From within the ranks rode King Gwynn and the Lady Creiddylad, impressive, stoic and every bit as regal as their titles befit them. They remained front and centre of the cavalcade, facing where Harry and Jade looked back at them from a distance of some 200 or so yards. Silent. Primed. Ready.

A cheer then rose from the direction of the town centre, followed immediately by a single piercing howl. That in turn was followed by a chorus of howls in response, and then, as the other-worldly sound echoed and reverberated across the valley, the baying hounds of the Cwn Annwn came thundering towards them, with Dormarch leading the pack. It was an incredible sight to see them thunder past and on up the slope towards the waiting Great Hunt, with at least sixty of the giant dogs sprinting and barking, around and eventually back to the front of the assembled ranks before lining up, one by one, behind the king and queen, and falling silent. They sat erect on their hind legs, their tongues lolling and steam rising from their panted breaths. Ready.

Jade squeezed Harry's hand ever tighter.

"So... what do we do now?" whispered Harry to Jade, feeling more inadequate than ever.

"I don't know. Should we maybe... " she began.

"Maybe what?" asked Harry, but Jade's attention was else-where, listening.

"What the...? Is that what I think it is?"

Harry listened too. There was something on the breeze, a sound coming from beyond the town and getting gradually clos-er. It set him on edge. It was an unnatural, terrible sound – a scream that was rising and falling in pitch. He turned wide-eyed to Jade, before adopting a puzzled expression instead.

"It sounds like... a police car," he declared.

Sure enough, as they turned to look back towards the town and the source of the noise, a pulsing, red light was reflecting onto the looming, sheer rockface behind as the sound grew. From behind the furthest outlying building, along the track and into the field screamed what appeared to be a red Gran Tori-no with white vector stripes running down either side, its si-ren wailing, a red light flashing above the driver's side, and the lights on full beam. As the engine roared and the car tore across the grass, Harry and Jade turned back to the assembled Great Hunt. It remained exactly as it was, primed and ready, utterly unmoved by this wild, noisy and ridiculous sight. The car au-dibly changed gear and raced past Harry and Jade, up towards the slope, following the exact same route that the hounds of the Cwn Annwn had taken moments before. Up it went, past the filed ranks of dogs, horses and riders, behind them all and then back down, gathering speed and returning before swerving to a skidding halt in front of Jade and Harry, who were preparing to dive out of the way.

This was a beautiful piece of machinery, shining as if brand new, its engine purring, and the whole thing fully worthy of the goggling eyes with which they were drinking it in. As the siren faded to silence, the driver-side window wound down slowly to reveal the beaming face of an ecstatic Clive, dressed now in an awful black-and-cream knitted cardigan and a black beanie hat.

"Alright, you two! Ready to face the hordes then? Your carriage awaits!" he announced.

"Clive? What in the dickens is this all about?" asked Harry.

"And you'd be perfectly entitled to ask, young fellow-my-lad. This'll be my ninetieth Great Hunt and to celebrate, and also by way of a thank you for all my centuries of service, King Gwynn himself has decreed that I could ride into battle in whatever form of transport I wished. So here we are – a 1975 Ford Gran Torino. She's a beauty. We're going to *Starsky and Hutch* the living shit out of this one."

"Oh my God, I fucking love it," said Jade.

At that, Clive chuckled before opening the door and pulling his seat forwards to allow her in. Little Stevie sat in the back seat, tongue lolling and eyes bright, clearly loving the whole experience every bit as much as his master.

"Harry, you hop round the other side and get in the front. Stick your rucksack in the boot for now, as it'll be safer in there. Stevie? Stevie, lad! Hutch up, will you? Give Jade room to get in. Ha! Hutch up! See what I did there? Ha!"

Once they were in, with the doors slammed shut, Jade cooped up behind Clive with what little room the giant dog afforded her. Harry strapped in to ride shotgun beside Clive Starsky, as the intercom buzzed and King Gwynn's rich voice came through the speakers. "Clive, I take it you're all ready to join us?"

Clive licked his lips, relishing every moment of his special treat. He grabbed the intercom from the centre of the dash and clicked it into life. "Ten-four, Your Majesty, this is Zebra Three confirmed ready to ride; VIPs on board and special cargo stored in the trunk. All set to rendezvous with Huggy Bear in Bay City, over and out."

"What?"

"Er, sorry, Your Majesty. Yes, we're ready to go."

Harry wasn't sure, but he thought he heard a sigh before the radio fell silent. There was no time to dwell on it, however, or even to get himself comfy in the leather seat, as at that moment a single, long blast on a horn was heard from within the Great Hunt. The sound hung in the air, reverberating around them, and as it did so, Jade noticed movement from the riders, who all seemed to be massaging their faces in unison.

"What are they doing? Moisturising?" she questioned.

"They're blacking up," confirmed Clive, looking ahead, focussed, with one hand on the gearstick and one on the steering wheel.

"Is that even allowed now, though? I mean—"

"It's just a couple of stripes on each cheek."

"Oh."

Another long blast followed, at which all riders – including Clive – raised their heads to the heavens and called, "ANNWN" at the top of their voices.

Harry and Jade yelped, Little Stevie licked Jade's face in response, Clive simultaneously pulled down on the gearstick and floored the accelerator, everyone in the car was thrown back into their seats, and the siren on the roof began to howl. Outside, the Great Hunt thundered forwards, riders roaring with swords raised, and the Cwn Annwn yelping their terrible barks into the night sky of the underworld as King Gwynn led the charge. Soon, they were alongside the Gran Torino – racing ahead, falling back and surrounding it – the cyclonic, whirling, red light illuminating determined, yelling faces; the blurred rise and fall of galloping hooves; gleaming weapons strapped across broad backs; and banners depicting ravens, wrens, red kites, boars and hounds proudly displayed. The Great Hunt powered forwards with a deafening rumble, as a single dynamic organism racing beyond the mountain, across the plains and up, up towards the surface of a sleeping, unsuspecting Britain.

The Great Hunt was wild.

28. Chesterfield

It was a quiet night across the peaks of Derbyshire. In the villages, people slept in their beds, with curtains tightly closed behind tiny cottage windows, shutting away the outside world. Bed-and-breakfast signs creaked on rusted hinges as they swung in the night breeze, animals huddled together as they slept in fields and barns, and there were no cars to be seen on the winding lanes throughout the county. From the looming shadows of the Dark Peak in the north, down to the White Peak in the south, across stiles and drystone walls that ran for miles and countless miles, everything was still.

The moon shone down, bathing the ground below in an eerie shade of blue. Nothing moved. Even the trees fell silent. The land waited, holding its breath.

And then came a change. Above the narrow entrance to Odin Mine – an ancient, disused lead mine to the west of the village of Castleton – a rock tumbled and bounded twice across the moss floor before settling on a clump of grass near what remained of the old crushing wheel. Everything was momentarily motionless again until another followed, and then another. From within the cave walls, a light – dim and distant, at first – began to glow. As it did so, there was an almighty and violent crack that tore through the soundless murk. A flock of sleeping birds in a nearby tree awoke noisily, crying into the void of night as their black silhouettes marked their flight skywards. Below them, the landscape was twisting, changing. The tunnel entrance was widening, opening and reshaping itself. Trees shook, the land heaved, and further rocks tumbled to the quaking ground. From within the cave, the light grew stronger, pulsing red and orange; unearthly shouts and screams echoed and reverberated; and then, as the enlarged cavern finally ceased to move, the Great Hunt of Annwn exploded forth from the underworld in a frenzy of noise, fire and muscle.

At the centre of the tribal explosion wailed the siren of a police car, a pristine 1975 Ford Gran Torino. Miraculously handling the rough terrain to an extent that would make even the most experienced Land Rover weep with ineptitude, it raced forwards with the pack, an excitable Clive at the wheel, and Harry, Jade and Little Stevie holding on for dear life. Across fields the powerful procession swept, heading north to Mam Tor; it ascended the steep sides of the slumbering grassy giant in no time at all until the Great Hunt had spread itself majestically along the Great Ridge, lining up to look down onto the moonlit Hope Valley far below.

The imposing outline of an ancient army, a pack of giant hounds, plus a somewhat famous police car, stood out impressively against the stars along the horizon. King Gwynn and his retinue paused and watched in silence, judging the lay of the land in the form of the weft and warp of the ancient lea and medieval strip fields all the way down to the town of Chesterfield, lying unseen in pitch darkness some twenty-five miles to the south-east. There, the twisted spire of the Church of St Mary and All Saints would be standing as it had for centuries, spiralling haphazardly towards the heavens as the clock beneath marked the passing of the seconds.

"Clive, are you ready?" enquired the voice of the king from the speakers inside the Gran Torino.

"Do you think he has an intercom at the other end?" whispered Jade to Harry from the back seat, where Little Stevie was starting to get restless. "I don't think that he does, personally."

"I don't think he does either," whispered Harry in response as Clive Starsky-*bach* responded into the mouthpiece.

"Yeah, ten-four, ten-four, chief; Zebra Three here locked and loaded, fully fuelled on gasoline. The big cheese is ready to roll."

There was an audible pause.

"Clive, I have absolutely no idea what any of that means. Not meaning to spoil your fun, but a simple yes or no in these situations is more than adequate, diolch. How are Harry and Jade holding out in there?" King Gwynn asked.

Clive, nodding in defeat, held up the white, plastic intercom for his passengers to speak into.

"Yeah, we're good, thank you, Your Majesty," Harry responded.

"Fine, thanks, Your Highness," concurred Jade.

"Are we going straight to Chesterfield now?" added Harry, a slight waver in his delivery.

"We are indeed, Harry. Yes. Now, as we get there, you'll see that everywhere is in darkness. Our source had time to tell us that the government now deactivates the National Grid every night from curfew hour until 6am to save power. So I hope you've been eating your carrots. Pitch dark suits us fine, but you should be able to see using the glow from our torch fire and the lights from Clive's vehicle. Like I said before, we're with you all the way until the crystal is in place, but from then onwards, the Great Hunt splits to go nationwide while I lead a party to London. We have very little time, only a few hours in which to get everything done, but I have every faith in you. We all do," the king confirmed.

"Thank you. I'll do my best."

"We can't ask any more than that. Riders?"

And with that, the intercom clicked off, and the Great Hunt began its descent of the darkened ridge, galloping first down the main road of the village of Hope and then on through the valley, silent now, with no shouting and no siren blaring, along country lanes that crossed moorland and brooks, and then on through the villages and hamlets, and down, down towards where Chesterfield lay waiting.

***

As the chargers arrived at the outskirts of the town, they slowed to a gentle trot. Making their way along the deserted and unlit A619 Chatsworth Road, the silent houses and other buildings of Chesterfield slowly began to rise about them. Garages stood idle while chip shops, takeaways and corner stores hid their wares behind steel shutters daubed in graffiti. From the gently purring Gran Torino at the centre of the procession, Harry and Jade peered through their windows at a town they both knew well, but that felt somehow stripped of all familiarity. They felt like aliens and that the whole world had changed irrevocably while they were underground.

"Blimey, what's happened here then?" whispered Clive as he edged the car slowly forwards.

Harry noticed that the street was strewn with rubbish, carrier bags and crisp wrappers crunching underneath the hooves of the magnificent horses while one or two of the hellhounds sniffed in curiosity at the litter bins overflowing onto the pavement. A wrecked bus shelter twinkled as the moonlight hit its shattered glass, and its one remaining plastic seat dangled from a single hinge. Further on, a pub appeared to have been looted, with its windows broken and torn curtains now hanging out over the jagged glass and into the night. Across a wall, someone had spray-painted "Screw the Aegis!", and as they passed the lonely car park of a desolate commercial estate, it was clear that something violent had taken place there too, with windows and doors smashed. A huge, dark pile of something lay in the middle of the parking spaces, with the faint, orange glow of burning embers visible within. Everywhere was deathly quiet. Nothing stirred. If the stories of a curfew were true, as they obviously seemed to be, then nobody in the town appeared to be bending the rules. The only cars to be seen anywhere stood motionless, parked on kerbs or drives.

"Jade?"

"Harry?"

"There's something I've been meaning to ask you," said Harry, an awkward note in his voice.

"Okay, go on," she answered dubiously. The car continued to creep forwards slowly.

"So, you ended up in Annwn after the lift fell down the shaft, and Clive took you in and made you watch US cop shows from the 1970s."

"Steady on, I didn't force anybody to do anything," came the voice of Clive from the driver's seat.

Harry continued, "Obviously, you and I went to get the crystal from Nia and Hedd inside the mountain together."

"We did, yep."

"Well," Harry paused, "how? The whole deal was that I was able to get into Annwn because I have this sliver of crystal inside me, and that also qualified me as the only person from above or below who was able to go get the big chunk of the stuff to bring with us tonight. So, does that mean you're a clone too? Or... what?"

Jade was about to say something, but only ever got as far as opening her mouth when Clive slammed on the brakes.

The procession had halted, with King Gwynn's left arm raised aloft to bring his men, women, horses and dogs to a standstill. As the shaken Harry and Jade craned forwards to peer through the windscreen, they were able to discern that, in the distance, where the road reached a large traffic roundabout, a bizarre barricade of what appeared to be neatly piled cars stood blocking their progress.

"You seeing this?" asked Clive as his passengers looked on.

"Yeah," answered Jade fearfully as Harry stared, transfixed.

"How in the hell did they do that?"

Family cars, hatchbacks, runabouts and the occasional small van had been carefully arranged as individual bricks by some almighty builder into a wall of steel and glass, blocking off each exit of the roundabout. It was like some bizarre work of industrial art, one car the right way up, the next upside down and so on, interlocking into each other to create a blockade, four vehicles high, preventing them from ascending towards the centre of town and the church. There was still no sign of anyone anywhere. The procession was alone in the night.

"If we back up, there's a one-way system into the town, back by the retail park. That might not be blocked off, so we could get to the church that way," offered Harry, pointing over his shoulder helpfully.

"Ha!" exclaimed Clive, "No need for that, *bachgen*. We didn't come all this way to be held up in traffic. Hang tight for a second, and keep your eye on the horses at the front."

Uncertain, Harry did as he was told. As he watched, five horses and riders trotted forwards from the cavalcade towards the wall, which stood there illuminated by the Torino's headlamps and the flaming torches of the riders. They lined themselves up in a row, and then, at a nod from their riders, the extraordinary horses reared up, whinnying loudly, their hooves slamming against the cars in the third, penultimate row of the wall. Those cars were dented, their windows smashed, and the cars in the final row atop them wobbled precariously, but – for now – the wall held. The horses fell back a few paces, before their riders drove them forwards again at a pace, and they rose onto their hind legs again to deliver another powerful blow. This time, two of the cars from the top row fell, causing Harry and Jade to gasp out the word, "Fuck," in unison, as the vehicles dropped towards the horses below.

However, in an incredible bit of horsemanship that went way beyond Olympic equestrian standard, the two horses nearest the tumbling cars stayed upright and hoofed them over the wall, like volleyballs over a net.

Clive broke out into spontaneous applause. "There we go. Now that's what I'm talking about! Annwn one, Chesterfield nil."

Astounded, the passengers in the back, along with an excitable Little Stevie, watched on as the five horses set about demolishing the wall before them, until only one row of cars remained. Dipping their heads, the horses concluded the spectacle by nudging the remaining cars aside, along with those they had already sent crashing to the tarmac behind where the wall had stood moments before. Within a minute, a path had been cleared that was wide enough for the Great Hunt and Clive's police car to advance through.

Looking down at them from the top of St Mary's Gate, the iconic church remained silent. The road between the temple and where the Great Hunt stood was both open and clear, and the procession began to move towards its goal.

The quiet around them all was absolute, snaking through the streets of the town and beyond, over the soundless fields and hills. Only the silvery moonlight provided anything for the senses to grasp on to. Harry pondered that this was what a weary and nervous traveller arriving at the town's edge centuries ago must have felt like – that is, apart from the tarmac road beneath them, the shuttered shop windows, and advertising hoardings plastered with phone numbers and website addresses – before he decided to ponder about it no longer, inwardly cursing his heightened sense of awareness and observation at that moment, and then being just as surprised as anyone else by the sudden arrival of an office photocopier and colour printer, which hit the ground amid the procession with a terrifying thump and broke into as many as five pieces.

"LOOK OUT!" yelled a voice from the rear of the procession, as a riderless motor scooter then flew over the roof of a nearby cafe and crash-landed noisily in among the heaving pack. Luckily, the shouted warning meant that no one had been on the receiving end of this strange missile. However, as the hounds began to bark angrily, it became clear that this and the photo-copier had merely been warning shots.

All of a sudden, a volley of bicycles, concrete planters filled with flowers, dustbins, a lawnmower and an assortment of household items were launched into the sky from behind the ascending row of shops, before crashing into the Great Hunt below. The street erupted into mayhem, with whinnying horses, yelling riders and howling hellhounds retreating from an air-borne washing machine, ironing board and settee. Immediately, Clive threw the Gran Torino into reverse.

Smoke flew from under the wildly spinning wheels as they sent the car and incumbent passengers hurtling back towards the roundabout. It was then that the Great Hunt came face to face with its appliance-hurling opposition. As horses wheeled in disarray, riders doing their best to both calm them and cling on for dear life, the hounds of the Cwn Annwn began barking ferociously in the direction of the church. From the surround-ing streets, marching malevolently towards them, came what on first glance appeared to be a group of enormous robots built from Meccano. At around ten feet tall, these cumbersome, metal frames of destruction lumbered towards the Great Hunt, each carrying a bulky and heavy item, which was most likely to be-come a projectile in the very near future. One carried a chest of drawers, and another a bench-cum-table that appeared to have been lifted from a pub garden. One even clutched a live and noisily protesting sheep in its vice-like pincers.

But there was something else. Each robot appeared to be being manipulated by a human, who was sitting at a set of controls within the cage of the machine's chest. As Harry stared in horror from the car, the first wave of the robots let fly with their freak-ish arsenal. Again, the Great Hunt was mostly able to avoid the opening salvo of splintering furniture, and the sheep was soon nowhere to be seen after it landed clumsily before righting itself, deciding to make a quick run for it and disappearing into the night.

The row of robots, their arms now empty and reaching menacingly towards their startled prey, continued forwards. From behind them came more of their brethren, which were armed in a similar fashion. At this, the Great Hunt roared into life and surged forwards to meet them. As the horses at the vanguard of the leading group neared them, the machines linked their scaffolding-like arms to form a defensive line. The noise of battle rose into the night as the Great Hunt piled in, swords and axes raised, and smashing into the steadfast metal barrier, horses neighing as they tried valiantly to break through the scrum. From behind the robots came a hail of further unlikely items – a microwave oven, a mobility scooter and a rabbit hutch – which all fell among the Great Hunt, breaking it up once again and even sending one rider flying to land in a heap on the pavement.

This time, the Great Hunt surged forwards once more, and where the line of linked machines had previously stood firm, it now buckled. As one robot lost its grip and flailed about trying to reconnect with the row, the giant, white hellhound Dormarch leaped snarling through the air and landed upon the unsteadied metal wretch, sending it clattering to the ground. From there, King Gwynn and other riders set about the remaining mechanical creatures as the Cwn Annwn snarled and raced forwards to tackle the next advancing bank of robots. Still things rained down onto and into the massed ranks of the army of the underworld – a concrete mixer, an oil-drum and another office photocopier, this time scattering sheets of A4 paper as it fell – all tearing into the horses and riders below. The concrete mixer struck a sickening blow to two riders, who were unceremoniously dumped from their horses onto the road below, with their horses wheeling away in panic.

Robots now grappled with riders on horseback, with powerful, metal arms swiping, grabbing and attempting to unseat them. Further on up the hill, the Cwn Annwn yelped and ran about wildly among the machines as more and more of the huge, mechanical brutes appeared from alleyways and from behind the church. The athletic hounds were working in pairs, one locking its strong jaws on to a leg and attempting to drag it over while the other would leap with full force onto the chest cage, barking venomously at the controller within. This in turn gave the riders the opportunity to work forwards on horseback, cutting through with their weapons. A few of the ungainly robots had already been knocked to the ground and were writhing on the tarmac like tortoises on their backs, struggling to right themselves again. Right now, it appeared that the Great Hunt had the upper hand, but it was a painfully slow and difficult process.

"They knew we were coming," said Clive angrily, "they were ready for us because they knew we were coming. Buggeration. This is slowing everything down. At this rate, we'll never get anywhere near London before daylight."

As if the king had read his mind, the intercom cracked into life. "Clive, I'm sending riders out in all directions to attempt to reach the church from a different approach," came Gwynn's voice abruptly, a little out of breath. "I want them to draw the walking machines too, to split them up. We need Harry to be able to get the crystal into the church as soon as possible, so that we can head south. Harry, I'm going to work my way back to come and get you."

Sure enough, a group of six riders peeled off from the back of the heaving pack, and as they watched, galloped through the beams of the headlights from their waiting Gran Torino and then off in the opposite direction before darting off up a side street and out of sight. Another six thundered past, this time to begin pounding at and breaking through another part of the car-wall at the traffic roundabout. It was mayhem. Horses and riders hurried about as more projectiles were thrown, joining the mountain of broken bits of furniture and other exploded bric-a-brac, as more and more robots marched forwards.

Then King Gwynn emerged from the heaving throng, his enormous sword held aloft in his left hand as his right hand gripped the reins of his racing charger. His red cape billowed impressively behind him, and Harry's heart soared at the sight of him. It was time.

"Go get 'em, Harry," encouraged Clive, "but don't forget your rucksack, mind."

Jade reached round the front seat to hug Harry round the neck. "Good luck, Salty. You've got this." She planted a kiss on his cheek, but then gasped in horror. "What the...?"

A well-aimed wardrobe unit had connected with the king, hitting him squarely on the head and shoulders, and sending him flying from his saddle. His mighty sword skittered to the side of the road in a shower of sparks, and as they watched in horror, their leader – dazed and very clearly confused – attempted to get up. But as he did so, an undulating tide of white fur and gleaming metal spilled down the road towards him from the battle beyond. A swarm of Alex robots, at least thirty of them, was bearing down on him, with their rows of sharp chromium teeth exposed maliciously.

"NO, YOU BASTARDS!" yelled Clive, slamming his foot down on the accelerator.

The engine roared, and with a jolt, Harry, Jade and Little Stevie were flung forwards in their seats. In a stroke of incredible bad luck and even worse timing, the car was still in reverse gear, and so instead of rushing forwards to the aid of his king, Clive sent the car careering wildly backwards, smashing into a section of the car-wall with a sickening and deafening crunch, throwing everyone inside about fiercely.

After a second or so, everything settled, and Harry – winded by but thankful for his seatbelt – turned to Clive. The aged sage lay unconscious, his head having connected violently with the steering wheel upon which it now rested. Blood spilled from beneath his beanie hat and spattered his chunky cardigan. From the backseat, Little Stevie whined mournfully.

"Shit! Clive? Clive?" Harry nudged him but he simply moaned gently, remaining out for the count. He turned his attention to the back seat. "Jade, are you okay?"

Jade was crumpled against the backseat, holding her shoulder. "I think so; my shoulder is killing me, though. Argh!" She winced as the desperate dog beside her licked her face.

At that moment, there came an ominous groan from above them. Harry peered upwards through the closed passenger window to see the looming shadow of an overhanging car, swaying precariously from the impact caused by the Gran Torino.

"Oh God, the car-wall. Jade, we've got to get out," Harry stated.

"Shit!" she replied.

Harry was already scrabbling at his seat belt. It clicked free, and he was out of the car door in a second and looking for the catch on the passenger seat. His fingers and thumbs searched anxiously before locating a lever at the foot of the chair. Little Stevie leaped over Harry's bent back, almost sending him toppling. Jade grabbed his hand, yelling in pain as Harry pulled her free.

"Right, help me get Clive out!" panted Harry.

In a moment they were round to the driver's side.

"CLIVE, CLIVE! WE'RE GETTING YOU OUT," yelled Jade as Harry worked the door open, glancing upwards in fear as he did so. "Clive, can you hear me?" She slapped him on the cheek, but he remained in a daze, brushing at her hand as if swatting at a drunken bumblebee.

Harry had Clive's seatbelt off and was now grabbing at him by the giant lapel of his cardigan, attempting unsuccessfully to heave the cumbersome Welsh ancient from the car. Jade joined in, grabbing at Clive's legs. Again, there was a groaning creak of car metal from above them. Now Little Stevie had reappeared, grabbing Clive's cardigan in his maw and tugging. Slowly but surely, the three of them managed to unfold Clive and haphazardly drag his dead weight away from the car before lying him down on a grass verge.

Immediately, Jade grabbed at Harry's sleeve and pointed. Where the king had fallen, the swarm of Alex robots had engulfed him. Some hung by their teeth to his back, his legs or his arms, wriggling to get a better purchase. Yards to his left, his giant, white horse was desperately trying to fight them off too. A couple had made their way onto its back, while another had taken a large bite out of its rump, which now was bleeding badly. As others teemed around them both, the horse reared up and crushed one with his mighty hooves. The king, heavily bloodied now, still fought on, struggling valiantly to get to his sword.

"GWYNN!" Harry yelled.

He made to run for the besieged monarch, but Jade held him back as Little Stevie shot forwards, his deafening bark freezing Harry to the spot. In a moment, the dog tore into one of the snapping robots, crunching it in half with one bite of his terrible jaw before casually tossing the remains aside with a flick of his enormous head. Immediately, he tore into another.

Jade shook Harry. "You need to get the crystal from the car. Now!" Harry looked to where the Gran Torino was still wedged into the car-wall, with a black BMW estate still hanging precariously over it, ready to tip at any moment. One of the Alex robots had broken free from Little Stevie, and was now eyeing them suspiciously. "If that car falls, it'll be trapped! I'll look after Clive, but you've got to get that crystal!"

"Gaaaah!" panicked Harry. He looked to where the king still fought, at the battle raging further on and at the twisted spire of the church beyond it all, which appeared to be craning round to get a better view of the carnage below. Harry ran back to where the Gran Torino stood, its doors still wide open and lights on full beam. He snatched the key fob from the ignition and edged to the back of the car, where it was wedged into a squashed yellow Skoda that formed part the bottom row of 'bricks' in the wall. The boot was completely inaccessible. The only way to get to the boot was going to involve getting the Gran Torino free from the wall.

"Shit! Shit, shit, shit, shitting shit!" he exclaimed in frustration.

"ARE YOU OKAY?" yelled Jade from where she knelt in the grass, tending to Clive.

"The boot of the Gran Torino is buried in the wall!"

"Well then, you'll have to drive it out to get to it!"

"I know! But... fuuuuuuck!"

"Just drive really bloody fast! Floor the damn thing!"

"AAAAAARGH!" Harry yelled at the heavens, and he carefully got into the driver's side of the car, closing the door gently once he was in. He felt every movement as the car reacted to his weight; it performed a gentle-but-terrifying rock as he settled. Gingerly, he put the key into the ignition and twisted it, with the brake pedal pressed underfoot. The engine rumbled into life, and Harry gasped. He took a moment to ensure he was in the right gear, with every vibration of the car setting his teeth on edge. Now Harry took a deep breath, whispered an internal prayer to whoever might be listening, and floored the accelerator. The engine roared, the tyres span, but the Gran Torino remained wedged.

"No!" said Harry through gritted teeth, as he took his foot away and then slammed it down again. "Come on, come on, *come on!*"

The passenger door was still wide open, and it was through this that Harry heard Jade scream. In a moment, he glimpsed her, now standing on the grass verge, pointing above at the top of the wall. He closed his eyes.

Miraculously, he felt the car break free and lurch forwards. "AAAAAARGH!"

Opening his eyes again, as the car tore towards Jade and Clive, he swerved to avoid them as, behind him, the wall of cars crumbled in a deafening cacophony of sound. He glanced into the rear-view mirror to see cars tumbling towards him, rolling like boulders as they fell, coming closer.

"ARRRRRRRRGH!" he yelled again.

One over the other they came; the BMW tumbled end over end, slamming into the bumper of the Gran Torino. The horizon suddenly disappeared downwards from Harry's point of view – he was looking at the stars momentarily before the front of the car slammed back down – but he was clear. He slammed on the brakes and stopped the car, panting and drenched in sweat. He leaped out, running to the rear of the scratched and dented vehicle, keys in hand. He tried frantically to get them into the boot lock, but his hands were all over the place, and he couldn't make contact at first.

"HURRY!" shouted Jade, but he didn't dare look.

Instead, he took a deep breath and tried again with the key, and this time he managed to work it in and turn it, and with a satisfying click, the boot popped open, revealing his rucksack. He grabbed it immediately, swung it over his shoulder and was reminded of just how heavy the crystal it contained was. Wriggling to ensure that the straps were in place around each of his arms, he popped the boot closed and took in the terrible sight before him.

The swarm of Alex robots had worked free of the king, leaving him lying prone in a heap on the floor behind them, his battered horse nudging sadly at him with his bloodied snout. With the king finished, they had now turned their attention to Jade and Clive. Even more worryingly, a Meccano robot had burst forth from the fray further up towards the church, and it was now striding over to join in. Jade was kicking out in terror at an Alex, which was edging slowly towards her, looking up with its chrome fangs glistening. Another had crept onto Clive's chest. Meanwhile, Little Stevie had returned and was laying into one of the small machines as Jade flailed.

"Harry, run!" she commanded.

"I'm coming!" He ran towards them. The lumbering, large, red robot was gaining on them, with the dark shadow of a person within manipulating the giant frame as it bore down on its victims.

"No, Harry! Run, take the crystal, for God's sake!"

More of the Alex robots were steaming in now, scuttling and

slithering their way to the isolated grass verge. Clive was stirring and then screaming, yelling as he abruptly came to his senses, and grabbed hold of the robot snapping at his face.

Harry continued to run, terrified but focussed on the red robot closing in. It was unclear who would get to them first, and there was nothing remotely resembling a plan in Harry's mind. They had lost. They had come this far, and they had lost without even making it to the church. King Gwynn of Annwn lay dead, and the last ragged remains of his brave Great Hunt was being overwhelmed by crawling, scuttling and missile-propelling technology.

"Harry, NO!" yelled Jade as she fell, with two of the Alex creatures pinning her down as a third wriggled its way up her leg and onto her chest.

The robot loomed over Harry now, a hideous dark and mechanical shadow that towered over him and blocked the moonlight. He could hear gears whirring and cogs grinding. He ran, shoulder first, into the metal giant and bounced off uselessly, yelling in pain and resigned frustration as he fell to the grass. The robot raised a mighty arm, ready to pulverise him and put an end to this sorry night. To this sorry life.

He had failed.

He heaved a terrified sob as the robot struck a giant, metal fist down, down – it would be a permanent end – past his head and straight into the carapace of an Alex robot, smashing it to its base components and thumping it deep into the soil.

"TARAMASALATA, YOU LITTLE BASTARD!" yelled an exuberant Newman from within the robot's chest. "Gotcha!"

29. Kebab

Between them, they'd managed to finish off the thirty or so Alex robots that had swarmed their way. Newman, from within his powerful robot casing, had dealt with most of them by snatching up the little swines and pulling them apart, or simply stomping on them. Little Stevie had played his part too, and appeared to have had a great time doing so, and he was now helping himself to a half-eaten and discarded doner kebab from a dustbin on the pavement. Harry and Jade had generally spent the time watching on in shock, as had Clive, who didn't quite seem to know exactly what was going on yet.

"Harry!" breathed a beaming and sweaty Newman, looking down at his former protégé from within the depths of his robo-suit. "Jolly good to see you, my old sport, my old chestnut, my young fellow-my-lad! And look at you, young Ruby!"

"Jade," she corrected.

"Jade! Of course, my little crystalline delight. How good it is to gaze upon your sweaty chops once again! Heavens to Betsy. Land's End to John O'Groats. London to Brighton. These are difficult times – difficult times indeed – and I fear I may be in part responsible."

"What are you talking about? Responsible? How?" asked Harry, "And what the hell are you doing wearing that... that *thing*?"

"Have you ever had your rectum filled with Worcestershire sauce and been hung upside down until it flows freely from your nose?"

"Er, no."

"Well, neither have I. However, I was tortured in agonising manners not too dissimilar until I talked and gave them what they needed: my knowledge of what was to come. But I didn't break! I didn't break, dearest Harry and sweetest Onyx!"

"Jade."

"That too! Yes, manhandled and panhandled, totally and scrotally electrified. But I didn't buckle! I didn't buckle at all. Well, I may have buckled. A bit. But only slightly." Newman paused, the illumination of the lighting from within his robo-suit revealing his face to look a little embarrassed. "Worcestershire sauce though, Harry. Worcestershire sauce."

"So you're saying somebody tortured you to find out about the Great Hunt? You knew about it?"

A mangled Alex, with only one half-open eye showing on its smashed facial display, was sluggishly trying to get at Harry's shoe with what remained of its jaw. With a whine of exquisitely engineered gears and hydraulics, Newman volleyed it into the night with a giant, steel foot, a gnat's whisker away from removing Harry's face in the process.

"Have that, you vile quim! Yes, I was tortured and, yes, I knew all about this, young Salt. The ins and the outs. Fortunately, I was able to escape their clutches using long-honed powers of sneakiness and derring-do, and requisition one of these OA-PRos – that's old-age-pensioner robots to the uninitiated – before they were all assigned and sent out."

"Hang on, rewind a tick," requested Harry, shaking his head. "How on earth did *you* know that the Great Hunt of Annwn was coming?"

"Roy? Roy Newman of Carmarthen, is that you?" came a shaky, Welsh voice.

Harry turned to see Clive, his face sorely swollen, sitting on the grass with Jade, who was rubbing his back gently.

There was a loud click, a whirr of machinery, and then – as they watched – the robo-suit powered down and lurched gently forwards onto both knees. The chest area popped open and Newman stepped forwards, hopping the short distance to the ground.

"Clive? Clive Owen? As I live and breathe, as I come and go, as I brush my teeth!" With that, Newman scurried across the grass to where Clive sat before diving on him as if he were an inflatable in the middle of a swimming pool.

"AAAAAARGH!" groaned Clive, thankful that his enormous cardigan had at least absorbed some of the impact from the flying Roy.

"For Christ's sake, Newman! The guy has just woken up from a concussion!" chided Jade, her eyes wide in alarm.

"I apologise, I apologise. I truly do." Newman was back on his feet, dusting himself down before crouching and gently cradling Clive's face in front of his own. "But this man – this wonderful, eternal man," he continued hurriedly, "this inspiration, this legendary paragon of wonder, this sea-bass of truth... "

"Oh give over, you daft, old sod," countered Clive, "you flatter me, you really do."

"Hold up, you two know each other?" asked Harry.

"Know each other?" laughed Newman, "Know each other? We're practically cut from the same clock! Clive and I go back years, begad."

"Harry, Jade – allow me to introduce our source from your world: Mr Roy Newman. I'll be honest, Roy, I seriously thought this was finally it and that you were a goner once things went quiet."

Harry and Jade looked at one another in disbelief before turning back to the conversation unfolding before them.

"In many ways, it was touch and, in other ways, it was go, dear Clive. It really was. But, yes, Harry, sweet Beryl—" rambled Newman.

"I swear, I'll fucking lamp him in a minute," muttered Jade.

"Clive and I have spent time together in the underworld. The overworld too. Underground, overground. Annwn has touched me in ways that other places simply could never do; it has altered me. Degraded me. Robbed me of my once powerful talents. Time, and time spent above the surface have not always been good to me and my beleaguered brain. You may have noticed inconsistencies in my mental states, incongruences even."

There was a pause. Nobody said anything.

"Right. Well then... " Newman cleared his throat. "Yes, for those I can only apologise, but it was indeed for the greater good that my time in and out of Annwn did send me to cerebral places that are somewhat foggy and indistinct. The greater good, I say."

Clive nodded sadly and with genuine sympathy, clasping Newman closely to him, patting him on the back. He looked up to Harry and Jade, who were unsure whether to laugh, cry or run. "You don't know it yet, Harry, but you and your family owe this man a great deal. A heck of a lot. You, especially. There was only ever one man who was going to be able to carry the crystal shard to the surface and see you right."

Suddenly, there was a deafening explosion from where the battle still raged towards the church, the ground shook, and they all looked as one in the direction of the continuing melee.

Clive immediately sat bolt upright. "Wait – what news of our king?" he asked frantically, rapidly looking about.

Harry and Jade looked at each other again, nervously.

It was Jade who spoke. "I'm so sorry, Clive," was all she managed before Clive's bearded jaw dropped, the colour instantly draining from his bruised face.

"No! No, it cannot be! Oh, for the love of sweet Brân the Blessed, no!" Clive groaned.

Harry repeated Jade's words sadly, "I'm so sorry Clive. He was overwhelmed. He was riding to come and fetch me and take me to the church, and—" Harry stopped mid-sentence, his eyes narrowing.

"What?" asked Clive, his eyes filled with tears.

Harry turned back to Jade, puzzled. "Actually, where *is* the king?"

Jade looked to where Harry was staring, the patch of grass where the king had fallen while under attack. It was empty. "He was there; that's where he fell," said Jade nervously, "and... his horse has vanished too. What the hell?"

They looked about them, but neither Gwynn nor his horse were anywhere to be seen. Clive was standing now, groggy but up on his feet, and he joined the two of them with Newman, his arm around Newman's shoulder for support. Little Stevie, his tongue busily licking chilli sauce from around his own mouth, trotted over to complete the team.

"Those vicious little sods," said Clive, his teeth clenched and doused in spittle, "they've eaten my king!"

Jade gasped, but Newman was quick to interject.

"Clive Owen. That cannot be the case, my man. It would take hundreds of the bastard things to devour a full human being; besides, their metabolisms are so efficient we'd be treading knee deep in Alex poo right now. It is more likely that King Gwynn and his stallion have been stolen. A stolen stallion and a misappropriated monarch, no less."

Clive let go of him and gave him a look. Newman chuntered and looked at his feet.

"Well, I came here as part of the Great Hunt, and it's time I rejoined it," declared Clive, clearing his throat and steadying himself. "Harry, we need to get you and the crystal to the church. We may be too late already, but we have to try. It's fifty years until the Great Hunt can rise from Annwn again. We've only got this one shot. Besides, I now need to recover the king's body so that we can take him home and... "

His voice broke, and it was a little too much for everyone to bear.

This time, it was Newman who reached out to shoulder his friend and give him a hug. "I'll drive, young Starsky. You need a bit of time away from the wheel."

Clive looked at his friend, and then across at his battered, scratched and dented Gran Torino, which stood there, its lights still on full beam and its doors open. He wiped his thick, woollen sleeve gingerly across his face and let forth a sigh. "Aye, okay then, Roy. One last charge, eh?"

Harry gave Newman a thoughtful look. "So, erm, will you not be needing this?" he questioned, nodding in the direction of the kneeling robo-suit. Newman gave his brow one of his famous furrows, and then his eyes lit up, delightedly. "Are you asking for a test drive, young Salt?"

"Bloody hell. Amazing!" said Jade.

Harry gave her a half-grin. "It'll mean us having to split up, Jade, but I reckon that thing could be my best way to the church. I'm sorry."

"Don't be," she stated, grabbing his hands, "I want to see you in that thing. It's a nice cut, tailored almost. I reckon you could carry that look off. Besides, I've got Little Stevie to look after me. I've never fought in a battle before. It'll be... a new experience for me, right?" On cue, the huge hellhound trotted to her side and nuzzled up against her elbow. "See. Man's best friend, yeah? Woman's best friend? Oh Saltychops!"

She kissed him – a long, lingering kiss that sent a warm feeling right through him – and then held him tightly. He did precisely the same to her.

"How the hell did things get so weird, Jade?" he whispered into her ear. "What the hell are we doing here?"

He felt a hand on his shoulder.

Newman's beetled forehead was gleaming in the moonlight behind him. "If you want to get the hang of an OAPRo, I suggest you get started now. I'm sorry to break you two up, Harry, Zircon."

Jade pulled away from him, momentarily eyeing Newman with a scowl, but determined not to cry. She shook her head, giving his hands one last squeeze. "Go on, Harry. Get your kit on for the girls."

***

After a few false starts and a couple of stumbles, Harry found that controlling the robo-suit was much less tricky than he'd feared. An arrangement of pads, which cosied up against his limbs once he was sealed in, responded to his every move. There was also a strangely faint smell of lavender.

While giving Harry his robo-suit crash course on the grass, Newman revealed that the suit was a distant cousin of a powered suit that had originally been designed to help warehouse workers with heavy items and difficult to reach storage areas. With a few tweaks, the suit and all its kin had been repurposed under government orders as the all-new OAPRo. Supplied under the pretence of being a wondrous technological aid to provide more mobility for the elderly generation, they had been an absolute boon for the Mabels and Howards of the world, who had previously struggled with their conifers. However, after a swift and unforeseen policy change that was passed quietly while the majority of the country was swept up in The Change, all OAPs in possession of the shiny, new suits were overnight deemed fit and healthy enough to work. Elderly people across the country were quickly snatched out of retirement, marched out of their care homes and warden-controlled flats by the newly violent and repressive Alex robots, and then put back into the employment machine, very much against their will.

As a public outcry followed, the Prime Minister muttered something unintelligible about, "easing the burden on the economy caused by people living longer," before adding that there was nothing to be done as the decision had been made, he was in charge and that was jolly well that.

The super-powered codgers now busily throwing home and office furniture at the Great Hunt also happened to be a specially harvested cross-section of those loyal members of the electorate who had voted for The Change, and who had been told only hours before to expect an invasion of foreign types, with their strange meats and cheeses, who were hell-bent on stealing British jobs and benefits once they had set up camp as asylum-seeking squatters in their local church. The Change-voting pensioners, suitably riled, had taken this call-to-arms at face value and suited up.

Needless to say, Harry didn't end up getting the amount of time to practise in his suit that he would have liked. Still, he was able to grasp the basics and find enough room in his cage to stow his rucksack with its precious cargo.

"You all set then?" asked Jade, looking up at Harry.

"I think so," he answered. "I mean, I'd give you a hug, but it would probably kill you."

"Quite possibly, yep. Listen, you just be safe, yeah? Get your task done, don't speak to any strangers, and I'll see you in the morning when the sun comes up."

"Okay. I'll try."

"You'd better. And Harry?"

"What?"

"Don't screw this up. A lot of people are depending on you, and, well, I kind of think you're alright as it happens, so it would be nice if we could at least hang out again when all this is done."

"I guess you're okay too," said Harry awkwardly. "Please stay safe, and stick with Little Stevie, Clive and Newman whenever you can. I mean it."

"Okay, Dad. Whatever."

Clive was standing by the open passenger door of the Gran Torino, his seat down, ready for Jade to hop in the back. Newman slammed his own door shut, already in the driver's seat and raring to go. Little Stevie was standing alert by the car, his back legs shaking with excitement.

Harry looked at them all with a sad feeling in his gut, wondering when he might see them all again, if ever. No, he had to step away from that thought. Jade was right. He had a job to do and a mean piece of working attire in which to get it done. This was his chance to make a difference – to alter things. To stop the rot. He was part of a team more than he ever had been before. This time, *he* mattered. Besides, there was Jade. She gave him something really wonderful to look forward to, and an ache for something that hadn't happened yet.

"Right then. Let's get this done. I'm off." Harry's suit hummed and whirred as he flexed his huge, metal fingers as if stretching them ready for action. As Jade looked on, his left fist crunched and clenched before his left thumb popped up.

She smiled as best as she could, gave him a thumbs-up in return and then a farewell wave before heading to the car. With a roar, the engine came to life, followed by the wail of the siren as the red lamp on the roof began to spin, and the car sped off towards the battle. Little Stevie, before springing after them, let forth a howl to the night sky that was as unearthly as anything Harry had ever heard, and yet it filled his chest with the resolve he so badly needed. There was no turning back or standing still. It was time to go.

***

As the car sped off towards the church, Harry – in his powered suit – strode off purposefully in the opposite direction. He had a plan to approach the church from a different route, away from where the main skirmish was still in full flow. With any luck, the riders whom the king had sent out earlier might have cleared a way through, or were at least still busy doing so, meaning that the level of opposition should be fewer in number. The suit was not as fast as he would have liked; Harry was pretty certain he could have outrun it on a decent day. What mattered was the protection it was hopefully going to give him, should he need it, and having the power to defend himself.

From the trading estate, he took a left up a small, cobbled lane, which was littered with the freely flowing rubbish that was now an unfortunate feature of the small market town. His metal feet clanged as he walked; he tried to place his feet a little more gently, but it was pointless. He was a hefty lad now, and he was just going to have to embrace his new body shape and get comfortable with it.

At the end of the lane, he reached an empty street that formed part of the town's pedestrianised shopping area. Black-and-white mock-Tudor frontages stood like rows of giant magpies, watching down intently from either side as this curious, new visitor walked among them. The sound of fighting was closer now, with the barking of the Cwn Annwn piercing the darkness as a constant reminder of the forceful energy and anger being unleashed only streets away. He could also pick out the shrill police siren, muffled by distance. His friends were involved, somewhere.

As Harry branched off to ascend another winding and empty lane towards the twisted spire, he saw movement and froze. There was nothing he could hide behind, given his ridiculous size, and for the first time since suiting up, he felt very exposed. Standing at the end of the lane and blocking his progress was a figure with a long weapon of some sort. In the dark, it was difficult to tell, but he was able to see that this person also wore a hat. They both froze at opposite ends of the lane, which formed a passageway of shuttered shops.

Quickly, Harry decided to rely on his size as a deterrent and he began to run at a lumbering pace up the alleyway. As he did so, he scrabbled around on a control pad that was built into the glove inside his 'hand', searching for a way to activate his shoulder-mounted searchlight. Sure enough, the figure at the other end thought better of the situation and darted back out of view, and by the time Harry managed to illuminate the lane, the figure was long gone. He turned right at the end of the tiny street to face the church and where the figure had gone, but the road was empty. He could still hear the noise of battle: the sounds of hand-to-hand fighting, of dogs and horses barking in anger or neighing in terror, respectively. But here, at least, there was no one to be seen.

He was close now. As he strode up Burlington Street, the church stood dominant at the far end, with the moonlight illuminating the warped and twisted tower and the clock face immediately below it. He could see riders on horses and robots grappling with one another at the foot of the timeworn building, one was galloping in circles as an enraged robot-suit grasped and tried to snatch the torch-bearing rider out of his saddle. Harry braced himself, knowing he would have to face a fight to gain access to the church, but as he did so, there was more movement again.

From the top of Steeplegate, a small alleyway that lay just ahead of him, a swarm of figures emerged and lined up across the street to completely seal it off. Harry was immediately blinded by a brilliant blast of reflected white-and-yellow light as the squadron assembled in the glow of his powerful floodlight. He staggered back, his eyes scrunched shut against the burning brightness. Fortunately, an unseen night-vision visor in his suit clicked into action, and when he steadied himself, he was greeted by the sight of his opposition.

A rank of thirty or so school crossing wardens clad in neon uniforms – lollipop ladies and lollipop men – stood facing him, their lollipops held forwards at an angle, like an armoury of yellow-and-black hooped spears, each topped with the legend "STOP! CHILDREN". Harry, ever the obedient fellow, had already come to a standstill, but clearly not to a sufficient standard. Without warning, the army of crossing guardians assailed him in a frenzy of hammering signs, smashing and jabbing at him furiously. Try as he might, Harry was unable to move forwards and instead found himself staggering backwards away from the church.

Despite the mechanical strength provided by his robo-suit, there were simply too many of them. As he picked one away and tossed him aside, he was battered and shoved from the other direction. With an agonising clatter, Harry realised he was now backed up against the wall of a bakery, and surrounded with nowhere to turn. He swiped at them desperately, connecting here and there, but it seemed that as soon as one fell to the cobblestones, he or she would shake themself down to rise again. Bizarrely, as Harry pushed and struggled against the relentless, neon tide, he became aware that a group of milkmen had joined the fray. A number of them were now tugging at his left leg in an effort to topple him, and both a milk bottle and a carton of raspberry yoghurt had exploded against his steel carapace, drenching him in delicious-but-cold dairy produce.

In a sickening moment of freefall, his legs were swept away from under him, and he crashed to the ground, his head slamming against the interior of his protective cage. They were on top of him now, with prying fingers trying haphazardly to rip apart his suit. Their faces filled him with terror; they were contorted by an anger and rage that he could physically feel, and yet their eyes told him another story entirely: they were empty, but with a hint of his own terror somehow reflected back at him. Harry grappled with a milkman who was compelled by fury to try to bite through the cage, and Harry managed to throw him aside, his teeth squealing horrifically against the metal as he was prised away. But now more crossing wardens were on top of Harry, clinging on grimly as he tried to wriggle free.

A sharp pain in his back caused him to yell out, and he realised he was crushed up against the giant lump of crystal housed in his rucksack. He tried to shuffle himself into a better position, but in doing so, he only succeeded in causing the stone to scratch and cut into the skin on his back.

As he gasped again, frustrated and frightened, he pictured the stone in his mind, remembering the distance Hedd and Nia had kept from it in the mountain cave, and how afraid of it they both were. It had to be worth a try. He swept wildly at the people currently on his chest, sending both a milkman and a crossing lady careening across the street. Having bought himself a few seconds, he clumsily wriggled his own arms free of the sleeves of the robo-suit, and he attempted to pull the canvas bag from underneath him. With no working space whatsoever, this was a difficult task, and to add insult to injury, a savage pair of rotund lollipop ladies had crawled on top of him and were both now trying to force their way into his cage.

As best as he could, he arched his back and was able to winkle the rucksack out a little further, but it wasn't nearly enough. If he was going to get it free, he was going to need more room, which was something that clearly hadn't been a primary concern for the designers of the OAPRo. He reached down with one hand to the small lever for the opening mechanism, and primed his other to grab the rucksack from under his back. Immediately above him, the two curly haired and completely identical crossing ladies, their hats having long since gone during the struggle, were actually growling and drooling in their attempts to get at him. He closed his eyes tightly and pulled at the handle.

With a powerful hydraulic whine, his suit opened, and the two lollipop ladies were flung both in the direction of and a good deal of the distance towards the moon that was shining directly above where Harry lay. Now with room to manoeuvre, he tried to force himself up and pull the rucksack out, but a milkman had already leaped onto his legs while a crossing man had grabbed hold of his left shoulder. He kicked and writhed, and then experienced the very horrible feeling of pain as the milkman bit him between his thighs. Hard. Harry wailed in agony as he pulled the rucksack to his chest and managed to open it wide enough to expose the top of the crystal.

At that, it was as if somebody had yelled out across the unlit streets and silent shops. Each individual milkman and crossing warden stopped what they were doing immediately and lifted their heads as though they were listening on the wind to the mysterious call. Their eyes were no longer empty, but alive and filled with confusion. They looked about themselves in complete astonishment, at each other, and then, one by one, to the sweating and shivering form of Harry lying in half a robot while a milkman lay with his head between Harry's legs.

"Oh God. Oh God, oh God, oh God. What on earth did I do?" asked the terrified morning delivery man. "Did I...?"

"No," gasped Harry, shaking his head. "You just bit me, that's all."

"Oh Lord," added the crestfallen milkie, "would you like a yoghurt? It's very cold and soothing; it would make a terrific unguent."

"I'm good, honestly. Thank you. I just need to get into that church."

The two crossing ladies who had been roaring at him moments before had since landed, dusted themselves down, and were now limping towards him.

"Young man," said one, a drop of blood hanging precariously from the tip of her nose, "I'm so sorry about that. I have no idea what possessed me. All I can remember is that I really didn't like you and that I needed to stop you, in the most horrible way available, from doing whatever you needed to do. I'm not normally that... growly... "

"Me neither," added her identical neon twin.

"Nor me," added a clearly embarrassed crossing man behind them, before adding, "To be honest, I haven't been feeling quite myself lately."

This was like a spark among them, and they all began to chatter and nod in agreement among themselves.

"Seriously, it's fine," said Harry graciously, resealing the rucksack and standing unsteadily. "It wasn't your fault, but I know who's behind this, and if I can get into that church, I can stop this from happening to any of you again."

"Curse, is it?" piped up the chompy milkman.

"What?" said Harry.

"Curse? With the church and all that? Knights on horses with massive swords and fire and stuff, galloping through the shopping precinct? Big dogs? End of days, is it? I've seen all the films with your Schwarzeneggers and your Keanu Reeveses. Oh ah."

"Well, something like that. A bit less grunty, maybe."

"Right, well that settles it then," concluded the milkman confidently. "All I know is that, a minute or so ago, I wanted to rip your knackers off with my bare teeth. I was going to kick your face right off and then turn your feet the wrong way."

"Yeah, I was all for pulling your entire nervous system out," chuckled a colleague in wonder.

Harry choked.

"But now I have an incredible desire to help you out," continued the first milkman. "Church it is, and if the Aegis or anyone else wants to give us any shit, we've got your back, youth. Now, get yersen back in your robot." He turned to his fellow roundsmen and crossing wardens. "Am I right?"

The hearty response told him that he was.

"You can count on us, young lad," said one of the curly haired crossing ladies, dabbing her nose with a hanky. "Getting you safely from A to B is what we do. Although I was going to knee-cap you back there and set fire to your hair. Anyway, leave those nasty buggers to us."

***

And so it was that Harry, surrounded by a watchful gang of milkmen and crossing wardens, was able to lumber his way up the remaining cobbles of the road to where the battle raged in front of the church. The ground was strewn with all kinds of skirmish detritus, flaming bits of rubbish blazed away here and there, while smashed crockery and broken garden furniture littered the grass verges. Members of the Tylwyth Teg lay along the pavement and on the tarmac, with the moonlight giving them the appearance of being asleep under the night sky, although Harry knew the reality was far more painful. Likewise, members of the Aegis were stretched out prostrate where they had fallen. Ahead lay the churchyard, where people fought hand to hand among the tombstones and under the enormous, ancient trees. Beyond them, the church stood silent, with its giant, dark, wooden doors shut against the carnage.

Harry was just planning how best to work his way through the melee when he leaped backwards, having at the very last second seen a terrified and riderless horse charging towards him, followed closely by a lumbering and grasping robo-suit. The white stallion missed him by a whisker, and it charged on down the road towards where further fighting was taking place, but the robo-suit was not to be as lucky. A coterie of six crossing ladies had already broken away from Harry's group and formed themselves into two rows of three, facing one another. They stood there resolutely, holding tight to their crossing signs, which were slanted from the waist to the ground, like dipped flags at a memorial. The robo-suit was in full flight and clattered into the sticks, which took its legs away and sent it crashing to its back on the ground.

The force of the impact caused the chest cage to burst open, revealing the tiny, terrified form of the pilot within. Harry was horrified to see that it was none other than poor Doreen Twigge, the old lady who waved him into work every morning, still wearing a plastic rain bonnet and a beige shopping mac, with individually wrapped boiled sweets from her pocket strewn about where she lay writhing arthritically.

"HELP!" she yelled, almost choking on her dentures. "I've been done a mischief! My rights have been violated! Goodness me!"

Harry directed a couple of milkmen to help her, and they lifted her gently from her deactivated metal prison before escorting the grateful pensioner to a nearby wooden bench, presenting her with a yoghurt, and being amply rewarded with a butterscotch each and a pat on the thigh.

However, Harry was already on the move. His full entourage of crossing wardens and milkies had now burst forwards into the battle, and were going head to head with the Aegis soldiers and other robots. One scooped up an Alex robot onto the circular face of her stop sign before launching it skywards and sending it to kingdom come – like a violent, furry baseball – once it had dropped back into hitting range. Harry waded in too, seizing an angry Aegis soldier by the shoulders, turning him upside down and planting him into a recycling bin. Around him, the remaining knights and archers of the Tylweth Teg fought valiantly, while pieces of kitchenware and a variety of office appliances continued to whistle past.

The robo-suit was giving him an edge he could never have achieved without it. He was now fully used to how it worked and how it could respond intuitively to his every move. Another snapping Alex robot was crushed under foot, and another pair of angry Aegis soldiers attempted to push him over, but after a short ruckus between them, Harry was able to peel them off and bang their heads together, knocking them both unconscious before casting them onto the roof of a nearby tavern.

A pair of figures, locked in a desperate struggle, then tumbled into his path. As he watched, one of the figures dragged up and overpowered the other, an Aegis soldier, before knocking him unconscious and sending him falling heavily to the ground. As Harry watched, the victorious figure turned to him and he was puzzled to see that it was Jason McDonald, the teacher he had interviewed recently at the MOP. With a defiant look at Harry, he raised his arms and yelled to the heavens, "THIS! THIS IS ANUS!" before roaring in delight and sprinting off in search of his next victim.

Harry was close to the edge of the churchyard now, but still the battle raged, and his way through was by no means secured. Without warning, three Aegis soldiers shoulder charged him together from his right-hand side. It was enough to knock Harry off-balance and send him crashing to the ground with a violent clatter. But where three Aegis soldiers had been enough to take him down, so too one milk float – piling into the action at a top speed of sixteen miles per hour, and with four milkmen throwing loaded bottles for all their worth – was enough to take the

Aegis down in return, albeit momentarily.

This gave Harry the time he needed to get back clumsily onto his stainless-steel feet, and as he did so, the crossing wardens scrambled ahead of him, forming a protective guard in two rows, one either side of the graveyard path towards the heavy double doors of the church. Sensing the change in the air, the fight itself had now turned in his direction. Mounted horsemen and women from Annwn pulled away from their cloned or robotic foes, and they gathered as best they could to defend the neon runway down which Harry was now attempting to make his way, with the scratched and snarling hounds of the Cwn Annwn at their sides, fiercely yelping their ire at anyone who dared to try to break through the shield of crossing wardens.

As the remaining robo-suits in the distance latched on to what was happening, they began to pelt the crowd with whatever they could lay their hands on or rip from the ground, but it wasn't enough. The protective ranks about Harry were under strain, but they held, with their crossing signs held aloft and interlocked as an impenetrable roof. He was able to squeeze ever forwards, inch by inch, pushing Aegis soldiers aside as and when he could, to lend support to those supporting him.

He was into the churchyard now, shoving his way through to where the heavy, old doors stood shut beneath the huge, stained-glass window, which depicted a holy battle from centuries past, with soldiers, chariots and horses struggling against one another under the watchful eye of God in the heavens. A badly wounded member of the Tylwyth Teg lay slumped against the trunk of an enormous plane tree, struggling to get to his feet. Still the debris rained down, still the neon lines of heaving crossing wardens held under the protection of the Tylwyth Teg and the Cwn Annwn, and still Harry was able to move forwards.

He was going to do it.

With his robo-suit being too big and bulky to pass through the doors, Harry powered down the metal monstrosity by the church doors and he flicked the lever to open the chest. The robot knelt down as if in submission to the God in the window above, its powerful searchlight illuminating the graveyard. Harry snatched up his heavy rucksack before leaping down to the path below.

"Go on, lad!" came the cry from a crossing warden nearby.

"Go on, Harry!" came the voice of a rider, and soon a chorus of voices was cheering his name as he set his hand to the bulky, metal ring set in the door before him.

Without warning, the ring turned, and the door burst inwards, sending Harry to his knees. As he looked up in shock, suddenly feeling completely exposed without his robo-suit, the menacing eyes of David Simeon glared back at him from behind wire-framed spectacles. He reached to grab at Harry, and although Harry did his best to get out of the way, Simeon had managed to snatch at his arm. Simeon then lifted him up to standing, before lifting him up off his feet completely.

Harry, rising skywards and in shock, was able to notice that Simeon's hand was at least four or five times larger than it should be, and it had wrapped all the way around his arm with ease. Not only that but as he looked down, he noticed that his tormentor was emerging from the church doors. Although 'emerging' wasn't quite the right word; he was *unfolding* himself out, all the while holding his terrified prey high in the air. Simeon was growing, extending towards the night sky. As his head came level with Harry, he sneered, his face an enlarged visage of despicable smugness. His arm then extended, taking Harry dizzyingly out over the tree below, his rucksack crushing into his back, with the crystal sharp and painful against his spine.

"What the hell have you done?" cried Harry, "What the hell—" He was prevented from speaking further as Simeon dropped him from one giant hand to the other, before putting them both around his chest and squeezing, hard. He could feel his ribs groaning under the pressure, with the crystal digging deeper as he struggled to breathe. Simeon again brought him up to his giant head, which was now as high as the intricate stonework that marked the top of the giant, arched window.

"Harry Salt," came the voice of Simeon, although it sounded somehow distorted – higher pitched, perhaps. "Well, I never. Funny who you bump into, isn't it?" he declared with a chuckle, a strange wheezing sound.

Harry scrunched his eyes shut for fear that they might pop out, and he focussed on trying to get air into his painfully constricted lungs.

"I had a feeling you'd see sense and come back," continued Simeon, "and with such an odd collection of friends. So brave and clever of them to rescue you in the first instance, but it's too bad we were ready for your return, eh? Stupid. So stupid."

Harry opened his eyes as wide as he dared and could see that, far below, the fighting had stopped; what was left of the shocked riders were now surrounded by Aegis soldiers with guns pointed. Even the brave milkmen and crossing wardens had been overpowered, while the hounds barked powerlessly, themselves surrounded on all sides by swarms of Alex robots, their white fur made blue in the moonlight. Everywhere, all open-mouthed attention was now on this horrifyingly augmented and warped version of what was once a simpering and weasely man of five feet ten inches.

"There's no limit to this technology, Harry. All it takes is a little imagination, a little daring, a dash of questionable morality and the willingness to experiment. There was no way a group of overblown horse riders could ever hope to compete with us and the power we now have at our command. Did you truly think that magic and superstition could overcome human ingenuity? Really? There is no magic. Not any more. Those days are long gone, centuries past, and the knowledge long forgotten or... " Simeon chuckled. "Diluted into madness. This is our time now, Harry. Ours. We are shaping the future exactly how we want it, according to our designs and our plans. It'll be glorious."

Simeon sighed delightedly – a horrible, unnatural whine. He held Harry up to his huge eyes, which were observing Harry like a pair of blinking and bloodshot satellite TV dishes.

He continued, "All the people at our command. Doing as we say. Saying what we want them to. Working as hard as we push them. Once they're done, we replace them. And so it goes on, Harry. We'll be immovable. Eventually, what remains of humanity won't be able to see the difference. The fertility crisis won't matter. Unemployment won't matter. The population will all fall into line and be just as compliant as we need them to be. They'll believe in us and only us. We'll be their champions. Voting for us when we ask them to. Silencing and discrediting the opposition when we need them to. Buying what we tell them to. Rioting on our command. Behaving on our command. Swallowing conspiracy theories like gospel. Order restored. Our order, Harry. Ours.

"They'll believe everything we say and do, knowing it's for the greater good of the people simply because we tell them it is."

He laughed his odd, rasping laugh again.

By now, Harry was close to blacking out, and he forced himself to focus on the terrible, gargantuan eyes that faced him.

"Now all I need is whatever exists within you, whatever it is that gives you life and the power to keep going where all the other clones fail. Whatever it is that makes you so different and so very damned special. Whatever it was your dear, old dad put in there." Simeon loosened his grip slightly around Harry's torso, as if reminding himself of his worth.

"You'll never get it," choked Harry, "Never, you bastard!"

"Actually, he will," came a voice from far below.

From under the cover of the London plane tree, the injured soldier of Annwn now ran forwards, screaming and with his sword drawn. As Harry watched, he plunged it deep into Simeon's spindly leg. The effect was instantaneous: Simeon recoiled in agony, emitting a sickening and painful howl to the sky. He flailed with Harry still clutched in his hand, first out over the churchyard and then back, slamming into the church wall and instantaneously letting him go.

As Harry fell to the grass below, he had just enough time to reflect on the fact that the sword that had stabbed Simeon's leg had glinted purple in the headlight from his parked robo-suit. Like crystal.

30. Dead

Jesus Christ.
Jesus on the cross.
Harry ached all over. He felt thirsty, his ribs were unbeliev-ably sore, and his head hummed painfully. Was he in danger? He wasn't sure. Should he be in danger? He figured he probably wouldn't like it if he were, and the warmth of the blackness was so good and such a comfort. He figured he'd go back there for a bit, and so he did.

***

There he is again. On his cross. Jesus. Doing his thing. What's he thinking? Is he judging me? Oh my head; my damn head. I ache so much. My head is throbbing, and I think I've done myself real damage. Did I fall? I think I fell. I can't be sure if I can take much more of this. I haven't even got my suit. I think I left it outside.
"Harry?"
I think I know that voice. "Jesus?"
"Harry, can you hear me?"
"Jesus. You're early. I'm not ready yet."
The blackness is coming again. Is this it? Is this the end of it all? Hang on, wait. Are you sure you can even let me in to be with

you? Will I be allowed? There's... there's a reason. I just... I just can't remember right now. I'm different. Oh Jesus. Besides, there was something I had to do before it got light, and there can't be long left.

"Harry?"

"What?"

"Harry?"

"Dad?"

***

Harry awoke again, on the cold, stone floor underneath the high-vaulted, wooden ceiling of the church. Bright, golden sunlight poured in through the stained-glass windows, turning them into a kaleidoscope of riotous greens, reds and blues. Noise was buzzing through his head, rattling his skull and making his teeth chatter. As he scanned through his body, he felt aches in all corners, and one of his arms felt like it was on fire. But he was definitely alive and, somehow, he had made it into the church.

He lay still a moment longer, trying to think. He remembered smirking eyes behind wire-framed glasses. Simeon. Simeon had been threatening him. Simeon had been big. Stupidly big. Was he still here? Something told Harry that Simeon wasn't, but he wanted to check. He tried to roll over. Colours from the windows had turned the floor into a glowing mosaic. His arm was in a neatly tied sling.

What the hell?

"Harry, careful now; lie still. You're okay."

This couldn't be right.

Harry looked up at the ornate, painted cross high above the altar, from which Jesus was staring down at him, in agonising pain yet full of compassion. This church was beautiful. Jesus was beautiful. His eyes swam a little, and the world turned.

What was that hum? Why was the sun so bright?

"Here you go. Lift your head, just a little."

He was lifting the back of Harry's head, and putting a soft cushion underneath. That felt so much better already. His hands were big, but the right kind of big. Friendly, working hands. Warm hands. Caring hands. One of them stroked him tenderly, smoothing the hair above his forehead gently, while the other cradled the back of his head as it lay on the cushion.

"Is that better?"

His only son looked up at him and began to cry. "Dad?"

"Hello, son," said Gregory Salt, who had tears running down his cheeks too.

Harry blinked away his own, smearing them away with the back of his free hand, so as to see better. He took in all he could see: the friendly, compassionate smile; the nose that matched his own; the love that radiated from those kind, green, laughter-lined eyes; and the receding hairline – the very face that had swum into his mind virtually every day since his death. Throughout the last days of childhood, throughout his teenage years and into his twenties.

They sobbed, holding tightly to one another; huge sobs that rocked their bodies.

Dad.

"I'm dead, aren't I? Again?" enquired Harry.

His dad, who appeared to be wearing the velvet robes of a citizen of Annwn, said nothing. He just continued to smile down at his son.

"Oh God, I'm dead. I'm in heaven and I failed." Harry looked about in panic. "I let them all down. I was... I was supposed to do something... Dad. I was supposed to finish something off."

His father shushed him gently, the way he had whenever his son was sad or angry as a child. "Harry, you were fantastic. You did everything asked of you."

"Jade!" he spluttered, suddenly remembering. "I lost her. I mean, I found her, but then I lost her again. Annwn... the king! Oh Dad, I need to get back! I can't be in heaven yet! I've got shit to do!"

"Harry." This time his voice was firmer.

"I love you, Dad! I love you, but I have to go back!"

"Harry, calm down. You're not dead. Not this time, and you haven't let anyone down. Not one person."

Harry blinked. "But... this place... you...?" He looked about the church, flooded as it was with the purest golden light from outside. Motes of dust danced in the air as they floated lazily by. The magnificent altar sparkled as if alive, and the ancient, wooden pulpit seemed to be watching him, calling him to prayer. And his dead father. As religious experiences went, it was almost cinematic in its perfection. The font. Harry sat up this time, getting himself woozily to his feet to stand back and look at where his father sat on the sunlit floor, smiling almost apologetically back up at him. He couldn't see his rucksack anywhere.

"Sorry to break it to you, but you're still in Chesterfield, Harry. You got the crystal into the church, exactly as King Gwynn had hoped you would."

"The crystal. Of course. But I have to... I have to get it to the font so that the Great Hunt can change everything. The crystal!"

Harry staggered desperately over to the ancient stone font – and there it was. The crystal. Rather than lying at the bottom of the large christening bowl, it was floating gently, rising and falling as if breathing. It glowed a brilliant purple, causing Harry to squint.

"I did it?" he queried.

"You did," confirmed his dad.

"And... I'm alive?"

"Very much so, I'm happy to say."

"And... you're alive too?"

"Yes. Yes, I am."

Harry felt relief at first. His task – he'd completed it. Against considerable odds and in the face of terrifying adversity, he'd done it. He searched for a feeling of jubilation, but he couldn't find it. It just wasn't there, even though it should have been. He stared at his dad, who had staggered over to sit on a pew facing him, staring back. His dad. Alive. Here. He didn't search for a feeling this time. Instead, he felt what seemed like a hundred different ones wash over him all at once. "Why?"

"Why what, Harry?"

"Why? Why are you here? Now? Why did you go? Where have you been? Why would you leave me on my own?"

"Harry, I—"

"I DON'T UNDERSTAND!" yelled Harry, who was then immediately shocked by the echo of his voice reverberating around the high, empty church. "You were dead. Gone forever. It took me years to get over that – years! All those times I needed you and all those times I wanted to talk to you! I couldn't. I had to suck it up and move on because you were dead. Now you're *here*. What the hell?"

Gregory, a fearful look on his face, attempted to stand up. He strained to get as far as halfway before slumping back to a slouched sitting position. He was hurt. "Fancy a pew, Harry? I'm sorry."

They sat together on one of the cushioned, wooden pews, arranged in rows to face the altar. Harry was struggling to get his mind into some semblance of order. The warmth of the sun on his face was welcome after what had seemed the longest of nights in the longest of weeks. Beside him, he felt the warmth of his father radiating out. He was real. He felt alive. He had felt his father's hands on his head. They had talked. His dad was just as real as anything else he could see, smell and hear right now, but his father shouldn't have been here.

"Is this... " Harry took a deep breath. "Is this really real? Or is it just another memory planted into my head? An algorithm? Should I expect a huge, black dog to come running up the aisle to get me?"

His dad's face dropped with the saddest of looks. "This is real, Harry. I'm here; you're here. Everything is real, and I'm so, so sorry that you had to question it. I'm so sorry that you had to spend all those years without me. I know it was horrible because it was horrible for me too."

Harry's voice shook as a giant sob overwhelmed him. "But you died. You're dead. You died in the car crash on the way home from Wales! God, we *both* died on the way home from Wales!" His dad tried to put his arm around his son's shoulders, but Harry pulled away, shuffling up the pew away from him. "Are you... are you a clone too? Did they make one out of you as well?"

"No."

"So then... what? How are you even here, Dad? I don't... I can't understand. I can't handle this." He shook his head, a frightened look on his face now as they watched each other from a few seats away.

"I'm alive, Harry. I always have been. I... I never died in the first place. Only you did." His dad paused. "I'm sorry. I'm so, so sorry."

Harry could only stare at his father. *I never died. Only you.* Suddenly, he felt the gulf of all those years since he had last seen him. The years living with his grandparents as he grew from a boy to a man. The years alone.

"What the fuck do you mean that you never died? You've been alive all along?"

"Harry, I—"

"This makes no sense. Somewhere... somewhere I feel happy that you're here, that you're real, but Dad... why would you leave me? Not actual me, but the cloned me – this me, I mean. I can't even work out who or what I am anymore! And yet you... you were here all along?"

"I wasn't here though, Harry. Not *here* as in Derbyshire or on the surface, even. I've been in Annwn ever since I brought you back. Ever since the sliver of crystal that Roy Newman brought to the surface completed you, and until tonight, when I was able to join the Great Hunt and return to your world. As much as I wanted to, I couldn't stay here. If I had, there's no way you could have survived, Harry." The sound of his last words, the name of his son, echoed around the church and reverberated into silence.

"What do you mean? What does Newman have to do with anything?"

His father gritted his teeth and sat himself up straighter. "It goes back to when Helen – your mum – when she died. That was wrong; her life was taken from her so soon, far too early."

"When I was born."

"Yes. It was the strangest time in my life. Inexplicably horrific. The most horrible time, losing Helen like that. But then there you were, this little bundle of hope. Such a beautiful boy. And I was determined that one day, somehow, the three of us would live together, like the family Helen and I had always dreamed of being. She deserved to see this amazing little boy she had created. To love him and to see him grow. I poured everything I had into my research, every penny and every available hour. Roy knew what I was doing. I'd always been one of his brightest pupils at the MOP, and we'd been working together on the early versions of what would eventually become a human cloning project. It wasn't always going to be that way, but I became obsessed with the notion that I could somehow bring Helen back, so it could be the three of us. I'm sorry to say it overwhelmed me, I know it did. But I got so close. So close." He sighed, looking upwards into the rafters.

Harry wanted to speak, but he held back, allowing his father to continue.

"I knew that my project – my research, what we were working towards – had hope in it. But it was so, so risky back then, and try as we might, we hadn't been able to perfect the formula or the technology – the very science of it all. Something was missing and we couldn't find it. However, I found it eventually, Harry. The others thought I was mad and that it wouldn't work, but I knew we had to look elsewhere. We were playing God, Harry. Science wasn't going to be enough. There had to be something else. In the end, I tracked down the source that could give life, and I combined with my science to make it all real. You came with me."

"Wales."

His father said nothing, but looked back at his son instead and nodded gravely.

"I wasn't sure if it was real or a dream," said Harry slowly, "but I remember. Wales. We climbed Cadair Idris and camped. I saw it; I saw you. It was night-time, but I saw *you*. Your eyes... There was someone else there... The red eyes... so many eyes in the valley... "

"That's right. I had it all planned, Harry. I would take the crystal shard to bring Helen back, and the three of us could live together as we were meant to before her accident. Our lives would be normal, and we could live the way we were supposed to, just like any other family."

"But, Dad, she was dead. I was what... twelve when we went to Wales? She'd been dead for twelve years. There's nothing normal in bringing someone back, let alone after twelve years."

His dad was insistent. "But that's not how I saw it at the time, Harry. I was hell-bent on bringing her back. I'd spent those twelve years convinced that I had to do this. The way I saw it, her future had been stolen from her; our future ripped away. But I was going to give it her back. I had the ability. Me. My knowledge and my skills, put to the purpose for which they were intended. All I needed was that something else, and I had found it. The books – everything my father, your grandad, had passed on to me. Annwn. It was all in there. It had to be real, and if it was, I could do it."

"Annwn?"

"Oh, there's so much everyone has forgotten, Harry. So much that isn't even seen anymore. But it's there; it's right there. It's all around us, and who we were is still who we are. Annwn below, and us above, and the universe all around us. Oh God, if only people could *see* it! It transcends borders, politics, religion and science. It's the reason the sun rises and the moon follows. It goes back beyond every one of us, every human, every animal and every bloody last bacterium! It's a part of us all!"

"What is?" asked Harry fearfully.

His father didn't seem to hear him. Instead, he rolled up his sleeve and looked at his wristwatch. "We haven't got long, Harry, but you need to see this while you still can." He stood shakily, wincing as he did so, and grabbed his son's hand. "Come on," he gasped mischievously, "you'll never get this chance again."

Harry followed, rising and joining his dad as he led him outside the church and into the sunshine.

31. Straight

It wasn't daytime. Harry was convinced it had been, but the night sky was still dark above. The light came from another, utterly astounding source. As they stood in the churchyard, shielding their eyes, the famous spire of Chesterfield's Church of St Mary and All Saints span impossibly fast, glowing from top to bottom and radiating the incredible golden light that had streamed in through the windows as Harry and his father had been reunited after so many years. There was an imperceptible hum – a bass almost, at the furthest range of their hearing – which they could feel through the soles of their feet. Tendrils of a mysterious, purple light crept out from the spinning spire and into the sky. But to Harry, a Derbyshire lad through and through, that wasn't the most shocking thing of all.

"Bet you never thought you'd see the crooked spire straight, did you?" Harry's dad asked.

Harry goggled, blinking with incomprehension and trying to take it all in. It was completely upright, with the famous kink in the spire having gone altogether. The light was so dazzlingly golden and it shone so brightly that it illuminated all of the churchyard, the pub and the shops round about. They were alone. Harry couldn't see anyone else; the horses, riders, Aegis and everyone else seemed to have departed from the scene.

"What... what's happening?"

"It's the crystal, Harry," explained his dad, looking down at him excitedly. "The crystal you delivered. Right now, the energy from that amazing piece of rock is radiating all across the country, and all of the clones who were brainwashed by the government are waking up. They're back to themselves again, capable of free thought, and able to make their own decisions and do what they want to do. Not what they're told or forced to believe. They've got their lives back, and the Great Hunt of Annwn is riding wild right now, putting everything and everyone back as they should be. The threat is over, Harry. It's done."

"It's... it's beautiful! I've never seen anything like it. And this is... the people of Annwn did this? Built this? How?"

"Oh Harry, it goes way further back than that. Right across Derbyshire now, the stones are singing: Arbor Low, the Grey Ladies and Robin Hood's Stride. Every place where the kingdom of Annwn punctures through and reaches above the land, in so many places throughout the Peak District, they stones are all glowing, all spinning like the spire and all alive. All sending their song to every valley, every street and lane, and every field across England, Scotland and Wales, restoring peace and reason to the land, with the Great Hunt and the hounds of the Cwn Annwn doing their bidding. This is how it's meant to be, Harry. This is the big reset!"

He threw his arm around his son, and they both looked on in wonder at the improbable spectacle that surrounded them. Harry laughed. He wasn't sure why, it just bubbled up inside of him and burst out. He felt more alive than he could remember, but his head was still swimming.

"I still don't get it though, Dad. If you were alive all this time, then why didn't you come back to me? Why did I have to live with Grandma and Grandpa, thinking you were dead? *Where were you?*" Harry questioned.

"I had to stay away, Harry, even though it killed me to do so."

"But I thought—"

"Well, no, it didn't actually kill me, Harry. I was just using a figure of speech. Oh gosh, this is hard. I didn't honestly think I'd ever be lucky enough to see you again and have to explain this."

Harry grabbed his father's hand and looked up at him, with the church glowing behind him like a halo. "Well, you're here now, so try me."

"Well," his dad sighed, "I had to make a choice. A horrible, horrible choice. I was so deeply involved in the lore of the Tylweth Teg and Annwn by the time I was given the shard of crystal that you carry inside you. I knew what I was getting into, sure, but it was part of something bigger – way bigger than anything I could have imagined." His voice faltered, tears prickling at his eyes again. "To take a shard from Annwn and use it in the way I planned, to clone and bring back your mum, I had to give up my life on the surface of the world and join the fair folk of the Tylweth Teg beneath it. It was an exchange, a sacrifice, my life for your mum's. That's the way it is; it was the only way a shard of the crystal could ever be taken from Annwn and brought to the surface to be used in this way. The price of the action was that I had to stay and give myself to life in the underworld. But to me, as painful as it was, it was enough to know that you two would be together up here. I'd give up my life so that you could both live yours with one another."

"But... when I died... "

They stood looking at one another in the golden silence, with no noise to be heard anywhere other than the low, throbbing hum pulsing from the eternally spinning spire.

His father bit his bottom lip before speaking. "Your mum and I had lived a happy life together, and the happiest point of that time was when she fell pregnant with you. When you were gifted to us. It was magical. Despite the horror of losing Helen, the joy of watching you grow was unlike anything I had ever felt before in my life. Then the car crash happened and... well... you had your whole life ahead of you. So, once I had recovered enough, I brought you back, Harry. I used the sliver of crystal alongside the technology to bring you back. I took my place with the Tylwyth Teg in Annwn, and... well, there we are. I've been down there ever since. It's an incredible place, and they're a wonderful people. I'm a farmer down there, believe it or not. I have my own little cottage on the hillside."

Harry looked hard at his dad, unsure of what to say. He felt unsteady, as if the ground could give way at any moment. The pounding and swirling of the hum rose through his shoes, rattling across his rib cage. "So all this time, I was alive up here and you were down there, five miles under my feet?"

"Believe me when I tell you, Harry, there hasn't been a single day that has gone by that I haven't thought of you. Or your mum. I have craved to be with you, with every single fibre of my being. But, Harry, there's no way I could have come to the surface and survived. It takes a special kind of someone to survive the enchantment. For me, the only way was to ride with the Great Hunt. Tonight."

"So, does that mean you'll have to go back with them when the Hunt is done?"

Harry's father looked away, staring into some distant space. "Yes."

Now it was Harry who faced away, not wanting his dad to see the upset and anger that he could feel flashing across his face. "But I only just got you back, Dad. I only just got you back!"

"I know, my son, I know." He took Harry close to his chest, wincing in pain as he did so, and they stood there together in the golden light of the church spire. "I only just got you back too. I would love to stay so, so much, but I can't. I'm sorry. It would send me mad, destroy my mind and destroy everything I ever was. Although I figured that one opportunity to spend an hour or so with you was better than none at all. I just hope I made the right call. Ugh... " He winced again, swaying unsteadily.

"Dad, are you okay?"

"I just need a minute. Do you mind if we sit down?"

They made their way, with Harry supporting his suddenly

groggy dad, to a bench in the church garden. There, Harry took a closer look at his dad's injury. Blood had turned much of his white vest red, seeping stickily into the purple velvet of his tunic. Harry looked on in horror. His father was getting paler as he watched.

"Jesus, Dad. What the hell?" Harry questioned.

"It's okay, it's alright—" his dad began.

"Okay? You've been stabbed!"

"Trust me, Harry. It's going to be okay."

"No, here." Harry attempted to take off his top, but was soon stuck as a bolt of pain shot through his damaged arm the moment he tried to move it.

"Harry, honestly, leave it."

"You need something to put pressure on the wound! You're bleeding like mad."

His dad was sighing heavily now, clearly in more pain than he'd been letting on. He gritted his teeth.

"Jesus, Dad. What am I supposed to do? I'll... I'll call an ambulance." He fumbled about in his pocket for his phone.

"You'll be lucky," said his dad, coughing, "There'll be no signal tonight. The power won't be back up yet."

"Then what the hell can I do? You can't stay here like this. You'll... you'll... "

"No, I won't," gasped his father defiantly, "I'm exactly where I need to be. Look. There." He pointed past Harry's shoulder.

Behind him, a tired caravan of horses, riders and hounds were making their way up the rise towards the church. Harry looked on in shock. The golden illumination from the church revealed that they were weary and blood spattered. Tunics were torn, banners hung ragged, and some soldiers held on tightly to one another for support, but they had returned. At the front of the pack – his face scratched and torn, but with a fiery, blue glint still sparkling in his eyes – King Gwynn rode atop his white stallion, with the ever faithful Dormarch padding along at his side.

Harry's heart leaped, if only momentarily. "Your Highness!"

he called, running to meet them, "It's my dad. Please, he's injured."

From his horse, towering above him, Gwynn smiled down wearily. "As are a great many of us, Harry. Some worse than that. But, thankfully, there are enough of us to return and make sure we can take the rest home with us. We ride together; we leave together as one. Geraint," he called over his shoulder, "Gregory is here. He needs help."

From the battered procession came a tall, middle-aged man with a kindly face and bright-aquamarine eyes beneath a strong head of white hair. He carried a leather satchel slung across his shoulder, and he gave Harry a pleasant and oddly familiar smile before nodding as he passed. "Harry Salt. Your da will be fine, believe me. You both come from a strong line."

As Geraint attended to Harry's father at the bench, King Gwynn leaped down from his horse to face Harry. He was in a bad way; the Alex robots had more than left their mark on him. Despite this, he smiled and rested his large hand on Harry's shoulder. "I'm sorry to see you got hurt, but I'm glad to see that you two... " He nodded towards where Harry's father lay on the bench.

"My dad? I know. I still don't know how to take all this in. Any of it. Did you make it to London already? And you... well, I thought you were done for."

Gwynn chuckled warmly. "It'll take more than a few furry robots to finish me off, as painful and unpleasant as that was. But, yes, everything is back as it should be in London. The mast is destroyed and it will not be rebuilt. Things have been set back onto the natural path, and the rest of the country will soon follow. We are ever grateful to you, Harry Salt. This couldn't have happened without you."

A feeling of immense pride was welling up in Harry, and it was something he hadn't properly experienced for a long, long time. He smiled up at the king, and then he heard it. Softly at first, but it was there. In the branches of the London plane tree that stood impressively in the churchyard, a wren was singing. It was a complicated, but beautiful song; long-held notes were followed by a rapid chirruping vibrato that then segued into a soaring call. From somewhere in the sleeping town came a delicate response, and with that, there was a murmur of acknowledgement among the exhausted riders. The ride was over, the Great Hunt was at its end. It was time to return to Annwn.

"I'm afraid our time here is at an end, Harry Salt. For another fifty years, at the very least." As he spoke, the golden light in which they stood faded ever so slightly. King Gwynn looked to the church spire and Harry followed his gaze. It still span round at an incredible rate, but the note of the hum that thrummed through his feet had lowered perceptibly already. "You have done your family proud, and Annwn will not forget you. Take this."

Harry flashed him a quizzical look, and the king produced from a pocket a small, blue, velvet bag, tied with a golden cord. Harry opened it clumsily with his one free hand, and was dazzled by the heavy disk of bright, polished bronze that he uncovered. Inscribed around the edge in Gaelic letters were the words "*Mae'r bryniau'n fyw gyda sain cerddoriaeth*" and at the centre was a Celtic symbol comprised of three hounds of the Cwn Annwn, interlocked forever in an eternal wheel. In the palm of his hand, the weighty medallion felt warm from within, as if it were conscious.

"It's beautiful. Thank you," Harry declared.

"Keep it safe always," warned the king. "It's part of your heritage, and it will one day afford you strength and protection when you need it most."

Not for the first time, Harry felt that there was something curious in the king's choice of words. He was about to say something when he felt a presence at his shoulder and was pleased to see his dad, who was up on his feet and staring down at the impressive piece in his hand. There was colour back in his face, and his breathing was steadier now.

The king gripped Harry's shoulder once more. "*Diolch yn fawr,* Harry Salt," he said, before returning to his majestic horse, which was nibbling at the churchyard grass.

"So, this is it then? After all that?" Harry asked his father.

"I'm afraid so. We've had our hour. Time's up. Well, for now at least," his dad confirmed.

Harry shook his head wearily, a tired smile on his lips. "I can't believe it. After all these years. Now I have to miss you all over again."

Harry's father looked back at his son fondly, and then beyond him. "Somehow, I think you'll be okay. There are plenty of good people in this world to keep you company."

Harry turned to where he was looking, and sure enough, a scratched and battered Ford Gran Torino was making its way slowly up the rise at the rear of the march, and at its side walked Jade with Little Stevie in tow. Upon seeing Harry, her face broke into a wild grin, and she ran the last few steps to throw her arms around him while the enormous, white hound skipped around them both.

"Erm, Jade. This is my dad. Dad, meet Jade," said Harry bashfully, once she had let him go.

"The pleasure is all mine," said Gregory warmly, shaking her hand. By now, the light from the spire behind them was much weakened, and it was possible to sense the first possibilities of sunrise on the horizon.

"Stuff that," said Jade, enveloping Harry's dad in the hugest of hugs. From the Gran Torino came a short "pip pip" on the horn. From within, a grinning Clive – still sporting his cardigan and beanie – waved. Harry returned it with a nod and grin of his own, before looking down once again at the large, glinting coin in his hand, and then slipping it back into the velvet bag and into his pocket. He could still feel the warmth emanating from within.

"FANCY A LIFT, GREG?" shouted Clive.

"You know what, I think I will." Gregory turned for the final time to hug his son.

When they parted, tears were already fighting their way to the corners of their eyes. Jade sniffed loudly.

"You've made me so proud, Harry," said his dad warmly. "You're everything I hoped you could be, and so much more. Be sure to look after each other, always be kind, don't settle for second best," he added, "and make sure you eat well and get plenty of sleep every night. Eight glasses of water a day too. That stuff's important."

"Okay, Dad. Got that."

By now, his father was in the passenger seat of the car, and the procession was lined up and ready to leave. Jade put her arm around his waist, and as they looked up, the spire of Derbyshire's largest church crunched to a halt, glowing faintly.

"I love you, Dad," called Harry, his voice faltering.

"I love you too, son. In another fifty years, eh?" his father suggested.

"I won't ever forget this."

"Ah. About that... "

But there was no time to catch what his dad said next. Clive revved the engine of the car as the Great Hunt itself roared into life in a series of whoops and cheers, followed by the clattering of hooves on the town cobbles. With the red beacon atop the roof flashing, the Gran Torino followed the galloping Great Hunt, and in a moment, they were gone, their noise lingering and fading as the sun began to break through to wake the town.

Harry and Jade stood and listened until they could hear them no more, enjoying the silence that was only broken by the morning chorus of the birds in the trees.

"Seems a nice bloke," said Jade. "I thought your dad was dead, though?"

"Yeah. Funnily enough, so did I," Harry agreed.

Jade took her hand from Harry's waist and instead threaded her fingers through his. The sun was rising, casting its light upon the church and the town, and the sky was warming up to a cloudless blue. The air about them felt fresh, crisp and renewed. The birds sang. The new day was beginning, and Harry and Jade breathed it in.

"I don't know about you, but I could murder a cheese-and-piccalilli sandwich right now. I've had one on my mind for ages, for some reason, and I just can't shake it," Jade declared.

Harry nodded thoughtfully. "Yeah, I could get on board with that. Followed by a week-long kip."

"Back to mine, then?"

At that, Harry felt a definite movement in his trousers. This time, however, it came from around his ankle. He looked down to see a knackered-looking white basset hound peering mournfully up at him while tugging at the hem of his right trouser leg.

"Little Stevie?" Harry reached down to fluff the hair on the dog's neck, noticing the flecks of red fur at the tufts of his ears. He was rewarded with a slobbery lick of gratitude.

"Bloody hell," said Jade, "are you any good with dogs?"

"Not traditionally, no." He shook his head, bemused. "Come on, Stevie."

As Harry, Jade and Little Stevie made their way home together, the spire of the Church of St Mary and All Saints groaned, creaked and then turned as if to watch them go.

32. Change

At the moment that the Great Hunt rode back through the entrance to Odin Mine, just outside Castleton, everybody forgot.

Those who had stirred in the night forgot the sound of horses' hooves they'd heard, thundering along the country lane past their bedroom window. Those in the town who had looked on in horror at the mass riot unfolding before them forgot the broken windows, the smashed shop fronts and the piles of burning office furniture.

The frightened pensioners never remembered that they had piloted robo-suits through the streets or had felt an irresistible urge to throw garden chairs at anyone they didn't like the look of. And across the country, from the smallest hamlets to the biggest cities, it was washed from the minds of everyone that there were those among us who were in any way 'different'. Nobody remembered the grudges they had once felt at the new office staff or the new policemen. It was no longer clear as to why it was so important to be nasty to one another, to look for arguments and to find fault wherever possible. People who suggested that it might simply be a good idea to be nice to one another for a change were supported rather than pilloried, and if anything, people remembered how to be pleasant once again. No one could quite remember why evening curfews had been enforced, and they proceeded to ignore them altogether. Anyhow, nobody seemed keen to enforce them all anymore. It was far more enjoyable to meet up with friends and sit outside for a drink and a bag of crisps.

Many people went to work with a banging headache that morning, and a very fuzzy recollection of what they'd done the night before.

At midday, the Prime Minister appeared on TV, looking somewhere between terrified and shamefaced, and bumblingly announced to the nation that he was resigning from his post due to 'issues'. It was never clarified what the issues were, but seeing as no one could quite remember why they'd voted for him in the first place or indeed whether he'd ever done anything of use, no one was particularly sad to see him go. Rumours in the press hinted at an insurmountable falling-out with the Eastern Coalition, but nobody seemed to be able to offer an answer of any substance yet.

Harry and Jade woke up at around 3pm, the sweet tang of piccalilli still haunting their palates from breakfast. Harry went to grab his trousers, and as he did so, he felt his phone in the pocket; after some rummaging beside Jade's bedside table, he located her charger, saw it was a match for his and plugged in his device. He then took a careful and rejuvenating shower, making sure not to move his damaged arm, while Jade fed Little Stevie, writing a note and sticking it on the fridge to remind herself to buy some proper dog food, a lead and, indeed, a dog basket. Why she hadn't thought to before now escaped her.

There was coffee and a vague amount of time spent doing very little, during which Harry flicked his partially recharged phone on and scrolled puzzledly through a number of missed messages. Alan, he of the fiery-red toupee, had been trying to get in touch over the space of the last few days, with increasing desperation, it seemed. "MATE, NEED TO TLK TO U. ALAN" was the gist of the first few messages, which then escalated a little to the likes of "HARRY, BEEN FOLLOWING PPL. SOMETHING BIG HAPPNG. UNDERCOVER ALAN", before taking on a more personal and worrying tone with "HARRY, U NEED TO GET OUT OF THAT PLACE. NOW. I'VE SEEN SHIT. ALAN" and finally ending with "FCK. NO MORE CREDIT. FCKING VODAFONE. GD LUCK. ALAN".

Harry had shaken his head, perplexed.

Eventually, he and Jade set off for the Chesterfield Royal Hospital to get Harry's arm looked at, determined as they were to get to the bottom of how he'd damaged it in the first place. It was still a sunny afternoon, and as Jade drove them both towards the town, Harry remarked on how he'd had the oddest dream that the famous spire of the church hadn't ever been curved at all, but was in fact straight.

Jade laughed as they sat at the traffic lights, and then turned to Harry. "But it was straight once wasn't it? I seem to remember it that way, recently even."

A lollipop lady had wandered in front of the car and was waving a line of school children across the road. Harry, however, was staring back at Jade, the colour draining from his face.

She blinked, trying to clutch at a memory in the corner of her mind. "It was... it... there was something odd about it. In my mind, it was on fire or something... no, hang on... "

"Glowing," offered Harry.

"Yeah. That's it. Glowing."

Harry flinched.

"What?" Now Jade was looking worried.

Harry reached into his pocket and pulled out a small, blue, velvet pouch that felt warm to the touch, as if glowing from inside. From it he pulled a heavy, bronze disk, engraved with Gaelic lettering and with a carving in the centre that looked like three large dogs in an eternal circle.

The crossing lady turned to nod and smile her thanks. Catching Harry's eye, her smile waned a little as she stared at him with an odd, questing look. He stared back. The lights changed, and from behind them, the cars began to honk their horns impatiently.

Acknowledgements

Thank you to everyone who has encouraged me, supported me and guided me during the time it's taken to put this book together and arrive at this point where it sits in your hands. There's a heck of a lot of you out there, scattered far and wide and I am eternally grateful, indebted (and more than a little bit in love) with each and every one of you.

Firstly, a huge thank you to Paul Handley at Bearded Badger Publishing for believing in my book, and for everything you have done to get it out into the world. You're an incredible guy with an incredible drive, and I'm not referring to the crazy paving outside your house where you park your car.

A massive thank you to my editor Kate Brown for encouraging me to push on and improve. I'm so grateful for your belief, time, skill and honesty – and a huge thank you with lots of love to the Monday night gang at The Reader, Berlin.

Thank you Lindsay Corten for your eagle eyes and important reminder that blue Penguins are the best Penguins.

Thanks also to Kathy and all at Balzac's Coffee Roasters on Market Street, Toronto (where Harry was re-born), Graham Tavener for knowing what is and is not anus, Chris Hutchins, Jennifer Lynch, Emma Collins, Lindsey King, Summer Bradshaw, Stephen Loynds, everyone at the wonderful ABCTales.com and everyone else who has supported me along the way and kept me from doing something more sensible instead;

Jay Taylor, my dear, dear friend, for countless hairy adventures across London and Wales but above all for that conversation in The Carpenter's Arms in Dale Abbey all those years ago, the result of which is, finally, this book;

Mum, Dad, Sheridan and Tom, for filling my life with love, encouraging me to imagine and to dream, and for wonderful childhood holidays and countdown calendars above my bed;

Reeganne, for, well, for everything. For turning my life the full 180 degrees, for your love, your belief, your kindness, your patience, your truth, and for making everything and anything not only possible, but fun. I love you.

BEARDED BADGER

PUBLISHING CO.

Bearded Badger Publishing is a small
independent press based in
Belper, Derbyshire.
We are committed to supporting writers from
our region, promoting innovative writing
and publishing brilliant books!

www.beardedbadgerpublishing.com